D0044565

THE SHATTERED VINE

Also by Laura Anne Gilman from Gallery Books

Flesh and Fire

Weight of Stone

THE SHATTERED VINE

BOOK THREE OF
THE VINEART WAR

LAURA ANNE GILMAN

GALLERY BOOKS

New York   London   Toronto   Sydney   New Delhi

Gallery Books
A Division of Simon & Schuster, Inc.
1230 Avenue of the Americas
New York, NY 10020

First Gallery Books hardcover edition October 2011

GALLERY BOOKS and colophon are registered trademarks of Simon & Schuster, Inc.

For information about special discounts for bulk purchases, please contact
Simon & Schuster Special Sales at 1-866-506-1949 or business@simonandschuster.com.

The Simon & Schuster Speakers Bureau can bring authors to your live event.
For more information or to book an event contact the Simon & Schuster
Speakers Bureau at 1-866-248-3049 or visit our website at www.simonspeakers.com.

Designed by Renata Di Biase

Manufactured in the United States of America

10   9   8   7   6   5   4   3   2   1

Library of Congress Cataloging-in-Publication Data
Gilman, Laura Anne.
    The shattered vine / Laura Anne Gilman.—1st Gallery Books hardcover ed.
       p. cm. — (The vineart war ; bk. 3)
    1. Magic—Fiction. 2. Vineyards—Fiction. I. Title.
    PS3557.I4545S53 2011
    813'.54—dc23   2011024966

ISBN 978-1-4391-0148-3
ISBN 978-1-4391-2690-5 (ebook)

For Geoff, who will read this,
and my twinling, who probably won't.
You guys have been my sanity
and my lifeline while I wrote this,
and I love ya.

ACKNOWLEDGMENTS

Over the course of these three books, so many people have stepped forward with information and advice, help and support, that at this point thanking them all individually would require another chapter, and my editor informs me the book is Quite Long Enough, thank you.

Thank you. All of you. For your answers, for your patience, and for sharing your enthusiasm not only for the final product but the *process* of winemaking. You are all magicians.

However, the trilogy cannot come to a close without again acknowledging The Jens—my agent, Jennifer Jackson, and my editor, Jennifer Heddle. Through trial and triumph, panics and partying . . . you guys rock.

*T*ruth, history, legend . . . they are all the same. The Washers, our self-appointed guardians, tell us a story, a lovely story, about gods and sacrifice, of the role that Vinearts play and what they may and may not do, to keep the world safe and whole.

I am neither Vineart nor Washer, but solitaire. I view the world down the line of my blade, not softened by legends of some demigod long dead and gone. Nor am I tied to the promises of a place or liege, to watch my fortunes rise and fall by how well my master weaves his strands of power. Solitaires give up House and hearth, have no allegiances save to ourselves and whatever oaths of employment we take. That allows us to see the world as it is, entire, and to hear much that would otherwise remain unspoken, or mis-said.

For history is written by the survivors, and each side has their version to tell. When you have no stake in choosing sides, if you pry away the gilding and the pretty words and look down the edge of your blade, what remains is this: that in the years before modern reckoning, a plague attacked the vineyards of the prince-mages, twisting and changing the fruit—and the magic within. Call it Sin Washer's blood, or the wrath of the gods, or merely a ferocious blight as comes by chance, it spread too quickly to be halted, too fiercely to be treated. What had been, was no more.

The prince-mages, who depended on magic to hold power, took their fear out on the people, and their cruelty became legend. Eventually the people rebelled, tearing down the vineyards and destroying the Houses of power. . . .

And the entire world suffered, because order was out of order. The Emperor died, the empire crumbled, and the lands were left to their own devices. I can only imagine the suffering that must have followed; the history books do not speak of it, and the Washers would pretend it never happened.

Slowly, over decades, the people and the princes came to an understanding. The magic passed into the hands of those chosen not from the ranks of power, but the children of the common populace, while physical might remained in the hands of the princes, and peace settled . . . or as much peace as man, ever restless, can know.

And thus the world moved on. Generations were born and died, towns grew into cities, armies marched, kings and princes rose and fell, some lands prospered while others faded . . . while on their plots of land the Vinearts tended to their vines and worked their magic, isolated from the strife and innocent of those cycles of power. The world remained steady, the gods no longer putting their hands into the affairs of mortals. We began to believe that this was as it always would remain.

We cannot choose the age we live in. The world of my youth was a simpler one—or perhaps I merely believed it to be so. But simplicity is not the natural state of affairs for man, and the whispers of past glory—real or otherwise—are forever in our ears.

I have been on the road nearly half my life, taking the blade the year I turned sixteen. I had thought I would end my service an old woman, with only small stories to tell.

Instead, I found myself on the outskirts of a great story, and was forever changed.

A year past, I accepted a commission to travel with a group of Washers, to bear them company, and protect them from the dangers of the road. Such men should not need my protection, not within the boundaries of the Lands Vin, and I wondered at it, but they were a cheerful group, eager to serve and share their learning, and I merely assumed they carried something of great worth in their packs, and wished to be certain.

But by the end of those two weeks, another Washer joined them, and the mood darkened. It was then I first heard the rumor of a violence growing deep underfoot, reaching its tendrils into the hearts and souls of princes and Vinearts alike . . . stirring the discord that had been settled long ago.

It was then that I first heard the name Malech. The first time I heard of the Apostasy. It would not be the last. Suddenly the ground under our feet was no longer steady, the tools in our hands no longer trusted, the world no longer safe.

A storm approached, and the winds whispered one word: magic.

I am a solitaire. I know that the road is dangerous, that my blade is meant to draw blood, even if it never does. Unlike Vinearts, we see who we strike at, know the damage we do with our skills. I did not envy them their lives, tied to one place and bound by such rules . . . but I sorrowed to see that innocence die.

Prologue

*P*rince Diogo *was* a cautious man. He took no action without considering the benefits and potential deficits, and thought things through the long-term. But the moment he first heard rumors of a Vineart who challenged tradition, undermining the Commands the Washers had shoved down their throats for centuries, he had known what it meant, and what he needed to do.

The Iajan land-lord was not a particularly superstitious man; he did not keep faith with the Silent Gods, and had no trust in any demigod who was fool enough to die. His sole faith and concern was with the land he had been born to, the title his family had held for seven generations, since the old *duque* had been slain in his sleep like the last emperor of Ettion and for much the same reasons.

Every action Diogo took, he did for Iaja, for its glory and its defense. His portion of it, anyway.

So while most land-lords chose to meet their visitors in grand halls, richly appointed and designed so that the supplicant was at a disadvantage, knew his place, and understood that all the power in that room resided with its owner, Diogo did not bother. He wanted those who came to stand before him focused on his words, not the richness of their surroundings, and he made no pretense otherwise.

For that reason, his meeting hall was a small, almost ordinary space, with three small windows set along the upper half of the wall to let in clear bands of sunlight during the day, and magelights flanking the other three walls for when darkness fell. The afternoon sun was fading now, but it still picked out the rich red hues of the table they sat at, catching at the inlaid mother-of-pearl designs. Richly appointed, yes, but somber, by most traditionally flamboyant Iajan standards. But this day, this meeting, Diogo had invited the first man to sit at the table with him, as though equals.

Vineart Ranji did not let himself believe it. His yards might be sacrosanct, but they were ringed by the land-lord's villagers, who in turn were caught between the crush and the fox in terms of who they could support, and who they need fear. Diogo had the power here.

But Ranji was seated, unlike the third man standing at the far end of the table, staring at them as though they had lost their wits.

"You cannot mean this." His voice was that of a well-educated man, controlled, melodious, and filled with shock.

"I do not say things I do not mean." In keeping with his surroundings, Diogo did not drawl his words, or practice the play-stalk of cats in his speech. Nor did he pretend unconcern or ignorance of what he was doing. This land-lord played the game, no denying it, but he did it with an honesty that Ranji found both disturbing and oddly disarming. You knew what trouble you were in when you dined with him.

Of all the lords in Iaja, when every soul knew that the lords had been in collusion, only Diogo did not deny placing the bounty on Master Vineart Malech's head to keep him from interfering with things—matters of power—beyond his concern. Only Diogo, after things went to ashes and rot, had not tried to hide behind tradition, but stood straight and said that he would do whatever was needful to protect what was given to him.

Common knowledge, among those who listened, that Diogo was dangerous to those he considered the enemy.

That was why Ranji had accepted his offer of Agreement, although he had refused similar overtures from the other Iajan lords. If you must choose among evils, choose an evil that admits itself. That way, you knew where you stood, and you could stand out of its way.

It was a pity, Ranji thought, that more of the world was not so forthright.

"This is unacceptable," the third man said, drawing his red robes about him, his left hand falling to rest on the wooden cup hanging from his belt. The closely trimmed beard adorning his swarthy chin seemed to quiver in indignation. "Surely you know that this is not allowed."

"There is much that is not allowed," Diogo said. "And much that happens nonetheless. So unless your prayers and invocations can prevent crops from failing overnight, villages from being ravaged by beasts, and men disappearing without a trace, then I suggest you leave the work to those of us willing to act, and go Wash something instead."

It was said lightly, but it was no joke, and the Washer stiffened again, this time in rage rather than confusion. "The Collegium will hear of this!"

Diogo stood, then, his temper finally frayed, and Ranji flinched, although the anger was not directed at him. "The Collegium *has* heard of this. Over and over again, for a year and more now, we have told them what is happening, warned them, and begged for advice, for some kind of guidance." He regained control of himself, tempering his anger into sadness and reproach. "We begged you for help when the sickness took our children, when the hives withered and died." The sadness slipped, revealing anger once again. "And all we received in response was the repeated droppings of Sin Washer's Commands, that we sit back and be patient, that the balance held, that all would be well, if we only trusted in Sin Washer's Solace."

Ranji lowered his gaze to the table, his fingers laced together in his lap. He would not speak against the Brotherhood, but he could not defend them, either. Diogo had the right of it. Once Malech had pulled that curtain aside, exposed the threat to their very existence, it had become impossible to not-see, to not-hear. Isolation was not protection.

"There is no more Solace in the world, Washer," Diogo said, more quietly now. "The Heirs are impotent, and now it is time for those with power to use it. Together, if that will accomplish our means."

The Washer turned to Ranji as though to implore sanity from him. "You cannot . . ."

"Cannot?" Diogo did not give Ranji the opportunity to respond, forcing the Washer's attention back to him. "Will you stop us all, Washer? Keep us from saving the people entrusted to our care? Will you stop the people themselves when, in their panic, they turn on you as well, having already destroyed the Great Houses?"

The Washer shook his head, denying such a possibility. "It is not that bad . . ."

"It is *worse.*"

The conversation, such as it had been, was over. The lord barely turned, but the subtle jerk of his chin was enough for the two figures standing, almost lazily, at the doorway. Firm hands were laid upon the Washer's arms, and he was led—not ungently—out of the chamber.

"We're sorry, sahr." The voice was low, but not soft; the woman might have been apologizing, but she was not going to refuse her orders. A solitaire, one of the hire-women fighters. Not young, with strands of gray in her dark hair, and a strong, pointed chin with a thin white scar across the tip; she had an air of determined patience about her. Her companion-in-arms wore Diogo's brand on his leather cuirass, rather than her simple star-sigil, and his hand held more tightly, as though worried that he might be judged were the Washer somehow to escape. A slender, brownish hound padded behind them, its dark eyes fixed on the Washer but its attention focused on the solitaire, awaiting her command even as it guarded her back.

The Washer addressed his words to the woman, judging the lad beyond any common sense, his loyalty too deeply ingrained. "You know what they do . . . it is an abomination against all decency. This entire city will—"

"This entire city is the only safe spot on the coastline," the solitaire retorted. "Sahr Washer, you are no fool. Diogo spoke only truth. The Collegium had its chance, and they wasted it, and now the people look to another to save them. You, your people, gave him this power; he did not take it."

They were in the hallway proper now, and she released his arm, shooting a glare at her companion until he followed suit. "Go back inside," she told the young man in a low voice. "I will see the Washer to the door."

The Washer had not been offered quarters when he arrived, as was traditional, nor given the chance to break his travel with a meal, or even to rinse his mouth with *vin ordinaire*. At the time, he had been too intent on the message he had been sent to deliver. Now, spent and tossed aside, he felt his exhaustion.

He would ask no favors of this apostate House, however.

They walked in silence through the hallway: two humans and the hound, the gray stone floors echoing their footsteps, the usual flow of foot traffic normal to a Great House absent.

"How bad is it, Daughter of the Road?"

"Bad." She did not hesitate, or ask him what he meant. "The past ten-month, it seems all has gone wrong or worse, but no one can lay finger on the cause or find any pattern. Lacking specific action or remedy, the people worry, chewing at themselves and any others they can reach. There are rumors in the street, and rumors in the powdered baths, and the rumors are the same. Something rises out of the seas and falls from the skies, crawls from the dirt and covers us while we sleep, invisible and with malign intent. Surely you have heard the same?"

He did not respond to her question. "And your hire-lord?"

The solitaire did hesitate, then. "A good man, as such men go. Strong, and looking to become stronger, always playing his own political games, but with cause and an eye to the long road. No more or less than any man of power. The Vineart with him"—she shrugged, but without a hitch in her stride or allowing him to pause—"the Vineart does what he must to survive, Brother, as do we all."

He might have argued the point, but arguing with a solitaire was the act of a fool: they did not care.

The guards at the main entrance watched them go, cautious but incurious, and they passed across the stone courtyard toward the front gate and the city beyond. There were more people gathered here, waiting their turn to see some official or another, or merely lingering to find the morning's gossip. The conversations were hushed but lively, the scene vibrant, and for a moment both Washer and solitaire could pretend that it was a normal day, that nothing was wrong, that everything, once they passed through the gates, would be well.

"Washer!"

A cry from one of the men milling about in the courtyard: a cartwright, from the guild badge on his shoulder, moving toward them at an urgent pace.

The Washer paused, forcing his escort to pause as well. "I am here," the Washer said, raising his hands in the universal cup and offering the man his blessing. "Zatim's solace be upon you."

The man was too upset to return the ritual greeting, his hands barely raising enough to indicate he knew whom he was speaking to before dropping down again, and then back up to wave in his anxiety. "Washer, you have been on the roads, you must tell us, what do you hear from Ternda-town? I sent three wains that way near a month ago, but no return and no payment has been heard, and messenger-birds will not fly there any more."

"What?" The solitaire snapped to alertness at that. "Bahn, heel," she said quietly when the hound would have surged forward, never looking away from the man in front of her. "How so, these birds?"

The man turned to her, responding to the command in her voice, although in normal time a guildsman might not have deigned to notice her, wrapped in his own importance. "It is true, my . . . it is true. The birds, when released, veer north or south, but will go neither east nor west to the ocean, no matter what magics we use. They veer, and then they return."

Messenger-birds were spelled to follow the flow of magic, were sensitized to the flow of magic, in ways only they—and Vinearts, who crafted the spellwine—could comprehend. If they would not go a certain way . . . something terrible came.

The Washer kept his hands steady, and only the solitaire saw the faint, fast twitch in his cheek. He had not known this.

Neither had she, nor any of her sisters, else word would have reached her, a warning. This was new, uncanny. A solitaire, trained to sword and hound, did not trust that which was uncanny.

At her side, the hound whined once, pressing its head against her knee as though seeing reassurance. Like the Washer, she had none to give.

Part I

Revenant

Chapter 1

The Berengia

Autumn

box edge hit against the rail, nearly cracking the wooden slats. "Ai! Careful with that!"

The hands holding the box curved in an unmistakably rude gesture, and Ao raised his arms in disgust. "Go ahead then, ruin it. It's not as though it were expensive, or rare, or . . ."

Mahault glared at him over the top of the crate, her arms straining with the weight. "You want to come here and handle it, then?"

Ao gestured grandly at the stumps of his legs, hidden under the blanket across his lap. "I am somewhat indisposed at the moment. . . ."

Jerzy leaned against the railing a few feet away, feeling the sway of the

Vine's Heart below him, his body almost unconsciously moving to the lull of the waves, and wasn't sure if he was too tired to laugh.

Probably.

It was good to hear the two of them bickering again. It had been difficult weeks since they fled the coastline of Irfan, and the disaster of their journey. The quiet-magic he had used to keep Ao from bleeding to death immediately after the serpent's attack had not prevented infection from setting in soon after, and between Ao's fever and Jerzy's own exhaustion, the mood had been grim enough without the others' overanxious guilt and fears bringing them down further. Even now there was cause for worry: Jerzy had stopped the bleeding that would have cost the trader his life, but despite Ao's determined cheer, the pain was still obvious on his face, and the risk of rot setting in still too high for anyone's comfort.

After the first week passed and Ao did not die, Jerzy had banned both Mahault and Kaïnam from the main cabin, treating the injured trader by himself. The others, worn down by the need to keep watch and keep the *Heart* on a steady course, aware that at any moment the Washer's ship—or another—might swoop down on them from the deeper ocean, were only too happy to leave him to it. Even when Ao recovered enough to sit up on his own, and come out on deck for the fresh air, the fear lingered among his shipmates.

Two months since they had fled the shores of Irfan, two months of steady sailing with only three able-bodied crew, and one of them him; they'd been forced to cast the weigh-anchor at night, when the winds died down, and sail as hard as they could dusk and dawn. Sighting the Berengian shoreline the night before had improved all their spirits.

The sooner they were home, the better.

"Children," Kaï said now, passing them by with his own packs balanced almost carelessly in his arms. "Play nice, or I'll throw it all overboard."

Kaïnam's attempt to pull a princeling's superiority did make Jerzy laugh. As they turned toward the welcoming harbor that morning,

Kaïnam had asked Jerzy to heat water for shaving, and Mahault had abandoned her trou and tunic for a more reputable dress that covered her arms and legs, while the others had brushed out their clothing as best they could, looking for something not faded into gray by the sun or worn to stiffness by the salted sea air. Despite that, all four still looked like rootless vagabonds, and certainly not a prince of note or the daughter of a lord-maiar.

Jerzy sobered. They were, in fact, vagabonds, as much as any brigand or beggar. If the Washers had taken him, he would never have seen his vineyard again, and the others . . . for their crime of associating with him? Ao would have died, his limbs infected without healspells. Mahl, disowned by her father, without protection beyond Kaïnam's claim to a distant Principality? Mahault had chafed even at her father's guardianship. She would have fought her way out—and died—rather than submit to any sort of imprisonment, much less becoming the property of any man who claimed her.

"You there!" Kaïnam abandoned playfulness and strode past Jerzy, vaulting over the railing and onto the wooden plank that had been extended from the shoreline and tied to the *Heart's* side for easy access. "Careful with those casks!"

The warning was not necessary: the men unloading the ship were Berengian docksmen who knew full well what a wine cask looked like. They would no sooner drop it than they would a crate of silks from Ao's people or silver beaten from the mountains. Less, perhaps, for fear of what the Vineart might do to them if his wares were damaged.

Although Jerzy, his skin finally weathered to a pale gold from the sun, his hair past his shoulders in a ragged fall of fox-red, and his clothing an odd mismatch of trou and tunic, low boots jammed over feet re-accustomed to going bare, his belt empty of the signs of his rank, would not strike caution or care into any man's heart.

Inside him, though, the magic pulsed strongly, almost overriding the calls of the dockworkers, the occasional scream of black-winged seadivers overhead, and the ever-present creak-and-slap noises of the *Heart* herself. The slave called Foxfur had not known magic, and even as a student the quiet-magic had hidden within him, waiting to be summoned. No longer. Since tasting the unblooded fruit of Esoba's yard and drawing on them to set fire to the sands so they could escape the Washers; since healing Ao and keeping him alive, using Kaïnam's supply of spellwines like tonics to maintain his strength and keep the others awake, alert, and healthy as well . . . Jerzy could barely remember what it felt like to not hear the hum and thrum of the quiet-magic in his bones.

But even over that, he heard Ao's quiet "uh," a sound not of pain but worry. Jerzy moved to where the other sat, his hand now fisting the fabric of the blanket in agitation, and tilted his head, about to ask what was wrong.

"Washers," Ao said, indicating the men gathering on the docks, clearly heading for them. The word had the sound of a curse.

Jerzy's gaze tracked the movement of the red-clad figures through the dockside crowd. Using Ao's trader-knowledge of port towns, they had chosen the town of Reoudoc, north of the border between The Berengia and Iaja, because it was large enough to hide their arrival but not so large that it would have a chapterhouse, one of the Washers' meeting places, of its own.

Washers, who had chased them from Aleppan to the coast of Irfan, and would have caught them were it not for the sea serpent whose attack had created enough confusion for the *Vine's Heart* to escape.

The same attack that had so injured Ao that they had no choice but to abandon any plan to chase down their enemy, and return here.

"Bad luck, or were they alerted to us?" Ao asked, his gaze never leaving the approaching men, all amusement gone from his voice now.

"Don't know," Jerzy said. "Bad luck would be better."

Ao laughed, the sound shorter and more tense than it used to be, even as one hand reached down to rub at the stub of his thigh, wincing at the touch. "Bad luck, we've got."

Ao had not meant it to sting, but Jerzy flinched nonetheless.

"A day until home," he said quietly. "Only a day to home." That had been the other reason to choose this port: a direct road to House Malech, Jerzy's home and the only place he would feel safe, protected by his own vines and the Guardian's stony presence. A place where he would have access to the healwines he needed to ensure that Ao recovered—although he would never be able to replace the limbs the serpent's teeth had torn away.

The guilt Jerzy felt at that was useless: it was a blow, along with Master Vineart Malech's death and Jerzy's own exile, to be laid at the feet of their enemy, the mysterious outland Vineart who had created the serpents and set them to the hunt, who had undermined the Vin Lands, sowed suspicion and death to further his own purpose.

Jerzy's gut burned with the need to make the man pay. They had a name now; Ximen, and a title, Praepositus, courtesy of the man he and Kaïnam had interrogated back in Irfan. With those, if it had not been for Ao's injury, they could have been out searching for him, putting the bastard on the defensive. . . .

Bad luck. They had that, it was true.

"Ho, the *Heart!*"

"That's torn it, then," Mahault said grimly, coming up alongside Jerzy. The former maiar's daughter might have put back her skirts and tied her long, sun-golden hair back in the complicated knot Jerzy had first seen her wear nearly half-year prior, but her face was thinner and harder than that girl could ever have imagined, and the way her hand rested at her hip, looking for the sword discreetly packed with her other belongings, was new.

"It might not be . . ." Jerzy stopped as the four men drew close enough to identify. Three were unknown to him, anonymous bodies draped in red. The fourth, and their clear leader . . . that face he knew.

"Washer Oren."

Any hope Jerzy had that this was purely coincidence or chance died with that name. The Washer had been the most junior of the three Washers sent to question him last spring. Neth, Oren's master, had been onboard the ship that hounded them on the coast of Irfan, had been the one who confronted them, ordering them to wait until the Collegium sent new orders on Jerzy's fate.

They had not been inclined to wait.

Jerzy scowled at the Washers, secure in the fact that he was far enough back they could not see him. If Oren was here, and Neth was there, where was the third Washer, Brion? The fact that the older man was not to be seen was slightly comforting, but only slightly. Oren was young, but the others gathered around him clearly looked to him for orders. And that meant Oren was taking orders from someone else.

Someone who knew the name of their ship, and that Jerzy was onboard. Had Neth gotten word to the Collegium already, quickly enough to muster a party to meet them? And how had they known . . . ?

Jerzy checked that thought. The same way the Washers had known to find the *Heart* along the Irfan coast: clearly they had access to tracking spells. The Collegium could afford to buy the precious aetherwine that housed that particular spell, if the need was great enough, and, clearly, they thought it was. Unable to find them on the ocean, the Washers had set tell-tales along the coast . . . and the *Vine's Heart* had sailed right into it.

Jerzy lifted his hand slightly in agitation and found Ao's fingers brushing against his palm, a brief, comforting touch.

"Ho, the party," Kaïnam called out in return to the hail. As the actual owner of the vessel, with Ao, it was his right to act as captain, and Jerzy did not envy him it. "What can we do for you, Brothers?"

Oren squinted up at the figure on the plank. "You are Kaïnam, Prince of Atakus?"

"I am." Despite hardship, Kaï's long, lean body remained loose-limbed, the sleek black hair shining under the afternoon sunlight and his grave beauty looking as though it would best grace a coin rather than a living being. In no way did he indicate surprise that this man should know his name; rather, he took it for granted that of course his name and title should be known to all.

Ao and Mahault had often found Kaï's power-born superiority grating, but occasionally it was a useful tool.

Oren did not bend before it, but returned arrogance for arrogance. "We request permission to board," he said in a manner that implied less a request than a demand.

"Indeed?" Instead, Kaï walked down the plank he had been standing on, meeting them on solid ground, in a move to keep all attention on him and not those still onboard.

"What do we do?" Ao asked, looking up at Jerzy for instruction.

"Do nothing," Jerzy said. "Play the cripple." Under the concealing blanket, Ao's stumps were still raw looking. If they were forced to move, the eye would be drawn to those scars, evoking sympathy and disgust, not suspicion. Anything that might stop an opponent, or even slow him down, could be useful.

"If we have to leave the ship before we're ready, there won't be time to get him into the handcart," Mahl said quietly, joining them. "They'll catch us for certain."

"I can work around that," Jerzy said, his attention on the tight group on the ground. Kaï's shoulders were still relaxed, and he had not gone for the sword that was weighted against his hip. So whatever was being said, it was still only words. "If we need to move quickly, I'll . . . do something else."

"Can you make me fly?" Ao had been asking that since he woke from his fever and accepted the fact that he could no longer walk, that all the magic in the world could not regrow bones and flesh from cauterized scabs.

"Fly, yes," Jerzy said, same as he did every time Ao asked, repetition turning it into an almost comforting exchange. "Landing might be more difficult."

"Vineart!"

Kaïnam was using what Ao called his "lordling" voice, and it carried over the bustle of the dock without actually silencing anything. Jerzy stepped forward automatically, almost jumping to respond, and then took a half-step beat to compose himself, moving more slowly as befitted a true Vineart, rather than a student pushed forward too soon.

"Look pathetic," he heard Mahl say to Ao, behind him, as the trader came with a thump down to the deck. "More pathetic than usual, I mean."

They were definitely feeling better. Despite the seriousness of their situation, it was difficult to keep a solemn expression on his face as he moved onto the gangway—opening the railing first, rather than leaping over it as Kaï had—but the sight again of those robes sobered him quickly enough. The last time he had seen Washer Oren, Master Vineart Malech had been alive, and he had been a mere Vineart-student, not Vineart Jerzy of House Malech. Was the Washer here to arrest him for the deaths and disappearances of the Washers and their hire-swords? Had the old charge of apostate been reinstated? Or was there some new trouble they were unaware of, waiting to come down on their heads?

"This is Washer Oren, here at the behest of the Collegium," Kaïnam said, stiffly formal as though they'd never adventured together at all. "He wishes to parlay with you, Vineart, and requests the use of the *Vine's Heart* as meeting space."

That, Jerzy had not been expecting. At all.

"You wish . . ." Jerzy sat back in his chair, staring at Oren, wishing desperately that the Washer had not been so adamant that it be only the two of them in this parlay. Although he now understood why.

"You have been at sea for months," Oren said. His voice, almost sullen with distaste, indicated that he was no happier than Jerzy about the message he carried. He might lead this group, but he took orders nonetheless. Jerzy's autonomy seemed to irk him worse than anything the Vineart had been accused of. "Things have . . . changed."

Changed in ways that Washer Neth clearly had not been aware of when he'd chased them to the shores of Irfan. Jerzy wondered, if they'd waited for Neth's messenger-birds to return, if this would have been the message carried back. Or was this even more recent? Jerzy was not the observer trader-bred Ao was, or like Kaïnam, trained in the ways of court politics, but he felt something was wrong.

"You wish me to join with you." And that, to start, was terribly wrong. Just as Vinearts were protected by their isolation, kept from power by their obligations to the vines, Washers wielded power to ensure that isolation, maintain it, as the very basis of their existence. Joining the two was anathema to Sin Washer's Command.

"The Collegium wishes you to stand with us," Oren corrected. "So that we may give a clear message to the rest of the Lands Vin, and prevent any further . . . unpleasantness."

Unpleasantness. Jerzy almost laughed, bitterly. Seven Vinearts, their names listed in a neat hand on the paper Oren had showed him, sealed with the mark of the Collegium, had joined with land-lords of their regions, placing their yards, their magic, at those lord's disposal. Seven that had come forward and publicly announced their decision— how many more acting quietly in tandem, as Kaï's father and their local Vineart had been? And how many had been forced, as the local lord would have forced poor Esoba, against his will?

And the Collegium called that "unpleasantness"?

Jerzy leaned back, resting the fingers of one hand against his lips as though to keep himself from saying anything before he had thought it through. Things had changed, indeed, in the time they had been at sea, and far worse than Oren was admitting, if seven—seven!—Vinearts had come forward publicly.

How many more were silent? How many, caught between frost and rot, were too afraid to move?

Remembering the muttered gossip he had overheard in the streets of Aleppan, of distrust, confusion, and fear among the merchants and workers, Jerzy leaned forward again and stared directly into Oren's face across the polished map table. "Let us be perfectly clear: in these days, when Vinearts are under attack from an unknown enemy, you wish me to reject any offers I might or might not receive from a land-lord, and cast my lot instead with the Washers. Yes?" He drew in a soft breath and asked, "To what purpose?"

The Washer didn't blink, his dark gaze steady on Jerzy's face. "We are asking you to remember your training, and the Commands, and do what is right, for the well-being of all the Lands Vin, to show the rest of your kind that there is still solace and order to be found in tradition." Oren's words, despite his obvious unhappiness, were well-rehearsed, with the weight of belief behind them.

Jerzy distrusted that weight, on instinct. He had seen too much, come too far from the ignorant slave in the fields. Tradition benefited the Washers more than it ever had Vinearts. More, Ao had taught him to beware any offer that spoke of what one side might gain, and not the other. What would he, or indeed any Vineart, gain by standing with the Brotherhood? While his master had been gathering evidence of things going wrong throughout the lands, the Washers had done nothing. When Jerzy had uncovered potential evidence of someone working against the Lands Vin, they had attempted to destroy it, and him. The Washers had accused him of apostasy in an attempt to draw out and destroy Vineart Giordan for petty politics, destroying a vineyard of such potential it made Jerzy weep to think of the loss.

And now they asked him to think of the Commands? To come to heel like a puppy, and settle for what scraps of protection they might decide to offer?

Now, when Giordan and Malech were both dead?

The taste of bile filled his throat.

What would Master Malech say? No, what would Ao say? *Think like a trader,* he could hear Ao telling him. *Let the other person spill their guts before you commit to a single agreement.*

"I will consider your words," Jerzy said, standing up without moving his chair to give the impression of a seamless flow, the way he remembered Master Malech doing. He was shorter than his master, and far less impressive, but Oren was no Washer Neth, either.

"But . . ."

"I will consider your words," Jerzy repeated, and with that the Washer had to abide.

"THEY WANT WHAT?"

Mahault's reaction mirrored his own, a gape-jawed incredulity that, unlike Jerzy, she made no effort to hide. The moment the Washer had left the *Heart*, the other three had crowded into the cabin, out of sight of anyone watching from the dock, waiting to hear what had transpired.

"They want Jerzy. That is interesting." Kaïnam had a faraway expression on his face, looking out and turned inward at the same time. The others left him to it, while Jerzy told them the rest.

"Seven Vinearts? Out of how many?" Ao frowned, his quick-ranging mind already worrying at the numbers.

Jerzy recalled the tapestry-map in his master's study and the paper one unrolled on the desk, with markers and colored stones placed across the Vin Lands, marking Vinearts whom might be counted on . . .

"There were eleven Master Vinearts a year ago," he said. "Including Master Malech. Now . . ." He did not know how many of those who had died or disappeared had been Masters, or if any new ones had come into their title since then. Mastery was not given, but earned; a Vineart grew into it, and none had ever claimed such before their time. Tradition, again.

His master had said that Giordan would have become a Master, given time. The Washers had taken that time away.

"And Vinearts who are not Masters?" Ao was still worrying at the numbers, trying to make something out of them.

Jerzy shook his head, frustrated at not having the information immediately in hand. He'd not had enough time to learn, before. "Thirty, mayhap, that I knew of. That Master Malech had noted. Far fewer now." Esoba, whom they had not known of until too late. Giordan, killed by

Washer decree. Poul in the desert lands, struck down by their enemy, and his slaves stolen. Sionio, the first known to disappear . . . how many others, gone?

It hurt, like a hot blow inside his chest, to think of the knowledge lost, the vineyards abandoned. If the Washers had listened, had done something, could that have been stopped? Jerzy did not think so, but he would never know, and that not-knowing was a continuing pain under his ribs.

"And now they want you to . . . argh!" Mahault threw her hands up in the air, her entire body seething disgust. Ao, on the other hand, started to laugh.

"It isn't funny," Jerzy said, annoyed.

"No . . . but it is. Suddenly, you're holding all the power, in their eyes, they need you to play along . . . and we haven't an idea what to ask for, in return. To a trader? That's terribly funny. Or just terrible. I'm not sure which."

Put that way, Jerzy could see Ao's point, and, reluctantly, the edge of his lips turned up and he shook his head. Even in the worst, most frustrating moments, when Ao should have had every reason to give up . . . he didn't.

"How do you do it?" he asked. The question lacked specifics, but Ao didn't pretend to misunderstand.

"What other choice do I have? What other choice do any of us have? You either laugh at something, or you let it laugh at you."

"I don't like it," Mahault said. "This change in their thinking. I can't tell you why, but I don't like it. Something makes my skin prickle."

"I don't like it, either," Jerzy said. "I have no love for the Collegium, any more than they feel love toward me." He tapped the table in front of him, frustrated that there was no room in the cabin to pace without bumping into someone else. "Rot and blast, I don't *like any* of what we're hearing. Vinearts are Commanded to stand apart for a reason. A good reason." Power and magic should not stand together; even with the best of reasons, it seemed all too often to go wrong. With bad intentions . . .

"Master Malech poked his nose beyond our walls because there was no other choice. Not because he believed the old ways were wrong."

"Standing with the Collegium would force them to support you in turn, yes?" Mahault was weighing the options, her face tight with concentration. "No more risk of apostasy . . . and maybe they could help us?"

"If they chose to. But if I agreed . . ." Jerzy tried to imagine it, and failed. "It would not soothe fears, as they wish. Not now. It would merely inflame them, each group seeing only the other gaining advantage, building fear out of suspicion. That is what our enemy wants, what he has been doing all along. To undercut traditions, to set us against each other. If I take this offer, I do his work for him. A Vineart cannot be part of the greater world, may not form alliances. Sin Washer commanded it."

Jerzy's words sounded hollow even as he spoke them; had he not already broken that Command, over and again? What had he done, here, if not forming an alliance, however informal?

"Aren't we already?" Kaïnam asked, returning to the conversation, picking up on what Jerzy had been thinking. "Look at us. Lord and Vineart. Trader and . . . solitaire, by heart if not training. If you added in a Washer and a farmer, we'd be every-folk represented at this table."

Exaggeration—a trader was not a guildsman, and a farmer could not represent the fisherfolk, but that did not make it false. Jerzy had formed alliances, had added his abilities to those of others, had used magic in ways forbidden. The fact that if he hadn't, he would be dead now, and no one would know that there was danger until it was too late, did not mitigate those facts.

The responsibility pressed against him, and Jerzy found himself instinctively reaching for the distant touch of the Guardian, the stone dragon who protected House Malech.

He had told himself to stop reaching, to not depend on that support: on the seas, in distant lands, the connection had been so faint as to be useless. But now that they were here, docked on the shores of The Berengia . . .

You are Vineart.

The reassurance came through, clear and steady, tasting of dry stone and fresh rain. It was raining, back home.

For the first time, the knowledge that the Guardian—as well as the Washers—considered him full Vineart was neither soothing nor disturbing, but merely another weight on his shoulders.

"I'm not supposed to be making these decisions," he said, hating himself for the too-familiar sound of uncertainty and fear in his voice. "I don't know enough . . . I don't know anything."

There was silence in the cabin, and then Ao, unexpectedly, slammed his hand down flat on the table, making it rock back and forth under the blow.

"Rot," he announced. "Twice-rotted. You think any of us know? You think Malech knew? I listen for my livelihood, Jer. I listen for survival. You know what I am hearing? I'm hearing that all the rules we ever knew have gone into the midden; everything's not changing, it's already *changed*. And us? Us four? We probably know more than anyone else what's really going on."

Everyone except the enemy who drove all this.

Jerzy felt the weight of the Guardian's confirmation push at his spine, and the pressure literally shoved him out of his chair. Once up, there still wasn't enough room to pace, the way he had back in his master's study, so he strode to the far wall and stared at it, not seeing the maps and instruments stored there, but his own convoluted thoughts.

The unknown Vineart, Ximen, had set all this in motion, attacking vineyards, using pawns to influence men of power, setting magic-born beasts to terrorize the common folk, undermine the ground the Lands Vin were built on.

How was Jerzy to know what the proper counter to all that might be? If he agreed to the Washers' terms, he would be safe . . . but at what cost, and for how long? He did not trust the Collegium, he would not take orders from a man of power. But was he strong enough to stand on his own?

So many others, more experienced, more powerful, had failed and died. What arrogance—what foolishness—to think that he could make a difference.

And yet, they had. The four of them had stopped Ximen's attack in Irfan, denied him access to the unblooded grapes he so clearly desired. They had kept one pace ahead of the Washers, had stayed alive despite sea-serpent attacks, and had made it back here . . . to do what?

"I could have stayed in my father's house," Mahl said, and her tone was quiet, as if she were speaking to herself, and the others overhearing by chance. "I could have stayed, and told myself I had no choice. But each thing we do is a choice."

Something in Jerzy rebelled at that. He had been a slave, taken as a child for the flicker of magic within him, sold to Malech for that flicker. He had no choice, had never had a choice in his entire life . . . and yet, Mahault was right. Everything had always been a choice.

He chose to live rather than die. He chose to learn rather than fail. He chose to run rather than be punished unfairly by the Washers. He chose to kill, that others might live. He chose to travel with these companions, rather than standing alone. And, now, he had to choose again.

A Vineart had no control over when the fruit was ripe. But his choice of when to harvest made all the difference.

Jerzy lifted his head, and his voice, when he spoke, was firm. "The first thing we need to do is get home."

AWARE THAT THE Washer's party was waiting for Jerzy's answer, the four did not hesitate once a decision was made. Most of their belongings had already been offloaded before that interruption, waiting only for the cart and hire-horses to be delivered. The *Heart* had been prepared for an indefinite stay at dock, and Kaïnam had paid her fees for the winter out of the last of his coins. If—when—they needed her again, she would be ready. All that remained was for them to leave the ship itself.

To do that, now, they needed magic.

"I wish there was some other way," Jerzy said, as they were preparing to disembark. "It's too . . ."

"Obvious? Noticeable?" Ao asked. "As opposed to the masthead you can't help but see and yet nobody notices?"

Jerzy looked back involuntarily. Their masthead was a living thing, dark-skinned hands stroking a wreath of vine leaves, the unexpected result of Jerzy's spell of protection when they had to leave the ship anchored and unguarded in Irfan. He did not know if the figurehead actually invoked any particular protection . . . but anyone looking at it would certainly assume that it did. They were counting on that to keep the ship safe again, since they did not have the additional funds to hire guards.

Jerzy touched the marker still hung around his neck. Once, merely showing it within the borders of The Berengia would buy him whatever aid he needed, on his master's reputation. Now, his master was gone, and he himself could not stand surety, not when he did not know if he would have anything to repay it with.

"Jer?"

"Yes, all right," Jerzy replied, finding the wine sack he needed and weighing it in his hand, estimating how much liquid remained within. The masthead had been unexpected, to say the least, and it still disturbed him to think about too closely. In contrast, what they were about to do wasn't even outside the realm of the usual . . . if anything these days could be considered usual or common. He unstoppered the wine sack, and then offered it to Ao.

"Me?" The trader looked half-horrified, half-fascinated. Behind them, Mahl let out a muffled laugh.

"You. You're the one the magic will be working on."

Ao swallowed hard, his throat working noisily, and then nodded.

Like the Kingdom of Caul, although for different reasons, his clan es-chewed the use of spellwines. Even though Ao had become comfort-able with what Jerzy could do, the thought of it being worked directly within him was only now sinking in. The realization made him clearly uncomfortable.

When he was a slave, Jerzy had been forbidden by law to so much as taste an unripe grape, or breathe too deeply of the fumes during crush. He had some sense of what was in Ao's mind.

"It will do only what you tell it to do. That's how spellwine works: the incantation frames the magic the . . . the same way you frame an Agreement, so that every detail is considered and every eventuality taken care of."

The explanation seemed to soothe the trader. In truth, it was more complicated than that, but Jerzy rather suspected a trader's Agreement had loopholes, too.

"So how do I . . ."

"You've seen me do it often enough. Take a sip, just a small one, and hold it on your tongue. Let it sink into the flesh, and the aroma rise up into your mouth . . ."

He watched, his gaze intent as Ao did as he was instructed. The other's movement was awkward, too aware of being watched, and he took too much wine with the first sip, choking a little as it ran out of his mouth and down his chin.

"It's all right. Everyone does that the first time." He hadn't, but he had made a fool of himself in other ways. "Hold it, and then say the decantation, the way I taught you."

Ao swallowed again, letting only a little of the liquid run down his throat, and then his lips moved. The words were barely audible, as he tried not to spill more spellwine, but that didn't matter. Loud or soft, the spellwine was crafted to respond to the shape of the words as much as the sounds.

"To the legs, flow. The legs, lift. Carry me, go."

The look on Ao's face as the windspell rose to do his bidding, lifting him upright as though carried on invisible legs, was worth every penny the spellwine had cost them.

"It won't last long," Jerzy cautioned him. "And you'll ache when it's done. But for a while, you'll be able to move by yourself." Enough to get them through the crowd and, with a carefully placed cloak over Ao's shoulders, without anyone seeing that the man was a cripple. The arrival of the Washers, and their demands, had changed plans beyond the need for haste: they could afford no indication of weakness, no hint of vulnerability others might try to use—or use against them.

Ao took a gleeful step forward—and pitched over into Jerzy's arms.

"Carefully!" the Vineart said, setting him gently upright. "Carefully. You're out of practice and these aren't your legs."

Ao nodded, and took another, more cautious step.

"But it doesn't last?"

"You know it doesn't," Jerzy said, picking up his own rucksack, keeping his free hand on Ao's arm to steady him. The words lingered in his mouth, like the feel of a spell, an ominous warning. "So don't waste it. Let's go."

Chapter 2

*T*he *dockside, like* most fishing villages of any size in The Berengia, was a bustle of people minding their own business, intent on their own problems. Jerzy noted a few older men, able-bodied enough to be out fishing, instead mending nets. They sat not down by the water's edge but up higher, where they had a clearer view of the horizon. As their small party passed, Jerzy saw fish spears on the ground next to them, and horns or drums at their feet. Sentinels, ready to warn the village should anything come at them from the sea. Serpents . . . or men? Jerzy felt a shudder of anticipation run down his spine.

Although a few folk stopped to watch them go by, curious, no Washer appeared to stop them. Despite that, all four were tense until they were out of the village itself, far enough along the rise and fall of the road that a man on foot could not catch up with them. Mahl relaxed first, settling deeper into her saddle with a sigh as they crested the first hill, while Kaïnam's shoulders eased a fraction with every step they took.

The ocean was hidden behind the ridge, although the tang of seawater and fish still carried in the air, when the spell wore off. Ao felt it just in time to brace himself, and then collapsed a little on the wagon's bench.

"Are you all right?" Jerzy, next to him, glanced sideways with a worried frown.

"Yes. Ow. No. You said ache, not . . ."

"Bad?"

"It could hurt less. It could hurt more." Ao's cheerfulness was strained enough to let them know that, in fact, it hurt a great deal, but he waved off any assistance, leaning against the cask packed up behind him and tucking the blanket around the stubs of his legs with a forced casualness.

The cart they had hired was larger and far more comfortable than the one they had been offered in Irfan; a full wagon, in fact, large enough for all their belongings and the remaining half-casks of spellwine they had taken from Vineart Esoba, from the now-fallen House of Runcidore. Jerzy held the reins of the placid piebald draft horse that pulled the wagon, barely having to guide it along, while Mahault and Kaï rode alongside on slighter-built brown geldings, their blades now lashed to the saddles, in reach—and, more important, in clear view, despite the apparent ease of their departure.

The others might have relaxed, but Jerzy found himself growing more tense as the road passed under their wheels. Once, those working in the field would have stopped to watch when a stranger passed by, their curiosity an open, easy thing. Jerzy himself, moving back and forth between the smaller yards owned by his master, rarely received more than a lazy wave if recognized, a long stare as he passed if not. Even the occasional troop of soldiers under Lord Ranulf's command, the lord who claimed these villages and fields, did not excite comment; there were enough villagers who had served, or sent their sons to serve, that the sight was familiar, if never entirely comforting.

In the time Jerzy had been away, that had changed. The few stooped figures working the fields now were conspicuous in how they did not look up, not ignoring the wagon and horses clattering by, exactly, but giving the strangers no cause to stop and notice them, either. There was a tension in their bodies that should not have been there, not here, where Sin Washer's Commands had kept strife to a minimum for more than a hundred years.

These were not trained warriors ready for battle, but ordinary folk, fearful of things they did not understand and could not predict. Unlike the fisherfolk, alert for trouble, Jerzy realized, these folk held themselves like slaves, aware that at any moment, without warning, the lash might come down on their heads.

Once Jerzy saw that, other changes were impossible to ignore. The comfortable, sloping fields and thick-leafed groves that Jerzy had grown up with remained . . . but it wasn't the same. The colors of encroaching autumn were the same, and yet the leaves seemed duller, the villages seemed more tightly built, once-open meadows now fenced to keep livestock contained, the areas between houses smaller, the herds grazing closer in, and more than one child visible, tending the flock or herd.

In less than a ten-month, the land had shifted.

"Something's wrong," Jerzy said, his voice tight as they left one such village, a cluster of a shared barn and five houses, three of them with their shutters closed against the mild weather. "The villagers . . ."

"They're afraid," Kaïnam said, swinging his gelding around to ride alongside the wagon. His voice was low, his free hand resting on the hilt of his blade. Mahault fell behind slightly, on the other side of the wagon, keeping pace with the back wheel, her sword now ready on her hip.

"They're not afraid," Jerzy said. "They're hungry."

Kaïnam was a princeling, Mahault grew up in a city, and Ao had more experience with roads than roots. But Jerzy had spent his entire life working the land, his fingers and toes in the dirt, and he could feel it oozing out of the land, and in the faces of the people they passed, their eyes too wide, their mouths too tight. He had thought to return home to gather strength. Instead, that strength had been sapped away.

"The crops are failing, the livestock not grazing the way they should,"

Jerzy went on, voicing what he saw so clearly now. "The land is under a blight."

A sudden fear for his vines shook him to the bone, and the urge to gather up the reins and cluck the beast to a faster pace had to be fought down: it would do him no good, not now. He had been away this long, another day would change nothing.

And yet, the feeling remained: unsettled and anticipating all at once, like hunger spiraled around his rib cage, the almost-forgotten wait for the overseer's crop to land on unprotected flesh. How could he not have felt it, before? Was it . . . was it because of Master Malech's death?

Even as Jerzy considered it, he rejected the thought. Vinearts died; the land lived on. This was Ximen's doing: the land itself sensed unrest.

They rode in silence, each wrapped in their own thoughts, the only noise the calls of birds overhead and the comforting sound of hooves on the packed-dirt road, and Jerzy had almost managed to convince himself that the fear was merely his own uncertainty and exhaustion playing tricks on him, when Mahault's voice carried forward from her post behind them.

"We're being watched."

"What?" Jerzy's entire body tensed up again, and he felt Ao shift in the wagon behind him, bracing his body against the sudden jolt of the wagon as the horse, sensing the change, slowed down.

"Don't stop, don't look around," Kaïnam said. Then, backward over his shoulder, still quietly, to Mahault. "Yes, I know. One?"

"One," she confirmed. "Hanging back a bit. On horseback, but staying off the road. I think he's one of our Washer friends. They can't seem to let go of the red, even when they're trying to be stealthy."

Jerzy chewed at his lower lip, instinctively pulling a hint of spittle from the flesh there into his mouth, feeling the bitter tang of quiet-magic waiting to be called. "Oren didn't like my leaving without an answer."

Kaïnam did not look impressed. "He's going to follow us all the way back to the vintnery? Poor use of available men. Why merely shadow us, if they're that worried? Why not force the issue?"

"They don't have the authority." It was the only thing that made any sense, their meeting him at the docks, using surprise and his own exhaustion against him, hoping to catch him off guard, before he realized that they could not force him to do anything. Whoever wanted him did not have the entire Collegium's support. But the thought raised another worry: if a smaller group within the Washers was looking to claim a Vineart of their own, if control of magic had become that contested . . . they would not rely merely on someone like Oren to woo him. What might a Washer with more authority do to those who rejected their offer?

True, Washers had always stayed clear of the battles other men might engage in; that did not mean that the Collegium could not be deadly in its own right. Even though Jerzy had been cleared of charges they had levied, he did not trust that would keep him or his companions safe if the Collegium again deemed him a danger. Or a risk.

"Lurker up front, too," Ao called, hard on that thought. Sure enough, a man had come to the side of the road, still as a tree. Unlike their follower, he was in clear sight, and obviously waiting for them. He wore a leather smock over his clothing, and his hair was close-cropped and gray, his face clean-shaven and jowly with muscles beginning to age.

"Blacksmith?" Kaïnam asked, squinting a little.

"Farrier," Jerzy said. "And he brought friends." There was a group gathered farther off the road, four figures . . . no five, although one was slighter than the others—a child, or a dwarf, perhaps, standing by a slight rise that looked recently built rather than natural, as though ready to duck behind it if they should prove unfriendly.

"Mahl. Come front. Ao, are you ready with that bow?"

"I haven't learned how to use it yet," Ao said, even as they could hear him pulling the small crossbow Kaïnam had given him during the voyage home. It looked like a toy, but Kaïnam claimed it was deadly, and more to the issue, did not need the archer to be standing.

"They don't need to know that," Kaïnam said, urging his horse forward a pace. Jerzy noticed, as he would never have months earlier, that Kaï's new position blocked Jerzy from a direct blow from the newcomers. Without turning to look, Jerzy suspected Mahault was guarding their rear in the same manner. The weight of the wine flask hanging from his belt and the warmth of quiet-magic ready in his mouth, waiting to be called upon, reassured him that he was not without defenses of his own, if need be.

"This road was safe enough for a child to walk it," he said. Not quite true—there had always been wolves on both two legs and four, and dangers besides, but once . . .

"Was," Ao replied. "Many things were, and aren't anymore."

The words stung, although they were not meant to. This was The Berengia. Even with the blight evident, Jerzy could feel the pull of the soil under them, smell the familiar notes in the air around them, hear the subtle sounds that told him he was home. Nothing should have changed . . . and Ao was right. Everything had.

The wagon and riders drew closer and the man's shoulders, tightened in expectation, slumped, as though he had suddenly realized they were not whom he was waiting for. He took a step back, ducking his head and lifting his arms to show that he carried no weapons. Out of the corner of his eye, Jerzy saw the small group with him likewise move, their disappointment as clear to him as though they had shouted it in his ear.

"Halt," Jerzy said to the horse, his voice carrying enough for Kaïnam to hear as well. Kaï lifted his reins, and the horse paused, obediently, just before the waiting stranger.

"You look for someone?" Jerzy asked the man in Berengian.

"The healer, m'lord." The man's gaze flicked over them, then his head lowered again, as though worried about being caught looking. Something in his pose shifted when he heard Jerzy's voice; he was no longer quite so ready to run.

"Someone's ill?" The only chirurgien in the area would not come to a small village, but there were a number of lesser trained herbalists who wandered from village to village, treating all but the most desperate or severe cases.

"You are a healer, m'lord?" The man looked up at that, and his gaze went first to Jerzy's face and then, with a widening of his eyes at Jerzy's red hair, dropped down again to his waist. Seated, it was impossible to see the flask and tasting spoon hanging there, but the man made the assumption nonetheless.

"Vineart Jerzy? 'Tis you, come home?" The man's voice was . . . Jerzy could not place the tone, and from the way Kaïnam cocked his head, neither could he. A hint of fear, tinged with . . . hope? Jerzy dared not look behind him to catch Ao's reaction, but he heard the sound of the wooden bow being lowered to the floor of the wagon and took his cue from that. Ao knew people, better even than Kaï.

"How did he know . . ." Kaïnam asked, bemusement overcoming his caution.

"The hair," Jerzy said. Among the slaves gathered from all corners of the Lands Vin, his dark red hair and high cheekbones had been odd but not terribly unusual. It did mark him, however. Especially on this road.

"I am Vineart Jerzy," he told the farrier, laying the reins down in his lap and resting his left hand on his belt, just above the wine sack and spoon, drawing attention to them rather than Kaï's sword or the implied threat of Mahault, coming up alongside the wagon.

These were no brigands. Someone was ill, or injured. Badly enough to warrant a healer, and a welcoming party to ensure the healer made it there safely.

A flutter of panic hit him, like one of Mahault's practice blows. Master Malech had been the true healer; it had been he who kept the plague from overrunning this area years before Jerzy was born, he who could coax every drop of magic from healwines to save those otherwise at death's door. Jerzy did not have that same skill . . . but they would expect him to be, to do what his master had done.

Jerzy had killed more than he had saved. The memory of the plague ship still festered in his memory, never mind that they had been dead men before he ever saw it, that he had halted their suffering. He had taken their last hope away. He had snuffed the life of a slave injured in a wagon accident, had set fires to burn, risking the lives of innocent sailors, and . . .

The face of a villager child in Irfan returned to him, the crusted edge of an eye clearing under his fingertips, others crowding around him, curious and trusting. He had made a difference there, in a foreign land, outside the Lands Vin.

This man, with his diffident posture and cautious voice, was Berengian. His responsibility. His legacy.

Master Vineart Malech was dead. He was Vineart of House Malech now.

He was no more free than he had been as a slave. "If I may be of aid?"

Jerzy's offer of help quickly ran into one difficulty. To reach the village, they would need to cross fields where the cart could not go.

"We should not split up," Mahault said, the four gathered off to the side of the cart while the villagers waited, impatiently, for them to come to a decision.

"I'm the only one who needs to go—"

"No." Kaïnam and Mahault both overrode Jerzy's offer, in unison.

"I don't need guards—"

"Yes, you do." Kaï's voice was flat, hard, and refused argument. "You think this is not a trap, but we can't be sure. You go nowhere unguarded until we have you back in your yard."

"I'll stay," Ao said. "Not as though I could travel with you, anyway."

"You can't . . ." Kaïnam hesitated, unsure how to state his objection without giving insult or sharing information these strangers should not know.

"Can't what? Can't defend the supplies? Can't keep someone from driving off with our cart?" Ao lifted his eyes to the skies, as though asking for patience. "Fine. Leave one of these stalwart folk with me, to be the legs if anything should happen."

"I will stay." A square-shouldered farmer, with a patient expression and a steady way of standing, volunteered. "Between the two of us, we'll have brawn and wit."

"Half a wit, perhaps," one of his companions said, and the tension broke slightly.

"Will that satisfy, O warrior?" Ao asked, and Kaïnam, with a sideways look at Jerzy, lifted his hands in surrender.

Without further delay, the others took up their packs and set out across the field, the child running ahead to alert them someone was coming, while Jerzy questioned their leader on the nature of the illness.

There was not one person in the village who was ill, but a dozen or so, in varying stages of misery. The farrier, Justus, also doubled as their healer, having learned how to set bones in his younger years, but he knew when he was helpless. When the illness appeared, he had sent a message to the herbalist who covered this area, asking him to come with haste.

"That was four days back," Justus said as they moved diagonally away from the road, following a narrow trail through the crops.

The remainder of the party—three men carrying glaives that had clearly and clumsily been made from plow blades—followed before and behind, their attention not only on the field around and underneath them, but the skies overhead. Kaïnam and Mahault took note and followed suit, forming an oddly shaped, moving guard around Jerzy. He felt like reminding them that he was perfectly capable of defending himself, but the look in the farrier's eye stopped him.

Hope, yes, but also a despairing sort of helplessness. If protecting the Vineart from some unknown threat gave him reason to feel useful, Jerzy would not take that away from him. No more than he would have pointed out how little defense Ao could give, if someone were to attempt to steal the wagon.

His earlier observation was not true for these men. They were not acting like slaves, accepting whatever was meted out to them. They needed to take action—to stand against what threatened them, however they could. He would not wrest that opportunity from them.

That thought, gruffly practical, sounded so much like Malech that Jerzy felt a sudden pang of loss, all over again. He had so focused on coming home, on healing Ao, and being somewhere he could finally, somehow, turn and fight, that he had almost managed to forget that he would be returning to an empty House.

Not empty.

No. Not empty. The Guardian was there. Detta and Lil, and Per and Roan were there. And he was not coming home alone. That thought did not ease the pain, but made it bearable.

Trying to escape further doubt, Jerzy focused his attention on their destination, quickly coming into view. The village was small, a series of two-story, red-roofed cottages between two roads, surrounded on three sides by fields and on the other by a longer, one-story building. In the distance beyond, a small herd of red-coated cows grazed on the sloping hill. The group entered the town proper without notice, other than a few sheep that gazed at them and then went back to pulling at the browning grass of the green.

The ill had been gathered in the main hall, kept away from the others and tended by volunteers, who also made their beds there. Jerzy nodded approvingly. Master Malech had taught the local folk that, back during the plague, and they had remembered, years later.

The farrier went into the main hall with them while the others stayed behind, unwilling to risk contact with the ill.

"This is your healer?" A woman rose from where she had been crouched at the side of one of the beds, her voice cutting through the faint gloom even as she moved toward them. A shadowed figure moved beside her, knee-high and muscled. Even before they could see the sigil on her leathers, that hound had identified her as a solitaire.

The dog stopped, and bared its teeth, shockingly white and sharp against black gums. The newcomers stopped as well, taken aback.

"Stand and let him approach you." The woman's voice was firm, not allowing any room for dissent.

The farrier passed by them, intent on checking the ill or spreading word of Jerzy's arrival, as the hound padded forward, deep-chested, the body covered with a rough, golden-brown coat that curled slightly, its tail a straight upward plume that did not wag but held itself still, a flag in windless air. Jerzy had heard of these dogs but never seen one up close. The hound, suspicious, extended its great, broad-skulled head to sniff at Jerzy's hand.

He held his breath, not sure what to think or expect. The hound's nose was wet but its tongue was almost dry as it swiped at his skin and then moved on to Kaïnam.

"What is it—"

"Shh," Mahault said, and Kaï subsided, letting the animal circle around him. The mouth closed around the princeling's fingers, but although it tugged slightly, did not break the skin. Kaï did not flinch, and the hound let go, releasing him and turning to Mahault.

Her face, tanned by so many months under the open skies, had gone pale, and her eyes were wide, as though she was frightened by this the way she had not been when facing men with raised blades, but Mahault did not falter. She went to one knee, almost as though she were making a deep bow, and raised both of her hands, palm up and layered left on right at even height with the hound's black nose, staying in clear sight. The hound looked her directly in the eye and took both hands in its mouth, the same as it had Kaïnam, but this time it did not let go but rather bore down, enough that Jerzy saw Mahault flinch slightly.

"Mahl . . ." A world of question in that one breath of air; Mahl managed to shake her head just enough to warn Kaïnam from doing anything and not yet dislodge the hound or lose eye contact with it. The stranger solitaire merely stood back and watched, so Jerzy took his own cue from that.

It happened so fast, nobody, not even the solitaire, could react in time.

From a nearly frozen tableau, the hound released Mahault's hands and lurched forward, knocking her backward onto the flagstone floor, her head making a hard thunk as it hit. Her hands, released, came up, but even as Kaïnam was reaching for his blade to kill the beast, Jerzy had his hand on the hilt, stopping him. The Vineart didn't remember moving, had not taken his eyes off Mahault long enough to see the princeling move, and yet his gesture had been unerring.

Mahault was laughing. The hound, rather than tearing her throat out, was laving her face with a great pink tongue.

"Codi, leave the sister alone," the solitaire said. Her posture was still alert, loose-limbed and ready to take action, but her voice was softer, less a command than a request.

The hound gave her face one last washing and backed off, taking a seated position just behind the solitaire's left knee. Mahault got to her feet in a graceful scramble and stood facing the other woman.

"I am not a solitaire," she said.

The fighter cocked her head, simply looking at Mahl. "Codi is rarely wrong," she said, and then seemed to dismiss the matter from her thoughts, turning to Justus. "Two more have fallen ill. I can do no more for them than make them comfortable."

Jerzy jumped in before their escort could respond. "What is the nature of the illness? Fever? Rash? Justus said that there was no warning, that people simply fell over, and had no strength?"

"In truth, yes. I would accuse them of malingering, save I have come to know these people, and they are not that sort. Such extreme exhaustion afflicts them that the act of merely moving their limbs brings agony." The solitaire seemed both worried and exasperated. "Other than bathing and feeding them, we have been able to bring no relief. That was when Justus sent for the healer."

"A spell, Jer?" Kaï asked quietly.

Jerzy didn't bother to respond, moving forward to where the cots had been gathered. The solitaire and her hound moved aside for him, her gaze flickering down to his waist, where the silver tasting spoon gleamed faintly in the spell-lights set in the walls. The lights had been set to half-burn, likely to spare the eyes of the ill, but Jerzy needed to see what he was looking at. As he passed, he raised one hand, the way he would going down the stairs to his master's study, and the illumination increased to near-normal levels.

A muted gasp from someone was overridden by Justus's quiet rumble as he explained who the newcomer was. He should not have used quiet-magic so casually, so openly; he was careless. The thought came and went, everything else fading from Jerzy's awareness, even as he sensed Kaï at his left shoulder, Mahault at his right, two paces back and waiting for any orders he might give them.

The cot nearest him held a man who should have been working out in the fields: ruddy faced, with close-cropped hair that was starting to thin; he had broad shoulders and thick muscles that, even now, looked as though he had only to sit up to do a full day's work. But the lines deeply indented in his face told a different story, one of exhaustion and pain.

Exhaustion, more than pain.

The next cot had a slightly younger, more slender man. He had a scar across his chest that looked as though it had come from a blade, but it was well-healed: a former solder for Lord Ranulf, perhaps, returned home after his term of service. Not one who would easily admit to illness, or failure. He did not open his eyes as Jerzy stood by him, as though even that was beyond his capability.

The next three cots held women, grouped more closely together as though to give comfort to each other. Two were Jerzy's own age; the third older. Their mother? Unlike the men, they were thin, as though they had lost the will to eat well before they took to their beds, or been ill far longer.

He moved on, moving more swiftly as he noted the consistent patterns, exhaustion and pain with no visible signs of illness or injury, only the faint scent of healwines lingering about them. Eleven cots in all, evenly split between men and women, no children. Eleven, in a village that could not hold more than a few hundred. The numbers were too high, Master Malech would say. Too high for coincidence, in times such as these.

Illness did not come out of nowhere; Master Malech taught him that.

Jerzy could sense the illness lingering within the structure, the way a traveler on the road could feel fog even in darkest night, but he could not discern its source.

"No animals died, or fell sick," he said, already knowing the answer.

"No, none. And there was no filth in the well's water."

When the sea serpents attacked The Berengia last year, those who came into contact with the dead body were struck by an illness that made them dispirited, unable to shake off their sadness. This did not seem the same, and there had been no reports of anything untoward occurring in the days or even weeks beforehand, but Jerzy could not rule out a spell, not after all that he had seen; they knew now that their enemy worked with a very long spoon.

To deal with the serpent-brought illness, he had brought Lord Ranulf a healwine for melancholia. Here . . . he had no access to his House's cellars this moment, but something stirred within him, sorting through the legacies within his quiet-magic, waiting for something to rise in answer. Healvine, yes. But that alone . . . not enough. Not here; not with an illness tied to an external cause, not if magic were already involved.

Jerzy tried to consider the bodies before him the way he would vines in a yard, assessing the vigor of new growth, the swelling fruit. Like the feel of the wine in his blood, the knowledge came to him.

The illness was a form of magic, yes, but it was settled within the victim. Deep inside, to show no visible signs on the skin, no fever or bruising, no buboes or patching, no loss of hair or skin. In the blood, perhaps, but he would not bleed them to discover it, not when the slightest movement caused pain.

He had to find another way to ease their suffering, while he tried to disconnect them from the spell's influence itself.

"Aetherwine," he said finally. "Mahl, the wineskin with the pale blue binding, and an aethersigil on the side." There were five sigils; water, earth, fire, healing, and aether, one for each legacy, for easy identification. Vinearts did not require them; all a Master had to do was pick up a skin or touch the side of a cask, and he would know whence the vine had grown, what sort of magic rested within. For others, though, the labeling was necessary.

"Aetherwine will clear the air," he said out loud, having fallen into the habit of speaking his thoughts out loud to his companions, even though they had no training, no skills to correct or guide him. He did not stop to think that there were others in the room as well. "If the spell lingers around us, it will be pushed aside, long enough for a heal-spell to work."

His fingers curved around the healspell at his waist. The vines that had produced this vintage were half a day's journey from here. The soil they had grown in was similar enough to the dirt outside that he could practically feel it humming in the soles of his feet, rising up through his body. Was this how Master Malech had felt, every day? Or was it the need that made him so aware, the need, and the time he had been away? The thought chewed at him; had the time away made him stronger? Or had it damaged him somehow?

The hum intensified, and Jerzy's hand fell away from the flask, reassured. He would not need this, not here. Not when it already surged through his body so quietly, as much a part of him as his blood and breath.

He moved through the room a second time, not looking at the bodies still on their cots, but rather following the traces of magic he could feel. None of it bore the taint he had been chasing, not obviously, and none of it had the feel of the unblooded vines of Irfan, that dangerous, untamed fruit, and yet there was something familiar about it all. Something that traced back to a shared root.

"Did anyone new come to the village, just before this all began? They might not have stayed long, even just an hour."

Justus consulted the others, briefly, quietly. "Only the solitaire. No, she came after the first illness."

"What about the Washer?" someone else asked.

"The what?" Both Jerzy and Kaïnam turned on the speaker, as though pulled by the same string.

"A Washer came through on his rounds, just before Harvest." Justus sounded surprised that they would question such a thing. "As he has done for every season I can remember. Surely he visits the vintnery as well?"

Each season a Washer came though to bless the crops, to praise the Harvest, to bargain with Detta for their usual shipment of barrels. As a slave, Jerzy had attended the ceremonies but thought more for the Harvest party than the prayers, had taken the Solace of Sin Washer's Heir but not looked closely at the man who offered it.

"The same man as previous years?" Mahault had a look on her face that meant she was thinking very hard about something, but wasn't ready to say what it was, yet.

"No . . . he was new, younger." Justus looked pained, his hands pressing against his rib cage as though the thought brought him pain. "But surely he could not have brought this here!"

Jerzy bit the inside of his cheek, feeling the quiet-magic flood onto his tongue, waiting to be used. Anyone might have brought illness, intentionally or otherwise. A Washer bringing harm was counter to everything Jerzy had ever been taught, but the world had changed. The greeting party at the dock had made it clear that the rules had changed, and no one—not even an Heir of Sin Washer—was beyond suspicion. Jerzy could not overlook the possibility that one of them might be involved, for reasons of their own.

"Illness comes in many forms," Kaï said, stepping in to cover Jerzy's uncertainty. His voice was princeling-smooth and soothing, redirecting attention away from the Vineart. "If he himself did not feel this exhaustion, he may never have known anything was wrong."

Or he might have been protected from it. This village was within House Malech's reach. If this was an attempt to force Jerzy's hand somehow . . . Washers, unlike lords and Vinearts, had no limits placed on how they might use either magic or power. Sin Washer had trusted his heirs . . . perhaps too much.

Justus did not care where the illness came from, or what power swirled outside his village. "Can you help them?"

The same words Kaï had used, when they watched the plague ship rising and falling on the waves.

"I think so," Jerzy said this time.

Mahl brought him the spellwine, and Justus slid a small wooden table over for him to use. Jerzy placed the wineskin in the center of the table, unhooked his tasting spoon, and placed it next to the skin, asking for a bowl of water to rinse his hands in before beginning.

Despite common belief, vinespells did not require ceremony to decant; his master had been disdainful of such flourishes, saying they distracted from the decantation, but Vineart Giordan had embraced them, claiming that people felt more reassured when they had something to watch. Justus and the others, even Kaï and Mahault, needed reassurances now, even if the ill would not see it.

His hands washed and dried on a rough, clean scrap of cloth, Jerzy uncorked the wineskin and poured a scant mouthful of spellwine into the shallow lip of the spoon.

The quiet-magic for healing already rested on his tongue, the soft red fruit of healwine filling his senses, the softness of it soothing the bitten flesh, making him feel stronger, calmer, even before the decantation was made. He didn't remember that happening before, but then again, every time he had drawn on it before he had been stressed, facing danger or uncertainty. Here . . . he was home, and although there was clearly trouble, he could sense no immediate danger, no flavor of the enemy's taint following him to these sloping, stony lands.

The aetherwine was stronger, right out of the skin; his nostrils twitched as the scent of it rose into the otherwise stale air of the sickroom and he breathed in deeply.

As a slave, he had been forbidden to breathe of the mustus, the crushed, raw juice of the grapes. Tamed and shaped, the spellwine could still intoxicate.

Behind him, he could sense the others, but if they spoke or moved, he could not say; all of his attention was focused on the dark red liquid resting in the spoon's depression, moving slightly as though stirred by a breath from within. No matter how often he saw aetherwine, it still awed him in a way no other legacy could, not even the cold, unblooded grapes they had discovered in Irfan. Aethervines, tradition said, had taken the brunt of Sin Washer's touch, had absorbed his anger and his sorrow, and turned it into something . . .

Magnificent. Stubborn, like weathervines. Deep and rounded, like healvines. Powerful, like firevines. And yet, as delicate as a morning's drop of dew, so easily ruined in the wrong or careless hands. And so very, very rare. . . .

He let the spellwine breathe a moment, then lifted the spoon to his mouth and let the liquid slide between his lips, joining the healwine magic already gathered there.

And something else, slipping into the warmth of the healvines and the sparkle of the aether, a building pressure of clean, tart power. Weatherspell. Giordan's vines, rising inside him without being called, as though it was his proper legacy.

This was forbidden. This was dangerous.

This was why Jerzy was apostate, not any reason the Washers could name.

He had taken more than his due share, his allotted-by-Sin-Washer legacy. Any man might use any spellvine incanted. Any Vineart might—secretly, unknown to outsiders—use quiet-magic to expand and increase a decantation. But quiet-magic grew from exposure to the vines, from being accepted by that legacy. To blend them; to absorb the work of more than one master; to twine the legacies into something more powerful than they were alone . . .

These were the mark of a prince-mage. These were the things Sin Washer commanded to end.

Jerzy let those thoughts go, focused on what needed to be done. "Into the air, rise and clear," and even as he spoke the words, forming them carefully around the liquid resting on his tongue, he was aware that he was asking, not commanding. The words were right, but the tone . . .

"Into the air, rise and clear," he repeated, infusing more command into the words this time. Magic, unformed or mis-formed, would do as it would, not as you would have it do.

The two legacies stirred, and he could feel the magic rise, sweeping outward from him, through him, into the air, waiting. His body shivered in response, but he focused on the next step, careful not to lose control. The command was everything.

"Clear the afflicted, set them free." As he said it, he visualized what he wanted each part of the magic to do: the aetherwine to wipe them clean, and the healwine to follow after and repair the damage done. And weathervine, to freshen the air around this town, flush the soil clean of its blight.

"Go."

The magic shimmered and then burst, a hundred drops off in twice as many directions. Jerzy felt his knees wobble and his head swim.

"Jer?"

"I think it worked," he said, before his body gave way entirely, and he collapsed.

Kaïnam caught the Vineart as he fell to the floor. He could not say what had warned him; some change in the way the other man stood, or the way his hand turned on the silver spoon he was holding, clenching the stem tightly, like a convulsion. Whatever the clues, his body reacted before his mind could put them together, keeping the Vineart from injuring himself as his body crumpled.

"Jer!" Even as Mahault cried out in concern, there was a motion from the bed, and the patient, an older woman with skin weathered from wind as much as age, opened her eyes and squinted suspiciously up at them.

KAÏNAM WAS WORRIED. He did not show it; to show his concern would be to cast doubt on Jerzy's decision, and Kaïnam was too much a son of Atakus to ever publicly disagree or doubt his captain, on the sea or off. And yet he cast sideways looks at the Vineart when he didn't think anyone else was watching, and he worried. Jerzy had recovered quickly from his collapse; had waved off their questions with a breezy explanation that made no sense if you knew anything of how vine-magic worked. The villagers and solitaire, overwhelmed by the nearly immediate recovery of the previously pain-racked patients, did not stop to question it: perhaps, despite their proximity to Vinearts, they truly did not know anything of them.

Kaïnam knew. He thought, perhaps, that Jerzy did not know how much he knew; the others took what Jerzy revealed so matter-of-factly, with no interest beyond the fact of what Jerzy did, that it was less evident the interest Kaï himself took in the how.

Not the magic itself: Kaïnam knew that he had no skills in that area. But the things that made other people powerful, that was something he studied. His sister had schooled him well: if you knew what drove another person, if you knew what gave them strength, you knew their weaknesses, too. Claiming exhaustion from spreading the magic among so many individuals—even had Kaïnam never seen a spellwine decanted before, he had traveled with this crew for months now. He had seen the Vineart do things that were not spoken of, subtle and overt, and drawn his own conclusions.

Jerzy was far stronger than he would admit. Possibly all Vineart were. If so, it would explain Master Edon, back on Atakus, insisting he could protect the island from danger, how he had managed to wreath the entire island in magic so that it could not be found by outsiders. Hidden strengths, magelike powers, kept for two thousand years of unbroken secrecy.

In another life, when he was only his father's son, that secrecy would have worried him, greatly. Now . . . he worried only that his friend's limits had been reached, and they were not yet safely at the vintnery.

And even when they arrived . . . it would not be safe. The sense of urgency drew tighter, the skin between his shoulder blades twitching as though someone danced the tip of a blade along it. Jerzy was so focused on returning home, he was not thinking beyond that, but Master Vineart Malech had been killed within the walls of his own House. They could not assume it would be any sort of refuge or safe harbor. They could not assume there would be any refuge whatsoever, until their enemy was found, and defeated, or they were all dead.

Kaïnam had been born to a family of power, but he had been a younger son, and as such had watched and advised, not led. Then his sister had been murdered, and his father pushed to madness, agreeing to Edon's foolhardy defense that had only made things worse, causing others to fear that *Atakus* was the source of the evil, the cause of this misery—drawing enemies who before would not have dared attack the region's sole safe-harbor. . . .

Kaïnam had abandoned his family, his honor, his future, to find their enemy and set things right again. He had given up everything; he would not allow anything to happen to the one man he thought could accomplish that goal.

Not that Jerzy was showing any weakness now. The Vineart had recovered quickly, what little color touched his skin returning, although his breathing was still too slow and labored. Jerzy had insisted that they be on their way almost immediately, refusing all hospitality with the excuse that Ao would be waiting for them. Kaïnam thought it had more to do with getting away from the site of his collapse.

If so, it was a matter of pride and magic, and not for Kaïnam to inquire about. Once they were back to the wagon, the volunteer guard sent back to his home, Jerzy seemed to have put the entire matter behind him, his mood lightening as they moved further inland, the land rising into low, rolling hills.

Kaïnam noted that the others had picked up his mood: Mahault rode up alongside the wagon, on the other side from Kaïnam, and tucked a sprig of tiny yellow flowers into Ao's straight black hair. The trader, rather than scowling, secured it better behind his ear and preened, making Mahl and Jerzy laugh. Despite his unease, Kaïnam smiled as well. They had been somber for too long, and would be so again—for now, this moment, laughter was good.

Distracted by his own thoughts, the sound of someone coming up behind them on the road was subtle enough that at first Kaïnam dismissed it as unimportant; they were not hoofbeats, not the heavier-shod tramp of Berengian soldiers, or the wagon creak of a caravan, merely one person, on foot.

One person, and one beast, coming fast.

"Greetings again," a voice called, just as the others took notice of the noise.

A stranger, but not unknown. He started to turn his horse to face the solitaire, then waited until Mahault turned and rode up beside him, letting her address the other woman. Solitaires were hardly man-haters; they chose the life of the road over one of Householding, but that was a legal matter, not a personal one. Still, she had nearly acknowledged Mahl as a peer, and so Mahl should be the one to respond.

Life in his father's court had taught him that a show of respect could solve more problems than a fleet of ships at your back. . . . Although he would have been happy with the fleet as well.

"If I may join you on your way?" The woman's tone was diffident, but her body language said she had no expectation of being refused.

"If your way and ours travel together," Mahault replied, and Kaïnam picked up both the rhythm of ritual in the words and the slight hesitation as Mahl spoke them, as though she was not certain of the phrasing—or how they might be received. The solitaire nodded once, and made a subtle gesture with her hand, down at her thigh. The hound, Codi, released from whatever bonds held it, loped on ahead.

A sentry. Or a hunter, to flush out anyone—or any thing—waiting ahead. For the first time, Kaïnam wondered at the hound's intelligence. Solitaires bred them selectively and kept the pups for themselves; he had never encountered one before, save at a distance. They looked ordinary enough . . . but then, so did Jerzy. Appearances deceived.

The Vineart had pulled himself out of his slump-seated position when the solitaire rode up and was listening intently as the two women spoke.

"I was on my way to Lord Ranulf's encampment when I paused in the village," the solitaire was saying. "He has taken on a full dozen of my sisters to supplement his forces and to use as messengers along the borders of his lands. Now that the illness has passed and there is no risk to my leaving, I plan to join them."

Mahault looked to Jerzy. The Vineart nodded. "He trains his fighters at Roget's Stamp, just north and east of here. If that is where you travel, then our road is yours, at least for a while."

"THERE IS FEAR in the ground." The solitaire's name was Keren, and if she noted that she was kept away from the wagon, with its casks and boxes, it did not seem to bother her. She hailed from the Northlands, further north even than Caul, and claimed to have traveled all over the Lands Vin in her years on the road. Mahault was tempted to brag in return that she had gone even farther south than Keren could imagine, but something held her tongue. No, not something; the knowledge that they were all being watched, that the wrong word or move might draw disaster down on them before they could reach shelter. Keren might not be a threat—but she might meet up with someone, later, who was.

"Fear, how?" Ao joined in the conversation, his natural curiosity closing in on that word like a hound to hare. "How can dirt be afraid?"

Mahault shook her head in exasperation. "Keren, may I formally introduce you to Ao, Trader of the Eastern Wind Clan, endless asker of questions, and my third travel companion."

The two of them exchanged formal bows, as best they could as the wagon continued to rattle along. "Forgive me for not standing, as is proper," he said. "I am a trifle indisposed." Ao's voice was wryly amused, but gave no further information, and Keren took it in stride, literally. The solitaire had likely seen enough in her travels to assume what was and wasn't hidden under the rough brown cloth.

"It is my honor to share the road, Trader Ao. And no, I do not mean . . ." She hesitated, clearly sorting through her own cautions. "There are some things of which I may not speak." Oaths of loyalty ended with the end of a contract-hire, but a solitaire who spoke too much was one who would not be hired again. "This I can and will say: beware any who ask your help."

"You mean, like the villagers?" That made no sense: Keren had been there; she had helped them as well. "You think that Jerzy should have left them to suffer?"

Keren glanced at Jerzy, who met her look evenly, until she turned away. "I think that what he did was the act of a good man, a caring man, a Vineart. These are his people, yes? His yard is within these hills? Then he was within his rights to act as he did. But these days are not as old, and there are those who would see that, even *that*, as provocation. As overstepping what is allowed, what is proper behavior."

"To heal?" Ao's voice ended in a squeak, the way it sometimes did when he was particularly outraged.

"He did more than ease their pain," Keren said. "He gave them solace."

The thought was absurd, and yet the look on the woman's face when she woke and realized it did not hurt to move . . . the moan of relief as a man sat up in bed for, Justus said, the first time in a week . . . those things came back to Mahault, and her forehead creased as she looked at the events the way Keren had seen them.

"Solace is the purview of the Washers. Jerzy would never . . ." Mahault's voice trailed off, reigning in her horse to keep pace with the wagon and the walker. "A Washer came, and left, and people fell ill. Jerzy came, and they became healthy again."

The solitaire did not speak, then: "Yes. It could look . . . bad, if one were inclined to look that way. There is fear in the land," she said again. "Anything that might feed that fear . . . is dangerous."

"And doing nothing is not equally dangerous?" Jerzy's voice, coming from the front of the wagon, sounded not angry or argumentative, but tired. As though he had already thought this through and come to no useful conclusions.

Mahault suspected that was exactly what he had done. Jerzy thought almost as much as Kaï, and twice as much as Ao.

The solitaire simply shrugged. She had clearly said what she meant to say, and the conversation moved on to less worrisome topics, Jerzy quietly driving the wagon, while Kaïnam rode on ahead, his gaze alert to every farmer in his field, every animal loping through the brush. In that manner, the day passed easily into dusk, and they came to where the road branched, one—their route—becoming a softer, grass-edged track, while the main road continued on toward the northeast, and Roget's Stamp.

After bidding Jerzy and the others farewell, Keren drew Mahault aside a few paces.

"You carry a blade with confidence, and ride far from your birthplace," she said to Mahault. "The lord here, Ranulf, needs more troops than he can gather. Another woman, with some skill and courage . . . he would not enquire as to where she received that training, or who her sponsor was. And once in . . ." She lifted one shoulder, as though to imply that no one else would be moved to ask such a question, either. "I have seen enough, and so has Codi, to judge you worthy of the sigil, if that's your desire."

Mahault felt a fierce rush of excitement. It *was* her desire, and had been since she was old enough to understand the extent of her own dreams. Traveling with Jerzy, the freedom she had discovered, merely confirmed that, however things turned, she would never be able to go back to what she had been, to the life her father had wanted for her. That tide, as Kaïnam would say, had gone out and would not return.

The others had paused to allow the two to make their farewells, but she did not pretend they could not hear, did not pretend not to see Ao's quick, worried glance her way, or the way Kaïnam sat more firmly into his saddle, as though preoccupied with the calmly grazing beast, or the way Jer let the reins of the wagon rest loosely as he studied the wide open sky, watching the gentle curve of a raptor overhead hunting for a rabbit in the fields stretching below.

Mahault had been given the chance to train as a solitaire once before, and abandoned it when something stronger than a dream had summoned her away, the whisper of the guardian's voice, telling her that she was needed. Her friends thought she had made a sacrifice; she knew they expected she would take this second chance, grab it with both hands.

She wanted to. She desperately wanted to.

But that tide, too, had gone out; that road would not be ridden. The solitaires could give her a future, a way to make her way in the world for the rest of her life, without uncertainty or fear. She would have a four-legged, faithful companion at all times, never be alone, never be subject to any restrictions save the ones she accepted of her own will, never bound to a situation she could not accept.

A dream. What she wanted, held against what she needed. . . . In the end, even if her father had disowned her, even if her heart called her one direction, she was still a maiar's daughter, born and trained to a responsibility beyond herself. The independence that she had craved, the freedom . . . she knew it now for an illusion. The moment she understood what was at stake, to consider what might happen if Jerzy were to fail, her loyalties had been struck.

"Thank you," she said to Keren, and meant it. "That . . . means much to me. But I will ride with Vineart Jerzy."

Chapter 3

The Grounding

Spring

One month each season, Ximen made a point of visiting with the men who stood watch over the Grounding, the Seven Fortifications who protected the holdings and fields their great-grandsires carved from this harsh landscape, and made their own. Three Fortifications were on the Wall to the west, two stationed to the north, one south, and the seabound patrol, historically and uselessly set to watch for aid that never came across the waters.

Traditionally, the visit was to ensure that the men kept up their guard, and to hear any mutters or complaints the men felt could not be brought to their commanders. The truth, he had discovered early on, was that each visit ensured that he, their Praepositus, did not become so entrenched within the walls of the Grounding that he forgot the world outside.

Or, Ximen thought grimly, stretching his legs as he walked and feeling a pleasant burn in his muscles as they climbed the stone steps to the top of the wall, that he did not go mad, bound up with the paperwork and petty arguments required of leadership.

"The Sixth Fortification, my lord."

Ximen nodded, acknowledging the troop leader's presentation. The Six walked the wall against the inner lands, the hills to the northwest, where harsh winter storms came down without warning, and loper-cats, who could kill a man with one swipe of their paws, prowled the night. It was one of the oldest Fortifications, and one of the proudest, the grandsons of men who served there vying for that assignment when they came of age. Aware of that pride-of-service, Ximen had taken extra time with his appearance this morning, adjusting the spotted loper's-skin belt that looped over his hips so that the jeweled knife hanging there caught the sunlight just so. The blade hadn't taken a true edge in over a generation, but it had been worn by the first Lord of the Grounding and thus did not require drawing, merely displaying, a link to the men who had gone before him. The belt itself had been made from a beast that tried to come over the wall and had been killed by a man of the Sixth in Ximen's grandfather's day. Every man standing to attention knew the story of how that man had died to save his lord's life from its poisoned claws.

Ximen would show them no less honor, now.

"Boys," the voice next to him muttered. "Weak-chinned boys hiding behind their little knives."

"Be respectful, or be silent," Ximen said, barely moving his mouth as he spoke, to hide the rebuke from their audience. He did not know why the vine-mage had chosen to travel with him; he had not summoned the man, had not told him of his plans, merely walked out in the morning to find him there, leg slung over a wild-eyed beast who shied away when a stable girl came to take the reins and would not settle until the mage was off its back and paces away.

The older man scowled, but fell silent. His cloak was raised to protect his skin from the sunlight, and the hood pulled forward to shade his aged face. If it weren't for the belt double-wrapped at his waist, the long-handled spoon dangling at his hip, he would look like a flesh-eating shade out of legend, hiding from the natural light, intent on doing harm to the living.

Ximen shut down the thought that such legends often came from truth, and focused on the men waiting for him. They were strong and brave, their features sharp and intent, their skins weathered from exposure to the elements, eighty-four scions of the strongest blood of the Grounding. Most had the broad cheekbones and bronzed coloring of the native families, but occasionally a narrow-boned face, pale-colored hair, or startlingly blue eyes like Ximen's own appeared, a throwback to one of the original Grounded.

"Next week is the Day of Grounding," he told them, letting his voice carry on the rising breeze, willing it to travel over the assembled ranks, down the line and beyond, out into the danger-filled hills and whatever might be listening there. "The day that commemorates how our forefathers came to this land, full of hope, only to be dashed against the shores by betrayal and greed."

Others might hear and believe only the softer version of history; how their forefathers explored under the flag of the old world, and, on arriving here, cast away that flag and struck out on their own. These men, though, who gave up their lives for the safety of others; they knew some of the truth.

Some. Not all. That alone was the Praepositus's burden to carry.

"But they did not let that betrayal break them," Ximen went on, warming to his speech. "They did not let that greed overwhelm them, or make them bitter. No! They landed on their knees but rose to their feet, and claimed this land they had been promised by the lords of the old lands. Here they built their homes, here they tended the soil, and made it into a home."

A home? A prison, more like. Bounded by the too-wide seas on one end and the hills at their back, where even these men went only in patrols of ten or more, heavily armed, and counted themselves fortunate if they were not attacked by things howling out of the night. . . .

As he, Praepositus, was bounded and hounded by the man at his side. Ximen kept a shudder of revulsion from ripping his skin as the vine-mage stepped a pace too close. The man was bathed and groomed as befitted his station, no different from any other day in all the years Ximen had been forced to deal with the mage, and yet there was something rotted in his smell today that made Ximen feel much as the gelding had; the need to throw the man from his back and race away.

Like the gelding, he could do no such thing. They were bound together, he and the vine-mage, for good or ill, to achieve their goals.

The thought made him ill, but now was far too late to reconsider the wisdom of that alliance; events were in motion and the men were waiting, hanging on his words as they carried through the air, down the lines. "Next week we will venerate those men who had such courage. And you will be with us on that shoreline in spirit and in courage, if not in flesh. We carry your sacrifice as we carry theirs, and we will honor you in the flames, even as we honor them."

His voice made it a promise; they would not be forgotten. They would not be abandoned. Whatever happened in the years to come, they would be part of it.

He could practically see the ripple pass through the lines as they stood a little taller, their spears and bows held so that the metal tips caught the morning sunlight and reflected it back off the walls rather than blinding anyone within—a gesture they must have perfected over the years and handed down to each new man on the wall.

These men were the best the Grounding had. He hated knowing that he lied to them.

*   *   *

"I need twenty."

"No."

"I am not here to Negotiate, Ximen."

The man's voice was like a snake, curling and uncurling, hiding under leaves until it could strike. The very sound of it made Ximen ill. The Praepositus took a deep breath, the way Bo always reminded him to, and let it out, slowly, carefully, listening to the sound it made, a soft puff of wind in the otherwise still room. "And I am not here to give you my men for your workings. Is that not why you have slaves? Use them." He did not know what the vine-mage needed the men for. . . .

No, that was a lie, and while he might mislead his men to achieve a further goal, Ximen would not lie to himself. He knew. He never spoke of the pits where bodies lay, unnamed and unmentioned. He never spoke of the sacrifices—the unacknowledged deaths—that fed both the vine-mage's magic and Ximen's own ambitions. But Ximen knew. He knew of the outbuilding where slaves went in, but did not come out. He knew that there were things that his vine-mage did that could not be condoned, and yet he condoned them by his silence.

"Pfaugh. Slaves are good for much. For most of my workings, they are what I require. But in this instance, I need not magic but strength, not sensitivity but courage. And I require the best. Give me twenty."

The vine-mage was serious. He sat there, a goblet in his hands, and asked for the lives of twenty men as though requesting a sheet of paper.

And it would be their lives; Ximen had no doubt of that. Twenty, plus the season's Harvest . . . no. Slaves were the vine-mage's to dispose of as he would, but these were his men. He would sooner give his own arm to a wild dog. The Harvest sacrifices were tradition, those chosen publicly honored, a means of tying the community together in shared loss and honor. This . . . this would be mere slaughter.

The vine-mage had no such qualms. "You owe me, *Praepositus*. For the plans you needed for your ships, for the safety I give your men, the ability to power your dreams . . . you *owe* me."

He remembered the look of the men on the Wall: proud, eager, willing to do anything he asked of them, because he carried that title. The smell that rose off the vine-mage had faded, here within the stone enclosure of the Wall-House, but it still lingered in Ximen's nostrils, making him wary and not inclined to give the other man anything more.

"You promise, and you reassure, and you demand . . . but you have shown me nothing, yet," he said instead. "We are nearly at the day of announcement, years in the planning, and all I have is your assurance that the Old World is ripe for the taking, that their lords are in disarray and distracted, that their mages are weakened to the point of being no threat. And, yet. I have no proof."

Ximen knew full well that there was no way to gain proof of the sort he desired; it was too far a distance to fly messenger-birds, and the few fireposts they had built carried news up and down the coastline, not across it. The Grounding had never been able to build ships that could cross back over the great waters, not safely. They had neither the skills nor the materials, their few ships slighter things that needed to hug the shoreline, not speed into the deeps.

That was why he had needed the vine-mage, originally, to conjure the sketches and plans, steal the knowledge of how to build the ships they needed. And now he asked his people to go beyond all that they knew, making ships that would carry them out of sight of the life-giving shore, to travel the waves that had brought them here seven generations before, without any idea what might await them in those far distant lands. All was ready, waiting only his announcement, the unveiling of his Great Plan, to tell them what they had been working for.

Ximen had thought, in the beginning, to return in triumph; surely there had been some there who mourned the loss of their men, who remembered the ships that did not return, and would welcome them, the long-lost sons and their new lands, claimed for the family's name. When, at what moment, had that dream turned to bitter mint in his mouth?

But if he did not know when, he knew full well *why*.

Everything, every plan, every dream he had based the future on was built on the assurances of the old man who now sat across from him and demanded the lives of free men, *his* men, as though they were naught but game pieces, of no value save the use he put them to.

For the first time in too many years, Ximen looked into the vine-mage's rheumy eyes and let himself see what lived within. They stared at each other, unblinking, and a part of Ximen wondered, uneasily, how much of that madness had infected *him*.

Chapter 4

erzy had seen the way Kaïnam looked at him, cautiously, studying him in the aftermath of his collapse in the village, and he understood the concern, but there was no need. The healing spell itself had been surprisingly simple, and once he recovered from the shock of what he had felt, his only driving desire was to put his feet down on familiar soil.

The thought crept in that mayhaps Kaï was right to worry, that he could not be certain the malaise had been entirely driven out, but he felt well enough to go on, and that was the important thing now: getting back to the House, and the yard.

Once they parted ways with the solitaire, he tried to lose himself in the familiar landscape. The road passed along gently rolling, plowed fields of wheat and barley, ringed by wooded groves whose trunks were thick around with age, their leaves turning with autumn colors. The villages became more scarce as the ground became less fertile, low fences running across the landscape at irregular angles, the occasional red-patched cow or shaggy-coated sheep stopping to watch them as they rode past. It all looked as it should, and yet the closer they came to home, the more uneasy Jerzy felt. The malaise in the village had not been able to touch him, driven out by the residue of magics within him, the tangle of legacies flooding his blood, but he could feel it now, everywhere around him. The village had been a pool, but the malaise seeped everywhere, slowly enough to raise no alarms, nothing more than a grumble of discontent at ill luck and bad weather.

How long had it been here? Had he been blind, before?

Jerzy shifted on the wooden bench of the wagon, first stretching his legs and then twisting, trying to work out a crick that didn't exist, causing the patient horse in the traces to stop and wait for new instructions.

"Enough," Mahault said finally. She swung off her horse, even as Jerzy pulled up the reins to the cart horse in surprise, making the beast stop once again. "You, take my horse and work out whatever's itching you. I will drive the wagon."

Rather than ride, however, Jerzy tied the horse to the wagon's rail and walked alongside, stretching his muscles and letting his feet make contact with the soil.

It wasn't the same as when he'd walked barefoot in the field, but even through the soles of his boots he could feel the earth respond, the sense of something alive, if not aware. Under the malaise, the land still knew him, responded to him.

That awareness brought home something else as well. So intent on returning to The Berengia, of ensuring that Ao would have access to the proper spellwines to heal and that he would be able to regain his own strength among the vines of his proper legacy, Jerzy had not let himself think overmuch about the passing of the seasons. Now, he could think of nothing save that.

He had left in the growing season. He had missed Harvest. The grapes would have been picked; Detta had promised him that, and as House-keeper she could make it so. But without a Vineart . . . the fruit would have been crushed and abandoned, the vats of mustus waiting in vain for a Vineart's touch. The things he had not allowed himself to think of, had not time or energy to think about, on their journey, settled against his neck now, as heavy as the wagon trundling along next to him.

As they walked, the wheels of the wagon and the clomp of the horses' hooves a steady accompaniment, a nightbird sang somewhere, and when he looked up, narrow blue and pink clouds gathered in the sky, giving a foretaste of night.

The days were becoming shorter, cooler. Soon it would be Fallowtime, when the earth lay still and Vinearts turned their attention to other matters, clearing away the debris of the growing and harvest seasons and mending their equipment, buying new slaves and sorting inventory in the cellars, incanting the slower-maturing spellwines, and deciding what to sell and what to keep.

Jerzy suspected there would be little of that routine for him; his time would of necessity be turned toward arts more martial than magic, of clearing the damage done rather than preparing it for new growth, and the thought was actual pain.

Guardian? he thought, almost barely daring to reach out for fear that he would still hear nothing, even this close, and was rewarded by the cool weight of stone slipping into him, taking some of the burden off his neck even as it pressed—comfortingly—against his heart and lungs.

Almost home, he told it, and felt the stone dragon let out a distant growl that rumbled down his spine, like a cat's purr grown immensely deep.

The moment the growl reached the soles of his feet, it was as though his awareness of the ground expanded, went even deeper, until he could feel not only the soil itself but the roots that still lay several hours away, the vineyards of the House of Malech.

His vines.

That easily, that suddenly, he could hear them whispering to each other, soft murmurings, like the morning wind over waves. The whispers said nothing, communicated nothing, but merely affirmed: *We are.* They were. And in their being, *he* was.

Jerzy called on the quiet-magic without conscious intent, the saliva filling his mouth until the sense of belonging became a physical taste, a ripe, full flavor of healvines, the spicier, darker fruit of firevines threaded like veins, the weathervine mingled within: a tart, pulpier flavor, carrying the salt of sea winds and a hint of yellow fruit, then a much lighter, brighter flavor, like a voice heard distant in the night. . . .

And, at the back of it all, tangled deep against the bones of his throat, the unmistakable jolt of unblooded vines.

The knowledge came to him, carried by the aroma of that blend. All there, carried within him. Part of him. Waiting—wanting—to be used.

He could do this. He could—he was—enough. Not himself, but what he carried, what he crafted. He could cleanse the land, protect his people . . . be a threat to Ximen's plans.

Jerzy shuddered, swallowing the magic back down, refusing to let the euphoria overwhelm him, distrusting the feeling. Distracted, he almost missed the sensation of the ground beneath him surging, dirt and stone replaced by the yawning sensation of roots, thicker than he was, wider than the seas, stretching not from him to his yards but everywhere all at once, spanning the distance, deep into the heart of the earth-stone beneath their feet.

It was, he realized with a shudder, the same sensation he had felt when he cleared the air back at the village, leaving him sweating and shaking, the same and yet more, underlying the taint, deeper and stronger, not drawn by his decantation but drawing him in, salivating with the need to consume *him*.

It was thick, and dense, and powerful, and . . .

And old. Deep and old, and he was drowning in it, feeling it fill him up from within. . . .

"Jer!"

The worried shout roused him from the dizziness, and he grabbed hold of the wagon's side with one hand, reaching automatically for the flask at his belt with the other even as he swerved to see what Ao was yelling about. The field to their left was clear, just a softly sloping hill covered with sheep—who, even as he watched, scattered, the two children watching them scattering as well, the sound of low yips in the air indicating the presence of herd dogs, as well.

Jerzy swung to the right, his side, but the road was clear there, too, as well as behind them. His eyesight seemed almost impossibly sharp, taking in the smallest of details, while his mind felt muddled, as though he had just woken from an unquiet sleep. Kaï had the road ahead covered, his blade out and ready, even as Jerzy heard Ao pull back the thick bowstring and notch a bolt to it. Where was Mahault?

Then a sharp cry from above dragged his attention back to the sky. Three, four dark figures coming out of the cloud, circling low—no, high, but falling quickly, shaped like raptors but larger than birds should be, pinions ragged, talons and necks angled to strike.

And with them, driving down out of the freshening sky, the taint of enemy magic, unmistakable even as Jerzy moved his hand away from the flask and grabbed in the wagon bed for his cudgel. His hand closed around the polished wooden heft just as the first of the too-large, misshapen birds reached them.

Glossy black, almost glittering in the sunlight, built like some gods-forsaken cross between a tarn and the giant seabirds that had glided over the ship each dawn, their wings spanning nearly Kaïnam's height across, their claws larger than Jerzy's own hands and tipped not with a bird's talons but metal-sharp blades, one of them raking across Jerzy's face before he could raise the cudgel to defend himself.

A horse screamed, and he heard Mahault swear, then the twang of a bolt from Ao's bow released into the air. Jerzy landed a hit with the cudgel, and the creature flapped its wings but did not retreat.

"What are they?"

"Don't know, don't care," he heard Ao say, even as the trader braced himself more firmly in the wagon bed and rearmed. "Jer, if they're magic, can they be killed?"

"Anything can be killed," Kaïnam said, but his blade, limited to his immediate reach, was useless in the dive-and-wheel attack, and his horse so terrified it almost unseated him.

"Jer?" Another bolt released, this one hitting with a fleshy thunk, even as Jerzy swing the cudgel up and hit something hard and muscled. He couldn't see where Mahault was, or how she was faring with her shorter blade, the birds wheeling around for another attack as though they shared a single thought or were directed like a pack of hunting dogs.

"If they're magic, it will take magic," he said, panting. That was how it had worked with the serpents. "I can weaken them; then you can cut them down." He hoped.

"Under the wagon." Mahault's voice, ordering him, even as her smaller hand took the cudgel from his grasp, her body checking his, knocking him to the ground even as he was rolling underneath the relative safety of the wagon.

A sudden memory: a wagon, shattered in two, the bodies of slaves lying broken as well, some dead, others dying . . .

Jerzy refused the memory, staring up at the narrow length of iron that ran along the bottom or the wagon, connecting the planking and giving it strength. Sturdy. Strong enough to carry their belongings. Strong enough to keep him safe—but not for long. He needed to . . .

He needed to bring the beasts down out of the sky, where they had the advantage, to where Mahl and Kaïnam could finish them off. Grounded, the beasts were no match.

A flash of panic filled him, burning away the last of the groggy sensation, then the knowledge of what he needed to do, and how, came to him: healspell, turned inward, to draw vitality away, tearing at the life that animated them, hard and fast so that they fell from the sky. Anti-healing. Something not-done but . . . possible.

Had the knowledge come from the Guardian? Jerzy had no time to reach for reassurance. He heard a grunt of pain, the smack of horseflesh against the wagon, rocking it on its wheels. Another thwang of the bowstring, and the scream, the terrible scream of an unnatural bird as it swooped to attack. Not being able to see was worse than seeing, unsure what was happening outside his temporary hiding place.

Jerzy called the quiet-magic even as his hand reached for the wineskin to augment it, and give him full strength. No time for subtlety or show: he uncorked the healwine and brought it to his mouth, spilling some over his lips in his haste. It stained the ground underneath him, the dry-packed dirt soaking it up. Instead of the usual smooth, warm fruit, he tasted harshness, as though the magic knew what he was about to do and was resisting being used in such a fashion.

"Forgive me," he whispered, unsure if he was asking the wine, or the birds, or Sin Washer himself. "Into their bodies, rise. Inside their bodies, break. Go."

The spellwine backwashed on him, resisting, choking him until he spluttered, but he could feel the magic working, *felt* it hit the creatures, sliding under their feathers, pricking into their flesh the way Lil salted meats for dinner, drawing the vitality out of them, magic drawing magic to itself. His magic, matching the taint measure to measure, not trying to fight it directly but clinging to it so that it could not cling to the bird's flesh any longer, dropping out, falling and dissipating . . .

He could not see the battle, but he could *feel* it working.

"Now!" he heard Mahault cry, her voice fierce and terrible, and then the singing of blades cutting air and the far more terrible sounds of them meeting flesh, meeting and diving, and the heavy thump of things falling, until there was silence, and the low coughing of someone throwing up over the side of the wagon.

"Jer?"

"Yeah." He rolled out from under the wagon—on the side without the puddle of vomit—and came face to beak with one of the grotesque birds. In death it still looked terrifying.

"You all right?"

"Yes," Jerzy responded, before realizing she wasn't asking him. He climbed to his feet, hauling himself up with a hand on the sideboard, and peered at Ao.

"I'm fine," the trader said, sounding embarrassed. His hair fell limp in his face, and there was a smudge of dark blood across the bridge of his nose, making it look even more lopsided. But it wasn't his blood—more of that dark, gooey liquid was splattered over his arms and the blanket, where a bird had fallen on him, and died.

Jerzy stared at the blood, thinking . . . he wasn't sure what.

"The serpents didn't have blood," he said. The only blood shipboard had been Ao's, thick and sticky on his hands and clothing. It wasn't Ao's blood this time; Jerzy looked again to make sure. "We cut them open and they were solid flesh."

Ao was too busy mopping himself up to hear, and Kaïnam was cleaning his sword over in the grass, but Mahault looked at him, her eyes still battle-bright. "Does that mean something?"

"I don't know. I don't know . . . anything." His legs were still wobbly, but he managed to turn and kneel down next to the bird on the ground by the wagon, looking at it without touching. It was clearly deformed, as though someone had taken its flesh and pinched and pulled cruelly, re-forming it, stretching the beak into a sharp, rending tool, hammering the claws out on a blacksmith's forge.

The malaise in the land was subtle. This was not. A weakness, a failure in their enemy's work? Jerzy didn't know. He couldn't think, not there, not right then. He got back up and rummaged in the wagon for something to gather the creature up in, finally dumping the last of their dried meats and using the burlap sack to scoop the bird-beast up, careful not to touch it with his hands any more than was necessary, then retied the top and went to attach it to the nearest horse's saddle— Mahl's horse, carrying the lighter weight. The beast, who had managed not to bolt during the fight itself, shied away from the sack, so Jerzy sighed and slung it into the wagon itself, careful to keep it away from the spellwines they still carried.

"Our watcher is still there," Kaïnam said, returning to them. His voice was low and casual, as though commenting on how far they had yet to ride, but his narrow face was ashen and his eyes a little too wide for true calm. "The coward saw us being attacked and did nothing."

"They don't care if we live or die," Mahl said, and her voice had a definite tremble in it. "Only that we don't ally with someone else. Keren was right. Everything's changed."

The watching Washer-spy was the least of Jerzy's concerns just then.

"How did those things find us?" Ao wondered, some of his normal vitality returning. He took a long drink from a waterskin, spitting red-colored phlegm over the side of the wagon onto the dirt, then splashed some more on his face. "Or was it coincidence. 'Look, people, let's try and eat them'?" His expression was doubtful, as was Mahault's. Kaïnam, as usual, was unreadable.

"It felt me," Jerzy said. "Out on the ocean, it couldn't find me, the same way I couldn't find him. But here . . ." It seemed hopeless; if the other Vineart could do so much, could send magic so fiercely, so secretly, how could any stand against him?

The sensation he had felt just before the attack was connected to the malaise festering in the village, which in turn connected to the continued unease he felt below his feet, he was sure of it.

He didn't speak further of it to the others and they, used to his sudden silences when it came to magic, didn't push him. While Ao sat guard, his crossbow at the ready, Kaïnam and Mahault dug a shallow pit by the side of the road and dumped the remains of the creatures into it.

Jerzy knew they should do something more, to ensure the corpses would not be dug up by dogs or other scavengers, but there were no rocks large enough to be useful but not too large to lift, and he did not want to use magic just then, to seal the ground more tightly. He certainly did not want to try the single drop of growspell he had anywhere near the creatures, even dead. Instinct told him that to poke at it again, here unprotected on the road, would not be wise.

When what little they could do had been done, the four started back down the road, each wrapped in their own thoughts, all intent on putting as much distance between them and the location of the attack as possible, especially as the last remnants of daylight faded entirely and the air turned a shadowed blue.

Jerzy took up the reins of the wagon again without comment, while behind him Ao rearranged the contents that had been disturbed during the fight, drawing the canvas cover back over them and fastening it securely before settling himself in a corner, and, to all intents and purposes, falling asleep. Kaïnam reclaimed the vanguard position, his body alert to any threat either around or above, while the clop of hooves told Jerzy that Mahault was doing the same behind.

"Be careful," he heard Kaïnam say. "Things come out in the dark that would avoid daylight."

Jerzy stared at the road, but did not see it, his thoughts chasing after each other, chewing on their own tails. The sense of being salivated over had come when he let the full force of his legacies fill him. The attack came soon after. Too soon? The beasts had found them, not by chance but malice. Jerzy had been identified as a threat, identified and . . . hunted?

Unlike the sea beasts, those birds had not merely followed along a shoreline until they came to a target: they had flown, looking. But not randomly; Jerzy had watched enough birds flying over the yards to know that a bird, no matter how twisted, did not fly randomly, but watched the ground, followed known trails and likely spots for a specific sort of prey. There were other, easier targets, had all these beasts wanted were food, or violence.

He had spent so much time wondering who and why, the how had seemed without purpose: magic, of course. But once decanted, once used, magic slipped away; as he had warned Ao, magic did not last. Even a master Vineart could not follow the magic back to the one who had used it: Magewine could identify the crafter, but that was all. It was not a pigeon, to return from whence it came.

Something else, then. Something that used the magic, but was not itself magic? That could reach across oceans, burrow into a distant land, bring illness and identify threats?

Possible, yes. Likely, no. And yet, if he concentrated, Jerzy could imagine roots tough and gnarled, stretching between everything, connecting Vineart to land-lord, coastline to farmland, cities of power to distant vineyards, and the Collegium in Altenne and all the red-robed Washers on their many roads . . . all connected through Sin Washer's Command. Even as he imagined that, the vision expanded to include a second set, creeping through the soil, reaching up to tangle and strangle the first set of roots, turning it to rot, spreading its dis-ease up into the stocks. . . .

All connected.

Master Malech had never even hinted at such a thing. But neither had he ever hinted that there might yet be unblooded vines left, or sea serpents, or . . .

There had been things Master Malech had not known. The thought caught in Jerzy's chest, as though it were a betrayal.

So. A thing unknown, but possible. It was assuredly no coincidence that the winged beasts had found them. Specifically, found *him*. *His* enemy had tracked him, traced him through that connection. Roots that were impossible, that deep and that old, but existed nonetheless, all the way through the earth: deeper than rock, deeper than ocean.

That was how the . . . Jerzy could no longer bring himself to call his enemy a Vineart, not after the abominations he had created—how the *mage* reached into distant lands, and struck.

Jerzy needed to consult Malech's records. He needed to know if anyone else had ever written of those roots—and if there was a way to cut them, before the disease spread further.

"Jer?" Kaïnam, his voice flowing back from just ahead. "Do we stop, or go on?"

It had become too dark for them to safely ride without risking a horse stumbling, or being attacked by something with better night sight. Jerzy looked up at the sky, now covered with clouds, and shook his head, although he suspected they could not see him.

"Light, come steady, light come low," he said, turning his closed fist palm side up and summoning quiet-magic into a pale light the same blue-white as moonshine. It slipped from between his fingers, spreading out in a ribbon to light the road just ahead of them.

"Anything more would attract attention," he said. "This should be enough."

"We split into two shifts," Kaï said. "Two resting, while one drives and one keeps watch. Switch at moonrise." He looked at the sky. "Or as close as we can tell, anyway."

The night passed that way, the steady clop of hooves and turning of wooden wheels broken by the calls of night birds and the occasional yipping of foxes, while someone stayed alert with Ao's bow in their hands or, in Jerzy's case, a small wineskin of firewine at the ready. None of them slept well, and the morning sun found their eyes rimmed with red and crusted with dust, their limbs aching from the aftermath of the fight and the hard jouncing of the road, but all that was forgotten when they made the turn off the main road and up to the vintnery proper.

As a slave, Jerzy had never thought that he would leave the confines of the low stone walls. As a student, he had gone only on his master's orders, checking on the smaller yards, or traveling to Aleppan, to study with another Vineart—and play the spy on their gossip.

Now, he thought he might feel much as Ao's people did, ever-leaving, ever-returning. It was a distressing, dizzying thought, compounded by how quiet it all was that morning, with only the occasional invisible but vocal songbird to keep them company.

The immediate yards ran sloping down to the right-hand side of the road, stretching across the Valle of Ivy. The valley itself was cut into a chessboard, half green with crops, the others brown and fallow, interspersed with the occasional gnarled fruit tree, and dotted with low stone buildings where the House slaves lived and the farming equipment was kept. In the distance, a river cut through the fields— the Ivy. The chessboard and the buildings belonged to the House of Malech, one of four Vinearts established within The Berengia.

Master Vineart Malech, once-student of Vineart Josia, who first planted these yards. Master of Jerzy. Dead now, months past, of an attack by the same force that had attacked them: an unknown Vineart, in an unknown land, with strength beyond anything Jerzy had been taught possible.

But he had not been taught enough.

Jerzy resisted looking to the left until he had no choice, the wagon drawing to a stop at the end of the cobbled road. Ahead, a narrower path led to the stables, the henhouse, and the coldhouse, set into the hill behind the House.

To his left . . .

The House itself.

He turned and looked back the way they had come, then toward the fields again. The slaves were out among the vines, working, while others tended the much smaller gardens. A taller, bulkier form strode among them: the overseer.

A slave came running down from the stables, its jerkin clean, if ragged, dark blond hair falling into its face. Its feet were bare, and the expression guarded, until Jerzy turned around.

"Master."

Something cold touched Jerzy at the sound of that almost casual greeting, and he fought to keep from shuddering.

Once his jaw unlocked, the words came easily. "Take the horses, and make sure they are all well-tended. Unload the wagon—carefully!—and bring the casks to the workroom door." Cut into the side of the house, that door opened into the storerooms and the study where he had taken most of his lessons. His study, now. His storerooms.

His slaves.

The slave bowed and sped off to gather help as well as spread the news that a Vineart was back in residence.

Welcome home.

Jerzy did not acknowledge the dragon's voice, not yet.

The others also dismounted, Kaïnam tying up his reins before lifting Ao out of the wagon. Jerzy watched the procedure, ready to assist if necessary, already running through the spellwines he would need to start the proper healing of that scar tissue. It was still painful to see Ao, once so exuberant and energetic, now reliant on someone else, but it hurt less than to turn around and see . . . what?

"I had forgotten how lovely it is," Mahault said.

At that, Jerzy looked.

The pathway led under a green arch, twined vines spelled so that no fruit grew from them, only thickly clustered leaves that remained green even during Fallowtime. He knew, walking underneath, that he would feel the welcome of the House, the sense of the Guardian marking him as he came home, although the dragon had known he was en route since before the *Heart* made port.

Beyond that, past the flowered shrubs and sloping patch of grass, up a golden stone path was the main building, its façade the same stone as the path. Two stories high, with narrow windows glittering with colored glass on either side of the entrance.

The great wooden door should have been open, as it always had been in the past.

It was shut.

Kaïnam looked at Jerzy, and waited, as a good guest would. Ao, however, had no such hesitation. Swinging carefully on the crudely made crutches tucked under his arms, he hop-stepped toward the archway, calling out, "Ho, the House!"

As though summoned, the doors flew open and a body ran out, down the path, her hair streaming behind her in an indecorous manner, and before Jerzy could think, Lil had thrown her arms around him, hugging him so tightly he could barely breathe.

Behind him, Kaïnam chuckled, and Ao grinned as though he were the one being greeted thus. Jerzy could feel his ears turn hot with a blush, but his arms went around the cook almost instinctively and, much to his surprise, he returned the hug.

Malech had been his master. Detta was House-keeper. But Lil had been his very first-ever friend.

"You're home, you're home," she was babbling now, letting go of him and dancing back a step, her hands automatically going to her hair, smoothing the tangled locks back down. Once she had worn a red kerchief over her pale hair, the same as he had while at sea, but now those blond locks were plaited in a narrow row at her crown, held away from her face and then left to flow across her shoulders, away from the work she would supervise. Her clothing was much the same, if of better wear: still a skirt and smock, soft house-shoes on her feet, and her face still broke into a smile, if not as easily as it once had. A change: there were lines around her eyes and mouth that had not been there before, and a shadow underneath her joy.

It had been a hard year, for everyone.

"All are well?" he asked, dreading the answer.

"All well, as well as can be," she replied. As though to confirm that, the rounded bulk of the House-keeper came down the path, moving at a more suitable speed for her age and position, but her eyes as kind and welcoming as they had been the first day she had taken him in hand and scrubbed off the last of the sleep house grime from his skin.

"Jerzy." Her welcome, quieter than Lil's, less formal that the slave's, made it all real.

He was home.

Somehow, it still felt wrong.

DETTA SOON HAD them organized and inside, the ancient tapestries and gleaming woods of the House a balm on Jerzy's exhausted nerves, the morning meal waiting on the table, fresh breads and cheeses and cold roasted meats sliced thin and spread with spices.

Detta had taken one look at Ao, balancing on his wooden supports, and sent one of the kitchen children to fetch Per, with orders for him to "bring 'round the chair."

"Old Master Josia, when he was older," she explained. "Not so much with the getting around, but still impatient, he was. Had this made for him, to move easier, and stored it when he was gone. No reason why, save now, I suppose. Never be rid of anything you might need, that's truth."

"I'm sure Kaï will be thankful not to be my beast of burden any longer than needed," Ao said. "My thanks, O Mistress of the House." He tried to bow from his seat, and Detta scowled at him until he settled down.

"Once the healing starts . . ." Jerzy said, and then let his voice trail off. He would not give Ao false hope; the best he could promise would be that the scar tissue would not become infected, and the pain would lessen. He could not give Ao back his legs.

There was an awkward silence, then Ao shrugged and went back to his meal, and the others followed. As they ate, Detta quietly brought Jerzy up-to-date with what had happened while he was gone.

"Harvest was unexceptional; it was as though they knew he was gone, the vines did." She was no Vineart, but she was House-keeper for decades, and knew more than most. "A fair amount of fruit was plucked and crushed, but I suspect it was no great loss you were not here to prepare it. I had the slaves cask it, anyway, but . . ." Her rounded shoulders rose and fell. "I'd no idea what to do, other."

"The fields were cleared and prepared for Fallowtime?" He felt no taint here, within the walls where the Guardian protected, but other things could and often did go wrong. It had been too early in the morning when they rode in to see if all had been done as it should.

"As always; the overseer knew what to do, there, and made sure the other fields were kept likewise. We had . . ." She paused. "It was a quiet autumn."

Meaning no visitors, Washer or otherwise. No attacks, once Malech was dead and he, Jerzy, was gone. The House had been no threat to what their enemy planned. That would change, now.

"I'll need to ride out to see for myself," he said, his mind leaving the impossible problems to focus on more well-traveled routes. "And let them know I'm back."

They know.

The Guardian, its voice cool and silent in his head. "They" might have been referring to the overseer, or the slaves, but they were not.

*　　*　　*

WHILE HE WAS away, Detta had moved all of Jerzy's belongs—a few trinkets his weapons master, Cai, had given him, the grammar he had learned his letters from, and a handsome glass bottle that Master Malech had gifted him with—to the rooms downstairs. Master Malech's rooms: a bedchamber, a small garderobe, and the study. Now Jerzy's. He could not protest: it was only right and proper. But the suddenness of it, to him, made his eyes sting.

Detta pretended not to notice as she sent Kaïnam and Ao up the stairs to what had been Jerzy's room, and arranged for Mahault to settle in with Lil.

"If I do not intrude . . ." Mahl said, clearly torn between being separated from the others and the pleasing thought of not having to share sleeping quarters with them any longer.

"You do not intrude," Lil assured her, tucking her arm into Mahl's and leading her away to the side stair without a second thought.

"Do you need help with the stairs?" Kaïnam asked Ao, who shot him a glare, and stomped off, awkwardly, on his crutches, only to stop at the foot of the staircase and give a heavy sigh. "Yes," he said. "I'm going to need help."

"I will have Per construct a railing," Detta said into Jerzy's ear, watching the two take the stairs carefully, Ao's upper body bearing his weight against the wall while Kaïnam carried the crutches. "And a pulley, perhaps: to slide the crutches alongside, so that he need not ask anyone to carry them?"

"You're wiser than everyone in the House thrown together."

"I'm older than everyone else in this House thrown together," she said, with a return of her customary tartness. "And you, go. It will take some settling in, don't think I don't know that, but soonest started, soonest done, and soonest ready for all that's to come."

Detta didn't know even part of what was to come, but it was good advice. Readying himself, Jerzy turned right where the others had gone left, and walked through the doorway and into his new quarters.

*　　*　　*

THE NEXT MORNING, Jerzy woke before dawn. The bed was too large, the ceiling unfamiliar, and for all that the room was more comfortably appointed, he missed the hard cot and the window with the view of the vineyards.

You don't need to see them. The Guardian, as puzzled as the creature had ever sounded.

"It's not need," Jerzy said. "Want."

The Guardian could not understand. It wanted for nothing, in that sense. It had never been taken away from what it was tied to and forced to rely on memory and hope.

The Guardian did not feel impatience any more than it felt any emotion, but it managed to convey a sense of exasperation, nonetheless. *Go.*

Like the command of a decantation, the word drove Jerzy out of the bed, into his clothing, and through the house on bare feet. The grass outside was covered with dew and tickled his toes, while the cobblestones cut at his skin as it never had when he was a slave. But he did not go into the yard, although they whispered to him; it was enough to stand there for a long moment, watching the mist rise at shoulder level, hearing the stirring of the nightwatch slaves as they came in and those in the sleep house rising to greet the day, while behind him the House started to wake. All was, for the moment, well here.

There was something he needed to do, first.

THE KITCHEN LOOKED the same as it had on Jerzy's first day in the House: large and warm, and filled with the smell of smoke and meats and the ever-present simmering kettle of tai. A small child was curled by the fire, making sure the tai did not boil nor the fire go out, while another servant was busily kneading dough in the far corner, where the air was cooler. Neither of them blinked at his appearance: the master had the right to be anywhere he wished. Jerzy placed his burden on a cleared portion of the long worktable, selected a knife, and set to work.

He had gotten halfway through when he heard a familiar voice ask, "What are you doing?" *In my kitchen* went unsaid, but Jerzy could hear it in Lil's voice, and almost smiled. He should have done this somewhere else, out of sight. Master Malech would have insisted on it.

But the knives were here, and the worktable was exactly the right height, and nobody would notice one more splatter on the floor, if it became messy—as it had.

He wiped his forehead with his forearm, sensing Lil pause by the fire, building the flames up and speaking softly to the child on watch before coming up alongside him, heaving an exasperated sigh as she used her own kerchief to clear his face. "If you wanted a roast hen for eve-meal," she started to say, then actually looked at what was on the table in front of him.

"Silent gods. Jerzy, what *is* that?"

"I don't know."

The wings of the creature had shredded during their journey back, the feathers molting all at once, the meat sliding off the bone as though it had been boiled to softness. Remembering the way those wings had beat down at his face, and carried the weight of the birds as they swooped, Jerzy doubted they had been that soft to begin with. Like the sea serpents, these beasts were meant to dissolve once killed so that none could find evidence, after. They had not needed to bury the others, at all; only the lingering effects of the basic healspell that created it had preserved this one, even this long.

The body, interestingly, remained intact longer; Jerzy suspected that the wings had taken the brunt of effort and so had used more of the magic—and therefore broken down faster. But it was only a thought; he had no proof, either way.

Using one of Lil's larger knives, he had cut open into the bird's flesh, laying it apart in sections.

The sea serpent had been solid flesh, no blood or veins, no bones to speak of. Master Malech had tested it and found nothing to indicate life at all, as though it had been pressed together the way a potter might press clay. This bird had bones—hollow bones, strong but light—and blood of a sort, although the way Lil was staring at it in horror added to Jerzy's feeling that it looked like no innards of any natural fowl.

"Don't touch it," he said sharply, when she would have poked at one dismembered bit, and her arm jerked back as though he had threatened her with one of her own knives.

"That . . . that's blood?" Lil, rather than being disgusted, was fascinated. She leaned forward over his arm, almost pushing him out of the way, although she was careful to keep clear of the sticky mess. "Ugh. It looks like night-meat."

Jerzy stared at the carcass, then turned his head to look at Lil. "What?"

"The goo. It looks like when I'm making night-meat, before it all congeals and cools. The blood and *vina* and the ground meal and the meat, all look like that."

Night-meat, so called because it was prepared the evening before, mixed and set in skins and left to cook overnight, to serve with breakfast in colder weather. Master Malech had liked it, although Jerzy never developed the taste.

"Blood and *vina*." Roots and vines, connected. His earlier thoughts suddenly collided in a new tangle. Nothing made sense, and yet there was a pattern. There had to be. Mil'ar Cai had said there was a pattern to everything; that was how you won a fight, by finding the pattern and controlling it.

"Jerzy?" She took another look at his face, and stepped away carefully, giving him space to think.

The pattern of attacks. From bloodless, compacted flesh, roaming at will . . . the cat's-paw of magic that had attacked him on the road months before, powerful and directed, but without physical form . . . and now this: flesh and form, directed to a single purpose. Puppets, played by a single, malicious will. Again, the question of *how*.

He remembered the sense of roots. Roots. Patterns. Methods. *Think like a Vineart*, Jerzy told himself. *Think like a soldier. Think like a man of power. . . .* If he had no Command to hedge him, what might he do?

"Not *vina*," he said finally. "Spellwine. Spellwine, and blood." Vineart Giordan had taught him that weathervines, only lightly blooded, required their Vineart's blood to bind them to an incantation; without that connection, they would fight him. Sin Washer's blood had been powerful enough to break the First Vine, shattering the power into lesser legacies, protecting the world from human folly and greed.

One god's blood, to shatter a world. Only a few drops, to incant an entire cask. How much would a skin of blood do? How much could a single Vineart give? How much, to create a spell that could twist and control so many beasts. . . .

Lil had been raised in the House of Malech, and she was no fool. "That . . . that thing is a construct of magic. Like the monsters that attacked the villages, last spring?"

Master Malech would not have ventured a theory, not without testing it with Magewine, to try and identify the traces. But Jerzy had seen more than his master ever had, felt the malign press of the taint often enough to recognize it, no matter how it was masked.

"Yes." He pushed the tip of his knife into the flesh, watching it part under the pressure, raw and soft. Spellwine . . . and blood.

How much blood, Jerzy wondered uneasily. And . . . whose?

KAÏNAM HAD ALSO woken well before dawn, feeling restless and too-aware. Rather than lay there, he had gotten up, leaving Ao still snoring in his bunk. Like Jerzy, he had been drawn to the outside, standing on the grassy verge just beyond the archway, but his attention looked not over the fields but back down the road, the way they had come the day before.

The weight of someone crossing the grass coming down from the house alerted him, but he did not move.

"Someone is out there," the House-keeper said.

"Yes."

Detta worried. Not obviously, and not without cause, but a House-keeper worried so that others could go about their responsibilities without having to do so. There had been no House-keeper in his father's House, as such, but Kaïnam understood the role; it must be even more complex in a Vineart's House, where the books measured not merely kitchen rations or purchased bales of cloth or servants' payments, but the purchasing and keeping of slaves. And how much did she handle the flow of casks and wagons to a dozen or more different ends?

And then, to carry on with the Keeping, in the absence of the House's master, never knowing if they might come under attack, or from where—or by whom? She had kept things working in Jerzy's absence, and had accepted his return with a smooth grace that most regents would not be able to manage, in Kaïnam's world, and so he did not snap at her or dismiss her fears when she stood next to him and told him things that he already knew.

"We had company on our way home. A Washer."

The older woman did not look surprised, but merely nodded her head, her gray curls bobbing slightly. She was rounded but not soft, this woman. "And they will not come to our door, because of . . . what happened here? To the other Washers?"

The day Malech died, struck down by a then-invisible foe, the Washers who had come to take Jerzy into custody had either been killed by that same hand, or disappeared.

Jerzy was master here, but Kaïnam knew more of strategy. "I believe he was set to observe, only," he said. "A few days wait, and then Mahault and I will ride out to confront him. For now . . ." He shook his head. "Let him watch. Where is Jerzy?"

"He went out just at sunrise," the House-keeper said. "Wanted to walk the yards, I suspect, although he did not say. It is what Master Malech did, whenever he was more than a day or three away."

Jerzy had been away considerably longer than that.

Kaïnam nodded. "I want to get Ao out and moving, before he forgets that he can. Is there a place where we might practice, away from the House itself?"

"Behind the icehouse," Detta said, without hesitation. "Jerzy took his lessons back there, when armsmaster Cai was still here. You can't do much damage, and nobody will see you without you seeing them first."

Kaïnam nodded, pleased. "Excellent. Please let Mahl know that is where we will be."

LIL FINALLY LEFT Jerzy be, with strict instructions to get rid of every bit of the creature from her kitchen or she'd not cook in there again. When he'd decided that there was no more to be learned, Jerzy scraped up the decomposing remains of the beast, and set it to burning in a pit behind the House, where they disposed of the kitchen scraps. Even the thick, smudgy smoke that rose from the debris made him feel ill.

He cleaned his hands in the washroom, scrubbing at his face to make sure any splatters were removed, and then walked out of the house, the fresh air against his skin a welcome relief. His feet took him, almost without thought, across the paving-stone road and down into the yard proper, looking for calm among the winter-quieted vines. The re-tinged leaves whispered against his hand, their sounds barely a low murmur of recognition, and Jerzy felt as though they were asking the same of him that he had thought to receive. Like him, the taint disturbed them, the uncertainty uprooted them. Vines, like Vinearts, were creatures of deep-rooted tradition, and unquiet did not bode well for the next year's Harvest.

Guilt pressed against him from within, guilt and regret. He was Vineart. The well-being of the vines was his responsibility. And he had been too long away. So he walked from one end of the yard to another, passing occasional slaves who ducked their faces and curved around his path as they went, until his feet were sore and the whisper of the vines had become a more contented, sleepy drone.

The vines were appeased. Jerzy was not. His soft-soled shoes in one hand, fine-grained dirt between his toes, and a sense of being unsettled in his own skin, he turned away from the sloping yard, meaning to

return to the study and the work awaiting him. Instead, caught by
unusual sounds, he turned away from the House proper and walked up
to the grassy area behind the stone icehouse and the stable.

The last time he had been here, the Washers had erected their
tents, and he had been questioned by Vineart Neth as to his actions in
Aleppan. Now, the space was empty save for a peg-and-rope circle tied
about an arm span off the ground, marking off a practice area and the
two combatants within.

Reminded of his own time spent within a similar circle, Jerzy leaned
against the low stone wall and watched.

Kaïnam was carrying a length of wood, crudely shaped like a sword,
his long black hair tied back from his eyes and his tunic off, his skin
showing a definite sheen of sweat although he did not appear to be
winded.

By contrast, Ao was breathing hard, and swearing harder. He sat in
a wheeled chair, a battered construction that looked like one of master
Malech's chairs from the study, affixed to three wooden wheels, two in
front and one behind. There was a small shield strapped to one arm
of the chair, just high enough to protect his midsection, and he held a
wooden sword-stick like Kaïnam's in one hand, moving the chair with
the other.

That must have been Master Josia's chair, the one that Detta had
mentioned.

"Again," Kaïnam ordered, in the same voice Mil'ar Cai had used
in this same spot, teaching a younger, flailing Jerzy the basics of fight
survival. Even as Kaïnam gave the order he lunged, swinging his mock
sword down with the same force as he might use in a true battle. Jerzy's
muscles tensed in reaction, his first instinct to voice a protest, to warn
Ao, but even as the urge rose, Ao's arm raised his own sword and
blocked the downward blow, turning the chair so that the side rammed
into Kaïnam's hip, driving him back a step.

"Good. Again."

They went back and forth, trading blows, until Ao misjudged his movement, and nearly tipped the chair over. Kaïnam dropped his own blade and righted him before the trader hit dirt.

"Rot and blast." Ao sounded both disgusted and dispirited. "In the middle of an actual fight, that won't do me much good, to ask my foe to stop and assist me, if he would be so kind."

"It was the chair, not you. It was built to move back and forth in peaceful times, not joust like a warhorse. We'll have a better one crafted for you."

"Best to have Jerzy magic me up new legs," Ao muttered, then saw the Vineart standing off to the side. "Jer, can you . . . ?"

Ao looked so hopeful, and so exhausted, that Jerzy found words he hadn't intended to say in his mouth. "I can't . . . not new legs, but there may be something I can do. *May.*"

Ao had lost his legs protecting *him*. Jerzy felt his earlier determination grind the doubt into dust. If his foe could create monsters, surely he could find a way to give Ao back mobility. The vines stirred, whispering to him of ways, stirring ideas in his mind. But it would have to wait a little while longer. His findings earlier weighed heavily on him, and he needed his companions' advice before he could decide the next step.

"We need to talk," he said. "All of us."

Chapter 5

*M*aster *Malech, when* he had things to consider, had gone down into the cellars. There, in close proximity to the stored spellwines, he said he could think best. Jerzy, with three others and Ao's chair to consider, chose instead the courtyard within the House. Open to the blue sky, the breeze tinged with the smell of rough dirt rather than the sea, the moment he ushered them all through the doorway, the rightness of his choice settled on him. He could think, here.

The night before, they had not done more than unpack the wagon and settle in, so Kaïnam had not had a chance yet to see the courtyard in the center of the House. He looked startled, then frowned at the bare ground as though demanding that grass grow underfoot.

"Over there," Jerzy said, directing them to the great spread-branch tree with the stone bench underneath that dominated the center of the courtyard. The branches raised all the way up to the second floor, creating shade against summer heat. Now, with winter approaching, the branches were mostly bare, and it appeared more like a skeleton than Jerzy was comfortable looking at.

Kaïnam sat down on the bench, still looking around curiously as though he were memorizing every detail, or checking it against something in his own memory. Mahault, who was familiar with the courtyard from her previous brief visit, pushed Ao's chair toward the tree, then started to fuss at him, making sure that he was situated out of the direct sunlight, until he mock-growled at her. "I'm legless, not witless," he said.

"There are days I wonder about that," she responded, but left him be, waiting for Jerzy to take the other edge of the bench. He waved at her distractedly, indicating that she should sit. He thought better while pacing.

"There is so much to do, now that we are back." The speech he had half-prepared felt awkward in his mouth, and he abandoned it. "This morning, I took apart one of the creatures that attacked us, on the road."

Jerzy had worried about how much to tell them. These were Vineart things, matters of magic, but they already knew the most dangerous things, about his quiet-magic. About the Guardian, creature of stone and magic, extending House Malech's reach in ways that surely the Washers would say contradicted Sin Washer's Command. Telling them what he suspected about their enemy's abilities, about how it was all connected . . . what he thought it meant . . . all that could be no worse an offense.

The fact that he worried at all, Jerzy knew, was laughable. He had already lost so much, had so much taken away while trying to obey, that had Sin Washer himself appeared and warned him to keep silent, he would have asked the god *why*. What else could he suffer, for telling?

"Our enemy has been sending beasts against us. You know this already. The serpents who prowl the seas, attacking at random, drawn, I think, by the scent of magic. And now these birds . . . and who knows what else that we have not yet encountered, or heard of. He is creating them, through some spell, some legacy I do not know."

Jerzy was prepared to explain, although he wasn't sure how he could describe something he did not know, but the other three instead went after the more practical details.

"Serpents and birds can cross the ocean," Ao said, leaning back in his chair and staring up at the sky, as though calculating distances. "If we are right that he comes from outside the Lands Vin, far outside, it's unlikely we have to worry about anything with four legs."

"Yet," Kaïnam said darkly. "Do we know how they are made? Can he create beasts from materials already here, or must he send them, intact?"

Jerzy wiped his palms against the fabric of his trou and tried not to think about the things he had seen. How much could he tell them? How much of what he told them would they be able to understand? "It began with things . . . influenced, here. Insects out of season, vermin and rot. That was where it began. The serpents came later, and the bird-creatures after that.

"When the serpents arrived, my master and I took apart one and found they were . . . solid. Like something carved out of flesh, or pressed together, rather than a living thing, and animated via a spell. My master surmised that they had, in fact, been made of dead flesh of other creatures, shaped to resemble serpents, animated by magic."

"Is there—"

"No," Jerzy said, knowing Kaïnam's question before it was uttered. "There was no spellvine, to Master Malech's knowledge, that could do such a thing." He did not mention the Magewine, the spellwine that could identify a particular legacy or Vineart. They already knew it was a different legacy, or a legacy that had been twisted, somehow, into new form.

"These birds, I suspect . . ." Jerzy did not have the right words to explain his fears, but pushed forward anyway. "I brought one back and cut it open this morning," he repeated. "Inside, it looked like a true-born bird, once, but enspelled so that its body changed. Was twisted, and more."

"Changed, how?" Kaïnam leaned back, as though expecting there to be a back to the bench, and checked himself. "Obviously, the bodies had been modified somehow, their size and those claws, that beak, but you're saying it as though there was something else."

"Inside. Not solid flesh but sinew and bone. Their bones were hollow, but thicker than a bird's should be." Lil's knowledge there, not his: he had never thought to wonder. "And their blood . . ." Even now, a wave of nausea threatened, and he forced it down with practice hard-earned while sailing. It was not the texture or the odd stickiness that bothered him, but the half-suspected knowledge of what it was, what it must be, and what it meant, that sickened him. "The blood was mixed with spellwine, as though the creature had been bled dry, and then some new mixture added in." But not only with spellwine. Lil had not needed to tell him that; the moment he had, carefully, cautiously, touched the blood, he had known that.

Human blood.

"A healspell, changed or twisted," Jerzy said, before they could ask. "It is the only way I can imagine. Probably when they were hatchlings, not adults. If it was possible, it was possible to do to adults, but they would then have to learn how to fly like that." He paced the length of the small courtyard, letting the familiar surroundings soothe him while the others digested the news. He did not want to admit how magic could be so misused. Did not want to admit to himself the small step from Vineart Giordan's means of taming his vines to this abomination. It was not new magic but old, the oldest . . . and more, a twisting of what had always been. Blood and vines. Blood and magic.

Master Malech had warned him against trying to change an existing spell. How much change was safe? A pruning here, a grafting there . . . If the spell that had poisoned the air in the workrooms succeeded, would he have created some living horror?

How close had he come to disaster?

What sort of price was this mage paying, to accomplish such deeds?

Jerzy turned, pacing to the other side of the courtyard, and saw a cool shadow land on the roof ledge, curling itself in a remaining patch of sunlight like a hard gray cat.

I am here.

The Guardian guarded. Against threats from without . . . and within. It would not allow him to go too far.

Jerzy returned to the other three, who were deep in discussion.

"Long-term planning. He is building his strength here, piece by piece, moving more directly with each increase," Kaï said, speaking with absolute certainty.

Jerzy squatted across from the bench, resting his wrists on his knees, balancing the way he used to, back when he was a slave, and considered Kaïnam's words.

"It seems probable," he agreed. "This Vineart, he has attacked directly before—with infestations, and illnesses, and shaped-magic." The magical attack nearly a year before that had killed his horse and nearly taken his own life had not been forgotten, despite more physical attacks since then. "But these are different: he is decanting magic into these creatures, mixing flesh and spellwine, not merely using the magic to send them . . . but it could have been done from a distance. We cannot assume any limit to his ability. He does not abide by the Commands, is not limited by the same laws."

Ao was silent, rubbing his hands on the polished wood of his chair as though looking for a splinter to catch. Mahault seemed to be thinking the way Roan unwound a skein of wool, following it back to the starting knot.

"Our enemy knew we were shipboard; he wanted some way to catch us. You." She frowned. "But he couldn't trace us on the ocean?"

"Running water dilutes spellwines," Jerzy said. "A creek or river, not enough to stop a decantation. A lake . . . if it is large enough. An ocean? We are blind. The currents confuse it, the winds diffuse it . . . the serpents attacked randomly. Even Ximen is blind, for all his magic. The birds did not attack until we were well inland."

"So he is blind on the sea?"

"He might be," Jerzy said. "It would explain enough to be reasonable."

"Then we can use that," Kaïnam said. "A physical attack, a fleet, could strike a blow against him and catch him off guard."

"Except we have no fleet, and we don't know where to find him," Mahault pointed out. "Two important details, in case you've forgotten."

"You were reluctant to use magic," Ao said, focusing on another angle. "When we were on the ship, coming back. Even healspells, unless I absolutely needed it." There was no accusation in his tone, only a slow understanding where before there had been dogged acceptance. "You think if these creatures were made from a healspell, however twisted, they would have felt that? Like calling to like?"

"It . . . seemed probable." Jerzy wasn't certain, not about any of it, but his passing thoughts and worries were being dragged from him, strand by strand, the most recent event merely clarifying what lurked in his thoughts, mustus turning to vina. "The times I have been attacked, it has always been after I used magic. Specifically, quiet-magic."

Kaïnam shoved his hands, palms down, on the bench, making a painful-sounding noise. "Why didn't you say anything? Why didn't you tell us, when you suspected any of this?"

Jerzy felt annoyance stir within him, as though Kaïnam were accusing him of having led them intentionally into danger. They looked to him to lead, but he did not know how. His hands fisted at his sides, and he deliberately kept his mouth still, refusing to draw on the quiet-magic he could feel welling within his flesh.

"How could I know?" he asked instead. "This is all guesswork and conjecture, shoving pieces together to see if they fit. You said it yourself: he has planned all this out, while we flail in the darkness. How could I know anything of what he does? You speak as though this should be familiar to me, and it is not!"

There was silence as the other three let the words sink in. Mahault bowed her head, while Ao gripped the arms of his chair even more tightly, until the knuckles turned white under the yellowish bronze of his skin.

"My failure, Vineart." Kaïnam did not stand to make a formal apology; the words were enough.

Jerzy shook his head, negating the need for any such, even as he accepted them. This was magic. They did not understand—did not know how much he did not understand. And it had to be that way, if he were to keep them focused, standing strong against whatever came. They trusted him, and even if he had to lie to maintain that trust . . .

"Master Malech . . . he could not identify where the serpents came from, or how they had been made. The spellwine was not one that was known to him."

That had been true, then. Now, Jerzy knew that the five legacies were not all that was left to grow. In Irfan, at least, unblooded grapes, feral grapes, still grew. And where there was one feral yard, there could be another. Esoba, the Vineart who worked those lands, had not known what he possessed . . . but their enemy had.

Irfan had changed everything Jerzy thought he knew. Unblooded vines, stronger and more fierce than anything he had ever dreamed, creating spellwines almost too subtle to detect. Vines that responded to his deepest-hidden wishes, rising up to throttle a man Jerzy had only meant to interrogate—taking his anger and turning it to murder.

Jerzy flinched from that memory, letting the Guardian's cool stone fill his thoughts instead, focusing on the question being asked: could they counter the attacks? Could they launch one of their own?

Jerzy stared into the sky, unable to look his companions in the eye. "Where he creates them, how he creates them . . . there is a deeper danger than even that. You asked me, once, if there was a spell that could make us do or say things we did not mean." Back in Esoba's House, when they had encountered mindspells, the most delicate and difficult of incantations that should have been far beyond that poorly trained Vineart's abilities, that had let slip the things they kept hidden even from themselves.

"You said there wasn't." Mahault had gone very still, and even Ao was focused intently on what Jerzy said next.

"Not for men, nor beasts; Sin Washer made sure of that when he shattered the First Growth. And yet Ximen is strong enough to force a creature that would normally not be violent to attack. To send a seabird, however remade, inland, and cause it to attack where there was neither threat nor food, following the trace of magic used hours before. That sort of bespelling must be made inside the creature, twisting more than its bones and beak."

"Twisting its thoughts, its instincts, to do what its master needed." Once again, Kaïnam followed his thoughts before Jerzy had a chance to speak them.

Ao swallowed hard, obviously remembering the beast falling on him as it died, the thick, spellbound blood splattering him. "Could . . . this be done to humans?"

Jerzy had spent the morning putting together everything they'd seen and heard, to one inescapable conclusion. "I think it already has."

He had thought to shock them. His companions, however, had been less sheltered than he, as a slave.

"The aide in my father's court, and the merchant in Irfan? You think they were . . . like that? Not coerced or seduced but twisted, changed? Like those birds?" Mahault's tone was doubtful, but more of her own understanding than the possibility of its truth.

"It makes sense. These birds, the twisted form he perfected with the serpents, the control he had over men"—and Jerzy noted how, despite having a name for their enemy, none of them used it now, as though trying not to attract his attention—"he's going deeper. He's not casting them onto his victims, he's . . . blending them."

Jerzy had tried blending spellwines before rather than using the established incantations or crafting new ones. They had gone wrong, filling the study with a noxious fume, or given back unpredictable results, like the masthead on the *Vine's Heart* that still left him uneasy for all that it seemed like a mark of Sin Washer's favor.

He was nowhere as skilled as their enemy. He did not use blood. Jerzy swallowed around a strangely dry throat, almost afraid to bring up moisture in his disordered state. What could their enemy do, if he had mastered that?

"The earlier attempts were lighter, touching only the surface of his targets. Like the spell used on us, it pushed a natural reaction, made what was already there stronger, more likely to be acted upon." Anger, or greed, or fear. They had resisted only because Jerzy realized what was happening, had felt the taint and warned them.

"The whisperers in my father's ear, the one who murdered Kaï's sister . . . they acted of free will." Mahault sounded less certain than she wanted to be, however.

"Ximen took what was there, fear or greed or anger, and used it to his own ends, crafting it the way I would the crush, into something more potent, something that could take direction."

Blood and flesh and bone and magic.

"If he has progressed to the point where he can twist living things to go against their base nature, twist his own desire into theirs . . ."

Magic could not make a person do what it did not want to do, merely bring forward thoughts, desires, that were buried deep. That was dangerous enough. Changing those desires to suit another's needs or desires? Forcing a being to go against its nature?

Abomination. The act of a prince-mage.

"To do such a thing, and at such a distance . . ." Kaïnam had already come to the same conclusion Jerzy had been circling around, unable to accept until now. They looked at each other, gray eyes and brown equally worried.

"How?" Ao asked, always curious, even when he looked a little ill at the thought of what that progression could mean.

"I don't know." Jerzy stopped speaking to them, and was talking to himself. "I need to know. If I can understand it, I can—" He could do what? Defeat it? Stop it? Use it himself? The thought, the memory, of the taint, coiled inside the bird, made him want to gag. What kind of man—and magic—could do such a thing? An ordinary man might decant a spell without harm or influence, but a Vineart could not separate the two: the man made the magic, the magic . . . created the man. Magic so twisted . . .

Jerzy did not have the time to chase that notion down further, as

Kaïnam had already gone to a more immediate, tactical concern. "Those beasts found you there, on the open road. Can you stop them from attacking here, from influencing us?"

Jerzy bit the inside of his lip, instinctively checking for his quietmagic, although he did not call it. "I think so." Malech had not been able to protect himself when attacked, but he had not understood the nature of what he faced. Once Jerzy understood, the Guardian had kept the taint out. Both of them here, forewarned . . . yes. He could keep this place safe.

"Then, while you do that, we will prepare a counterattack, taking advantage of his ocean-blindness." Kaïnam, for the first time in weeks, looked as though he anticipated something rather than dreading it. "Our knowledge, our contacts, and your magic. We are stronger than any single man, no matter what he has done."

Jerzy, still worried, nonetheless felt some of the weight slide away. He was Vineart. But he was not alone.

He could feel the Guardian worry, not certain that this was wise, but it did not interfere.

"We're going to need more information," Ao said, claiming his own role with relief. "Jer, you have a pigeon coop?"

"In the stables. One of the slaves handles them; he will be able to bring you whatever you need." He looked at the three of them: Kaïnam, the fierce and proud prince, as much advisor as warrior; Ao, equal amounts worry and mischief in his eyes, his body canted with excitement; Mahault, cool and strong, like a well-tempered blade waiting to be brought to bear. In that instant, Jerzy understood something he hadn't before. He didn't know quite what it was, had no word for it, no incantation to make it take form. But it made his throat sore, and his eyes itch.

"What we're doing . . . whatever comes now . . ." He tried to make them each understand, meeting their gazes as he spoke. "There is no justification under the Commands; I will be in complete apostasy. We have no proof of Ximen's existence, no court of judgment we may appeal to. The Collegium will have no doubt and no hesitation in killing me, in taking down all of House Malech. I don't know what they might do to you, perhaps nothing, but . . ."

"And the other option is what?" Mahault tucked a strand of pale yellow hair back into her braid, her gaze steady on his even as her hand shook a little. "To sit and wait, and let whatever happens, happen? To hide, and hope it blows over without touching us? That whatever our enemy wants, it will end well?"

"The Washers," Jerzy tried again, and Ao made a wet, rude noise, and the words came out of him like a flood, cutting off anything the Vineart had meant to say. "The Washers have chosen their ground, Jer, and it's right smack in the middle, like merchants who have nothing to sell and don't want to buy, but don't want anyone else to sell or buy, either." The weight of frustration and fear pushed his words out hard, as though it were all he could do to keep up. "I'm not a Vineart, or a lord, or anything that's important, by Sin Washer's rule, but I didn't go through all this"—and although he didn't draw any attention to his missing limbs, they might as well have been bleeding anew for how aware the others were of the hard-scabbed stumps under the blanket—"to sit back and let someone else decide my fate."

He took a heavy breath, and Mahault added, "If we stop now, then what was it all for?"

She did not specify "it." She did not have to. They had all sacrificed to reach this point, this place.

Jerzy looked at Kaïnam, who merely looked back, waiting. The princeling had his own reasons for being there, for wanting the mage not only stopped, but exposed.

They had been running so long, trying merely to stay one step ahead of those who chased Jerzy, trying to discover what had caused all this, who was behind the attacks, and then to come home, one question had never the chance to surface, much less be asked.

"Why me?" he said finally, as much to the Guardian, or the vines, as the three around him. "Why do you trust me to decide what we will do, where we will go?" He was Vineart, he knew magic, but they were all more experienced in these things of power and conflict, even Mahault. He was a slave, who—no matter what he had seen or done—knew the stone boundaries of his yard, the slats of a wine barrel, the cycle of a Harvest, not what happened in the outside world.

He wasn't expecting an answer. To his surprise, he got one.

"Because you transform us," Ao said, and for once there was no humor in his voice, no spark of mischief hiding in his eyes. "Jer, before I met you, all I ever wanted was to be the same as my father and brothers. Being part of a trader delegation, thinking only of the deal and the advantage, planning of the day I'd lead a caravan myself, it was enough, until I saw you in the hallway in Aleppan. I thought I could teach you something, for a laugh, and instead . . ." he searched for the words to express what he meant, but floundered. "Whatever it is that makes grapes into spellwines, you do that with people. You give us something to make us greater." His nose and mouth scrunched in dislike, as though his words tasted off, and added, "Or, at least, different."

Mahl had obviously thought about this before, as the moment Ao paused, she leaped in. "You're not afraid of change. We've all done the same thing for so long, calling it tradition, or Commands, or whatever reason we had, that even when someone else came in and changed things, we were stuck in our same responses—or worse, we panicked, flailed around and made things worse. Are still making things worse. Something is wrong, and we circled around it, but couldn't see, and couldn't do anything. You saw; you did something. And you made your choices out of what was needed, not fear. That's why."

Jerzy listened to the words, but did not recognize himself in them. Fear? Since returning home, since opening that creature and seeing what waited inside, decaying even as he studied it, he had been afraid, and not even the weight of the Guardian's presence against his mind or the rooted strength of the vineyard could counteract the growing fear that they were too small, too weak, and too unprepared, that the coming storm would blow them over, all of them, and beat them down until there was no chance of recovery, no opportunity to regrow.

"With your permission, Vineart." Kaïnam was in formal mode, standing like a soldier in front of him, or a captain, waiting for word of the tide. "If we are to build a defense against our enemy, we will need ears and hands in the world beyond, as well as magic within. I would follow Trader Ao's lead and make use of the pigeon cote in order to send messages out to those who might answer our call."

And there, Kaï hit at the heart of the matter. Vinearts were not meant to interact with the rest of the world. Their lives were contained within the walls of their vineyards, their efforts concentrated within the limits of their legacies. The command of men was forbidden them.

If Jerzy had changed his companions, they were changing him as well. He looked up to where the dragon crouched on the roof, its stone claws curled around the edge, tail curled around its hindquarters. Slave to student. Student to Vineart. Vineart to . . . what? His earlier uncertainty bloomed again. There was no tradition here, no legacy to guide him. He had no idea what he was supposed to do.

The dragon's blunt gray muzzle turned, the blind eyes looking directly at him.

Vineart crushes what the Harvest brings.

Jerzy turned back to Kaïnam and nodded once, his face stiff, trying to remember how Master Malech had looked when he came to Agreement on something, aware that on his face such an expression looked more foolish than formidable. "Yes," he said, not only in response to Kaï's formal request. "Yes."

Ao exhaled, a relived gust of wind. "Let's get to it, then, O Princeling." He turned his chair, intending to leave, but the back wheel jammed hard enough that Ao winced as a shock ran through his stumps. Jerzy and Mahault watched as the trader tried to get the chair moving again, both of them straining to help, but aware that it would not be welcomed. Finally, in disgust, Ao had Kaïnam back the chair up and lift the younger man through the doorway, careful not to jar his upper body. The princeling did so without comment, coming back to reclaim the chair and push it easily through the door.

"It must hurt," Mahault said softly. "The pain, every day . . ."

Jerzy felt guilt push at him, that he had not immediately found the right healspell to complete Ao's healing. Never mind that they had been home only a day and the beast-bird had taken priority, never mind that the serpent's teeth had torn away Ao's legs mid-thigh and he had been bleeding so fiercely all of the quiet-magic within Jerzy had been spent sealing off those wounds before he had no more blood left to spill, that the trader would have died on the spot had Jerzy not been there. If Jerzy had not been there, Ao would not have had to rescue him in the first place.

"Hurts less than dying," Jerzy said brusquely, now. It was the answer Master Malech or Detta might have given. It was the answer he believed. He wondered, not for the first time, if it was the answer Ao would have given.

"It wasn't an accusation," Mahl said softly, her hand warm on his shoulder, fingers curling against the cloth of his shirt. "This is war. People get hurt."

But Ao was not a fighter, had never trained in anything save the battle of words and wits. If he had changed Ao . . . was it for the better?

Jerzy looked at Mahl, remembering the last time they had been together in this same place, the day she had said there was no place for her within the walls of the House of Malech, when she had gone to chase after her dream of becoming a solitaire.

Everyone made sacrifices.

"Do you regret it? Not going with the solitaire?"

"With Keren?" Mahault took the question under consideration, not dashing off a response the way Ao might have, but it was only a minute before she shook her head, her smile sad but sweet. "Mahault, daughter of Niccolo, maiar of Aleppan had dreams. Mahl, sword-second to Kaïnam, honored in service to the House of Malech? This is . . . real. This is where I am meant to be."

Jerzy met her gaze, his face composed and calm, and something in his throat eased.

"I don't know what I'm going to do," he admitted.

"You'll figure it out," she said, letting her hand fall away. "You always do."

MAHL'S WORDS, AND the sight of Ao carried like a helpless babe, drove Jerzy not to the vineyards, although he felt the urge to return, but down the stone stairs to his master's workrooms. His workrooms, now. His cellar.

His cellar.

"My cellar."

Yours.

The Guardian had followed him down the steps, its wings moving slowly although it had no actual need, the magic that animated it giving it the ability to fly as well. The dragon went over Jerzy's shoulder into the workroom a flicker ahead of the Vineart, and settled into the hollowed-out niche over the doorway where it spent most of its days.

Jerzy reached up, an old habit, and touched the tip of the stone tail that flicked down as he passed through the doorway.

The room within was dusty; it was clear that no one had come down here since Master Malech died. Here, within the thick stone walls, away from anything and everything that might distract, Jerzy expected to feel the greatest sense of loss. Instead, he found a hint of comfort. But the true test was yet to come.

The vines had reached out, their leaves brushing against his skin, their roots murmuring to him of welcome, yes, but also of need. Of things undone or missed, of the longing to slip into their Fallowtime slumber and recover from the stress of the harvest.

Let others think that the Vines served the Vineart; the truth was more complicated than that. Unblooded grapes like those in Irfan had no need of a Vineart, but these had been trained to the line, crafted over generations to obey incantation, and demanded his obedience, in exchange.

Magic makes the Vineart.

Mahault, and Ao and Kaïnam, thought he would know what to do. The vines expected him to be Vineart. Detta expected him to protect the House. He, Jerzy, didn't think he was strong enough to sit in Master Malech's chair, much less *be* him.

But the spellwines ... He could not pretend to them, could not bluff or dodge or put up a strong face. They would see him as he was.

There was no mustus this year; the harvested juice had been placed in the tanks but there had been no one to punch it down, no one to follow its progress, to determine the moment when the skins would be separated from the juice, to ensure that the magic was strong enough to warrant keeping, to be refined and crafted into *vina*. He was afraid to look to his right, where the vatting chamber waited. He would have to look, soon. But not right now.

Instead, he turned to his left, facing the cellar proper: the Vineart's treasure of spellwines; wines he had helped craft, spellwines he had helped harvest as a slave, spellwines that recognized him now. They did not welcome him the same way the vines did, with the constant whisper of demands and needs, but in a quieter way, the way the Guardian pressed against him from within, the magic in it recognizing the magic inside him.

Home, the Guardian said, and finally Jerzy nodded. This, here, was home.

He turned again, standing in front of Malech's desk, the battered wooden table where he had sat so many times on his stool and listened or responded to questions, had taken cuffs to the ear when he was particularly stupid, or received the rare but precious praise when he said something that pleased his master.

"He is gone."

The spellwines did not recognize his grief any more than the vines had. The Vineart was not gone.

"I am apostate," he said out loud, letting the word settle on his skin. "Everything we have been taught, everything we have learned, to protect ourselves, to protect the Lands Vin. I have betrayed." To survive, yes. But . . . if in surviving, he destroyed everything, what had he been surviving for?

The spellwines did not recognize his concerns, either. There was no apostate, there was no hesitation, there was no doubt. They saw the slave and marked him, brought the magic forward, and were in turn brought forward by the magic within him. The magic was not . . . it was not something he used, something he did. It was something he *was*.

Magic makes the man. The man makes the magic. There was no difference between Vineart and vine.

Jerzy shuddered, feeling, for the first time, the danger that surrounded him, not from any outside threat, but himself. What he was.

A slave. Once chosen, *always* a slave. A Vineart was driven by the needs of the vineyard. Jerzy had abandoned the yards to follow another need, had left a Harvest to falter and fail. And now he had returned, not to take up the duties and responsibilities tradition demanded of him, but to . . .

To survive. If—a sense of something vile, an abomination, a blight worse than rot—*comes here . . . if it changes the Lands Vin to suit itself, to serve it . . .*

The Guardian's voice faded.

"I have a choice." Even as a slave, he had a choice: to live or die. To follow the instinct that had made Malech choose him that day in the markets, to embrace the spark that had made the slavers buy him from his parents, to lead his companions in an impossible battle against an invisible, unknown foe.

Choice, but no assurances. Even if he chose what seemed the inevitable, unavoidable option . . . it might not be enough.

And in the end . . . what will he have become?

"You make us greater," Ao had said.

"You'll figure it out," Mahault believed.

Kaïnam stood at his right shoulder, offered his sword and his strength not in service, but shared command. Shared responsibility.

You are Vineart . . .

Jerzy nodded, hearing more than what the Guardian was saying. But the Guardian, made of stone and magic, did not understand. It could not change, could not grow beyond how it was shaped. Jerzy alone was Vineart, and Vinearts stood alone.

But he *wasn't* alone. They were together, all four of them. No, six. Lil and Detta, too. It was an odd feeling, a fearful feeling, but one that gave him hope, all the same.

And, with that hope, the courage to do the next thing that needed to be done.

"I HATE LOOKING at them."

"Then don't."

Jerzy tried to keep his voice calm, to counter Ao's obvious apprehension, but even he could hear the curtness in his own tone. "Would it help if you closed your eyes?"

Ao let his shoulders relax and dropped back onto the padded frame. "Not really, no. I'd just wonder what you were doing."

Jerzy barely heard Ao's last comment, already focusing on what came next. There was no place within the House set up for this sort of thing; Master Malech had crafted spellwines but rarely used them here. The last time Jerzy had to do any healing within the Household, it had been an accident on the road outside, when a cart had broken and injured several slaves.

He had been younger then, with less understanding of the wines, and himself. He could do better now.

But then, the injuries had been raw, amenable to being worked. Ao's stumps, cauterized by Jerzy's own magic mid-thigh, had since scabbed over, the flesh forming a barrier he was going to have to undo in order to work.

He needed Ao to feel whole, complete. Hopefully this would work.

"This might hurt," he said, even as he reached for the tasting spoon.

"Might?"

Ao's low scream of agony was answer to both of them, as the healspell invaded the scabbing, softening it, and opening the wounds to the cool morning air.

"I'm sorry," Jerzy whispered, trying not to let the knowledge of his friend's pain interfere with his concentration, waiting while the hard white tissue resolved back to pink and red. Normally the patient would be the one working with the spellwine, his own awareness directing the healing, but this was different, and the material . . . Jerzy thought it better he perform the decantation, and Ao had agreed.

A second spellwine was poured into the silver cup of the spoon, and the spoon was lifted to Jerzy's mouth.

Opening the hard-dried scab had been the simple part.

"Ready?"

Beside him, Detta nodded. He could have asked any of the others to help; there was little of the Vineart's art that they had not seen, by now, but he would not ask them to inflict pain on Ao, even indirectly. The trader needed to be awake and alert: there would be no avoiding the unpleasantness for anyone involved. Jerzy had suggested that the others spend the day elsewhere, perhaps go with Lil to bargain with local farmers. But they had refused, quietly, and were even now waiting somewhere else in the House.

He hoped they could not hear Ao's cries, as much for Ao's comfort as their own.

The decantation for what he needed was in one of Master Malech's books, but there had been no notes written in the margin, and so he did not know if his master had in fact ever used this spell or merely noted it for some future use that never came.

Decantations were for show, Jerzy reminded himself, his own hands sweating slightly despite the cool temperatures. The incantation was the important thing; if the spellwine was properly crafted, a Vineart could do anything. . . .

The taste of the spellwine was rounded and cool, bringing the faint flavor of spring fruits and sweet smoke. "Wood and flesh, find."

He nodded, and Detta lifted the wooden limb, carved by the groundkeeper Per the night before, out of vinestock that had been old when Malech was born. There was magic in its grain that would echo that of the spellwine.

If this worked, Ao would be forever bound to the vintnery. He had not told Ao that.

Detta placed one limb against the sore and bloody flesh, pressing firmly, wincing as she did so when Ao cried out again in agony. The taste of the spellwine in Jerzy's mouth changed, turning sharper, with the faintest hint of spice against the back of his throat.

Jerzy placed his own hands over the line where the two bits met, feeling the wet hot trickle of blood against his skin. "Wood and flesh, bind."

His quiet-magic surged, trying to join the spell, and he forced it back. There was too much mixed there, too many legacies lurking, to trust it with something this delicate. He swallowed the sip of spellwine, and felt it burn down his throat.

"Go."

Ao's next scream echoed within the room, and Jerzy flinched, even as he pressed more firmly, willing the magic to seal the connection, the living wood to take root within bone.

"WELL?" MAHAULT HAD been lurking, pouncing the moment Jerzy emerged from the workroom. Detta remained behind to watch over Ao, who had mercifully passed out during the second spellcasting.

Jerzy was exhausted, covered with sweat, and his mouth tasted as though he'd been drinking spoiled mustus, not one of their most expensive, finely crafted healwines. He wanted to bathe, and to sleep, and not be interrogated.

"He's asleep."

"Did it work? Is he . . . did they . . ." She stepped back, suddenly aware that she was crowding him in her impatience, and schooled her body to a more composed pose.

"My apologies, Vineart."

Jerzy exhaled, too tired to care if she gave him the respect due his position or not. She was worried, he understood that.

"Get Kaï," he said, rubbing one forearm across his eyes, wishing they felt less gritty. "I only want to talk about this once." He left her, heading for the bathing room.

Once it had seemed an odd, unnerving place, the idea of submerging his entire body in steaming water foreign to a slave who washed only when needed, in a cold-water stream. Now, as he shucked his clothing, wincing as he saw the blood streaking the sleeves of his shirt, Jerzy could only bless the servants who had thought to prepare the bath, buckets of water already drawn and waiting, a clean towel and clothing folded on the wooden bench beside the tub. A hand on the surface of the water and a small pull of quiet-magic was enough to heat the water, and Jerzy almost smiled, remembering the first time he had tried that, and set the water itself on fire.

Master Malech had merely, calmly, told him to put it out, and gone on with the lesson.

As Jerzy sank into the tub, letting the water cleanse the sweat away and ease his knotted muscles, he reached out to touch the cool awareness of the Guardian.

All is well, the dragon assured him. In that connection there was more than a sense of quiet on the land—all was well within, too. Ao was sleeping, healing. He had done what he needed to.

And there, hidden by the bath, supported by his Guardian, Jerzy let go of the worry and fear and sorrow he had been holding, being strong for Ao; his own saltier tears mixing with the bathwater, his body shuddering as he cried.

THE SUN HAD finally set, but the air was still heavy and warm. The vine-mage sat on his haunches, staring at the stone wall of his workroom, and let his gaze rest on the bloodstains splattered there. Some were old, the colors faded to a muddy brown, while others remained a thick, sticky wine-red, the remnants of a slave chosen that morning. In a child's tale, the stains against the cold stones would have told him something, spoken to him of what he needed . . . but the wall was silent.

"I feel you. I know you are there. Where are you?"

Rage simmered in his words, but the blood did not speak. Dried blood, dead blood, was of no use to him. If he still had his poppet, he could have pulled answers from it . . . but the clay figure had decayed rapidly with the death of its human anchor, the Irfanese merchant, and been dumped in the gully with the rest of the debris. The merchant's failure meant the vine-mage would have to find another connection to the old world, and that would take time. Each poppet had to be constructed of blood and flesh, and then the lure cast out, to tie a willing fish to the line. The merchant had been the last of his viable poppets: another cost to cast at the heels of this upstart who would challenge and wreck his plans.

"Where are you," he asked again, but with less venom in his voice, knowing that nothing listened.

A week since he had asked that whoreson Ximen for more men— and been given none, forcing him to rely on his own supplies. It had not been enough, the single poppet he created too weak to lure anything. There were a few slaves in his yard who had enough of the sense about them that their blood might be enough, but the vine-mage was not yet so desperate to use them. He might yet need them alive, and one, some day, might be his successor.

"I can feel you, moving below, disturbing the roots of all that I have done. Twice, thrice I have struck at you, and yet you do not fall. Why do you not fall?" He had taken the feel of the upstart from the remains of the Irfan lordling, but it was not enough to forge a connection. Had the fool survived, he could have told more, but the body was too badly managed, unable to withstand the force of the magic used to pull him from the scene of his failure. The vine-mage could move flesh and blood across great distances, but nothing had lived through the process. Not yet.

Thus, this Vineart had remained elusive, slipping away the moment he was touched as though slicked by oil, or hidden by mist, his own identity as cloaked as the vine-mage's own. The thought made the vine-mage's seamed face wrinkle more deeply. The taste of the upstart was strong, with the deep tones of older vines and the tang of younger fruit, but of no discernible legacy, no direct root he could follow, no fragment he could snatch and keep. That frustrated the vine-mage, and what frustrated him made him even more determined to destroy it.

The mix of soils; could there be more than one old-worlder? Could they be banding together, looking to stand against him? No. Not impossible, but unlikely, improbable. They hewed to the laws that limited them, willfully castrated themselves in the name of a long-dead godling, and refused to lift their eyes from the mud they trod.

More, he had ensured that their historical distrust had been driven even deeper; they would look upon each other with suspicion, expend their strengths in defense against shadows, until, too late, the true danger showed. Too late, then, for those left to resist.

And then they could call on their blighted Sin Washer until the last drop of blood drained from them, for all the good it would do.

The vine-mage forced himself to breathe calmly, letting his heart slow to a more controlled rate. Anger would not suit his needs. He was the closest thing to a god these lands had, the only god they needed. One Vineart, however crafty he might be, however skilled, was no match for a lifetime spent preparing for this. No, he should not worry overmuch, and he should not waste his anger. There would be time yet to pluck this irritant and crush him, as he had done all others.

For now, he had other things to bind up his time. Today was the Day of Grounding, when the Praepositus would be making his grand announcement, the final stage of their long-laid plans, and he would be needed for more ceremonial purposes. The vine-mage bared his teeth at the thought, somewhere between a smile and a snarl. Let the younger man make sport today with his speechifying, lording over the people with their games and their ritual burnings. Let the Praepositus pretend, a while longer, that the future would be his to determine. The motherless pup would learn soon enough, when his part in the Return was done, and he was no longer needed.

But the vine-mage needed him, now, to coax the people into working, to lead them with the call of glory and respect, the hopes of some future where they would be feted and followed. He could not transport himself to the old lands, any more than he could bring his victims to him, yet alive. He needed that fleet. And if that meant he must dance a tune and say a blessing . . .

The vine-mage laughed, a crackling, creaking sound that hurt his throat. They were fools, all of them. The old world would soon be bereft of their toothless Vinearts, distrustful of their Washers, and trembling in fear. Then they would be reminded of what it meant to be a mage—reminded of where the power in this world, old and new, truly rested. Then . . .

Oh, then.

The vine-mage smiled, a skeletal thing that stretched the skin across the bones of his face so tightly his skin looked almost white, his teeth crooked, stained shards. Holding the pleasure to him like a coal in winter, he wiped his hands clean with a wine-soaked rag and stood, allowing his attendant slave to drape him with the robes of occasion, and strode out into the evening light to join his companion.

He would not enjoy this foolishness, but he could endure it, for what was to come.

XIMEN WATCHED THE vine-mage walk toward him, even as the evening breeze brought the man's scent to him well in advance. He managed not to make a face, but it took effort: once again there was an unpleasant odor wafting from the man, a stale, musty smell like overheated metal and rotted fruit, and the hint of decaying flesh. The smell of a carrion-eater, of a dog that wallowed in its own kill. It seemed as though the closer they came to the end, the more the smell grew. Not even days spent wrapped in the thick salty air of the shoreline, watching his ships take form, could numb his nostrils to that stench, nor could he pretend he did not know where it came from.

His own guilt, perhaps. After their confrontation on the Wall, he had not been able to shake the unease sliding under his skin, keeping him company even down into his dreams, making him send his lovely, patient Bohaide from his bed unsated, his own desire dead.

"Ximen. An excellent evening for the unveiling of all your plans."

"Indeed." Ximen's skin prickled a little. There was something about the man tonight, something beyond the usual unease he felt around the vine-mage. Or perhaps it was merely Ximen's own nerves. It was hardly the first Grounding remembrance he had overseen, but it would be the most significant. As the vine-mage said, tonight would be the unveiling of his plans, years in the making. No, generations in the making.

Ximen was confident in what he had done, in the logic and the future that impelled him. What he did not know, could not know, was how his people would react when he unveiled the breadth of his plans, not merely to explore but to *retake*. They would follow him, but would they do so willingly, sharing his vision, or . . .

He would not allow that thought to continue. He would convince them to support him joyfully, enthusiastically. He would not be able to take ship, take the cream of their people, leaving the rest behind, if he did not believe they understood, and shared the dream.

"The carriage awaits," he said now, only, indicating the cart, draped with black, red, and gold cloth. Traditional colors, the colors the original ships had sailed. The colors of the Grounding were reversed: white to signify the betrayal, the loss and the fear they had come from, blue for the water, and silver for the pearlescent, deceitfully beautiful beach they had been dashed down upon.

His choice of the old colors would be remarked upon, he knew. He was ready. Once he explained, they would understand.

The cart was barely large enough for the two of them, standing behind the high-walled front. Drawn by two thick-muscled dogs, their black coats brushed and gleaming in the dusk, the servants would run alongside, keeping pace and announcing their arrival to those who waited on the shores below.

Waited for him to set fire to the remains of their history, following tradition, and to set them afire with the dream of a better future.

"It might have been more apt," the vine-mage said, as he studied the cart thoughtfully, "to have children pull it. Harnessed to our whim, drawing us to our destiny . . ."

The unease prickled more fiercely, even as the idea struck Ximen speechless. Children *were* the future, the only one the Grounding ever had. To speak of them in such a way, as though they were no more than dogs . . .

The vine-mage laughed, a low noise that had no humor in it, and his breath carried more of that charnel smell.

Behind him, his guards shifted, uneasy although—too far away to have overheard, or indeed understood what the vine-mage meant—they could not have said why. Ximen had noted before that they did not look into the vine-mage's eyes—they would not dare.

The common folk were protected from close contact with the vine-mage, unless and until they were chosen for the Harvest. The slaves, though, they knew; you could see it in the way they walked—no, crept around the man, not afraid but resigned, aware of the reality the way they were aware the sun rose and set, the rains fell, and the vines grew.

They knew that the vine-mage was insane.

If—no, *when* they escaped this bitter, hard land, Ximen swore to himself. When they were free of this accursed land, that demanded everything and gave so little, he would kill the vine-mage.

No, he would kill every mage left alive, when they were done; slaughter them like wall-beasts, and for the same reason. Magic was poison, rotting everything it touched. He would not let future generations live with that madness among them.

But for now, for now, until the ships sighted their destination, until the distant seas were traversed and the end in sight, he needed the madman.

But only until then.

Part II

Rebel

Chapter 6

IAJA

Winter

The first touch of winter was firmly on the Lands Vin, with snow coating the mountains, while in the lower regions, although the weather had been neither exceptionally cold nor overly wet, the winter crops were not growing as well as they should. The flocks had all been brought to winter shelter or bound up in paddocks, safe from hungry predators running on four legs and two alike.

Set at the crown of a low hill along the curve of the Iajan coast, a stone-walled House looked out over the waters to the West and a prosperous city to the south, and a solid defense of mountains to the east. It was a House of secure foundations, and obvious wealth. A

Lord's Hall, designed to protect and awe. As night slid over the region, the lights visible in the windows slowly flickered and were put out as the residents gave way to sleep, and even the guard on the walls dozed in the early morning chill.

Despite the hour, light shone brightly in a stone-walled room deep inside the structure, in a room where no windows showed to the rest of the world.

In that room, the lord of that House stood, his empty hands cupped in front of him in a seemingly unconscious echo of the Washer's blessing, and looked down at the man in the chair in front of him with a sorrowful expression on his face.

"Eulálio. You were not truthful with me."

The man in the chair, older than the first speaker but still young enough to sit straight-backed and defiant, met that sorrowful gaze without flinching. His face was tanned from years in the sun and his hands were gnarled from a lifetime of work, but his body had begun to soften around gut and thigh, his years as a slave decades behind him. "I gave you everything you asked for."

"Ah, yes." The lord, dressed in somber but finely woven cloth of gray, nodded. His hands were smoother, but hardened as well from years with blade and rein. Neither man underestimated each other, at all. "But you did not tell me everything I needed. I call that bad Agreement, Vineart."

"I call it"—the Vineart's ribs ached, although he was certain nothing was broken, merely bruised—"the exact terms of Agreement."

He had known that this would not end well. Two weeks back, he had been summoned to this lord's home—summoned, like a slave—and he had come, because what other option did he have? He did not think the man would force him—but the fact that it had to be considered showed how times had changed, and not for the better.

Once he presented himself, they had quickly come to Agreement: he to put his magics to use defending the lord's holdings, the lord to offer protection for his person, and, as needed, his yards. It had seemed a fair move, a cautious and sensible move in light of recent events, the whispers and reports of attacks, of disappearances, of entire crops destroyed, and villages laid to waste by some unknown, unseen enemy. In light of things that moved in his dreams, lurked around the stone wall of his yard . . . These days, even a Master Vineart was not safe in his own House. Eulálio was not a master, and he did not wish to become one of the missing.

Whatever stories he had heard of this lord, whatever had happened to the Vineart who made Agreement with him last—and nobody spoke of that, not at all within his hearing—his new master had for years carried a reputation as a hard but honest man. The Agreement had seemed the best option out of a bad situation.

Whatever and whoever the Iajan lord had been, he had changed. The world had changed. Such a short span of time, to feel the ground beneath you slip away, everything you knew to be real suddenly false as mist. What the lord now wanted, what he demanded . . . no. Eulálio would not put his vines to such a use.

His mouth was too dry to call up quiet-magic. He did not think the withholding of water was intentional, did not think Diogo that wise to the ways and workings of that last recourse of Vinearts, the quiet-magic. But intentional or not did not matter; with no spellwines to decant, no ability to call more than a trickle of magic to him, he was helpless in a way he had not been since the mustus marked him for its own.

He knew what would follow.

Diogo turned away, as though to consider the lamp hanging from its post, its natural light flickering and bending in a way no mage-light ever would. "I asked if you could do such a thing. And you said no."

One last chance, to recant, to confess, to do what his master demanded. "I cannot."

The lord's hand snapped out once, cracking across Eulálio's face, and he heard the crunch of his nose breaking even before the pain began.

Heat sparkled through his skin, and when he shifted weight from one buttock to the other, his spine protested like an old vine bearing too much weight.

The Vineart did not utter a sound, neither in pain nor protest. The law was on Eulálio's side, the law and tradition that protected him from a lord's raised hand, but he had broken tradition—shattered it—when he accepted Agreement, and the Vineart had no hope that the law would appear now like a silent god to save him.

He had known that something happened to Vineart Ranji, something terrible, and he had come, anyway.

There were no gods left, no law, nothing save fear and force. Eulálio had hoped to stave off the fear by aligning himself with a man of power, but he had not truly understood that the fear was everywhere. Not only in the towns and farms, but here, in the fine halls and Houses of power.

It might even run deeper here, where there was so much more to lose.

Eulálio cast his gaze down to the dark red mark on his wrist. He had been so proud of that mark, once. Had truly believed all the suffering and pain had disappeared forever, once he was chosen, once the magic whispered in his veins. He had trusted the world, and it had betrayed him.

It was not the man's words or even his actions that left Eulálio resigned to his fate. Where once he listened only to the whisper of his vines, he had learned, quickly, to put his ear to the wind and listen to men as well. Diogo was terrified: Eulálio could smell it on him now, even hidden by his fine musks and powders. Terrified not of a thing, no beast or man, but of rumor and whisper. Of the suggestion, a worm in his brain, that even those sworn to him would betray him. The man who had been, only a few months before, was gone, hollowed out by fear and uncertainty the way insects would eat at a tree. And so he wanted that of the Vineart: to bring men to him, to ensure their loyalty by taking away their will.

Even if Eulálio could do such a thing, he would not.

It was a fool's wish, a madman's request. Spellwines coaxed and cajoled the elements, from aether to fire, flesh to stone. There was nothing—not even the memory-wine Lethe—that could force a man to do something he would not.

There were rumors, true. Vinearts did not mingle nor gossip, they shared no confidences and built no alliances among each other, but even before these uncertain times they watched, and they listened, and Eulálio had heard things: A student, too strong for merely one master. A Vineart who disdained the Commandments, and challenged the Washers themselves. Rumor claimed that this student had killed his own master, that his quiet-magic was not quiet at all but shouted its power to the skies, healing and destroying like the silent gods themselves.

Impossible. Mortals could no longer work such magic—Sin Washer had ensured that when he shattered the Vine, blooded the first growth and left them only the legacies to work with. But such power was exactly what Lord Diogo asked for.

For two weeks he had been a valued guest in Diogo's home, treated with respect until the question—no, the demand was made. That had been three days ago. Three days, two nights, and the Vineart had not slept in all that time, had not eaten, had only the occasional sips of bitter ale to keep his body going and his head fogged.

Another man, in Eulálio's position, might give up the rumor, give up a name, the promise of someone who could do what Diogo asked, to deflect the lord's cold anger away for at least a while. If this Vineart was so powerful and so strong, then he could save himself.

But Eulálio could not bring himself to be that man, any more, he suspected, than Ranji. If the rumor were true, then such a Vineart should not be the servant of one such as Diogo. And if it were not . . . Eulálio would bring no other soul to this end, not by his words or actions. He had that much honor left.

Diogo had not been foolish enough to bind him: nothing so crude, or so visible. But the Vineart had no illusions that he was free to go; the burly man standing at the door could snap his neck without sweating, and even if he were able to call on his quiet-magic . . . what could he hope to accomplish? He could strengthen young bones and clear water, but not as he was, dry and exhausted and confused.

The only thing in the room, other than himself, the lord, the chair he sat on, and the burly guard, was a single, simple bowl of water. Just a bowl of water, shaped like a basin, barely a handspan deep. It could have been made for any bathhouse, to rinse hands or splash a face.

There was no reason that the sight of it, sitting on a low table barely an arm's length away, should fill the Vineart's bowels with the need to empty themselves. He was no fool, however, and did not think that any hands would be clean when this was done.

He also knew that he would not—could not—do what the lord wanted of him, even if his quiet-magic were strong enough.

He would do anything to survive. But not that.

"An it please you to give me such solace," he whispered. "Sin Washer, make it swift."

Outside the door, a hired solitaire making her patrol heard the muffled sounds of splashing, like a man at his bath, but the quickly muffled cry that accompanied it was nothing at all of pleasure, only fear. Her hound stopped, its flopped-over ear even with her knee, and looked up at her inquiringly. She was not uncertain, merely undecided.

There was another splash, this one heavier, more sodden, and a hoarser sound, like the pained drawing in of breath, and then a third splash.

There was no sound after that. She hesitated a moment longer, then heard the low noise of one voice, male, asking a question, and another, deeper, answering; then a low, water-choked cough, and the sound of water being poured from one vessel into another.

Another place, another time, she might have stopped to investigate, rapped on the wooden door and inquired if someone within needed aid, if only to let the villains know that they had been heard, observed. Her position protected her: anyone who harmed a solitaire in their own employ would never hire another, nor would they work within his lands—save with his enemies.

Here, now, she stepped forward, moving down the hallway again, her hound without protest trotting at her side.

Bahn might accept her decision without hesitation—that was what starhounds were bred and trained to do—but she was less certain, even as her steps took her away from that door as though nothing at all were wrong.

Much was wrong in this place.

Her contract with Diogo was to guard against strangers, not against things that happened to those already within—particularly not within the lord's own chambers. Her own personal thoughts had no place within the bounds of the contract: that was the solitaire's way.

But she did not like it, did not like the mutter and swirl of this place, had not been comfortable here since the day Diogo turned the Washer away at the door, had become uncomfortable the morning she was told that Vineart Ranji had departed, without a word to anyone, his belongings suddenly, mysteriously gone. And now the new Vineart, who seemed a kind, soft-spoken man . . . no one had seen him in two days. His belongings were still in his chamber, but she did not give good odds that being the case come morning.

Whatever darkness haunted her contract-lord, it infected others close to him as well. She shuddered, as though the fact of their contract was enough to taint her, too.

She took some comfort that the Washer was safely away and none of his cloth had come to the city since. The people might suffer by that, but she could not blame the Brotherhood. The moment her contract ended, she, too, would depart this place, and find somewhere else to serve. Surely, somewhere, there was a place in all the Vin Lands that had not gone insane?

IN THE CLOSED room behind her, Eulálio, his throat and lungs filled with water, let the quiet-magic seep onto his now-wet tongue, and brought it forward one last time. When the pull came again, sharply yanking him by the hair back into the blessed, burning air, he opened his eyes and looked up, his water-sore mouth curving in a grin that made the lord drop his pose of indifference and raise his hand to the guardsman, intending to cry an alarm.

Earthvines, his legacy. Growspells, his gift. His voice was gone, choked and drowned, but Eulálio did not need his voice to send the magic, deep into the lord's head, deep into his skull, and command, with all the violence a dying man could muster, *Grow*.

And as his face plunged back into the bowl for the last time, his vision graying at the edges and his thoughts turning to mud, Eulálio felt the quiet-magic leave him, wending its way through the flesh and bone of Diogo's skull, the enlarging tissue already pushing against the skull from within. It would not be swift, no. First, a headache. Then a stutter, a slowness of speech. Weakness, vomiting. A shame, a disgrace. Then . . .

Revenge.

Chapter 7

HOUSE OF MALECH, THE BERENGIA

Fallowtime

A crash startled the predawn silence of the House, then a flood of cursing, a woman's voice, irate without actually being angry. A flock of birds that had been roosting on the roof over the kitchen took flight, their wings rustling shadows in the dark air.

Jerzy, who had gone outside to let the morning air soothe away the sweat of his dreams, shook his head and sighed. In the days since they had returned to The Berengia, the calm, peaceful House he had lived in under Master Malech had been replaced with a place of noise, confusion, and barely controlled chaos.

"What did he do this time?"

It was not his fault.

The fact that the Guardian took Ao's side did not surprise Jerzy. Ao's new-gifted legs were stumps of vines that had born their last fruit before Jerzy was born, grafted to the flesh sealed to them by healspells crafted from that same fruit. Magic now tied him directly to the House, making the Guardian inclined to include Ao within its protections just as it did the servants and slaves, and Jerzy himself.

The sun reached the point it became visible over the far ridge, a pale glow touching the cobalt sky, casting the ridge of ancient trees into shadow and touching the rows of winter-dormant vines with a faint glow. From the House to the farthest reaches, where the low stone wall marked the ends of Malech's—his—yard, the ground was clear. He had walked every pace of it the past week, dropping to his knees to dig his hands into the cool dirt, to make sure. Beyond those walls, into the copse of trees that had stood since before Malech's master Josia cleared the land? Jerzy dared not go beyond to check.

"But what did he do?" Jerzy asked again.

The Guardian did not sigh, or show any signs of true emotion, but there was a *sense* of a sigh and a laugh, all the same, like a low wind under leaves, and the visual of copper pans scattered over the stone floor, and Lil, her hands on her hips and her pale hair backlit by the fire so that she looked like Jacia, the goddess of the hearth, glaring down at someone.

"The chair needs fine-tuning," Jerzy said, shaking his head. Ao still had little control over his new limbs, and the pain when trying to stand kept him confined to the chair. A week before, Per had appeared at the edge of the training ground, stared at Ao and Mahault trading awkward blows, trying to maneuver the chair over the rough ground, muttered something nobody could understand, then disappeared again.

Jerzy had told the others not to worry about it: such behavior was not out of character for Per, who lived almost like a wild beast outside the House by his own choice, preferring to spend his time tending to the grounds rather than interacting with other people. The next day, however, he had returned with a smaller, lighter version of Josia's chair, not carved from solid wood, but woven together with branches and rope, narrow enough to fit through all the hallways without scraping and light enough that Kaïnam or Jerzy—or even Mahault—could haul it somewhere, when Ao wanted to work on controlling his new legs.

The one thing it couldn't do very well, however, was turn quickly. If Ao was not careful, he would either knock into something or, more often, knock himself sideways. Ao, as ever, was impatient, and in the two days he'd had the new chair, Lil had threatened to burn it under him at least five times.

"Why was he even up so early?" Jerzy wondered now. "No, never mind, I know that you don't know why."

The Guardian, not being hostage to uncertainty or fear or uneasy dreams, could not understand, but Jerzy did: the same reason he was standing out here, staring at rootstock he had checked thrice already. Because it was better than not sleeping, lying abed and thinking of everything that needed to be done, everything they did not know how to do, the tension winding inside them like a rising storm. Within these walls there was an almost uncanny peace, but they all knew what waited beyond.

Eleven days since they had come home.

Jerzy let his gaze fall over the yard spreading out in front of him, trying to see it as a stranger might, as Kaïnam or Ao or Mahault did: the gentle downward slope that ran all the way to the banks of the river Ivy, the wooded slopes of the ancient trees, their leaves now orange and brown, that bordered his lands. The low stone structure of the sleep house and work shed. The ordered, gathered clusters of vines, their fruit stripped, their leaves shading to match the trees up on the hill, preparing to sleep for the winter.

His lands. His vineyard. Jerzy wasn't prepared for the rush of emotions that filled him: pride, possession, worry, affection . . . fear.

Normally in the Fallowtime, a Vineart would be working with the mustus from the Harvest, crafting it into that season's vintage. But with no Vineart to handle it, the mustus had not settled. He trusted Detta, that she had done exactly as she said, but she had admitted herself that she was no Vineart and the mere action of crushing and vatting did not a spellwine create.

Without the Vineart's skill and sense . . .

The fourth day after their return, Jerzy had forced himself to siphon off a small dose, intending merely to test it, to see if anything could be salvaged. As he had feared, the magic was too wild to handle, refusing to settle to his touch, and the effort had left him shaking and ill for hours after.

Since that attempt, every night he slept, he had dreamed—terrible dreams, torn from his worst fears and memories. This morning he had been convinced that Master Malech again sat behind his desk; only his master had risen from the pyre the others had burned his body on, down in the vineyards, after his murder. In the dream, a crumbled, soot-covered hand reached for Jerzy as though to administer one of the familiar cuffs to the head that had been as much a part of his training as the wine itself, familiar and comforting, but when the hand actually connected, it cut like Kaïnam's blade, slicing open the top of Jerzy's head and revealing not spluttered brains and blood, but the same thick flesh as the serpents, covered in the wine-blood goo of the bespelled birds.

Jerzy woke covered in cold sweat and reeking of spoiled mustus, the taste of the taint deep in his mouth, so thick that even repeated rinsings with clear, cold water had not been able to clear it.

A Vineart was meant to be focused, centered within his own vineyards. A Vineart stood alone and did not meddle with the world beyond his walls. A Vineart did not take power, but crafted it for others to use. . . .

He was apostate, and there was a fear, deep within him, that the vines would know that, would turn from him as the mustus had; that in trying to save others, he would never become master of his own vines.

The bitter taste of his dreams showed him that fate.

A vision, not his own: a vat, dumped into dark soil, covered with more soil, and set afire.

Jerzy shook his head. "I can't do that."

Magic that cannot be tamed must be diluted.

Once, the Guardian had been silent, when Jerzy was still a slave. Now, Jerzy often thought he would enjoy those days returned.

I was not silent. You could not hear.

"I don't trust this mustus," Jerzy said, ignoring that last comment. "Not to release it like that." Pouring the mustus—powerful but unformed—loose back into the soil . . . a more experienced Vineart might have been able to tell him what might happen, but Master Malech was dead, and Jerzy could not, dared not reach out to another. Not without knowing if they were in Agreement with a land-lord, or partnered with the Washers, or a puppet to their unknown enemy . . .

He could trust no one save those within his own House.

They do not have the knowledge you need.

"I know."

The Guardian was silent after that. The responsibility lay on his own shoulders. The Guardian would support him, share with him whatever it knew, but it was not a Vineart and could not tell him what was right or proper. It was a creature of tradition and what-had-been, not what-would-be.

Tradition. Commands. Words that had shaped the world for two thousand years, since Sin Washer was born of anger and despair . . . words the Collegium had used to keep the world balanced, a three-handled wheel of power. The earlier emotions were joined by a more familiar one: despair. How could you maintain balance when tradition worked against you and commands were broken?

A raptor flew overhead, no longer looking to feed a nest, it might merely have been stretching its wings or looking for an early-morning snack. Jerzy, the memory of the deformed birds that had attacked them still clear in his mind, tracked its progress over the fields until it dove down and disappeared into the tree line that ran across the upper ridge.

They had not seen nor heard anything from the lurker on the road, although Kaïnam, after a quick sortie, was of the opinion that he yet lingered, watching them. For what purposes, nobody could say, and Jerzy saw no reason to send anyone out looking. If the Washers wanted to find them, well, here they were.

Jerzy had come home for a purpose. The beast-bird, Ao's injury, all necessary elements to be dealt with, but they were done. The Guardian was correct. Jerzy's fear and uncertainty, like mustus, needed to be punched down, and crafted into something useful.

He was Vineart. It was time to act as one.

The air was filled with noises now; the slaves waking, the distant voice of the overseer getting them moving, the clatter and crunch of the livestock being fed, up the hill, and the sound of footsteps behind him. He recognized the feel of Mahault's presence even as her voice reached him.

"They've started dishing up breakfast in the hall, if you're hungry." Her voice took on a slightly scolding tone. "And even if you're not."

He turned then, and shook his head. "Second to Detta as well as Kaïnam?"

He meant it as a tease, but it was truth: since they had returned, every aspect of life in the House now seemed to run through Mahault, no matter who managed it. A true Second, she knew where everyone was at any given time, what they could be called from, and when they were not to be disturbed. And, in his case, when they had not eaten recently. Between Mahault and the Guardian, he had even less space for secrets than he'd been allowed as a slave.

Mahault, as usual, refused to be baited. "If you won't sleep, you need to eat. And not just tai, either. And Kaïnam wants to see you in the practice square this afternoon, for weapons practice."

Kaïnam. Sober, dry-humored Heir, denned up in a vintnery far from home and need. It would not have surprised Jerzy if, at any point, Kaï had left them, gone hunting on his own. Instead, he stayed, using his skills and knowledge to find them allies with the same solid determination he approached everything, one methodical step at a time. Including, it seemed, beating a Vineart and a trader-boy into half-decent fighters.

"I'll be there," Jerzy said, because if he didn't she wouldn't go away, and if he wasn't, Kaïnam would come into the study and drag him by the scruff of the neck anyway. Vineart dignity meant little to weapons masters; Mil'ar Cai had taught him that.

"Does he really believe that it's going to come down to a battle of arms?" Jerzy could hear his master's voice in his own words, but Mahl simply shrugged.

"We've been attacked . . . how many times now? You've armed us"— and her hand touched the palm-sized wineskin of firespell that hung on her sword belt, although the scabbard next to it was empty in deference to Detta's refusal, even now, for weapons to be carried within the House—"so he's making sure you're equally prepared."

Jerzy had no answer to that, with the memory of his nightmares still lingering, the sense of time passing, and pressure building beyond the low stone walls of the vintnery reminding him that, for all that it seemed peaceful at the moment, they could not afford to believe it was so. His yards were healthy, but his—or, more likely, the Guardian's—protection extended only so far. Reports had come in from the secondary yards of damages along the boundary lines as though something were gnawing, trying to get in, and he had not forgotten the feel of the land as they traveled, the feel of something under a slow, draining attack. A blight, undermining the well-being of the land itself and all who dwelled there . . . the people who were his responsibility as much as any land-lord's.

The Washers would say it was not so, that Sin Washer's Command left the care of men to lords and bound Vinearts only to their vines. But Malech had saved these people during the plague, had placed his mark on them . . . and Jerzy could do no less. The fact that there was more that he felt obligation to, over a greater area . . .

He had traveled farther than Malech, as well. Had seen more. Touched more.

Been touched by more. People, places, voices . . . the lands itself. His fingers had dug into dirt that grew vines he was not called to, and he had tended to them, listened to them.

The Lands Vin entire hummed within him. He could no more turn away from it than he could his own vines.

You are Vineart, the Guardian kept reminding him. But the shimmer of magics within his blood told Jerzy he was more, too. If he would accept it. If he could accept it. The thought was like a circle of fire under his ribs, burning every time he shifted, never allowing him to relax, or find true calm.

The sun was up in full over the hills now. It would be a clear, cool morning, the kind where you could see a fox move across the road a hundred yards away, or an enemy swordsman riding at you from a full league distant. Or a monstrous beast diving out of the pale, winter-blue sky.

But you could not see, even in such clarity, what was happening beyond this valle. For that, you needed eyes elsewhere.

Jerzy turned his back on the vista and followed Mahault inside.

THE SCENT OF twice-brewed tai steaming on the table still made Jerzy's lip curl, but he gladly accepted a bowl of the meal-and-milk Lil handed him. The wooden spoon was the same one he had used as a slave, the smoothness of the handle familiar in his hand, and he was able to feed his body without gagging while a mug of warmed *vin ordinaire* wiped the last of the night's dreams away. The sense of urgency driving him remained, however, as though the decision to abandon the spoiled mustus had allowed him to move on to what must be done.

Master Malech would not, perhaps, have approved. His master had been a cautious man, even as he bent Commandments and risked censure to uncover the truth. But the time for caution and care might be past, beyond reclaiming. Jerzy himself could not do what needed to be done. But he was not alone.

"So, what do you think?"

The question jolted Jerzy out of his thoughts, until he realized that Ao had not been asking him, but the others, as he lifted one of his grafted legs onto the bench, pulling up his trou to better display it.

"They look better than your original legs," Kaïnam said.

"Kaï!"

"No, he's right. I think I'm taller now, too." Ao tried to stand up, and rocked unsteadily.

"Careful now," Lil warned him through the open doorway that led into the kitchen, as though Ao were about to knock over something other than himself. "You're still no more in control of those things than you are that blighted chair."

"Give me some time, I'll—"

"You will break your neck," Detta said firmly. "Sit down and finish your tai."

Ao sat, half a breath before he fell over. Jerzy shook his head and nursed his *vin*. He had warned the trader: vines were slow to grow; it might take years, if not decades, before Ao had true feeling in them.

And yet, of them all, Ao—who would have been perfectly within rights to be angry at the world—had been the one to cheer them all up, to encourage them when things went badly, to be forthright in his belief that, if they could only find the key to their enemy, that they would be able to defeat him. Ao was learning to walk again. Jerzy needed to do the same.

The past ten-day had been necessary, healing and preparing, but events moved on in the world outside, and their enemy was assuredly not resting. It was time. Looking sideways at Detta, he saw her usher Lil and her helpers back into the kitchen proper, leaving the four of them alone, as though she knew what he planned.

Perhaps she did.

"It's time." He spoke quietly, but the others in the dining hall heard him, and stopped what they were doing as though struck by a lash.

"Finally," Kaï said, sitting back with quiet, if grim, satisfaction.

Mahault, by contrast, leaned forward, her elbows resting on the table, her face intent and hungry. Ao pushed aside his plate, and cradled his mug of tai between his palms, his expression as blank as though he were observing a trade session, giving nothing away, taking everything in.

The feeling of being the center of attention, of everyone looking to him for leadership, caused only a flicker of panic this time; although Jerzy could still feel doubt thrumming under his skin, it was not them nor their abilities that he doubted. Although he had been occupied with other matters, he knew that they had not been idle. Now, just as he had gone through the cellar to determine what spellwines he had to-hand, he would discover what their cellars contained—and how it could all be used.

"Kaïnam, you updated the map of where attacks occurred." It wasn't a question; the other man had asked for the map soon after their earlier discussion, and Jerzy knew how the prince's mind worked. Kaï liked proof, detail under his hands, a pattern to observe and predict.

"I have. Both the vineyards that have been touched, and all seats of power where the lord is reported acting out of character, or there has been actual unrest. I have also marked the sea and land routes between all those places, looking for a possible connection. There are . . . possibilities, but nothing that seems useful, yet."

Jerzy nodded, already moving ahead. "Ao, could you add the trade routes to the map, as you remember them?"

"Remember?" Ao sounded insulted, as though Jerzy had asked if he knew his mother's name. "I had every route memorized by the time I was—"

"Yes or no, Ao."

He grinned, his teeth white against his still-tanned skin. "Yes. And I've already added them to Kaï's notes."

Jerzy let out a small laugh. Of course Ao had. They had been waiting on him, but they had not been waiting. "And?"

"The routes he sorted do not match the routes my people take; we tend to prefer the profitable route over the simplest one. There is some overlap in each instance, but nothing to indicate our enemy might be using a caravan for transport. Some of the other clans might have deviated in recent years but . . ." Ao shook his head. "A trading route, once set, tends to stay set, unless there is massive unrest, or a market disappears entirely."

"And none of those connects directly with Caul," Kaï added. The northern island kingdom of Caul was outside the Lands Vin, disdaining the use of spellwines. A sea-going nation, they had sent a fleet against Kaï's home of Atakus in what had seemed like a purely military move, but when Kaï and Ao went to investigate, they discovered that the Caulic king, too, had whispers in his ear, the influence of their enemy attempting to undermine the men of power there, including the spymaster. As unlikely as it sounded, magic-hating Caul might be their best ally, now.

Jerzy started to pace. "I want to know every single connection between all the known lands—and any unknown ones, as well. Not only where he has been but where he might go next." Predicting the pattern. Learning it, so that no new move came as a surprise.

They had been playing catchup since the beginning. That needed to end.

Mahl had unpinned her braid, tugging at the plait as she thought. "Would he be following some line of magic . . . ?"

As though the word summoned it, Jerzy again felt the sense of a vast, impossible presence underneath his feet that he had encountered in the village, ancient as the Lands Vin itself, but he refused to acknowledge it. Now was not the time for theory, or distractions. They needed facts.

"If he were merely attacking Vinearts, then he might be. But he's been reaching into villages as well, and towns where there are no Vinearts. So there must be something else."

"The spellwines?" Mahl suggested. "Everyone uses those, especially in seats of power."

"Too faint, too . . . fleeting. Magic doesn't linger, doesn't leave a trail." Jerzy shook his head. "I'm working on it."

"The question I have," Kaïnam said, "is why does he choose those specific cities, those towns, those ports? There are other cities with more immediate or obvious power or wealth, others that, if they fell, would open serious gaps in the land's defenses. And, yes, why is Caul the only Outside Land afflicted by whisperers among their men of power?"

Three nations outside the Lands Vin: Caul, Inistahn, the great plains where Ao's people hailed from, and the snowbound islands of Ithysa, north of Caul.

"There has to be a connection, some market or route in common, perhaps some alliance," Ao said. "I sent a message to my clan elders, asking if they will help, but they . . ." His mouth twisted in a reluctant admission of defeat. "They have not acknowledged it, or me."

"No response at all?" Mahault did not sound surprised. She had been disowned by her father for her part in Jerzy's escape from her home city of Aleppan, giving her no family left to claim.

Ao shook his head. "We can't expect more. In their eyes, I'm . . . back in Aleppan, I abandoned my trading party not only without warning, but leaving them trying to explain why the junior member had absconded with an accused criminal."

"Have I thanked you for that recently?" Jerzy asked, distracted.

"You never thanked me, actually. Don't worry, you still owe me. But the only way they will acknowledge me now would be if I brought them something of equal value to the trade agreement I'm guessing they lost when we scampered. Until then . . ." Ao shrugged. "I am dead to them, and never mind how bad things may get because they won't help. We're nothing if not stubborn when it comes to value owed."

There was a breath of silence, a sense of disappointment in the air.

"Tell them about Irfan," Jerzy said.

"What?" The others looked shocked, Kaïnam standing abruptly, but only Ao protested. "Jer, you can't. I can't!"

Jerzy felt a warning push from the Guardian, but he ignored it. It was a risk—a terrible risk—but Jerzy was beginning to understand the way this new world worked. Master Malech had been cautious, careful, had kept within the limits, if stretched, of the Commands . . . and what had it earned them? He had to think beyond the vines, think as more than a Vineart. Esoba's vineyard, the unblooded vines, were dangerous, to be kept out of their enemy's hands at all cost, but Ao's people did not trade in spellwines, did not use them for themselves. They knew and cared nothing for vineyards or legacies.

Traders cared about profit. About trade. And, if Ao was representative of his people, about getting in a step ahead of anyone else. Irfan was outside the Lands Vin; the northern ports were known to experienced travelers like Ao's people, and its western coastline had been charted by the mad explorers of Iaja decades before, but none who had gone deep into its territory, up into the mountains, had returned. Even their foray, following a false trail to the Vineart Esoba, had barely poked into the unknown lands. A safe landing site, a friendly village, would be a tempting prize to a people constantly on the search for new markets, new opportunities.

And if the risk of their discovering Esoba's vineyard, of spreading the news of unblooded vines, was the price to save the Lands Vin? Jerzy would take that risk.

"Give them Irfan," he said again. "Tell them of the villagers we encountered who were generous to strangers. Tell them of the land-lord we encountered, with his greed and willingness to deal with outsiders."

The village was far enough away from the vineyards, unless the traders asked specifically, they would not be told of the vines, and traders would not think to ask. The land-lord who had attacked Esoba's House was dead and could tell no one of what he had done, of why the vines had been so important to his master. It would be safe . . . safe enough.

The Guardian still disapproved, but Ao was nodding his head thoughtfully. "Yes. New territory, a new market?" He pursed his lips and made an approving noise. "That would prick their ears, at least . . . Hah, I said I'd make a trader of you someday!"

Sending outsiders into the area might distract Ximen, keep his attention focused away from what Jerzy was planning, but it would also put Ao's people in danger. And there was no way to warn them, without mentioning Esoba, or Ximen himself, which might lessen the value they put on Ao's information. From the considering look in Kaïnam's eye, the princeling had thought of that as well. Jerzy heard the echo of the prince's earlier words: everyone they had would be used, no one could be protected.

"It may be that I have something to offer as well," Kaïnam said, instead of what they were thinking. "My father may not acknowledge me, my people lost behind their magic-shield, but my name still carries some weight among the sailing folk of that region. If our enemy is indeed blind on the sea, it is time we use that to our advantage. There are captains who travel freely even now, crossing the seas at their own whim and fortune. Like Ao's people, they move around, are used to seeing the larger view, the wider horizon."

"You mean brigands," Ao said. "Pirates."

"Useful men," Kaïnam said. "They come to port in certain towns, certain merchants supply them. Send messenger-birds to those merchants, asking for assistance. Asking these useful men to stay alert to anything they might see or hear that might be significant. These . . . useful men know that peace is better for them than war, when the pickings are slim. If this Ximen moves ships or men, or disrupts routes or routines, we will know."

Jerzy nodded, his thoughts racing ahead. Too much depended on the information they could gather, too much resting in the hands of others. But there was no help for it. He had tried going out to gather information himself, but the Lands were too wide, too scattered. He had wasted time, trying to do it alone.

"I am the only one who has been able to add nothing," Mahault said, her voice heavy with regret. "I have no dowry to offer."

Jerzy turned to look at her, sitting still and upright in her chair. Without speaking, without moving, she was so clearly the daughter of wealth and power, it seemed impossible that she should be here, with them. And yet the maiar's daughter had been disowned more dramatically than Ao, with no real hope of return. She had no ties, no connections to call upon, no way to add to their knowledge . . . but she had been the first to *do*; it was her courage that had saved him in Aleppan, her courage, and her common sense.

And that gave him an idea. "There is something I need you to do for me."

THEY LEFT THE other two unrolling a new map on the desk, placing markers on it, and he led Mahault to the one part of the House that she had not yet seen.

The House looked imposing when seen from above ground, but the true work of the vintnery was done out of sight, in these cool, stone-lined rooms below the ground. Part of that space was accessible through a double-hung doorway in the side of the House, to allow for the casks to be brought in and out, but the workrooms were off-limits to everyone save the Vineart.

And now, those who worked with him. Doubtless, another mark against his name.

Jerzy went down the narrow stone steps with easy familiarity, while Mahault moved more cautiously behind him, clear mage-lights coming on as Jerzy raised a hand to them, then flickering off as they passed, leaving the passage behind them in shadows.

They passed through the main workroom, a portion of the wall sliding away as Jerzy touched it, and entered the hidden space. "What's down here?"

"The vats."

"Vats?" Mahl stopped as they came into the main room, then followed Jerzy to where the secret door slid open easily when Jerzy touched it, and the larger room beyond was revealed. Five vats waited, each nearly twice times his height and three times his reach in girth.

"Oh," Mahl said, taking a step forward, her head tilted as she tried to see how deep the room went and how many vats there were within.

For Jerzy, the only thing of importance was what he felt *inside* each container. After a normal Harvest, these would have been filled with fresh mustus, sorted from the crush and ready to become *vina*. But Malech had been murdered well before the grapes were ready, and the mustus had failed. The great vats might be empty—or, if Master Malech had not had time to finish his spring preparations, they might contain *vina*, primed but still waiting to be formed into *vin magica*. He had put off coming down here, hesitated for fear of knowing the answer.

Jerzy knew the moment he passed through the hidden door, the moment he passed the thick stone walls, that the vats were full.

He waited, breathing in the slightly damp, musty flavor of mustus and dust, old stone and cured wood and the history of the House filling the air, acknowledging that it had been more than hesitation that kept him away. It was in this room that he had passed the second test, the mustus of that season deeming him worthy of his magic, washing the slave-mark off his wrist and replacing it with the stain of a Vineart, visible for all to see.

Returning to the vintnery, he had not known what to expect. Each touch, each reconnection, reintroducing himself, had been a risk. What if they did not acknowledge him? What if he had been too badly damaged by his time away?

Not for the first time, Jerzy wished his master had put aside a bottle of the Iajan foreseer wine, to give him a glimpse of what was to come, but Malech had believed in letting things unfold in their own time. "What will, will," he had said.

Jerzy had thought he understood, at the time, but even a clouded hint would have been welcome, now.

The vines themselves had known him, but vines were deep-rooted, tied to the history of this place, taught to wait for a Vineart's hand. The spellwines stored in the cellar were crafted, ready; they would respond to anyone who knew how to use them. The mustus had refused him, but that was a flaw in their nature, their handling, not his own. It had spoiled from his not being here, not because of what he was becoming.

And yet, he had been frightened, had hesitated coming into this room, focusing his attention on the things he knew, or suspected, were damaged beyond repair, making sure that Ao would heal, and the yards were clear and healthy, properly prepared for Fallowtime. Excuses, all of it, afraid to face the possibility of even more loss.

The *vina* in these tanks had already given way to a Vineart's touch, had accepted preparation, begun the transformation from raw magic to useful. Delicate, filled with potential. If they did not accept him, if they rejected him . . .

I'm back, he told the *vina* waiting in those tanks. I'm home.

If they had somehow gone bad, the way the crush had, ruined by the lack of a Vineart's touch . . . if they did not recognize him as House Malech, as Vineart . . .

His heart paused, mid-beat, until the response came. It wasn't a voice or a touch or even a smell, but an awareness that filled him, like the feel of the sun on skin, taking you from the cold of night into the warmth of day. The *vina* was not spoiled, responding to his touch and his authority as it should.

Mahault forgotten for the moment, the uncertainty and exhaustion of the days preceding faded, and Jerzy moved closer, placing one hand flat against the weathered wooden staves, the finest work of the carter's guild. The magic within pushed at him, demanding entrance. Instinctively he breathed out, and then in again, letting the aroma fill his lungs, touching the quiet-magic within him.

Like the living touch of the vineyards, the stone-heavy sense of the Guardian, the *vina* filled spaces within him that had been left dry by the weeks at sea, unsatisfied by the cool awareness of the unblooded grapes, who cared nothing for the humans moving around them. This was home. This was him.

"Jer?"

Reluctantly he moved away, forcing his attention on the needs of the moment, not his own desires. "These are all healwines," he said to Mahl, indicating the first three tanks. "Probably meant for heal-all and bloodstaunch." Those were the most basic of their healwines, the ones most in demand in normal times. In normal times, the largest portion of the crush would be reserved for these, he would have been crafting them even now, while Malech worked the more specific incantations requiring more experience, a stronger hand.

These were not normal times. He moved on to the two last tanks, placing a hand on each one in turn. Their greeting was more subdued; he had not worked these vines, but he knew them, and they knew him.

"These others, they are firewine." Master Malech's secondary legacies, these would have gone to make drylights to be used in fine houses, and on shipboard to reduce the risk of fires. But Jerzy had another use in mind for these *vina*.

Firewine. Master Malech had been a healer, had focused most of his life on the healvines. The fact that he grew firevines was simply because the land there best suited them, and there was always a need.

There might be even more of a need, now. The idea was yet faint, unformed, but the urgency within him grew, even as he stood with his hand against the vat and felt the magic stir. Yes. Action and pause. Push and pull. Heal and destroy. Calm and roil. Incanted spellwines could defend, protect, or cause harm, but they were not destructive, in and of themselves. A healspell might cure, or it might ease the way into death when hope was lost, but its main purpose, its reason for existing, was to heal. The use of spellwines as weapons, crafted for no reason other than to harm, to kill, had ended with the vine-mages themselves.

He had undone a healspell, used it to defend. What might he be able to do, then, with firewine? What could be done with *vin magica* that had not yet been incanted to a specific task? It was not forbidden simply because it had not been thought of to be forbidden. Only a Vineart could use an un-incanted *vina* and no Vineart would have cause to craft a weapon . . .

"Mahault."

She came up behind him, and he noted that she was careful to leave a cautious space between herself and the vats: Mahault might be willing to follow the Vineart into his lair, but she did not let herself forget where she was, and what she was surrounded by. She was wiser than Ao, less cautious than Kaïnam, and had one advantage over them both.

She eyed him curiously. "What?"

"I need you to trust me."

"Phrases like that, my father always said, are the mark of a man who should never be trusted." But she gave him her hand, anyway. Her skin was warm and firm, and he could almost feel the vitality within it, surging like waves beneath the hull of a boat.

Was this how the mage felt, when he . . . no. Jerzy refused the thought.

"Don't worry. It's important that you trust me, and don't worry." And he sliced open her palm with the fingerlength blade that hung from his belt, a blade meant to be used to cut wax seals, not human flesh. She let out a cry but did not jerk her hand back or protest as he lifted them both to the cask's rim and pushed her bleeding hand into the open cask of firewine.

His master had tossed him in, headfirst, and left him to drown or thrive, whatever the mustus decided. But he was not giving her to the raw juice but the *vina*, fined and aware. She would be fine—he hoped. He kept his hand on hers nonetheless, feeling it quiver as the magic slipped into her veins, familiarizing itself with her.

And then she let out a little sigh, the tension flowing out of her body, and he pulled her arm out, using his own sleeve to dry her skin.

The cut had already healed, a narrow purple scab left behind.

"What did you do?" She was more curious than angry, examining the skin, sniffing at it, as though able to smell the wine inside her.

"Forged a connection. If it works, I will be able to reach you—protect you—when you leave."

That got her attention. "I'm not going—"

"I need you to go. I need you to go to the outer vineyards, the firevine yards up north, and tell the overseer that we will need them to increase the crops this year by half again. He will argue; you will tell them it must be done."

He handed her the sigil that hung around his neck, the coin bearing his master's mark. His mark, now. "This will convince him."

It was not merely the message that needed to be brought. He needed someone observant, who could see things that were missing or odd even without knowing what she saw, and tell him, without hesitation. Mahault could do that, and see it without judgment, fear, or prejudice. That was her skill, to see things as they were, not as she wished them to be, or how they might become. Unhindered by doubt, she would be able to tell him, on her return, if anything had been interfering with the yards themselves, or if his overseers had been infected with the taint.

Ideally, Jerzy would go himself, but he could not; even if there were not other things that needed his attention here and now, the attack on the road had showed him how dangerously exposed he was, when he left the House proper. If she was Kaï's second, and Detta's, she would be his, as well. Ao was observant but could not ride, and while Kaïnam could ride swiftly and defend himself, it was not the sort of errand he could send a princeling on, even one who was willing. It would raise too many questions about what Jerzy intended, cause others who were watching to assume the worst.

With luck, his precautions would not be tested. A woman without obvious rank or importance, especially one bearing the Vineart's mark around her neck as surety, would be accepted, and heeded, and not considered a threat.

Jerzy hoped.

FIVE DAY'S RIDE to the southwest of House Malech, two men were standing outside a large, dark red tent pitched between the wide packed-dirt road, and a narrow creek that curved around to skirt a small town built of timber and stone, backed by good grazing lands and a patchwork of crop-bearing fields. It should have looked welcoming . . . but they had not been invited to stay within.

"The rumor says that a Washer killed them."

The taller man, in robes that matched the tent structure, snorted in disbelief. "Impossible."

Brion, who wore riding leathers instead of his robes, shook his head. "You know that and I know that, but these people . . . they hear the rumor, and they do not know what to believe. Not after this year past, of unrest and uncertainty. Too many whispers in the wind blaming us for not interceding with the gods somehow, for not stopping the unstoppable. And now, when they see us ride through, when we camp by their homes, they do not come for the speaking and they do not ask for solace."

Neth scowled at his brother but could find no comeback. The truth was that there had been few at the morning's service, in this village of several hundred, where once every soul would have come to hear a Washer speak. Before, Neth would have been offended. Before they had heard of the illnesses in this town, and others, before they had seen the mass graves, a dozen at a time, across the countryside.

"A single man in the robes of a Washer came through two months before and spoke briefly, and in the days thereafter, nearly two dozen sickened and died." No rumor reported here, merely dry fact.

"All?"

"All, down to the last child." Brion had ridden out to see the graves himself, on Neth's orders, and called for solace on the departed souls. "Just as before. I felt the gaze of the families on me as I walked through the village, but none spoke to me."

Neth supposed, under the conditions, he should be thankful none of them had attacked him and that this village had allowed them to camp here overnight, rather than asking—demanding—that they move on.

If this was their enemy's work, if a Vineart were seeding illness, using a Washer's robe as disguise, then it was dastardly well done. In towns like this, people moved on to other towns to find spouses, intermarrying among families over generations, out and then back, until it was a braid that could not be unwoven. There would not be a single family in all

Corguruth that did not feel this loss. And the rumors would spread, no matter what soothing noises Neth might make. He could not tell them who their enemy was, could not give them a target for their rage and sorrow, and so they would strike out at the nearest target.

Much, he thought wearily, like the Collegium itself. Correspondence was restricted to what could be coiled around a messenger-bird's leg, there being no time to send a *meme-courier*, even if one could find him, and he was feeling his way around orders, trying to do what was right, what maintained Sin Washer's Commands. Every day, it seemed harder, every day brought him a greater sense of being out of step with his brothers, of being pushed onto a road he did not know, and had not chosen.

"Have the men sleep in shifts," he said. "But tell them not to be obvious about it. I don't want anyone watching to think we are at all worried, or alarmed." There were only eleven of them, off the boat at long last, thank Sin Washer, and mounted on hire-horses. Neth had wanted to return to the Collegium, to discover firsthand what was happening, but his updated orders—sent by a pigeon spelled at great expense to find him—had been quite clear, for all they were brief: the House of Malech was still his concern. Vineart Jerzy, who had disappeared after setting the very sands on fire and stranding Neth and his men on the beach, who had called up some monstrous serpent to aid in their escape, was to be brought into Agreement with the Collegium, or ensure that the young Vineart would not become a problem.

Neth had not shared the details of that communication with anyone, not even Brion. Let them believe whatever it comforted them to believe about their mission. An innocent mind gave solace better than one weighted down by the reality of the world.

"It would require magic to do something of that sort," Brion said thoughtfully, as though he were working the logistics in his mind. Neth smiled, despite the seriousness of the matter. Knowing Brion, who had come to the Brotherhood only after years as a soldier, he was doing exactly that.

"What, a cursewine? An illness-spell?" Neth meant it to be sarcastic, but the words came out more curious than not.

"You don't believe there is such a thing? All these years, you think the Vinearts have shared every spell they ever crafted with us, open-handed and guile free?" Brion turned his head to spit, explicitly giving his opinion on the likelihood of that.

Neth had, once. Before he had seen the things he had seen. Before he had learned what his own Collegium was capable of hiding behind the cup.

"I believe . . ." Neth paused. "I believe we're not going to find any answers here," he said finally. "Be ready to move on in the morning."

Brion nodded. If he had doubts of his own, they did not show.

After his second-in-command strode off to make the camp ready, Neth should have gone back to his tent, to deal with the rest of the paperwork that had come with his orders, prepare for the day ahead, and the day after that. Instead, he stood watch over the freshly turned mound until full dusk fell. Only then, his hands cupped and poured for whatever solace he could give those lost souls, did he return to his own tent.

In four days, if they rode hard, they would be back on the doorstep of House Malech.

Chapter 8

*T*he troubling dreams that had plagued Jerzy since he tasted the spoiled mustus should have, he thought, ended once he confronted the *vina* and set the first stirrings of a plan in motion. In some sense, they had: no longer nightmares, these dreams were slower, softer, filled not with fear or disgust so much as longing, an almost physical ache in his body. His limbs felt heavy, but his groin stirred, blood flushing into his lower regions, sending urgent messages back through his brain.

Come, the dream whispered every night. *Come down, come into, be one and be free.*

The first few nights, he resisted. The sensations were awkward, uncomfortable, and even asleep he knew it was not the Guardian whispering in his thoughts, although the voice sounded similar, as though the dragon's stone had melted into something softer, more malleable. Like the Guardian, but not. Jerzy distrusted anything that was not known, proven.

Then one night, after going over new and essentially useless reports with Kaïnam and Ao until nearly dawn, with too much tai and *vin ordinaire* in his veins, Jerzy was so tired, so frustrated, that when the touch came again, promising comfort, Jerzy relented.

In his dream, then, something touched him, gnarled and hard as an old root, curling around him, burrowing into his skin, drawing him down. A sense of power overtook him, the sense of flying, of snapping and crackling like flames, the rush of dashing through waves like the sea-skimmers who had followed the wake of the *Heart*, and the sudden heart-stopping dive of a tarn as it snapped its claws around a rabbit. It was too real to be a dream, too intense, too powerful. All he had to do was give in, the dream whispered, let go, and this would be his.

Temptation, seduction, and a tinge of unease: something was wrong.

Jerzy woke, covered with sweat, the ache in his groin unrelieved. He stroked himself, hand wrapped around his organ, knowing already that it would do no good: the flesh might be released, but the hunger remained. Whatever he craved, it was not to be found here.

He turned in his bed, the oak-hewn structure too large, too soft after years of the sleep house, his narrow bunk as a student, the swinging hammock of his shipboard exile. The pillow, pummeled into a wedge while he slept, was pushed to the floor, and he lay facedown, forehead resting on crossed arms. His breathing was muffled, but he could feel himself panting, as though he had just run from the ridge to the river, or gone a full workout with Kaï in the practice ring.

Unlike his room upstairs, there was no window in this chamber, but he could still sense the slow rise of dawn outside, *feel* the birds chirping and fluttering their wings, the slaves moving, the cookhouse fires beginning to flare. He should get up; there was much to do—plans to make, messages to send, and the daily details of the vintnery pressed on him, even in the quieter winter months. He was Vineart; he had responsibilities.

Under rational, waking thought, the sense of that seductive, urgent pull faded, and his breathing returned to normal. Jerzy did not pretend, he knew it was still there, deep under the soil; waiting, patiently waiting for someone to slip into its tangled ways and lose themselves. He did not know what it was—some magic his master would have told him about had there been time? A trap laid by their enemy? Some leftover magic, like the unblooded vines, coming to the surface now, spurred by the unrest in the Land? He did not know, and the temptation itched at him to find out. It could be something useful, something that would aid him understanding what he was, what he needed to do, give him the answers he had not learned from Malech and could not find in his master's books.

But if it was a trap, he could not afford to set it off.

Not yet, anyway.

With a muffled moan, he pushed himself out of bed, letting his feet touch the cool stone floor.

"Light," he called, and the room filled with brightness, the sconces set into niches in the wall glowing with a steady light. The air was chill; frost had settled overnight. He would need to check the vines this morning; the slaves had been busy under the overseer's watchful eye, readying the yards for winter, but even the most conscientious slave could miss something. A Vineart would not.

Dressed, his head was cleared by cold water splashed on his face and a quick mouthful of healwine. He could hear Master Malech's disapproval at how he treated the heal-all: it was not proper, using a spellwine like tai, he could hear his master say, but the lack of sleep and weight of worry bore him down too far for anything less.

Dressed in working clothes, rough-woven trou and hard-soled shoes, and a thick, loose-sleeved tunic, Jerzy wrapped his belt around his hips twice, hung cup and knife properly, and left his quarters intending to check on the yard before breakfast and the morning's work.

Instead, he stopped just outside the front door, finding Mahault already there, sitting on the ground under the low-spreading branches of the trees that shaded the front of the House. She was bundled against the chill in a cloak and had a sheet of paper resting on her lap.

Normally, anyone in search of quiet went to the courtyard. For Mahault to be here . . . she doubtless looked for privacy, thinking no one else would come out this way. Jerzy should have let her be, gone on his way. But something made him cross the white-frosted grass and stand beside her.

"Mahault."

She looked up, her eyes bright with what might have been tears.

"When did you get back?" He had heard nothing from her while she was on the road, not even a hint of anything from the vines. That might have meant all was well, that there had been no difficulties—or it could have meant that the bond had not taken. He had been too busy to worry overmuch, trusting her to return safely, as she had. Still, she should have reported in the moment she returned.

"Late," she replied. "You had already gone to bed. I left my report on your desk this morning. I thought . . ."

He indicated the papers. The rider had come the afternoon before, sent from a ship just into port, bearing a leather sack of missives and letters from Ao's trader folk, the first result after his offering of information on Irfan, and the one missive, sealed with the sigil of Aleppan, for Mahault. Clearly, Detta had passed her the packet this morning.

Questions about her trip were banished by the tears in her eyes. "Is the news bad?"

She shook her head. "No. Or, not truly. My father refuses to speak my name but my mother . . . she hopes that I am getting enough to eat, and that I remember my manners when speaking with strangers."

Jerzy frowned, not sure what to make of her words. "That is . . . a good message?"

Mahault laughed, and the tears slipped from the corner of her eye, causing her to dash at them with the back of her hand. "For my mother, it's practically an outpouring of love and affection." She folded the message and slipped it into her belt, resting her hand over it briefly, as though to ensure that it was there.

"What else was in the packet?" she asked, discussion of her home and family clearly over.

"More of the same," Jerzy said. In truth, he had left the other two last night busily amending the map, adding and subtracting markers, marking alliances old and new-formed throughout the Lands Vin, as seen by Ao's folk.

The offering of trade routes into Irfan had been remarkably, although unsurprisingly, effective.

"Jer?" She was looking at him now, the expression on her face one of suspicious alert. "All this information you have Ao and Kaï gathering, the ships and the spies . . . You're building to something, I can tell, but what?"

Kaïnam had asked him the same thing, the day before.

"I'll explain everything soon," he said, as he had said yesterday. "Soon."

MAHAULT HAD NOT been satisfied, although she said nothing more. The question lingered in Jerzy's mind as he spent the rest of the morning in his study, rereading his master's notes on firevines and what they were capable of. Mahault's report on her trip was indeed waiting on the desk, closely written in her neat handwriting. The overseer was worried, clearly, but claimed that the yard was healthy. They had lost two slaves to illness and would need replacements in order to meet Jerzy's request for a full Harvest.

Jerzy drummed his fingers on the table, staring at the far wall. There had been no other reports of slaves dying, but there was always that risk. He would have to summon the slavers and hope that something in their offerings matched his needs. But that would have to wait—he would bring no new bodies to the vintnery now. Not when so much was at risk. Slavers were single-minded, and it was in their interest for Vinearts to remain safe and wealthy, but even a single chink in a roof could let in rain.

A Vineart protected his vines.

Kaïnam's comment came back to him. No one was safe, and no one could be protected. This was a battle—no, a war, the likes of which had not been seen since. . . .

Since before Sin Washer. Since before the breaking of the First Vine. Since the last vine-mages used magic—and people—as markers in their endless, pointless battles.

This was not pointless. This war was for survival. But to those around them, who knew nothing of what was happening, who would likely never know, because how could he explain it to them . . . what would they believe? There was, after all, no proof that Ximen would be any worse a master than an existing lord, any less capable a Vineart that any here . . .

But those people had not seen what Jerzy had seen. Had not felt the fear, the cold, bittersweet touch of the taint.

He knew what needed to be done. But, despite his words, would he know when? How much information was enough, how many possibilities could they adjust for? He knew when the grapes were ready for Harvest: was he waiting for a similar sense here? What if it never came?

"Past noon."

Kaïnam stood in the doorway, looking expectant. Jerzy, shaken from his unpleasant thoughts and made aware of the day passing, felt the aches in his body: his shoulders were too tense, his lower back cramped, and his left leg was sound asleep. He rotated his shoulders gingerly, wincing when he heard something crack.

Kaïnam heard it, too. "Come on, Vineart. Time for practice."

"All right." Jerzy pushed away from the desk, then stopped. "I want to try something new today."

THE WEAPONS PRACTICE served more than one purpose, Jerzy had discovered: when his body was in use, his mind was, for a short time, quiet, the doubts were put aside.

Doubts about magic, anyway. After the third time Jerzy found himself facedown in the dirt, feeling his soreness from sitting replaced by soreness from being thrown down like a sack of grain, he had doubts as to other things, including if he had actually learned anything from Mil'ar Cai.

Kaïnam's style of fighting was decidedly more aggressive.

Jerzy paused, mid-movement and Kaï landed a blow that stung, using the flat of his blade. "Watch yourself," his opponent said, and they circled again, gazes wary, judging distances and muscle tension, weighing each observation and selecting a counter to each predicted move. As Jerzy turned, he let the quiet-magic rise, imagining it running down the length of his cudgel even as he swung.

The blow landed hard enough to make the prince stagger back with a pleased-sounding "oomph," but nothing happened.

"Rot."

Kaï frowned. "Nothing?"

"No." Today he was using firespells against Kaï as well as his cudgel, trying to pair them into one smooth movement. Ideally, the quiet-magic scorched the practice blade and drove Kaï back with white-hot flames. When he tested it at rest, it worked. During battle, even practice, it failed. Magic, or muscle. The combination of the two seemed beyond him.

"Hrm. Steady on, we have company," Kaï said, changing his stance and letting the wooden blade rest point down in the dirt.

"I know." Jerzy paused, then turned over slowly, spitting out the taste of dirt. The two figures ducked lower, but not before he had seen them, the tops of their heads clearly visible over the low stone wall that ran alongside the road between vintnery and House.

When he had been a slave, the thought of going near that wall would never have occurred to him. Had the overseer seen him, it would have been the lash for daring leave his task; even worse to be caught spying upon the Vineart.

Jerzy tried to imagine ever daring to lift his eyes to Master Vineart Malech, even in hiding, and failed utterly. Either the overseer was slacking in his duties, or these two . . . Or these two were drawn by something they could not resist, to risk the fear of discovery.

"Two of them," Kaïnam noted. "Companionship breeds courage."

Jerzy merely shook his head, his voice curt with worry. "Slaves don't think like that."

"Well, you at least are not lacking for courage." Kaï was still uncomfortable discussing slaves and was clearly glad to leave off the topic. "But you're still thinking too much. You need to keep your mind *off* your moves, not worry at them like . . . like Lil over a roast."

Jerzy, stung, tightened his grip on his cudgel. "Come at me again."

Kaïnam grinned tightly and lifted his sword, clearly preparing another strike. The day had warmed up slightly; after the cold start the two of them were stripped down to sleeves and trou, and sweating slightly with their effort. Their steps left imprints on the browning grass, until a neat square was beaten down by their workout.

"Full-bore?"

"Full and a last minute turn," Jerzy said, thankful that he didn't need to take time out to explain what he had in mind, that the princeling would accept and follow his lead without question. Kaï nodded and, with a harsh shout that didn't make Jerzy blink anymore, charged at the Vineart, his sword swinging through the air with deadly intent.

The blow landed, despite Jerzy's best attempts at any sort of defense, and had the sword carried a sharp edge, the world would have been less one Vineart. As it was, the blow drove him onto his stomach, the air leaving him with a painful whoosh.

"Mil'ar Cai would disown me for that," he said when he could speak again, rolling over and staring up at the sky.

"You're doing better than you think," Kaïnam said, not offering him a hand up this time. "Your weapons master taught you to defend yourself from beasts or brigands. I'm teaching you to attack another fighter. There's a difference."

Defense, and attack. Turn and step. What is visible and what was hidden, out of sight . . . or underground. The worries of earlier swept back as though they had never been gone. Kaï accused him of thinking too much, but how could he not, with so much to think on?

His hair had come loose from its band when he fell. Jerzy rolled over and got to his knee, reaching up to pull the long strands back again, making a face as the hair stuck to his sweat-damp skin. As he raised his arms, a slight movement caught his eye. The two slaves, still lurking, in a place they knew they should not be, nowhere near careful enough, frightened enough, for being this close to their master.

They were out of place, acting wrongly; something new and different when too much else was changing, and therefore a concern.

He finished securing his hair and bent over, his left arm reaching out for the cudgel driven into the dirt by the force of Kaïnam's blow.

"Again," he said, rising to his feet, his thoughts not on the movements but magic. It wasn't working. Why?

Winespells were controlled, crafted to do only what they were intended for. All of Malech's notes on firespells referred to the level of control built into the incantation process, to keep a mis-decanted spell from sparking a wildfire, or burning flesh where it was meant to warm. Even the firespell he had used to burn the plague ship had been limited; when the fuel went out, so, too, would it. Only when he drew on the sense of the feral vines, the unblooded grapes, had he been able to set the sands on fire, and even then . . . despite his fears, they had not leaped beyond his control.

But he had used them against others—he had used a spellwine against the serpent, that first time, to bring it down. He had used a spellwine to kill, in order to end suffering not once but twice. So why would it not work as a deliberate weapon?

Vinearts do not use . . .

I know, he thought back at the Guardian. *I know.*

Vinearts did not use weapons. Vinearts did not engage in battle. Vinearts did not engage in matters beyond their walls. He had broken all those rules already, and the world had not ended. What other choice did he have?

"Again," he repeated, when Kaïnam looked hesitant, summoning the quiet-magic one more time. "Now."

Unlike previous exchanges, this time Jerzy did not lift his hand to counter the blow, nor did he attempt to direct his quiet-magic against his attacker, but spun, trusting that Kaï would make that last-minute turnaway, and instead looked toward the stone wall and the two figures trying to remain inconspicuous behind it.

"Go," he told the spell, looking toward the wall, and without further order it went, following the tumbling arc of the cudgel, the quiet-magic sparking and shimmering along the length of wood as though lightning were trapped within.

Pulling it so quickly and releasing it without pause left him shaking and weak in the legs, but the crunching sound as wood and spell hit stone was satisfying, as were the terrified yelps from behind the wall, as two terrified slaves took to their heels, racing down the hill back to the shed where they were, clearly, supposed to be working.

"I didn't know you could do that," Kaïnam said, having finished his pivot unnoticed, and returning to a ready, waiting stance.

"I've kept some secrets," Jerzy said, equally calm, although in truth he had not known he could do that, either. Letting the magic fly like that, undirected, had been an impulse move, and already he was regretting it, regretting that he might have seriously injured the slaves rather than merely frightening them. Because they were easily replaced did not mean he should be careless.

And yet, he had done what he wanted: had used the new firespell offensively, without hesitation or failure. Why now, and not when he crossed blades with Kaï? Was it useful only against someone who would not, could not fight back?

"Not so brave after all." Kaïnam sounded disappointed, and it took Jerzy a moment to realize he had been talking about the two slaves.

"Braver than you could ever imagine. You might lurk, out of sight, of a schoolmaster or visiting dignitary, secure that none would do more than yell, or perhaps a blow in rebuff." Jerzy had no idea what sort of discipline Kaïnam had faced as a child; no swordsman or sailor grew up soft, certainly, but he had been a prince, nonetheless.

"A slave has no such security; disobedience could easily mean death."

Slaves did not fight back. Slaves did not fight, period. Vinearts did not go into battle, but left that to the lords and common folk . . . it wound around the problem like vines on a post. The answer was in there, somewhere. Jerzy simply was not wise enough to decipher it.

The loss of Master Malech was a fading pain after so many months, but Jerzy felt it keenly in that moment.

"Again?"

"Again," Jerzy agreed.

He reclaimed the cudgel, and they resumed position for another round, Kaï looking thoughtful under his sweat, Jerzy trying to focus again on the task at hand, putting all other thoughts out of his head, as Cai had taught him.

It came with no warning; a faint indrawn breath, and then the wooden sword came swinging at him, Kaïnam's entire body in the blow, with no intent of pulling back at the last instant, no practice involved but a killing move, a fighter's strike. Jerzy had no time to do anything other than react, raising the quiet-magic in an instinctive defense against the weapon, even as he was aware of Kaïnam shifting his balance, one foot sweeping out to catch him off guard.

Instead, Jerzy stepped over the foot as he would a tangled vine, and found himself within Kaïnam's inner guard just as his first weapons master had taught him, close enough to lay hands on the other man.

Dropping his cudgel, he did so, palms flat against Kaïnam's chest, the magic rising within him even as he moved, instinctively calling on the quiet-magic, feeling not only the firewine but healwine as well move to his command.

"Sin Washer!" Startled, Kaïnam leaped backward, his sword still clenched in his hands, his eyes wide in a suddenly ashen face. "What the rot did you just do?"

Jerzy's mind had gone blank. "What did it feel like?"

"Like . . . like all the warmth in my body fled, all at once."

"I wasn't trying to hurt you." Jerzy was sweating, as though he were standing under a summer's sun, not pale winter light. "It shouldn't have hurt you, only made you stop. I think."

"You think?" Kaïnam shook his head, letting his sword lower slowly until it was in resting pose, while Jerzy struggled to find the words to explain what he didn't understand himself. "No, don't tell me. Sin Washer had the right of it, there are some things it's best ordinary folk not know, nor poke fingers in. Just remember what you did, when you knew it was for real, and see if you can do it again."

"Yes." Jerzy looked thoughtfully at his hands. "But not today. I need to think about this."

Chapter 9

*J*erzy *ended the* session sweaty and his head still filled with too many questions. Rather than heading back to the House, he skirted the yard, walking around the great stone sleep house where he had spent so many nights, avoiding the slaves who were working outside, down to the river that bordered the House lands. The River Ivy was a rushing torrent in the spring, but in winter slowed to a steady flow, the water cold enough to pucker skin, and just deep enough to douse a body without risk of drowning.

Jerzy had learned to swim, slightly, when they were at sea, but he felt more comfortable when his feet were firmly on the ground. Plunging into the currents over and over again until his skin and thoughts were both washed clear, Jerzy put his clothing back on, and headed back to his workroom.

While the other three went about their work of gathering information from beyond the vintnery walls, the Household staff pretending that there were no concerns other than preparing meals and caring for stock and tools, Jerzy pulled down every text and manuscript in Malech's library, poring over the pages until his eyes crossed and his head ached.

What he had done with Kaï, that touch, that had been purely quiet-magic. He could repeat it, if he were ever in close combat again, as he had been with the merchant back in Irfan. Had he known that trick then, the man would not have escaped. If the man had not escaped, they would have more detailed information than what his assistant had knowledge of, and Jerzy would know where to direct the attack the others were urging him to make.

The regret was useless, and put aside.

But why had the spell worked against the slaves, and not when it was directed against Kaï, during practice?

"Guardian. Is there anything you know, anything to explain why the firespell works some times, but not all?"

A sense of cool, blank stone came back to him. If the Guardian knew anything, it was not sharing it. That meant it did not approve, or felt Jerzy was doing something wrong . . . but he was no longer the slave or student to be scolded, but master, and as such the Guardian was tasked to follow and protect, not instruct. Jerzy reminded himself of that, but the sense that he was somehow wrong stayed with him.

Vinearts stood apart. And yet . . . there was the text about Bradhai, who had defeated the sea serpents generations ago. He had not stood apart, but had gone in search of battle . . . against beasts, true, not men, but was there a difference? Jerzy searched through the papers until he found what he was looking for, not even noticing when several priceless sheets were pushed off the table and onto the stone floor.

"And the Vineart stood in the prow, a vat of the strongest weatherwine to be found, and called upon the storms, and called upon the seas, and called upon the flame . . ."

Three legacies. The Master Vineart had braided three legacies into one, on the seas, no less, surrounded by water, to strike a blow to destroy an entire pack of sea serpents.

Bradhai. No one bothered with "Master Vineart" before his name, because there was no need. There was only one Bradhai. None before, none since, had managed anything close.

Of course, the text Jerzy had in front of him was not a history, exactly. It was the retelling of a man who had been told what happened. Master Malech would snort and say it was merely a legend, as useful as a story of the silent gods.

But it was all Jerzy had to work with.

He stared at the text, his finger tracing the brown lettering, the gilt-picked design at the edge of the page, the slight stain at the corner, and felt an uneasy twitch on his skin, as though a spider walked along his flesh, only deeper. There were other stories in these pages as well, references to the horrors committed by the vine-mages when they ruled the Lands Vin. Stories of mages who ordered a town destroyed to expand a yard, or sent men to their death in a battle that meant nothing save ego and bragging rights for a season . . . and more, of women taken from their homes to breed children for the prince-mages, and children who disappeared, and worse. Rumors, legends, stories to scare those who came after into obedience to Sin Washer's Command.

Jerzy let a sigh escape him. Vinearts did not take part in the world. And yet, if he was to keep Ximen from destroying the Lands Vin, what choice did Jerzy have but to take part, to do as Bradhai had, and turn his magic to counter it?

The Guardian worried, but said nothing.

The question weighed on Jerzy's mind through the evening meal, making short answer to conversation until the others left him alone. It kept him company on his evening walk through the vineyard as he felt the ground sleeping under his feet and the cooling breeze on his skin. It even pushed aside the usual dreams that night, leaving him awake well before dawn, staring at the shadowed plaster of the ceiling, exhausted and shattered, his eyes so grainy he could barely open them, his muscles slack and aching.

He could feel the answer moving, deep, out of reach but coming closer. He could not rush it, any more than he could rush the fruit ripening, but the need to *do* something screamed at him.

When the first sounds of dawn began, Jerzy got up, washed his face, drew on warm clothing, and walked quietly to the front path, where Mahault was already waiting, her face turned up to the starlit sky, watching a dark-feathered bird as it rustled its feathers sleepily, perched on a bare tree limb. They had fallen into the habit of walking together before the morning meal, both of them in need of some time where no conversation was required, comfortable with their own thoughts and each other's company, the way neither Ao nor Kaïnam ever could.

She turned to acknowledge him, and they started walking without a word, heading down the cobbled road, away from the yard and toward the main road. Never past the marker, never off safe grounds, but as far as Jerzy could go, without risk of exposing himself.

The point of decision was coming. Jerzy could feel it in his skin. No matter if he was ready or not, he would have to act. The months they had sailed, their enemy would not have been idle, and while it was winter in The Berengia, they had experienced firsthand how the seasons were reversed there, which meant the enemy would be coming into the Harvest.

If Jerzy were to launch an attack, it would be then, once there were no more worries about weather—

"There was no damage to the yield."

"What?" Mahault stopped to look at him, her expression curious.

"Detta said the harvest went smoothly. There was no damage. There should have been damage."

"Jer, you aren't making any sense."

"There haven't been any major storms in . . . years," Jerzy went on, now speaking to himself, pacing back along the edge of the road, his gaze scanning the top of the sleeping vines, occasionally lifting up to the shadow-dark ridge beyond. A slave, carrying something from the sleep house across the road to the stables, was caught off guard by Jerzy's sudden change in direction and scurried out of his way, but the Vineart barely noticed. "Not since the hailstorm that destroyed the secondary field in the north. And nobody else has reported anything, not beyond the normal. In all that has been odd, that has been utterly . . . quiet."

"And that is a bad thing?" Mahault was trying to follow his thoughts, and failing. "Aren't storms bad?"

"Very bad," he said, halting in his pacing long enough to answer her. She did not seem to take offense when he started walking again, merely waited for him to come back.

"Grapes are fragile," he said on his return, speaking intently, as though he could make her understand by force of will alone. "Too much rain, not enough rain, too much sun, too little sun, a fungus or insects or a hundred other things can destroy the yield, make the grapes unusable, or drain the roots so much that all we get is *vin ordinaire.*"

"And . . . ?" Mahault shook her head, still not following. "You're worried because you've not had any disasters?" Of all the things they had on their platter, that obviously seemed foolish to her.

"Think about it, Mahl," he said, his voice tight with impatience. "If you wanted to undermine Vinearts, spread fear through the lands, cause the lords to snap the restrictions placed on them so that they were in clear violation of Sin Washer's Commands . . . sending a drought, or a terrible storm, would cripple that Vineart for the season, force him to rely on older stock, if he had it, or do without, if he did not."

"Weaken and distract the Vineart so that he would be caught off guard by a later strike." Mahault began to see where Jerzy was thinking, now. "But there hasn't been any of that."

"No. Nothing that caused anyone significant worry, weather-wise. This is a man who sends out sea serpents, who drove root-blight into vineyards and swarms to attack travelers. Who had seabirds dive out of the sky, hours from the coastline. Think like Kaïnam for a moment. Our enemy is dangerous, but he is not subtle, nor does he favor any one tool. So why is he not using this particular tool?"

Mahault had no hesitation about her own intelligence, or how much she had learned since leaving Aleppan, but she had also learned when to wait, and listen. The air was still and cold, and she pulled the sleeves of her heavy hide jacket down over her hands. Normally by now they would be walking quickly enough that the cold would be an incentive, not an annoyance.

She started walking again, thinking it through out loud. "No rain or winds . . . when we were at sea we encountered one storm, but only the one."

Jerzy, caught off guard, had to stretch his legs to catch up. She was referring to the storm that had wrecked their first ship and driven them to where Kaïnam met them.

"I had assumed that was his work," Jerzy said, "our enemy, but I never was certain. There was no way to prove it, one way or the other. A spellwine carries trace, quiet-magic carries a trace, but the effects of the magic itself . . . it fades as soon as the magic itself does. More, windspells travel so far, and if Kaï himself had been using one; all it would take would be a few to match . . . and the smell of the taint could have been from the serpents." He was speaking to himself again, his mind turning over what he knew too quickly to explain to Mahault, even if she could understand.

Puffs of air appeared and then disappeared in front of their mouths as they breathed. The sun had risen enough now to cover the valley in a clear purple haze, and the air was still chill; Mahault was shivering, even under the jacket, but Jerzy had forgotten all about the cold.

"He has no weathervines."

Jerzy's tone was so triumphant, Mahault forgot about petty things like chilblains, waiting for him to explain.

"A WEAKNESS." KAÏNAM'S voice was low and fierce, like a cat that had just pounced on a particularly clever mouse.

"Not a weakness," Jerzy corrected him, tearing off a chunk of bread and then waving it at Kaï as he gestured for emphasis. "Vinearts rarely are called by more than two legacies, and most are limited by skill and soil to a single one. And you must never forget that any Vineart can do more with a spellwine than merely decant it."

Quiet-magic: the greatest secret, kept nearly two thousand years, and he, Jerzy, had told not one but three outsiders. That was the very least of his worries now.

"More, I would not dare call this Ximen weak, given that he has learned how to reach across distances to work his spells, something that should have been impossible. But this—if I am right, he lacks at least one legacy, and that is the first real information we've learned. He lacks them, and he needs them. Either weathervines or—or the feral vines, like those in Irfan."

Jerzy could see that he had lost them, and tried to explain.

"Weathervines are the least touched legacy. When the Vine was broken, the roots were shattered, each one drenched in Sin Washer's blood, changed by that touch. Weathervines were . . . somehow, they were less touched."

"That's why they're paler," Mahault said, with the tone of someone putting two unexpected bits together. "Giordan grew weathervines," Mahault said now, the first she had spoken since they had gone back inside, meeting the others in the dining hall. "My father offered him the lands around our city because they were best for those vines, and he used them to protect us from the storms that came over the mountains, to divert them. . . ."

Her breath caught as she finally understood. "That is why—you think that Sar Anton was one of this Ximen's tools, and targeted Giordan not because you were there, not because he associated with Master Malech, but because of his vines. And the same for poor Esoba?"

Ao poured himself another cup of ale and sipped, listening intently, ignoring the platters of food that had been set out for them.

"Yes. But it wasn't Sar Anton," Jerzy said. "The Washer, Darian." Darian had been the one to accuse Jerzy of interfering with another Vineart's yard, who had forced events in Aleppan to their eventual conclusion. "It had to have been him, else Sar Anton would not have saved me from the servant who tried to kill me, to keep me from reaching my master and telling him what was happening."

The Washer, the servant, the aide who had the maiar's ear and twisted his mind to believe Darian's accusation, to see conspiracy in every glance, even his own daughter's . . . all thin roots, offshoots of a thicker one, pushing them one way or another. In the aftermath of the accusations, it had been a tangle, all confusion and fear. A step back, and he could see the patterns, just as Kaïnam had first seen the pattern in the attacks, a net, drawing more tightly around them, driving them to . . . what?

Roots, underneath, spreading . . . why did that image stay with him? The reassurance of the stone-walled hall kept Jerzy from feeling quite the same apprehension that grew every time he looked at the map, the lines and pins drawing ever tighter around the Vin Lands, but the unease that had become his constant companion would not be dispelled by the comforting, familiar smells of roasted meats or bread.

"So he does not grow weathervines. Neither do you, Jer, but you've used them." Ao wasn't seeing the pattern. "What does it matter, if they have less bloodstain? Why can't he just . . . ?" Ao waved his hand in the air, unable to vocalize what he thought Ximen might do.

"He has no access. I was invited to work Giordan's yard, and they . . . they . . ." Those vines had taken a liking to him, allowing him full access, but he could not say that out loud. There was no way to explain to anyone who had not felt the touch of the vines what that meant. "That, and I have weatherwines available to me, the same as any within the Vin Lands with coin to trade. Wherever he is, we know he's beyond the Lands Vin . . . he has no access to the work of other Vinearts, save what he can steal. And he has not been able to steal weathervines. Giordan was killed"—and it still hurt, to think of the energetic, occasionally foolhardy man, dead—"but the vines were uprooted, his cellar immediately destroyed."

That was the punishment for apostasy, the same fate that had faced Jerzy and the House of Malech, until the Washers relented. Had Ximen thought to put a puppet of his own choosing into that vineyard instead? Or had he planned to have Darian take the spellwines already racked and somehow send them to his master? He ignored the Commands— did he even know of them? How far removed was their enemy from the Lands Vin and its centuries of tradition?

Too many questions, and no answers. Not yet.

But the mage had known of weathervines. Had he known that they, like he, used blood in their crafting, to bring those stubborn vines into obedience? Or had the mage been blindly reaching, searching, as he had in Irfan, for grapes with the least touch of Sin Washer upon them?

Sin Washer had protected the Lands Vin, to keep those vines from the mage's grasp, until now. But they could not count on that protection lasting.

"If he's seafaring, the lack of weathervines would be a true hardship," Kaïnam said. "It would explain why our ships were attacked by fire, instead."

Master Malech had not used weatherspells, finding them too risky because of the way they spread, the magic caught up on the very winds they controlled. They had weatherwines in the cellar, but only a few. Jerzy had worked Giordan's vines, had touched them, and they had touched him. They lingered within him, changing the quiet-magic of fire and healing he had been sold to, giving him access to not two, but three legacies in his blood.

Three. Like Bradhai.

Purest coincidence, that Giordan had been the one Master Malech sent him to. It had to have been coincidence, there was no other explanation . . . unless Sin Washer wished it so. Unless all this, everything that had happened, his being sent away, his encountering Kaïnam in the midst of the seas, had all been driven by the gods, to keep Ximen from his plans.

A shudder passed through him. The silent gods did not interfere in the acts of man. But that had not always been true, and there was no reason to believe anything would be so forever simply because it was so now.

The thought was both disturbing and exhilarating.

"So we know that he couldn't send storms, before. Does it matter, now?" Mahault, practical as a knife.

"Not everything that is important is useful, true," Kaïnam said, picking up a piece of fruit and running his thumbnail along the skin. "This feels important, though. Even if it's not a weakness, as such. Jer does have access to weatherwines, so we have magic that our enemy does not. The question becomes, does he have access to magics that we are missing?"

The *vina* they had drunk in Irfan had abused their thoughts, their emotions. Those had been of Esoba's making, though, his fecklessness and ignorance blending with the power of his feral grapes. Their enemy had manipulated Esoba, but he not been allowed access to those grapes; they had stopped him, unknowing.

The memory of those vines, the subtle power in the *vina*, made Jerzy shudder again: this time not entirely in distaste.

Guardian? Jerzy reached out to the stone dragon, but received no answer. The dragon did not know, or could not tell; there was still much about the Guardian that Jerzy did not understand and suspected even his master had not known. Like the masthead on the *Vine's Heart*, a spell that had worked in ways not intended or expected. Perhaps even the prince-mages had not controlled their magic entirely.

"So what does all this mean?" Ao suddenly seemed to remember there was food available and slid a cut of meat onto his own platter, but did not eat, just yet.

"We can't know," Kaïnam said, "and so worrying about it does us three no good. Jer, if you discover anything—"

"I will tell you, of course." Master Malech would not have accepted orders from a man of power, but the world had changed, and only a fool—or a dead man—did not adapt.

Jerzy was a Vineart, but he had learned not to be a fool. An alliance of equals was different from being forced into an Agreement.

"The question that we need answered is, can we use this against him?" Kaï moved back to his own area of knowledge. "In battle, I mean."

"What, send a storm against him, to blind him during an attack? We would need to know exactly where he was, to do that, and not even Jerzy could send a storm all the way across the sea." Ao paused, then turned his head to look at the Vineart. "Could you?"

"No." Something shimmered in his thoughts, not the hard, cool influence of the Guardian but something fainter, softer. The memory of the feeling when he had struck Kaï with the magic, the open palm. The scent of the soil under his bare feet, as a slave. The feeling he had, within these walls. The other mage had gone to great lengths to gather other Vinearts' magic to him, stealing their wines, their slaves . . . why? "No, but I don't have to send it against him. I just have to let him know I have it. That my blood-magic, my quiet-magic, carries the vines that were destroyed. Giordan's vines, and the ones in Irfan both."

"Not a weapon, but a lure?" Kaïnam looked thoughtful, while Mahault's eyes lit up

"'Tcha, Ximen, look at what I have,' make him come to you, and then we cut him down?" She approved, that much was clear.

Only Ao, leaning back in his chair, seemed to have a sense that a straightforward attack was not entirely what Jerzy had in mind.

THE MEAL FINISHED, they nonetheless lingered in the dining hall, as though the comforting, homey sounds from the kitchen made them reluctant to leave. Work continued, however: Kaïnam and Mahault had unrolled a map of the Lands Vin and were moving markers around as though it were a game of Go, while Detta came in, cornering Jerzy for a discussion of something that made her wave her rounded hands in exasperation, and him scowl. Ao felt a moment's pity: no matter what went on in the greater world, the Household budgets must be squared.

That thought nudged another into shape: leaving magic to the

Vinearts, still even a mage needed supplies, services. That meant people, ordinary people, and ordinary people were vulnerable. . . .

Shaking his head at his own obtuseness for not thinking of it before, the trader picked up a scratch-pen and three sheets of paper from the pile at Mahl's elbow and wrote out three quick notes, then maneuvered himself back into the wheeled chair, and headed through the kitchen, ducking Lil, and outside. The day was full lit now, the sky a pale blue, the sounds of the slaves working at whatever winter chores they maintained familiar enough that he barely registered it.

He could have made himself walk, exercising the still-weak connection between his body and his false legs, but instead Ao pushed the chair up the hill enough that he could be seen from the pigeon coop, and raised a hand. "Boy!"

The tousled head of the slave appeared, and Ao showed him three fingers, then a single, which he pointed to the south, indicating that he wanted three birds capable of flying to the first outpost directly to the south. The slave nodded and disappeared again, then the entire body appeared outside the coop a few minutes later, carefully carrying a wicker basket in both hands. Inside were three gray-winged doves, cooing and restless.

"Trustworthy, Master Ao," the boy said. He could not quite say Ao's name properly, pronouncing only the last syllable, so that it sounded like "ow." "As you want."

"Good, good. They're only off to the next posting, no need to spell them elsewhere. Here's the first, then," and he handed over one of the bound messages resting in his lap, waiting while the boy tied it carefully to the first pigeon's leg. Two more were attached to their respective messengers, and the slave climbed back up into the coop and sent the birds on their way.

Ao watched them flap their way into the darkening air, then circle once, as though looking for their destination, before setting off. He did not fully understand what magic was used to train these birds, allowing them to have a multiplicity of destinations rather than flying between birth-coop and training post, but their usefulness could not be denied. At the first outpost, the messages would be transferred to other birds, and sent on the next leg, covering the distance faster than a horse and rider.

"Silent gods put wind under your wings, and keep you from harm," he whispered, staring up into the sky even after the birds had disappeared from sight. All three messages were for members of his clan: Tel, his cousin, who was a caravan leader and a woman of rare good sense; Ret, who had been Ao's own teacher and might still have a kindness for him, despite Ao's behavior; and Kaji, the clan elder.

After his first message, promising news of a great and useful—and potentially profitable—sort, the elder had finally begun sharing information. But while Kaïnam and Mahault seemed satisfied with what trickle they had been fed, Ao knew there was more. Not fact, but gossip, was what traders thrived on. Gossip, which moved so much faster than fact, and could be used in more ways. That was what he needed, now, if they were to move one step ahead of Ximen's games, and lure him into a trap. For, surely, that had to be Jerzy's intent?

Ao's messages asked for that gossip, while warning them of consequences, should Jerzy's plan—whatever that plan night be—fail, to not believe what was unspoken in Kaji's responses so far: that no matter what fate befell the Lands Vin, the Eastern Wind trading clan would come out with a good bargain. They thought they could negotiate with whoever ended up in power.

Ao, having seen in Irfan how their enemy treated those he bargained with, thought his people were fools. Hopefully, Tel and Ret could counter some of that, with what he told them about the danger to come. . . .

"Master Ao!"

Ao turned his chair back to look toward the coop, where the slave was waving his arm. "One's coming!"

Sure enough, there was a speck in the sky, coming in at a direct angle to the coop. Ao held his breath, suddenly sure that an owl would swoop down and take the bird before it reached them. But in a few seconds the pigeon had landed with a flurry of wings, and the slave was removing the message from its leg, bringing it back down to where Ao waited.

The message was sealed with the tree-and-vine sigil of the Principality of Atakus.

Ao's breath caught in his throat, and he forced the sudden hope down, not allowing himself to expect anything. His people looked to the main chance, but men of power were different beasts. Kaïnam had sent a bird to his father when Ao's first salvo went out but had warned the others that it was unlikely his father would respond.

"My father is a proud man, and I am dead to them, or worse than dead. He will have named one of my brothers as Heir, in my place, and . . . and that is assuming the birds can break through Master Edon's spellcasting, to start."

"If he incanted the spell to keep out animals," Jerzy had said, "your people will be starving to death, as no fish will be able to pass through your waters, either. Master Edon is not so foolish."

Kaïnam had seemed unconvinced.

"If not him, then perhaps others," Ao had said, refusing to be cowed by Kaïnam's pessimism. "We need a man of power to stand with us, preferably more than one. Jer might think he can solve this all on his own—"

Jerzy had let out a harsh bark of laughter at that.

"But you and I know more will be needed. Magic is a tool, but to win a war, you need men."

"Men, and ships," Kaïnam had said.

"And ships, and money," Ao acknowledged.

The memory of that conversation stayed with Ao as he started back to the House, the wheels of his chair jolting on the uneven ground. The scarring where his legs were joined to his wooden limbs still ached, but it was familiar now, the way his arms ached and his backside seemed forever sore. Men, ships, and funds. Money to move the men and ships to buy information. To move the pieces into place, so whenever Jerzy made his hidden move, struck the blow he was preparing with all his magic and research, the Lands Vin would be ready as well. Now, if he could only convince Jerzy to tell him what he was going to do, and when.

Ao turned the chair—moving carefully, unwilling to risk a fall—and headed at an angle down the road, preferring the uneven cobblestones to the rutted and uneven grass. Intent on not flipping the rattan-work chair on its side, he almost missed the rider coming up the road toward him until the sound of hooves reached his ears.

Ao stopped, his hands resting on the wheels of his chair, feeling the rough wood under his fingers. He could not see the figure clearly until they came into the vintnery's grounds proper, and another few paces before they were close enough to be identified. The first thing he noted was that the horses of House Malech were brown-coated and hard-muscled, not the sleek gray form coming toward him.

Sleek gray . . . with red trappings at rein and saddle.

Washer.

"Oh, rot."

Chapter 10

"*Vineart Jerzy.*"

The rider leaned forward in his saddle and addressed not Jerzy but Kaïnam, who raised his eyes skyward as though in entreaty for patience, and then stepped to the side, wordlessly indicating Jerzy beside him.

The Washer, corrected, tried again without a hint of embarrassment. "Vineart Jerzy."

Older than any of them, a man in the prime of his life, the Washer carried himself with the assurance of someone secure in the knowledge that he was welcome in any House or village he rode into.

Any save this one.

Ao had barely time to recognize who approached before Jerzy and Kaï had joined him, both quickly dressed in their available best: Kaï in a dark blue tunic and trou, his boots polished, his hair pulled back with a ribbon that was probably one of Lil's from the way it fluttered rather than tying in a neat knot. Jerzy, on the other hand, had merely thrown a somber robe over his attire, but the belt at his waist was oxblood leather, and the silver spoon and knife that hung from it gleamed under the subdued winter sunlight, for any with the wit—or experience—to look. He was less gaudy than Kaï, but Ao did not understand how the Washer could not sense who was master here.

Whatever his failings, the Washer had the look of a hard man to him. Ao didn't know how the others had known company was coming, but he was just as glad not to be confronting the Washer alone. If he was here to try and take Jerzy . . .

The trader felt the solid weight of the cudgel in his lap where Jerzy had placed it as they walked past him. He might not be able to walk without wobbling, yet, but his arms were strong, and he could by-the-gods hit.

It was one man against the three of them. Four, if you considered Mahault, who was not visible but doubtless waiting in a window of the House, bow at the ready. One Washer, no matter how hard, could not be a challenge. Yet Ao could feel the tension building.

"I am Vineart Jerzy of House Malech."

The Washer dismounted, again showing the ease of a horseman and the stiffness of someone who had long been in the saddle. Was this their watcher? Ao didn't think so.

A slave appeared out of nowhere, taking the reins of the horse and leading it a few steps away, waiting to see if the visitor would leave again, or stay.

"You are doubtless surprised to see me—"

"Not particularly," Jerzy said, his voice cool. "You followed us from the docks; we have been waiting for you to work up the nerve to approach us."

Jerzy did not mention the fact that the Washer had not helped them when they were attacked by the beast-birds. There was no point: if the Washer knew they had seen him then, he also knew that they knew he had not come to their aid. Not mentioning the incident gave it more weight, not less, and put the Washer on the defensive.

Jerzy did not let his expression show it, but Ao could tell that he was rather pleased with himself. A Vineart might not dabble in politics, but he was not doing so badly, for all that.

"That was not I," the Washer said, bearing out Ao's suspicions. "But one of my Brothers, yes."

Jerzy showed no reaction to being corrected, or the news that another Washer still lurked beyond the boundaries. "What is your purpose in being here, Washer? Are you here to offer us Solace?"

"If there is need, a show of violence will not stop me from offering," the newcomer said, his voice steady even as his gaze flickered from Jerzy to Kaïnam, then back up to the House, bypassing Ao entirely. Ao took solace in that—he could do more damage, if needed, if he was not counted as a threat. Off the horse, the Washer was short and wide across the shoulders, and looked to be from one of the lands north of Mahault's home, with skin the white of river foam and hair only a shade darker, like cream. His eyes were light colored, and cold. "But, no. Neither Solace nor violence is my purpose in approaching you, Vineart. My name is Edmun. You avoided giving my Brothers an answer at the docks, and left without further discussions. It was feared from these actions that you . . . misunderstood our intent. To clarify our position, I bring a message from . . . certain members of the Collegium."

"Certain members?" Kaïnam's voice had the distant, cultured quality to it that had been absent lately, the Named-Heir of the Principal of Atakus coming out of the shadows for the occasion. "I was not aware that the Collegium was allowed independent thought."

The Washer flushed an angry red, but held his ground, refusing to be baited by a man half his age who bore no obvious signs of rank, despite—or perhaps because of—his earlier error. "My business is not with you, young master, but the Vineart."

"You speak with us all, or not at all," Jerzy said. That comment earned him a quick, startled glance from Kaïnam beside him. This was Jerzy's home, and no other held sway in another man's House. Certainly, no lord could claim any rights at all within a vintnery. For Jerzy to state that, so bluntly; he was telling the Washer that he broke the Commandment of isolation to work with men of power, even if it was merely the disinherited son of a small Principality. And what the Washer would think of Ao and Mahault being included in that . . .

The Washer didn't seem at all taken aback by such heresy; perhaps it was no more than they expected from someone like Jerzy, accused apostate, masterless student, and threat, in the Collegium's eyes, to all that was. Or perhaps it was such a common thing now, that affront against Command, they could not afford to blink.

"If we might go inside, then?" the Washer suggested gently, keeping his shoulders soft, his hands well away from his body, as though to indicate that he was no threat.

Jerzy nodded and inclined his head to indicate that the Washer should walk with him. To Ao it was as though he had observed a player's scene, scripted and yet somehow unrehearsed, each so careful not to fumble a line.

The two seemed an odd pairing: a quick glance might think that the Washer was the master of the House and Jerzy the acolyte, but it was clear, as they moved under the green arch—still in full leaf even well into the Fallow season—onto the House grounds proper, who was master there.

"WHAT DO YOU think this means, him coming now?" Ao rolled his chair next to Kaïnam, the sound of wood moving against stone an oddly comforting noise, like the slap of a hull against water. Never tall, and now seated as he was, Ao's head barely came to Kaïnam's shoulder, but his voice carried easily to the princeling's ear.

"I have no idea. He was surprised that we were waiting for him, expected Jerzy to fall over in awe the moment a man of age and experience showed up, rather than the boy they sent before. That tells me he's spent most of his life within the Collegium walls, not on the road."

Most Washers were wanderers, spending their lives moving from one wayhouse to the next, preaching and giving Solace. But there were those who stayed behind, handling the day-to-day life and training of the next generation. Like House-keepers, maintaining the Collegium building and its daily affairs, save that there were no women among the Washers.

Kaï stared after the two men, not yet ready to follow. "In my experience, House-bound life breeds men prone to politics and overplayed manipulation, as much out of habit as need. But that does not mean we should underestimate him." The prince sighed. "Jerzy's playing out the courteous host . . . I suppose that means I get to be the abrasive lord."

"And me?" Ao kept pace with Kaïnam as they moved toward the House, the wheels of this new chair moving more easily than the old. "How shall I play it? Meek, unassuming, useless cripple?" Ao's voice dropped into a self-pitying tone, but his expression was bright, almost cheerful, the mischief that seemed to perpetually live in his eyes in full view.

"If it's possible for you to stay quiet that long, yes," Kaïnam said. "Until Jerzy decides otherwise." Kaïnam might have been Named-Heir, but he had been one son among many for most of his life, scion of a man who ruled the principality of Atakus without hesitation, and he had no difficulty giving the Vineart the lead on this.

The words of an old Atakuan prayer, a child's recitation to a sea god leagues and centuries distant, to give his liege good-sailing, came to Kaïnam's lips, unbidden, and he mouthed them silently, almost without realizing it.

In truth, Kaïnam did not *want* the lead in this. He might have been the one to first spot the greater net being thrown over them all, but his interest, even now, was to save his homeland from the disastrous course his father had steered it on to and have his revenge on the man who ordered his sister's murder, as though she were nothing more than a pawn to be sacrificed to lure out the king.

If he had to abandon other interests to accomplish that, no matter how dear they had become to him, he would, without hesitation. Jerzy knew this, even if the others did not.

"Right," Ao said, maneuvering his chair under the green archway, unaware of the way the leaves stretched, as though moved by a breeze, to touch his hands and hair as he passed by. Kaï noted, but when he touched the leaves, they did not react to his presence.

INSIDE THE ARCHWAY, they found Detta standing alone, scowling, at the open doors of the House, and no sign of the other two, or Mahault.

"They've gone into the courtyard," she informed them, her hands fisted at her ample hips, her voice harder than they had ever heard it before. "I would not let that snake into the master's rooms, not even if the dragon led him there itself."

Master Malech had died when last Washers entered the House. The fact that Washers had also died, or disappeared, at the same time, did not ease the House-keeper's anger.

Ao touched Detta's hand as he rolled past, lifting his hand from the wheel to do so, and the older woman's lined face smoothed out briefly. "Go then, both of you. I'll feel better if that man's soundly outnumbered."

There were only two ways to reach the Courtyard: through the kitchen or via the square chamber that led into the Vineart's private chambers in the right-hand wing. Ao's chair required the wider span of the kitchen entrance. They went through the now-deserted dining hall, the great wooden table now cleared and empty, the benches pushed back against the wall, and came out into the open space to find Mahault seated on the bench under the single tree, its bare branches draped with cloth to create a makeshift canopy against the midday sun.

She was dressed in a simple blue gown, and her feet were demurely shod in soft shoes, her golden-blond hair pinned back in a neat coil. No one looking at her would ever suspect she had only moments before been holding a crossbow aimed at a man's heart.

The Washer was seated opposite her in a chair that must have been pulled out from storage, a gracefully carved wooden piece far more formal than they had seen in daily use here. The two were already chatting softly, seemingly sharing nothing more important than a reflection on the weather of the day.

Clearly, some hurried scurrying had been occurring inside the House while they confronted the Washer out front.

Another chair, similarly shaped, was set at an angle to it, and Kaïnam took that, allowing Ao room to place his chair between the two so that he could watch the Washer without being in his direct line of sight. Clearly, the Washer's overlooking of Ao had been noted, and made use of.

Jerzy was pacing slowly, seemingly preoccupied with his own thoughts, waiting for the two latecomers to arrive and settle themselves.

"All right," Jerzy said, without turning around to see if they were listening, and Mahault leaned away from the Washer, subtly isolating him. He merely turned slightly in his chair to face Jerzy's back, aware that he was being manipulated, possibly still feeling wrong-footed and unwilling to protest.

The Vineart continued without turning, refusing to give their visitor the honor of face-to-face. "You had someone follow us from the docks, lurk and watch, spy on us, and, for all I know, send a message back to your Brothers to come with more men and weapons to take this vintnery by force."

"I assure you—" the Washer began, as though to protest the accusations.

"Be still," Kaïnam said sharply, falling into his role with ease.

"We have not been unaware of you," Jerzy continued, "nor have we left ourselves unprotected. Did you truly believe that you could walk a Vineart's lands, and not be discovered, and watched in turn?"

Jerzy turned then, his left hand raised. A pool of blue flames flickered, cupped in his palm. It was drylight, the same illumination that lit keeps and Houses throughout the Vin Lands, nothing to take the breath away, save for how tendrils of it moved up along Jerzy's bare arm, as though following the lines of his veins, as much a part of him as blood or flesh. And the fact that he had not touched a spellwine to create it.

"Did you truly believe that I would trust any man who wore the robes of Sin Washer, ever again?"

"We do not expect your trust," Edmun said softly, forcing his gaze from that flickering flame to look the Vineart directly in the face. "Not immediately. But you need to know that not all the Collegium agreed with the steps that were taken . . . before. Not all were behind the actions carried out. And there are . . . no small number who believe that the stance the Collegium has taken, officially, is . . . not wise."

Whatever they might have expected, or feared, the Washer's words did not match.

"Dissention within the Collegium?" Kaïnam asked, slightly incredulous.

"A difference of opinion on the best policy to implement," the Washer said, picking through his words like a man treading on sharp stones.

"A fine distinction," Mahault said. "And have those with this different opinion raised their voices to the Collegium elders?"

Edmun grimaced. "They . . . have not. We are few in number, still, and need . . . support, before we make our move. Those who met you at the dock were chosen because they had . . . shared views. We had thought that sending Oren, someone you knew already, would be better."

"Not particularly." Jerzy's voice was dry as dust.

"No. We see that, now."

"Oh-ha," Ao said, rubbing his hands together like a player's villain, unable to stay quiet, as Kaï had predicted. "Jer, they come to you for help in o'erthrowing their elders!"

Jerzy closed his hand around the flames, and they extinguished, silently and instantly.

"Is this true?" he asked, and only his gaze gave anything away, a fierce spark seemingly leaping from his hand into his eyes. "You would use me, use magic against Sin Washer's Heirs? Against the will of the Collegium itself?"

"No." The rebuttal was immediate, and the Washer stood as though to throw himself at an attacker, although to attack a Vineart in his own home would be suicide.

"No," he said again, visibly forcing his body to ease. "Not to overthrow. To . . . work around. To prevent the disaster that we, at least, can see coming. The disaster you know is on its way. We wish to protect the Collegium, to protect that which has served the Lands Vin well and faithfully for nearly two thousand years."

Edmun paused, his words chosen more carefully now, aware that he had not convinced any of them. "Washer Neth is on his way here, bearing his own orders—orders that we believe to be wrong, that will harm the Lands Vin, not save them. Of a certainty, they would bode ill for you, Vineart."

If not meant as a threat, it nonetheless had the edge of one.

"You have shown yourself to understand the enemy, to be aware of the threat. And so we would ask you to join us. To defeat the enemy that threatens us all."

Jerzy turned then, one hand resting lightly on his double-wrapped belt, his face still and cold as the Guardian's stone.

"You have delivered your message, Sahr Washer. Now I ask you to leave."

"Vineart . . ." The Washer swallowed, then nodded once. "Of course. You need time to consider your position. I will await your response. But I advise you, Vineart, not to take too much time, as Neth will likely arrive within days, and at that point . . ."

He let the words trail off and gave an eloquent shrug.

"Kaï, please accompany our visitor back to his horse."

The prince nodded, waiting until the Washer had gathered himself, and led him back out through the kitchen.

"Jer—" Mahault started to say, but he held up a hand to stop her.

"No. Just . . . no."

Jerzy was almost blinded by rage. Now, the Washers would come to him, ask his help? *His* help? After they had destroyed Giordan with their refusal to see what was happening, after they had allowed so many to die, to be destroyed? And then to threaten him with Neth's arrival, as though that was the worst fate they could offer . . . He paced back and forth, one end of the courtyard to the other, his anger increasing with every step. How dare they?

They had no idea what was coming. No idea what had already happened. More, they did not want to know, merely to sidestep it, make it all fade away. Did the others at the Collegium understand the magnitude of what they faced? Or did they see it all as mere game playing and politics? Was he, even now, being played? That thought cooled his temper, if not his anger. If he lost control of his emotions, he would be at their mercy. He needed to stay cool.

The news that Neth was coming this way did not surprise Jerzy; the older Washer would have known he would return to the vintnery. It also did not surprise him that Neth would be bringing orders, most likely, to take Jerzy into custody. That, Jerzy would not allow to happen. He had things to do here, not play whatever game the Collegium concerned itself with. Especially if the roots of their enemy were already set within that soil.

Roots. The thought stirred something again, a subtle worry. No, the roots were fine, the yards were ready-banked for the winter. There were no disturbances, there.

"What benefit would they gain?" Ao rubbed his palm against one knee as though it were true flesh, thinking out loud.

"They are afraid they are losing control," Kaïnam, having returned already, answered with confidence. "Any man with power seeks to hold power. Washers are Sin Washer's Heirs, not Sin Washer himself. The power they have comes from his name, their control over Vinearts rests upon the strict obedience to Command. Two thousand years of having the final say . . . stripped away by rebellion, if Jerzy is not contained. If they have a whisperer among them, that is assuredly what he says."

"Then why shouldn't we use that? We can manipulate them a fair sight better than they can us. Have Jerzy pretend to come inside, join them, and then use their contacts—"

Jerzy couldn't bear to listen any longer. Leaving them to their discussion, he went out the far doorway, through the small square hallway that led to his master's quarters—his quarters, now—and out into the yard. He did not stop to think, letting his anger and frustration carry him down the path, across the road, over the grass and into the neatly tended rows of vines where a handful of slaves were resetting the smudge-pots against the risk of frost.

The soil was cool, the vines bare, their rough-twisted texture harsh against his hands, and he gripped them as though he could pull a solution out of them by sheer force.

"What use are the Commandments, if they can be broken at will?" His voice sounded harsh as the vines, as though he had been screaming for hours, and he had no idea who he was asking—the silent gods had long since abandoned the world of men, and he could not bring himself to blame them. "If all there is, is power, then why should we not take it? If power is all that will save us, should we not save ourselves?"

He stopped, his jaw snapping shut, and there was silence; even the wind seemed to drop into silence, and the few slaves working nearby cowered, as though terrified that they had somehow caused his anger.

A flash of memory: *seeing the Master in the yard, his every step the sound of doom, trying so hard not to be noticed, not to draw attention to himself, knowing that not being noticed was how a slave survived . . .*

No matter how Jerzy tried to think of another way, it always came back to this. Sin Washer had given them each a role to play. Ao was taught to maneuver, to be quick and clever. Mahault learned to be strong and brave and true. Kaïnam was trained to be thoughtful and cautious, to inspire loyalty, and reward it in turn.

A slave learned to survive.

A Vineart was commanded to provide.

And there, the heart of the injustice of Sin Washer's Command, the subtle but iron-fisted punishment meted out to all who worked the vines. From slave to master, a Vineart did not get anything from this world. A Vineart *served*.

The thought rumbled inside him. He sacrificed, and served. Why should he not earn something, in turn? Why had Sin Washer cast them so far down, that even the most intimate aspect of themselves, the quiet-magic, needed to be hidden, denied? After all that Vinearts gave, how was that—he shied away from the word "fair," and finally wondered, as Ao might, how was that equitable trading?

Jerzy walked blindly for hours, taking rows at random, from the near edge to the furthest, stopping to stare up at the sky or listen to the night birds, and the rustle of small things hunting and being hunted in the underbrush. Slowly his thoughts cooled, and his body calmed, but he did not return to the House until the moon had risen full into the sky and the chill in the air drove him inside.

There would be frost by morning; he could feel the roots readying themselves for it.

The others were waiting for him in his study, as he had expected; the single steady light over his desk added to by the flickering tongues of two thick candles they had brought with them, still not knowing how to work the quiet-magic lights Malech had installed. Jerzy cast an uneasy eye over the open flame: he had nothing against fire, but not near so much wine, or so many important papers—and extinguished it with a cupping of magic even as the other lights came to life. The magelights filled the room more evenly, with less flickering, and yet the room seemed oddly dark.

It was not the light in the room but the shadows inside him that made it so.

Jerzy was not fanciful by any means, but he could almost sense the same shadows filling the Lands, coating the winter sun and casting everything into uncertainty.

And he did not know if he fought the shadows . . . or was part of it.

There was a tray with a pitcher of tai and several mugs on the side table. Jerzy might have wished for *vina* but acknowledged that he might need the stimulant more. Mahault and Ao already had mugs in hand, she curled with her legs underneath her on the old wooden stool Jerzy had used as a student, he with his chair against the wall. Kaïnam had taken the only other chair in the room, a battered structure that usually held a clutter of wineskins and manuscripts Malech had forgotten to put away. They had been talking about something in low tones, but the conversation faded when he came in.

"What are you going to do?" Mahault asked, even as Ao interrupted.

"You can't trust them."

Jerzy looked to Kaïnam, who was holding one of the discarded wineskins in his hand, turning it absently as though he had forgotten he had picked it up. "They might be telling the truth . . . the Collegium is made up of many men, and just as many opinions." The prince shrugged, setting the skin aside. "If there are those who believe that it is time to stand and fight . . . isn't that what you wanted? To drive a wedge between the factions of the Collegium, force them to confront their whisperers, and take action?"

"No. Or, yes. But Ao is right, we cannot trust them. Fortunately, that trust is not required, only a willingness to do what needs be done. If that is what we need to do."

"And what needs to be done?" Kaï asked.

Jerzy still had not told them his plan, mainly because he did not know it well enough to verbalize, yet. He thought he knew what was right, but . . . it was not merely this place, this moment he feared. Whatever he did, it would change everything. Everywhere. And he had not anticipated the Washers taking an active role, not in such a way.

"They have trained fighters," Mahault said, calculating, when Jerzy did not answer right away. "Not many, but enough. And wealth, enough to buy the contract of every solitaire, and freebanded fighting men. They could field an army, if you convinced them it was needed."

Jerzy started to sit in the chair behind the desk, then changed his mind at the last moment and remained standing. It had been what he wanted, the chance to strike back, to place a blow against Ximen that would stop him cold, keep the Lands Vin free of his manipulations. But now, the Washer's words in his memory, and the sensation of a world tangled in knotted roots, tangled and tied together . . . he was less certain.

"No. The Collegium may struggle within itself as much as it pleases. To bring Vinearts into that struggle, to put magic on one side or another, even if it were to lead, to do what we are agreed must be done . . . It would not end there, and it would not end well."

He had asked the Guardian once before: if Vinearts fought back, revealed their secret, the quiet-magic they had not shared, shown the true measure of their strength . . . what would happen then?

You would be powerful . . . and hunted, the dragon had said. *Feared . . . and abused. The structure would break and chaos would rule.*

The world was in balance. Two thousand years, on Sin Washer's back.

"The balance needs must be maintained."

"What?" Ao was staring at him as though he had suddenly started speaking an ancient dialect of Ettonian.

Jerzy made a helpless, frustrated gesture with his hands, then let them fall loosely to his sides. They didn't understand. They had never been slaves, forced to stand aside and accept what was done to them, without recourse, without argument. They did not understand how delicate a wedge the world rested on, how close they were to tumbling into the violent abyss the dragon had warned of. He barely understood it himself.

"If I stand with those who would break the Collegium, however well they word it, if I raise magic against Sin Washer's Heirs, what have I become?"

There was a reason the First Vine was broken, the roots shattered into legacies. The memory of what he had read, how the vine-mages behaved, turned into tighter and tighter knots with every example of their enemy's actions.

All that stood between men like that, and the Lands, were the Commands.

"Does it matter?" Mahault's voice was cool and practical, and Jerzy was reminded of what Kaïnam had said, how she saw the world as either allies, or enemies. "They are the only ones to offer any aid whatsoever. If we four are not enough to beat back the tide, might we four, plus even a splinter of the Collegium, be enough?"

"Jer . . . if they released you from the Commandments, you could . . ." Ao made a motion with his hands, a complicated swirling gesture. "You know . . . stop Ximen. Interfere. Use—use all the magic you've been gathering. Isn't that what we need to make happen? Isn't that the point?"

Jerzy began to pace, barely finding enough room, with three others in the room with him. He wove around their chairs, trying not to pay attention to the way they watched his every move, as though the answer might grow from his actions. Were they right? He had gone so far already, was this simply the next step? From slave to Vineart, his training would hold, as Sin Washer intended, and keep him from abusing that power. Or would his next move tumble him into an abyss? Did it matter, if the First Vine was truly gone, if he were able to bind up the fragments into his own quiet-magic? Three legacies . . . who was to say he could not use four, or all five?

Only to save the day. Only to defeat Ximen. Only to keep the peace. . . . No. It would not end there.

Those thoughts were not his, cool-hard and unspoken. The Guardian was inside him, leaning against him until his heart itself felt stilled to stone. The seductive pull of his dreams returned, winding tendrils around that rock, whispering of magic just beyond his reach, magic that could do all that he needed, and Jerzy did not know what to believe.

They had been going nearly nonstop since dawn and it was near midnight now: it was no wonder his head was spinning.

"They have no right to release him," Kaïnam said, cutting to the heart of the matter. "If they set aside the Commandments, they are as apostate as any. They would lose whatever authority they claim, and all the wealth in the world would not appease them for that. No matter what they need, they will not release him, and they will not be led by him."

Ao tilted his head, looking as though he wanted to argue the point.

"It's not a trading session, Ao," Mahault said.

"Of course it is," he said, surprised. "They want Jerzy, and want to know what he wants in order to agree. That's as basic a lesson in trading as it gets."

Jerzy felt his head tighten and ache, as though something were pushing and twisting it. They didn't understand. All of them, treating it as though it were a question of favors and alliances, weapons and strikes. They used magic, but they did not sense it, did not feel how it flowed . . . had no idea of the things that bound them all together, balance for balance. Sin Washer was a legend to them, a myth. Magic was a tool, a weapon. They did not understand, the way Jerzy was beginning to, how very much more it might be. How much more connected to the world it was.

A vine might be shattered . . . but the roots remained.

"The Guardian warned me," Jerzy said. "It saw worse to come, if the Commandments were broken." Specifically, the dragon had warned him against revealing how Vinearts were not bound by incantations the way others were, how they could adapt and expand the magic, using their own nature, the quiet-magic, in their blood.

It all came back to that. The quiet-magic.

His companions did not know how much he had gained working with Giordan, from interacting with the unblooded grapes. His experiences on the ship, using a legacy he had not been trained in. Invoking the figurehead into something near-living. Twining legacies to stop Kaïnam from attacking him on the training ground. All these things, small, important . . . and, when he paused to consider them, unnerving.

What worried him most, however, what turned his sweat cold and his bowels to water, was what they did not know of the tendrils of power he could feel spreading underfoot, across every part of the Lands Vin, how they haunted his dreams, haunted *him*. They did not know, could not understand, even if he tried to explain to them, how it all seemed to be changing his quiet-magic into something else, something not entirely under his control.

Slave to Vineart, stressed like the vines he tended, crushed and crafted like mustus, used like spellwine. Magic makes the man. But when the man is reshaped from what he was meant to be—what then does he then make of the magic?

The Guardian's weight pushed against him again, making it harder to breathe much less think. The dragon was there to advise, not enforce, but it disapproved, strongly, of where Jerzy's thoughts were going. He rubbed at his forehead, trying to make the ache in his head disappear. Part of him was desperate to share his fears, but the hard weight of the Guardian stopped him, even as the words clawed into his throat.

You are Vineart.

It was a reminder, and a warning. Others might use magic, but only a Vineart could shape and control it. Only a Vineart understood the risks, the responsibilities. A Vineart stood between power and magic, protecting one from the other. People did not matter, feelings and friendship and even suffering did not matter, only the balance. A Vineart served.

The thought struck him as though he had taken one of Kaïnam's flat blows to his chest. There was no reward. There was no equitable trade. There simply was obedience, to prevent the annihilation the prince-mages had once threatened. That was why he recoiled from the offer the Washers had made, why the thought of joining with them, even to protect the Lands Vin, even to protect himself, made his mouth turn sour. The Washers should have understood this: it was their legacy, to maintain the balance. To protect the Vinearts—even from themselves.

So what would happen, after he rejected this offer, when Neth arrived?

The Guardian had no helpful—or unhelpful—advice there.

"Blast and rot!" Ao's exclamation shook him from his worried thoughts. "Jer, in all this, I forgot! A message arrived, just before the Washer. From Atakus."

Kaïnam moved faster than they had ever seen him, on his feet and in Ao's face, his hand outstretched. "Give it to me."

"Yes, all right, hold on," Ao said, digging into his belt pouch. "I shoved it in here when red riding boy came up. It didn't seem like the kind of thing we'd want to discuss, just then." He found the message and handed it over with a careful relief, as though feeding a wild cat with his fingers, unsure how many digits he would draw back.

Kaïnam slit open the seal and unrolled the message, a long, narrow sheet of paper covered with a careful hand. He turned away from the others, reading intently.

"What?" Ao started to ask, then hushed as Mahault looked at him fiercely, warning him off. She and Ao had received word from their families already. Kaïnam had not. "Kaï?" she asked, more gently.

"My father is dead." The princeling's voice was wooden, his body stiff and awkward, at odds with his usual sailor's grace. "My brother Nilëas now is Principal of Atakus."

Jerzy felt himself retreat a step, although he did not move. A slave did not have family, a Vineart belonged only to his vines, so although he could hear the pain in Kaïnam's voice, he did not know what it meant, or how to respond to it.

Ao lifted his hand, resting it on Kaïnam's arm, and the other man did not shake it off, still staring down at the missive. "Your brother . . . is that . . . a good thing?" For Atakus, for them . . . the question remained open for however Kaï wished to hear it.

Kaïnam put his hand up to his forehead, fingertips touching his brow, covering his face briefly as though to hide from the world, then he reached back and pulled at the leather thong holding his hair back, letting it fall down into his face in a gesture of mourning. Despite that, his voice remained steady as he continued speaking.

"Nilëas informs me that the barrier remains intact . . . but whatever resources I need to bring our sister's killer to justice are mine, and the moment I am convinced that the danger is gone, he will order Edon to remove the protective spell and restore Atakus's name among the Lands Vin."

What Kaïnam had wanted, hoped for. All it took was an old man's death.

They were frozen, four figures, uncertain of what to do, how to respond. Ao moved forward, his hand lifting to rest against Kaï's back, but for once, even he was silent.

"Master Edon will do this?" Mahault's practical nature overcame the sorrow of the moment. Kaïnam flinched, but nodded. "He has agreed," and his voice was confident enough that it put their doubts to rest.

There was another silence after that, as each of them considered what this would mean.

"My folk, and the sailors of Atakus . . . the information they could gather . . . And patrols! No ship would pass undetected through that." Ao was clearly tallying up the game counters, thinking in terms of attack and counterattack. Suddenly, they did not need the Washers. Ships and coin, driven by the undoubted anger of Atakus at being used, unblemished by madness and counseled by Kaïnam.

"With Jerzy to lend his magic in defense, maybe bring other Vinearts as well, if we can convince them, we could strike a blow that would draw Ximen's attention, make him aware that we are not to be plucked like overripe fruit." Mahault latched onto Ao's thought, her voice sharp and strong, determination so fierce Jerzy could taste it like the spice of a firewine. "And then follow through, sail into his own harbor and defeat him on his own lands."

"Stop him and his folk from ever trying this again," Kaïnam agreed, his usually measured thinking washed under by fresh grief and the renewed desire for revenge.

Vineart, you must be careful.

The Guardian was a creature of pattern, of tradition; its stone moved, and spoke, but it did not live, while it displayed new abilities at need, it did not grow, or change. Jerzy clung to it with one hand, but his thoughts ranged beyond. They were thinking like soldiers. Fighters. But they faced a mage, not swords or cudgels.

The Commandments prohibited the blending of magic and leadership of men. Never again were there to be prince-mages, never again such a danger to the world, unchecked. And yet, was not Ximen a greater threat than even that? Sin Washer had been a demigod, but the gods themselves were not infallible, and they took no care with humanity, now. He could not challenge the Washers, he would not upset the balance, but neither could he sit back and allow another to do damage.

Jerzy's quiet-magic surged within him, uncalled. There was too much building inside him, the trickle only recently discovered grown suddenly into a rushing stream, pushing at the banks of his control.

And under it all, the gentle, insidious pushing of his dreams, tendrils wrapping around his legs, pulling him down into a seething vat of power.

Magic was power. Power was meant to be used. The temptation to pull the magic from his flesh was like an actual thirst, and he shuddered, even as the magic urged him to use it.

Vineart.

"I know, Guardian," he said out loud. "I know."

The desire tempted, sorely tempted, with a flush throughout his body he now understood was akin to the lust a man might feel for sex. But a Vineart was nothing more than a slave. And slaves learned control.

That thought spawned another, and the pieces shifted and grew in his mind, the vague plan of luring the mage within reach suddenly clear in his mind. It could work. But not the way the others were traveling. . . .

"If we are to do this, it must be subtle, as our enemy is not. Roots underneath him, reaching up to the surface, to catch and tangle him unawares."

Like the roots that trembled in his nightmares. Were they meant to suggest not a threat to him, but a threat he might become?

"Kaïnam. The man you spoke with in Caul, who disliked the way his king was thinking."

"The Spymaster?"

"Yes. Contact him. Offer him the chance to be known as the man who reopened the port of Atakus. But first, he must help us. . . ."

As he played out his thought, an evil grin grew on Ao's face, and even

Mahault looked intrigued. Kaïnam's body eased slightly, and when the Vineart was finished, turned and made a formal bow to Jerzy, a war-lord acknowledging his leader.

Vinearts might be slaves. But a wise slave used whatever it had, to survive.

THE *HOPE OF RAIN* was a scouting vessel, not the pride of the Caulic Navy by any shot, but she was a strong ship, fast and agile, and accustomed to odd orders. She carried no troops, only a scaled-down crew who could, at need, fight, a captain with ties to the High King's sister, and a small, white-haired man who was not as old as he looked, not as harmless. His name was Aron, and he reported directly to the Spymaster of Caul.

And in their hold, they carried three passengers who took no food, only water, and slept restlessly, one awake while the other two dreamed. Witches, the men called them, and spat on the ground at the very thought. Bad luck to carry magic, for all that no harm had ever come to the *Hope* while the three women traveled below.

"The fish have gone elsewhere," the Captain said, his weather-beaten face worried. "No spinners, no birds, either. Bad sign. Something's lurking. Another damned sea-beast, I'll wager."

"Anything that big will follow the fish," Aron said, barely paying attention to the conversation. The Captain had been grumbling since they entered Atakuan waters that morning, obeying orders carried direct from the lord spymaster via the three corbies below.

Aron distrusted magic on principle; he was old-fashioned enough to spit when Vinearts were mentioned, but his master commanded he use the witches, and so he obeyed. The Captain preferred to trust in the stout timber and trained crew rather than any amber liquid soaked into that timber and women's nonsense-chanting, and so he simply ignored it, as much as he could. But even he, with his royal connections, knew who gave the true commands.

"And what of above-surface?"

"Crew reported one flag, a few hects to the eastward, just before dawn."

Aron nodded, and noted that down. "Colors?"

The Captain hawked and spit onto the weathered planks of the deck. "Black."

Pirates were on the rise since last winter, but that was none of their concern; these were not Caulic waters, and since the destruction of the fleet sent to find Atakus, few Caulic-backed vessels came this way to be disturbed by brigands. Let the local islands deal with these intruders, if they wished.

The *Hope* did not want to be here, not so near where their kin had disappeared, but Aron's orders, and the Captain's responsibility, were to follow any ships coming from outland, and note what they did, where they went, and if they interacted with any others on the seas.

Aron did not know why they had been set to this duty, and he did not wonder at it; he merely did as ordered, and trusted his master to make sense of his reports.

"Should we follow?"

Eastward was back toward the Vin Lands, back toward land. Odds were that the pirates, having also failed to locate the hidden port of Atakus, were now looking to raid the outlying islands to make some profit. They would not lead the *Hope of Rain* to anything useful.

Aron looked out over the endless waves, his eyes squinting closed against the reflection of the sunlight. On the other hand, if the pirates were truly desperate, they would not hesitate to attack another ship were they to encounter it, and might even go after one deliberately. The *Hope of Rain* would not tempt them, but any ship carrying an unknown banner could be carrying untold wealth in its hold. What surer way to find a school of fish than to follow a fish eater?

"Old man?"

Aron did not take affront at the sailor's words, or his tone: he was, in fact, an old man, and had seen and heard far more offensive things in his time.

"No," he said finally, dropping his gaze from the glittering waves and back to the relatively soothing maps on his hand. "We are here now to watch over Invisible Atakus, and so we shall."

Chapter 11

The morning after the Washer's appearance, Jerzy began writing the details of the unfolding plan into the leather-bound journal he had found among his master's belongings, the pages empty, as though waiting for him to begin. His lettering was not smooth, but Detta had taught him well enough to be legible, and he was determined to mark down as much as he could remember of what had occurred. Some day, however this ended, he might need to refer back . . . or someone else might need to know what happened.

He was the master of a House holding a conspiracy to undermine the Commands, laid down by a demigod, meant to safeguard the Lands Vin, for the good of the Lands Vin. Even if they succeeded, and survived, it would take some explaining to, well, explain.

The thought, in his exhaustion-thick mind, made him laugh, a short, harsh bark. If the Washers did not burn the vintnery, and everything in it, before they were done. If Ximen did not defeat them, destroy all traces of what had been, and take the Lands for his own, some prince-mage of old come again.

Jerzy put down the pen, blotting his work carefully, and stretched his arms over his head, feeling muscles crackle. His eyes felt gritty, his face remained flushed no matter how much cold water he splashed on it, and somehow the facts seemed both muddy and clear in his mind. Only magic could defeat magic. Yet, magic could not be used—not in the quiet-magic form, the way it was most powerful—as a reliable, consistent weapon. Why not? Jerzy did not know—he was no scholar of Altenne, and he had no access to them, now, to ask.

"Rot, I don't even know if they still *are*." There had been no communication from that part of the Lands, despite birds sent to postings there. For all Jerzy knew, anything beyond the mountains, Altenne, and Corguruth, had fallen into chaos.

There was a pitcher of twice-brewed tai at his elbow, and he poured another mug and gulped it down, not even noticing the taste.

Somehow, Ximen was using blood to intensify and corrupt his magic, sending tendrils into unsuspecting lands, worms into unsuspecting ears, destroying even Vinearts who should have been protected. But how could they have known? So long in the balance, how could they have expected one of their own would war on them?

Jerzy knew him now, guarded against him. Was ready to turn the war back onto him, to balance the Lands again. Magic to magic.

Ximen would come. He could not refuse, not if he wanted— needed—the lure Jerzy held out, the hint of weathervines and unblooded grapes to graft onto his own twisted magic, the one piece he still lacked to become as the prince-mages of old.

And when he took the lure, when Ximen came looking for Jerzy directly, what then?

Magic to magic. Vinearts were not as the mages of legend. Quiet-magic, the innate strength of a Vineart, could not be used to attack, to initiate a strike. That had been the lesson of the fight session, Jerzy suspected. To defend, to repel, to injure, yes. The firespell, used offensively, to warn slaves off from where they should not be. A healspell, turned backward to cause weakness in an attacker. Defensive moves . . . no. Passive moves.

There was something in all that, the solution to everything, waiting for him, tied somehow to the awareness in his dreams. But unlike magic, the answer did not rise up when called, and unlike fighting, it did not come with practice. It merely lurked just out of reach, until Jerzy's head ached from the effort of coaxing it closer. Or that might have been the lack of sleep; even as a slave, Jerzy had gotten a full night of sleep. Now, he was fortunate if he managed half that, and no amount of tai could compensate for long.

Jerzy shook his head and turned the page of the journal, inking the next letter with careful deliberation, letting the worry fade to the back of his mind. You could not harvest before the fruit was ready. Focus on the task at hand.

The slaves.

"I know." He kept writing, trying to let himself think only of what he wanted to say, careful not to blot the page. Trust the Guardian to remind him of yet another problem to be dealt with. Not that he had forgotten it. Like Neth, the uncertainty of what that man's arrival might bring, the unease nibbled at him.

A slave that would leave the yard without direct order, who would spy on his master . . . unusual. Two? Impossible. Even in these uncertain times, even with the changes occurring . . . it should have driven them to stay low, out of sight, not risk everything.

They were drawn to you.

The Guardian said no more, and Jerzy shook his head, not understanding.

They sensed the magic.

Understanding came, not from the Guardian's words, but his own memory. They sensed it the way he had sensed it, as a slave, in the grapes he tended and harvested. The way he had known, somehow, that not-so-distant day, that the mustus from the first crush he had worked was not acceptable.

They had the Sense. They were potential Vinearts, being shaped and formed by the vines they tended.

Or they are being pushed by something else. One slave with potential was rare enough, Malech had told him. Two at once, and willing to lurk and spy? It was out of the natural order. Jerzy had not sensed a taint around them, had not felt it anywhere other than in the birds that had attacked them, but that did not mean it did not exist. Jerzy could not bring himself to believe that the stone walls of the vineyards, and the stone wings of the Guardian, could protect them forever, or even for very long.

The world beyond pressed closer, the unrest in the world touching even here; his nightmares attested to that.

As though he summoned it, the sensation of roots growing and stretching upward underneath his feet returned, stronger and closer than before; a sense that all he need do was reach down and touch it, and . . .

And what? Jerzy hesitated, desire and fear holding him evenly. The Guardian pressed a sense of caution at him, a need to be careful. This was unknown, and therefore dangerous.

Jerzy twitched, for the first time feeling the Guardian's weight not as comfort, but imposition, frustration. The nightmare frightened him, but at the same time it was seductive, the fear almost a thrill, the hint of something to come, if he would only take it in hand, take it into himself. Power. The kind of power that he needed, to match his enemy.

Driven by impulse, the need to prove that he was not afraid, that he was no longer a slave to stay low and hide from notice, that he knew what he was doing, Jerzy let himself reach out, following the seductive whisper that stroked along his skin, reached into his chest and pulled him in.

Power. Cold, fierce, and unrelenting, it rushed into his veins, scraped his skin, and made his mouth pucker as though he'd just taken a gulp of *vin magica* when he expected *ordinaire*, had inhaled fire instead of air. Roots, thick and twisting, deeper in the earth than any roots could grow, wrapped around salty rock and twisted through heavy flame, surging with a magic Jerzy had felt only once before, when he touched the feral vines of Irfan.

No. His body shuddered as though under assault. Not the unblooded vines, but similar. Deeper, wider, more vast; like being immersed in a vat of mustus that never ended, that constantly moved, bringing skins from the top and sending raw juice to the top, sucking in air and turning itself continually into something new, something fierce and cold and strong and too much for Jerzy to bear.

He dropped the connection, willing himself away, shooting through the dirt and back into the air, gasping for breath even as he shuddered, certain that there were tangles of root around his ankles, trying to pull him back in. It felt as though an entire day must have passed but the study was the same; the ink still wet on the page in front of him.

Jerzy waited for the dragon to say something, but it did not seem to notice anything unusual, still in its customary place over the doorframe, looking as though it had been carved out of the wall itself. Whatever he had just experienced, it had been his alone, so deep within his quiet-magic that even the Guardian could not follow.

Jerzy felt as though he should be staggering, woozy from too much ale, sick from the motion of the sea, although the ground was firm under his feet. Unblooded. Magic itself, unblooded. The word suddenly took on a new meaning, the taste of it flooding his mouth and nose. Envined magic, even the unblooded vines of Irfan, were softer, melded to those who worked it. Tamed and controlled, as Vinearts were tamed and controlled, each broken to the yoke of the other.

This was not a feral vine. This was *wild.*

"Dragon."

Yes?

"When the First Vine was broken . . . what happened to it?"

There was a long silence, and a sense of puzzlement.

"I mean . . ." Jerzy struggled to explain what he was asking. "The stories, the way the Washers tell it, they all say that Sin Washer's blood ran through it, breaking it into the legacies."

Yes.

"But what happened to it?" Not all the unblooded vines had been changed; he knew that now, although he had not shared that fact with anyone, not even the Guardian. Did it know, anyway? How much did it simply take from his memories?

It changed. Became lesser.

And that, for the Guardian, was as far as the answer went. What had been was no more. But Jerzy, with the awareness of what lay deep underground, in the core of the world, was not so certain. Something remained there, fierce and cold, too powerful for any mortal to touch, much less use. But its existence might explain how Ximen reached so far, yet remained safe-rooted within his own yard.

The Vine: not broken but shattered. Not the First Growth, but what remained, ungentled by Sin Washer's blood. Deep-seated roots, sunk into the bones of the world. Power, waiting below the surface.

Had his master known of it? Was this something he, Jerzy, would have learned, or would they have averted their eyes, letting what was beyond Command stay untouched, unused? Or had it been hidden for ages, the secret of apostates and fools?

And if a Vineart were to match that cold power, and blood?

Giordan's single drop of blood, to tame an entire cask of mustus. Ximen's creatures, filled with blood. Magic in their blood, the connection between magic and creature. Whispers in the ear, whispers in the blood, turning men from their traditional roles, cracking the foundations of the world.

His own blood felt cold, sluggish in the aftermath, the power he had touched leaving him raw and small.

Something bothers you.

Jerzy paused and glared up at the Guardian. Had he known it, he was a perfect echo of Master Malech, caught mid-thought by the Guardian's prodding.

"Something? Everything." The sickness turned from cold to heat as Jerzy let his anger rise. "Call me Vineart if it suits you, let others treat me as I am, but in truth I'm scarce more than a student myself, and no idea if we'll survive another week, much less a year. We play at magic, we play at power, but the truth is as far beyond us as the valley is to a worm, the ocean to a single fish. And the others, they think I can . . . I can do something. Anything. And I can't. Not without destroying everything I'm supposed to save."

The fury ran down from him as suddenly as it came, leaving him panting like a tired dog. Lashing out against the Guardian served no purpose.

"And now these slaves . . . anything that is out of season, now, is suspect, Guardian. Even slaves."

There was a sense of something moving in the air around him, slow and heavy. *If they are a threat . . .*

Jerzy felt hollowed out and dry. Too much piled onto him, too much to bear. But the Guardian was right. If the Washers themselves had been influenced, then nothing could be secure. A slave who was drawn to magic, who had even the merest glimmer of the sense, was a potential Vineart. Rare, searched for. Worth all the rest of the slaves together. Two, in one season? It might be to balance out those who had been lost . . . or they might be tainted. A slave who had the Sense could so easily be pulled in by Ximen's whispers, taken whole, without the ability to resist.

Jerzy had no way of knowing. And he could not take the risk.

You are Vineart.

He had not seen them, not clearly, but it was enough; the Guardian was able to find them: huddled against the near wall of the sleep house, knees bent, their heads bent together. They had a piece of machinery in front of them and files in their hands: they were sharpening the tiller, so that it would be ready come spring, when it was time to break up the soil and weed the rows again.

Ordinary work, the sort of thing he might find any slave doing during the slower hours of winter. There was no scent of the taint around them, no feel of wrongness or danger.

Too much at risk, if he was wrong. He could allow no weakness within his walls. This was not attack, but defense. But how . . . ?

The memory of the servant in Irfan came to Jerzy. How simple a thing it had been to let the vines that wrapped around his chest, holding him in the chair, tighten. The sound of his rib cage as it cracked, the gasping of breath as a vine around his neck turned into a noose, the way his dark-skinned face had become tinged with blue, and his jaw had hung open, white froth on his lips . . .

Jerzy had not touched him. He had not needed to. The unblooded grapes had surged at his lightest thought, had done what was needed. He had blamed the vines, let it take responsibility.

"These are healvines," he said, barely a whisper. Vines he had tended, weeded, harvested, and protected.

What heals may also kill.

The Guardian's mental voice was as it had always been: cool, uninflected, unjudging. It had acted once without directive, when it brought Jerzy back when the House was attacked and Malech killed. If Jerzy did not act . . . would it?

He closed his eyes, but the realization remained, burning like spellfire, cold and bright. "I am Vineart," he said quietly. The Guardian might do many things, but not this. It was a tool, created to protect, not destroy. If what Jerzy had touched was indeed the remnants of the old magic, if Sin Washer had softened that cold, fierce magic with his blood, warmed it to malleability . . . he had also made Vinearts fierce enough to match it. To do what must be done.

Vinearts stood alone. Vinearts served. Vinearts stood between the cold power and human flesh. That realization did not shake Jerzy this time so much as ground him. This was his purpose, to shape the magic, make it useful . . . keep it safe.

His sense of the dragon remained, cool and firm, but his thoughts were his own. Jerzy felt his mouth water, quiet-magic rising, a mingled sense of healwine, firevines and weathervines, and the distant bitter-tart flavor of the unblooded grapes, lingering at the back of his tongue. Firewine, to dry and sere flesh. Healwine, reversed to deny vigor. Earthwine, solid and steady, the pulse of the earth, to make things grow . . . or fail. And the faintest remnant of aetherwine, the memory of it still in his awareness, to draw the very spark of breath and cast it away. Only weather stood apart, present but not needed.

He knew all the elements, how each moved and flowed, the ripened swirls of power. All the legacies, the taste of the unblooded grapes, tangled in what already existed, forming something new, fierce, terrifying.

There was no decantation for this, no learned words to direct the magic, only an innate understanding of the magic within him. The magic that was him. The two figures blurred and faded, the files dropping from their hands even as their eyes widened and their chests heaved.

"Die," Jerzy said, his voice soft as an evening breeze, gentle as the newest curling leaf, as unyielding as the sun at summer's peak.

In that instant he *felt* the House move around him, the beat of the dragon's wings, the heat of the kitchen's hearth, the shifting of the horses in their stalls, whisking tails and flickering ears as a slave moved down the aisle to groom them, the sound of Mahault's voice as she spoke to someone within the House, and the clatter of Ao's wheels, the feel of a map unrolling under Kaïnam's capable hands . . . Detta, her feet a steady rhythm against the worn flagstone steps, the slap of the House keys at her waist. A heady sense of disorientation took him, his thoughts dizzy, his body trembling.

And then he was back in his study, ink staining his fingertips where he had clenched the pen, a blot on the page he had just completed.

He felt . . . cold. Dry. Hollow inside, like rotted wood and empty flask.

The overseer, or another slave, would find the bodies. They would be disposed of, and nothing would ever be said. Slaves died. Had anyone known what he had done, had he gone into the field himself and cut their throats, nothing would ever be said. He was Master. His was the hand of life or death.

The dragon rested, cool and heavy, within his chest.

Jerzy licked his lips once, tasting the sweat on them, and carefully tore out the blotted page, resetting the pen and beginning the report again.

The act of writing anything now seemed like folly. The likelihood was high that their enemy would win; that he, and the others, would die in some fashion in the very near future; that the Lands Vin would crumble and fall. If he, Jerzy could not find some way to strike back, that likelihood was near-certainty. And yet . . . Vineart Giordan's master had left behind only books of drawings, the lifetime of study. Giordan had treasured those books, and given them to Jerzy. Jerzy had left them behind, when he fled Aleppan, and he regretted more than seemed reasonable, losing that connection to those who had gone before.

Jerzy had possibly just killed the slave who would have followed him.

Seh veh. The seasons do not end.

Jerzy didn't know what the Guardian meant, but somehow it eased the dry, hollow feeling inside him, filling him with a sense of inevitability. Malech had foreseen the need for the Guardian—had he known why, what role it would play?

It did not matter. He trained the vines, crushed the grapes, crafted the wine, incanted the spells and let them loose into the Lands. What he had done was done.

Jerzy picked up the pen once more, dipped it into the inkwell, and completed the page, a methodical recounting of every detail, the way he had been trained. For whoever might come, after.

Finished, Jerzy left the last page open to let the ink dry, and stood up, stretching his arms overhead again until he could feel his spine crack, his shoulders pressing down the way Cai had taught him, to prevent his body from becoming too stiff after sitting so long. As he did so, his thoughts slid into place as well, and an idea occurred to him.

Jerzy moved around the desk to look at the map that hung on the far wall in place of the ancient tapestry that had been there. The tapestry had shown the known Lands Vin, as they had been centuries ago. Where once the lands had been torn apart by prince-mages waging war against each other, there had been two thousand years of relative peace and prosperity, the ambitions of the land-lords kept in check by the Vinearts' control over available magic.

This map, more recently drawn, was the result of Ao and Kaï's combined work, the trader's careful hand marking the results of their recent journey. Jerzy now had the location of every vineyard and every lord or prince who had reported disturbances, or been somehow marked by the taint. Points of attack. For Ximen—and for them.

Jerzy studied the map, noting how each point connected to the other, tracing the invisible lines between with his finger. Kaïnam's original theory, that the attacks were a net, drawing the Lands Vin into some kind of confrontation, seemed born out. They had been maneuvered, all of them: Washer, Vineart, and land-lord. Driven by fear, panic, the way a wolf might harry a flock of sheep, but instead of picking off the weakest, the strongest were taken. The strongest . . . or the most useful.

His plan would work. If he could make himself such a target, something too strong to be resisted, to useful to ignore, Ximen would come, ignoring all else.

The Guardian protected House Malech too well. For his plan to work, Jerzy needed to flaunt himself. To do that, Jerzy needed not to avoid Ximen, but find him.

"Foreseer wine would be useful about now," he said to the Guardian. "I don't suppose Master Malech left any hidden in the racks?"

No.

No, of course not. It was among the rarest of the rare aethervines, and a wonder that Malech and his master Josia had enough to see the need for the Guardian. He would have to do this some other way. Turning back to the pile of journals he had pushed to the side of the desk, Jerzy flipped through the pages until he found the passage he had been looking for. Not a decantation, but the offhand mention of Master Vineart Bradhai, who had rid the world of true sea serpents by tracking them to their undersea lair.

Jerzy didn't have foreseer wine, and the last time he had attempted scrying he had been sent not toward the source but the strongest taint, but that did not mean he was giving up.

Master Malech had not been able to identify the legacy used to craft the serpents, and Jerzy had not been able to find the source of the magic, distracted by the taint itself. Up until now, Jerzy had tried to trace the path of the taint, tracking it back to the source. But if what they had learned was true, and this Ximen worked through others, channeling his magic across the Western Sea, then it was doubtful a straightforward scrying spell would lead them directly to the source. Ximen had covered his tracks too well for that.

The traditional means did not seem to work against their enemy.

To find him, Jerzy would have to step away from tradition. Willingly, knowingly break Commandment. No way to hide behind ignorance or half measures. There was one step yet he had not taken.

He swallowed, raised his hand to the back of his neck, threading his fingers through his hair. The urge to talk to the others, to seek their opinions, came and passed. He walked over to the rack of bottles against the wall and selected one, a golden-brown glass with a wax stopper in the mouth. Aetherwine. He could sense it, even stoppered, untasted. It did not linger within him the way his own legacies did, nor the weathervines he had taken from Vineart Giordan, but an awareness, like voices in conversation, heard from another room.

These were not foreseer wines. But that might not matter, for what he needed. Knowing what he knew, and what he had to do.

Jerzy uncorked the bottle with his teeth and, with his free hand, lifted the silver tasting spoon from his belt and poured a portion of the spellwine into the shallow cup. It glittered darkly, shifting shades of red. Holding the spoon with one hand, Jerzy recorked the bottle with his teeth and placed it back into the rack, moving with the smooth motion of long practice.

Tied to the map with one of Detta's needles was one of the feathers taken from the bird-beast that had attacked them, while just below it hung one of the long fangs scavenged from the sea-serpent corpse. Flesh and magic, bound together. Jerzy studied them, considering their nature, their origins. Two items were not as good as three, and five would have been better, but two was what he had.

"Blood. Blood . . . not his blood, but passing under his hands." The habit of speaking through his work remained, and he could feel the Guardian's intent presence at his back, although the dragon did not speak. "The blood was on his hands."

Jerzy raised the spoon and let each item dip briefly into the spellwine, just enough for the color to stain the tip of the dun-colored feather, and the slender, curved fang to set up a swirl of motion across the spellwine's surface.

Decantations were for pre-set spells, to trigger the incantation already pre-set. For the second time in an afternoon, what Jerzy was about to do had no decantation that he knew or had been able to find; if it existed, it was lost, along with all the other spells he would never learn from his master.

But this time, it was not merely a question of redirecting a spellwine he knew well, but crafting something new, entire. It was possible; tradition aside, all spells came from nothing, once. But that never meant it was safe.

"Guardian?"

Here.

Jerzy leaned against that rock-solid reassurance. Once before, when he had miscast a spell and caused near-disaster, the dragon had held off the worst of the effects, kept anyone within the House from coming to harm. Master Malech had not known the dragon could do that, had never had need for the dragon to do any such thing. In one long year, Jerzy had discovered more to the spellcrafted Guardian than even the Guardian itself knew it could do.

The Vineart sent a quick but heartfelt request to Sin Washer, that they would discover no new ability today, and placed the spellwine onto his tongue.

"Old to new," he said, careful to enunciate each word, even with the liquid resting on his tongue. A much-used decantation carried itself, despite the speaker; this new decantation needed to be clear. "Blood to bone. The one who looks for me, mine to find." He paused, letting the magic gather itself, burning as brightly as he could manage, visualizing himself as a beacon in the night sky, and then, remembering to speak softly, an entreaty as much as a command, whispered, "Go."

THE NEXT MORNING, as dawn lifted over the ridge, Jerzy sent a slave running down the road, a red kerchief tied about his arm and a short message on its tongue. Several hours later Mahault, wearing not the graceful dress of his last visit but sturdy trou and vest like a solitaire, met their guest at the door. She exuded a steely grace that did not allow him time or opportunity to gape at his surroundings as they passed through the main hall and into the Vineart's study.

"Vineart Jerzy."

"Washer."

"Please," Jerzy said, making a gesture with his left hand, "be seated."

The Washer, his face older-looking than the last Jerzy had seen him, adjusted his robes and sat in the single chair set opposite the desk.

They stared at each other, assessing: Jerzy sat in the high-backed wooden chair, his finest robe over a shirt and trou, polished boots of smooth leather on his feet, and the ring that had been his master's on the third finger of his left hand, the only finger it would fit, the others being too thick. The metal felt cool against his skin, and he resisted the urge to twist it.

He was not a Master Vineart. He had no right to wear the ring, taken from his Master's hands before he was placed on his pyre. But it had been there, on the desk when he came down to prepare for this meeting, and the Guardian would not have placed it there if it were not the right thing to do.

"I will not accede to your proposal," he said abruptly, before the Washer had the chance to speak again.

"You cannot—"

"Do not tell me what I can and cannot do, Washer." Jerzy's voice was a low growl, startling even himself. "You have asked me to abandon all that I have been taught, all that *your kind* have taught, in order to . . . what?"

"To save the Lands Vin."

Jerzy could not remember the last time he had slept well. The first night home? Or had it been onboard the *Heart?* The lack of sleep coupled with the draining aftermath of his spell the day before made Jerzy too irritable for diplomatic speech. "It is too late to save what was. It was too late when your Collegium refused to hear what my master and I warned them of. Too late, when Vinearts felt they had no choice but to break Commandment to survive, when land-lords turned to take magic with an open hand, and no one slapped them down. Too late, when people died, and the Heirs of Sin Washer were too busy playing games to hear their cries."

Jerzy's voice stayed even as he spoke, even as the Washer's face turned an unpleasant shade of red, as though he were coming down with the plague.

"Your words are . . . not unfair," the Washer said, letting his own anger fade away. "I think that you are making a mistake, but I will not belabor the point. Nor will I threaten you—it would be both pointless, and foolish. Brother Neth will arrive soon, as you have been warned. Whatever your arguments with him, he has remained aloof from the tremors within the Collegium; we are agreed that he need know nothing about this?"

Odd, that they wished to protect him—or protect themselves from him? Either way, Jerzy did not care. He nodded once in agreement, and the Washer stood as though to leave. "This was a situation not of our choosing, a time not of our wishing. If we meet again, I hope—"

"Sit down," Jerzy said, his tone mild but unmistakably a command. "I said I would not accede to your proposal. However, I have one of my own."

The other man sat back down, and listened.

*　　*　　*

SOME TIME LATER, the Washer exited the study, his expression thoughtful, nodding curtly at members of the Household as he passed but not speaking to anyone. Mahault watched him leave from her position in the main hall, then ran for the study.

By the time she made it through the door, Ao and Kaïnam were already there, Jerzy having set them to wait in the courtyard, out of sight but within reach. Once they were all settled, Jerzy stood, and began to pace.

"Well?" Mahl said, leaning forward on her elbows, careful not to disturb any of the papers on the desk. "What did he say?"

"He agreed. There is no way he could refuse," Kaï said, confident even before Jerzy spoke.

"There's always a way to say no," Ao said. "If you're willing to walk away. If they thought Jerzy's plan was more risk than profit—"

"He agreed," Jerzy said, his voice hard.

The tension in the room did not ease; if anything, it heightened. They were listening to the sound of his voice as well as the words, and were not sure they liked what they heard.

"He will inform Neth that I behaved in a suitably mild manner, cowed by my experiences and the death of my master, and then he will return to the Collegium and tell *his* masters that I refused their offer, that I scorned everything the Collegium stood for, and held them responsible for Malech's death."

Jerzy did, in fact: had they left magic to Vinearts and not interfered well beyond their own legacy, he would have been by his master's side when Ximen attacked the House, and the two of them could have fought him off, not been distracted by Washers and their hire-swords. But it was gone and past. If a vineyard died, you uprooted it and planted anew. The Vin Lands would not return to what had been, no matter how events had turned.

"He will also tell them that I have begun gathering my own allies, continuing the work my master started, and that he believes I have knowledge of the source of our difficulties and am planning a strike."

The other three nodded; he was thinking like a fighter, like a trader, like a man of power. It also had the advantage of being true.

"He will advise his master—and any others who might be listening—that I be left alone, and that they follow me, when I do strike, thereby taking the glory of saving the Lands Vin for themselves."

"Doubtless, you suggested that he put it in more welcoming terms, for their gentle esteem."

Jerzy grinned at Kaïnam, for a moment shedding the cold weight he carried. "Of course."

"And then what?" Mahault leaned forward, her elbows on her knees, her chin resting on her knuckles, looking as though she were ready to leap for her sword in an instant. He was not the only one who had become something else. The girl who had been caged behind city walls, heeled by an older woman to ensure she did nothing to shame her family, was long gone, and in her place was a warrior. Jerzy saw it clearly, as he turned to answer her; the difference was that she had chosen the road she walked. He felt a lurch of envy within himself, for that choice. Not that it mattered, in the end.

"And then we attack," Kaïnam said with satisfaction, too caught up in his own emotions to notice anything wrong. "Ximen will turn his attention to Jerzy, leaving gaps in his defense, and we will be ready to strike."

Jerzy stopped his pacing in front of the map that had been covered by the old tapestry while the Washer was there, studying it as the other three broke into intense discussion about the details of such an attack, what pieces should be moved where. He smiled, not the carefree grin of earlier, but a grimmer, thin-lipped expression. They thought like a fighter, like a trader, like a man of power, and did not notice he had told them the beginning of the plan, but not the end. They thought he had set the Washers on a fool's chase; they did not realize he had done the same to them.

The distractions were in place, he had dangled the lure. All he waited on was for Ximen to make his move.

THE SUN ROSE earlier each morning, the days warming, the dirt turning to thick black mud when it rained and caked brown dust when it dried, while the reports from the wall increased in seasonal urgency, as breeding season drove more beasts to look for easier, two-legged prey. Ximen had not slept in two days. He had not been home in almost a week. While he might be able to steal a nap at some point during the day, the comfort of his House-hearth seemed impossibly far away, right then. The ships were readied, the men being trained. Two of his sons were among them, sturdy and capable boys who would come with him when they sailed. They seemed thrilled to spend their days learning how to climb rigging and be useful shipboard, never giving a thought to their brothers who would be left behind.

Ximen wished he could say the same.

"Another man was lost off the border last night," his adjunct said, giving the worst news first, as Ximen preferred.

Ximen rubbed his eyes tiredly, feeling as though that were simply the latest blow struck against him. He hated summer, even in normal years. The night air did not encourage sleep. "Did anyone see the beast?"

One shake of the man's head was his answer. "No, of course not." The damned hill-beasts were quick, quicker than a sneeze and twice as hard to stop. Every generation they seemed to grow more fierce, more deadly, as though the very fact of two-legged invaders on what had been their land made them mad. It had not mattered so much before, when there were enough troops to keep them cowed. Now, with half their men taken off, and too few remaining to fill the holes . . .

"Pay the death price to his family, and close ranks," Ximen said, knowing that it would already be in the works. He had good people on the borders, from the coast to the Wall, and up into the hills itself. Good people who trusted him. Who followed him without hesitation, no matter how dangerous the order, how mad the scheme.

"And this is madness," he said, once the adjunct had bowed and left the room. "Madness of the most poisoned manner."

None of the servants or staff still in the room could share his concerns or soothe his guilt at those who would be abandoned, left to the tender mercies of the vine-mage when he set sail. His the responsibility. His the burden.

Months before, he had stood in front of the Third Fortification, who covered the low border, and ordered nearly a third to lay down arms and pick up saws, to cut down trees and haul them to the shoreline. There had been no dissent, no uproar, merely obedience. His people had been trained since birth to accept sacrifice as the cost of survival, and the word of the Praepositus was more than law: if he wished them to learn to build ships, after decades of avoiding the sea, then they would do so. If he wished them to abandon the patrols that they had kept sacred for seven generations, they would.

If he had given way before the vine-mage's demands and sent twenty of his best to be slaughtered, they would have gone without protest or hesitation.

The vine-mage had not forgiven him for refusing. There had been no words said, no dark looks sent, but Ximen knew, the way a guard knew when a dark-beast lurked in the branches beyond the wall, watching and waiting for the opportunity to strike.

A determination grew in him. He could not afford to take the vine-mage out yet, not while they still needed him. Not until the ships were set on their way, safely across the seas. His men had training, but the ocean was vast and the mage their only source of protection.

Not yet, but soon. When they were safely in possession of their ancestral rights, he would rid his people of this monster. Once they were free of this place, and back in a civilized land.

Until then, his hand was stayed. The season's Harvest was due. He would watch the names being drawn, would stand at a distance and observe the Sacrifices made. He would allow no one to see how the act disgusted him, having seen the travesty the mage turned it into with his year-round, seemingly endless hunger for victims. There was no nobility, no generosity in the sacrifice anymore; they were simply tools, used and discarded. But his people needed to believe, more now than ever before, that they were a part of something greater. A man who believed in his own destiny was a man who would fight for it. A man in control of his life would accomplish things that were otherwise impossible. And if that control was illusion, fate a fickle wind under another's command?

He would keep that knowledge to himself.

Ximen cast his gaze down on the desk, where the plans for the fleet—the first fleet the Grounding had ever built—were unfurled. Meticulous planning and precision work had them ahead of schedule, all five ships and their crew. The crafters and builders had thrown themselves into the challenge, and he was unutterably proud of them.

Once summer ended and the Harvest was in, the first stage would be undersail and away. They were too few to storm by force—the ground needed to be prepared first. The early ships would sail, while more ships were built, to take those who remained once it was safe.

Those who survived.

"You had best be right, you flea-bitten bastard," he told the vine-mage, distant in his own yard, as though the man could hear him. If the Lands Vin were not in disarray, their small force would never reach their goal, much less reclaim their family lands, lost so many decades before.

It was still bitter on his tongue, that secret history. Once, the founders of the Grounding had listened to the betrayer, had heard his honeyed words and believed that they were on a mission to increase the glory and might of Iaja, their families joined together in marriage and exploration, to seal the ruling of the land under one banner. They had believed it right until the sighting of land, when the very spells that held their ship together came undone, wracking them on this unhappy shore.

Nearly a third died that first, firelit night. More died after, from starvation and wild animals, before the local peoples came to the shore and saved them, taught them how to survive.

Survive, but never thrive. Not in this land, which did not cherish their blood. His lovely Bohaide's words, so many months ago, came back to him: "And then you will be gone?"

He looked down at the plan for the ship, and then looked at the map of his land, ringed by inhospitable mountains and depthless ocean, a narrow strip of land that had taken so much, and given . . . nothing but suffering and sorrow.

He was Praepositus, and as such he must do things that an ordinary man need not. He would bear the weight of that on his conscience, and call it the fair weight, if it brought his people out of this damned exile. He would bear the weight for all decisions he made, to the very fingertips of the silent gods.

Seven generations they had been forgotten, and seven generations was eight too long. He shook his head, reaching for a sheaf of orders that needed to be signed, when noise in the hallway below took his attention.

"Ximen. Ximen!"

Of course. The afternoon had been going too smoothly; Ximen had almost anticipated someone shouting his name, in exactly that tone. "What is wrong? Did the entire shipment of wheat become infested with mice? Has everybody in the Grounding come down with river sores? Or, no, wait, I know, the sky has finally fallen?"

"Ximen!" Erneo came in through the doorway, his thin chest heaving from dashing up the stairs, his eyes panicked. His travel-aide was not a man given to panic; Ximen had seen him face down an enraged bull-hog with nothing more than a spear and a scrap of cloth, a calm smile on his face. "The mage, he has taken . . . he has taken children."

The noise and bustle in the room ceased, although Ximen was not sure if everyone had indeed stopped, or he simply could not hear them any longer. Inside him, something already cold turned into ice. "Did he," Ximen said quietly, even as he stood, touching his aide reassuringly on the shoulder. "Did he indeed."

There was surprise, but little shock, as though Ximen had somehow known this moment was inevitable.

Three times now he had refused the vine-mage sacrifices. Every man was needed, he had told the mage. Every body that could hold the walls, or sail a ship, was needed. The mage would have to look to his own slaves, until the quarter's Harvest was due. He would give no more of his people to feed the vine-mage's hunger.

And yet the vine-mage could not cease, taking what was not his, not by tradition nor need. Like a wall-beast, he answered only to his own hunger. And, like a wall-beast, he needed to be stopped.

"Where is he?"

"The road returning to his yards," Erneo said, his breath calming now that his lord had been informed of the situation. "He took eleven, between the ages of nine and eleven. Seven boys, four girl-children. All from different families."

Slaves were taken before the age of three, and the families were proud to see them go, proud to have the magic found in their family, even if the child did not grow to be chosen. There was protocol, tradition, as there was around all things magic. They might be far from Sin Washer's gaze, but there were things that were not done, nonetheless....

And he, Ximen, had allowed them to be done. He had thought he'd come to an accommodation with his own actions, accepting them as necessary, needful.

No more. The mage might not have been mad enough to take any of Ximen's children, but they were *all* his children. And he would put an end to this, now.

"In my quarters, there is a blackwood box." It was not hidden nor locked, the better to ensure that no inquisitive noses sniffed it out. "Fetch it, and bring it to me in the stables. Hurry."

By the time Ximen had a horse saddled—refusing any accompaniment, much to the distress of the House's stablemaster, a square-shouldered, hawk-nosed man who seemed more worried about his horse than his Praepositus—Erneo appeared with the box.

"Good man. Keep them working, don't let anyone worry. I'll deal with this and be back before dawn."

"Ximen . . ." Erneo had run with him as a boy, in the endless mixing and alliance-forming the Grounding families did. "Be careful."

That last request—not an order, Erneo would never dare order his Praepositus—echoed in Ximen's ears as he caught sight of the dust trail the vine-mage's caravan left behind. It was a heavyset wagon that might have been used to carry casks or farming equipment, save for the metal loops set into the side of the wagon itself.

"Tradition," Ximen had been told, when he asked why the children were chained into the cart. "Tradition."

There was nothing of tradition about the chains binding the eleven in the cart today. As Ximen drew nearer, he could see several of them still tugging at the chains, while the others sat glumly, slumped against the sideboard, resigned to whatever fate would bring them. None of them were crying, and Ximen felt an insane flash of pride: even the children of the Grounding knew that tears solved nothing.

"Mage!"

His shout carried up the road, and the two slaves walking alongside the wagon certainly heard him, but the vine-mage neither looked nor stopped.

"Mage, cease!"

That time, with Ximen's horse almost even with the wagon, the vine-mage pulled down on the reins and the thick-set pony pulling the wagon obediently came to a halt.

The vine-mage turned in his seat and pushed back his hood, so that he was fully visible in the warm afternoon sun. A trickle of sweat ran down the side of his narrow, close-cropped head, and his eyes were cold and dead. "Yes?"

"It ends here, mage." Ximen wished the man had a name. He did not want to give him the respect of a title, did not want to emphasize the differences, but bring him back under the laws that all of the Grounding lived under. Remind him that magic did not excuse him from obligations—did not excuse him from the need for human compassion.

Except, of course, that it did. It always had.

"Is there a problem, Ximen?"

The whoreson smiled at him. Smiled, as though they were meeting over *vina* and roasted hill-deer; wives at their side and children playing behind them, rather than chained to a sweat-stained wooden cart. Ximen swallowed, feeling bile rise up, trying to choke him.

"This ends. This ends now."

"So close to your goal, my dear friend? Oh, no." The vine-mage tutted at him, a father to his impatient son. "You have sown and pruned . . . will you not Harvest, as well?"

The bile flooded his mouth, and he clenched his jaw against the need to spit. "No more. Not children."

The vine-mage pursed his lips, as though he, too, were tasting something sour. "You would not give me what I needed, Ximen. You knew, oh, yes, you knew what I needed, and you would not give it to me. And so I have taken. But not the ones you needed, not the ones you warned me off. No warriors, no householders, no mothers who might yet bring new life to your little lands. I understand, yes, I do. I take only those which cannot serve our plans any other way. Will you deny them the chance to serve?"

Ximen forced down the bile, tried to put a placating, understanding tone into his voice. "I asked too much of you." He had asked nothing but what the other man offered, the crumbs of his own ambition. "The strain of so much magic has taken its toll; you are stretched too thin, too far from your soil. It is healthy rain and sun that we need, not—"

He choked, unable to say it.

The vine-mage's eyes brightened. "Not what? Not blood? Sin Washer gave his god's blood to break us, to shatter us to less, but our blood rebuilds, makes it stronger. Are we not like gods? Are we not more than gods, that we create where they only destroyed?" A speck of froth appeared at the corner of the mage's mouth, tinged with red as though he had bitten the inside of his mouth in his excitement.

"We are not gods," Ximen said, not daring to look at the slaves, or the children staying still as frightened monkeys. "There are things we must not do."

"There is nothing I *must* either do or not do," the vine-mage said. Ximen's gaze went instinctively to the man's hands, to make sure that he was not reaching for a wine sack, even as his own hand went for his blade.

"Blood flows," the vine-mage crooned, his mouth barely moving. "Blood chokes."

A decantation—but the whoreson had not sipped . . . had he been keeping the spellwine in his mouth, had he been waiting, all this time? Even as panic reached his thoughts, Ximen felt something change within him, the sensation of something crawling inside his body, like spiders inside his skin, and shuddered, his hand falling away from the sword even as his vision started to dim. He could not feel his face, and something heavy pushed against his chest.

"Go," the vine-mage said, almost lovingly.

Ximen convulsed once, and quiet-magic flooded him, turning his blood to sludge, slowing his heart and lungs until he was merely flesh, mounted on a suddenly nervous horse.

One of the slaves caught the reins up before the horse could bolt, and patted its neck, wordlessly calming it down.

"That was easier than I expected," the vine-mage said, neither pleased nor surprised, but merely noting a fact. A pity he had to rush things, it would have been easier if he'd waited. But you harvest when the grapes are ripe.

"Bring the body," he told the slave, already lifting the reins to start the wagon moving again.

The slave showed no emotion, slinging the body over the front of his horse, then bringing the reins over the horse's head and leading it slowly as they picked their way down the road. In the back of the wagon, the sound of muffled tears slowly faded, until there was only silence.

PART III

Regent

Chapter 12

THE ATAKUAN SEA

Early Spring

"*Captain! Red flag* on the horizon!"

Aron lifted his spyglass to where the bird's-eye, hanging from rigging like a madman, was pointing. The lad had spotted it first, but it was visible to all against the clear sky. Distant on the horizon, a red stripe fluttered, then another, dark smudges underneath them the forms of ships. His eyes were old, though, even with the glass, and he could make no more detail than that.

After so many months on the water with only the occasional pirate or Eastern trader-ships to report, he had almost forgotten why they were here. The crew was accustomed to long stretches of boredom, but he was not. Aron had filled his hours making sketches of the seabirds and fish the sailors caught, and noting the display of stars, all useful and valid expressions of his supposed existence, that of a man of inquiry with a wealthy—and lenient—patron. But now, in a rush, his true purpose and identity returned.

"Two ships?" Two ships, out here, at the edges of the Lands Vin, bearing the red banner . . . not that anyone would tell Washers where they might or might not go, but the Brotherhood did little, if anything, without deep reason, and any parlance they might have in these waters was certainly within the course of what he had been set here to observe.

"Mil'ar? What do you see?"

The cabin boy's voice had barely broken, and he looked very young, staring up at Aron, old enough to be his twice-grandsire.

"Trouble, lad," he said. "I see trouble."

The boy's face lit up as though the spy had told him of some great treasure, and he dashed off to climb a little ways up the rigging, to see if he, too, could see what was coming.

"A true son of Caul," one of the sailors said, laughing, even as they heeded the Captain's orders to turn the ship about and match direction with their visitors.

His master needed to hear of this. Without taking his eyes off the horizon, Aron reached down to the folding table in front of him, unerringly finding the small metal pot waiting there, as it had waited every single day since they had set sail, tucked under his pillow for safety, while he slept. It had no sigil on it, no wax stopper or indication that it held anything at all of value, and yet it was worth more than the entire ship and crew combined. The taste burned as it went down his throat, but Aron had been trained to control the automatic grimace that accompanied the *uishkiba poitín*.

He did not like it, did not like any stench of magic—a true son of Caul he was, too—but he would use it, as ordered.

Deep in the hold, the three women came to awareness, their months-long sleep broken by the summons of the *poitín*. Like the claws of birds, their mind gripped his, and knew all that he knew, saw all that he saw.

He heard them whispering in his brain, shuffling about in their sealed box of a cabin, draped in the black cloth that earned them the nickname of corvines, the black-winged birds of battlefields. Witches. Abominations, twisted and changed by exposure to the *poitín*. But whatever battle it was Caul now fought, it required new weapons, and the corvines were part of it.

"Washers sighted. Two ships." A quiver of excitement that was both his and theirs fluttered through the link, to suddenly, unexpectedly, be useful. Finally.

"Hold, Captain, they're coming about—Captain!" The bird's-eye's voice rose from his usual shout to something showing true excitement and . . . fear? Aron paused, still feeling the tingling burn of the brew in his throat, and waited for news, aware of the three birds waiting with him.

"Captain, I don't know those flags!"

"Sound the colors," the Captain called back.

"Red on gold, sir!"

Iajan colors. Iajan ships out here would not be terribly unusual— the whoreson explorers were Caul's match on the oceans, although they had managed to stay out of each others' way, for the most part. But two, together, here, might mean trouble. . . .

"And black!"

Aron snatched up the spyglass again, trying to see what the eye was maddening on about. There were no colors that ran red and black and gold . . .

Except there they were, snapping sharply, clear now as the ships came closer. Old-fashioned ships, the sort Aron had not seen since childhood, bearing a flag he did not know. Suddenly, the foul taste of obscene magic caught in his throat was matched by the taste of bile rising from his stomach.

Aron had been a scholar before he was a spy. He knew that flag.

"Tell our master," he said even as the pot-magic began to fade, unsure if the witches were still sending. "Tell him the Exiled have returned."

Chapter 13

Spring

The village, just south of the border-range of Corguruth in the hills of The Berengia, had built the icehouse in the time of Lord Ranulf's grandfather, bringing each stone from the riverbed and placing it just so into the hillside, building walls twice a man's height and filling the chinks in so that even during the warmest months, the air stayed cool within.

Normally great blocks of ice rested on a bed of wood chips a handspan thick, and slabs of dried meats and wreaths of vegetables hung from the rafters year-round. A wealthy House might use spellwines to keep their food fresh, but despite their relative prosperity, such a thing was beyond the village of Foulantane. An icehouse was good enough for their grandsires, and it had been good enough for them . . . until the lord closed the mountain passes, the last of their ice melted, and the blight ruined the winter crop they had expected would sustain them.

They had survived the winter, but spring had not brought with it the expected relief: they had eaten all their seed and had nothing now to plant, too few lambs born to butcher, and still expect the flock to grow and thrive.

The elders appealed to the town one over, a day's travel down the Great Road, and were told that they had no grain to spare: the blight was there, as well, the early crops stunted and frail, and their children needed to be fed, first.

A delegation was formed; the reeve and one elder from each village went to Lord Ranulf, seeking news of what relief they might be afforded in the meantime. It was a lord's right to close roads and mount guards as he deemed needful, but it was his obligation to care for those affected as well. Or so the elders had said when they set out on their mules, their mood determined but confident.

They returned, shaken and empty-handed. The lord had been too busy to see them, riding the borders with his troops. Well and good; the lord was a busy man and it was well that he knew what was happening on the outskirts. But the man he left in charge had refused to see the delegation, making them wait all day before sending them home.

"It's a hard time, he said." The reeve had repeated that phrase half a dozen times since their return, and it made no more sense than it had the first time he'd said it. "Hard time, and we all must wait and be patient. Patient is easy for him to say, in his House with his servants and his spells. What about us?"

Disaster in one town was a problem. In two, trouble. But when it happened in three, it would doubtless be happening in more, and there would be no help from others—and more worryingly, from their sworn lord.

"Vineart Hugues?" one of the men suggested.

"Phagh. He has already packed up his House and gone to cover within the lord's House, like a tame dog. His slaves tend his yards; you would suggest we take food from their plates?"

The speaker had been about to suggest just that, but a look at the expressions of the men around him kept him from voicing such a thing. Slaves were lower than any freeman, but to be pitied, not preyed upon.

Not yet, anyway. The seven men in the room knew that, if conditions changed, they would protect their families first.

"Sharpen your scythes and be ready," the reeve said, finally, his voice thick with regret. "If we will not be given aid, then we have no choice but to take it."

The House of Malech

The Berengia

"Vineart!"

The shout was loud, well-modulated, and bordering on insolent. Jerzy had encountered Prince Ranulf only once before; he had been sent with spellwine to heal the villagers struck ill by the afterstink of the sea serpent's flesh. He had been intended as a messenger, his master's foot, to run errands. Instead, he had helped Ranulf hold off the attack of another serpent, using spellwine to support and modify Ranulf's decantation.

Jerzy had told no one what he had done, allowing Ranulf to take the credit for the destruction of the serpent, but he had suspected even then that the prince knew that his decantation alone could not have been enough.

From the look in the lord's eye, now, Jerzy suspected that suspicion had grown into something more pronounced. And more problematic, for Jerzy. He would not antagonize the man, not yet. But neither would he be conciliatory. Not when the man rode onto his lands, accompanied by armed guards, and shouted for him in that voice.

The winter had been no kinder to Ranulf than the others; his face was still clean-shaven but the skin sagged around the jowls and under his eyes. But he still sat his horse with an easy grace, his shoulders proud and his elbows relaxed. The two solitaires in their distinctive brown leathers, hounds trotting alongside, were the only guard he had brought, and Jerzy inclined his head once in acknowledgment, even as he stepped down the path and under the ever-green archway to greet his visitor.

Kaïnam had given the party a careful once-over before allowing Jerzy to leave the House. In a way, bringing solitaires rather than his own fighters was a sign of Ranulf's respect—for Malech, if not Jerzy. Bringing warriors could have been construed as a threat, showing his force, or it might have implied that Ranulf did not trust the Vineart, to come alone. Either was an insult to his host. Solitaires were perhaps more deadly, but they were more expensive to hire, and would not be thrown into battle lightly; therefore, they could be seen as merely a courtesy, escorts to a prince who could not be expected to travel alone. Ranulf came to talk, not fight. For now, anyway.

One of those solitaires was Keren. She made no sign, however, that they had met previously.

"Welcome to my House, Lord Ranulf," Jerzy said. Unlike when the Washer had ridden up, he had not taken the time to change, but rather came out wearing leather trou and an open-neck shirt with sleeves that folded back, suitable for working with *vina*. To appear otherwise would give too much importance to this visit.

That had been Ao's advice, and Kaïnam had agreed. The two of them waited in the hallway, while Mahault took the side route through the vineyards and waited behind them.

"This is not a social visit, Vineart." Ranulf might have considered the implications of offending the Vineart, but he was clearly unwilling to give up his ground, remaining on his horse where he had a tactical advantage.

Jerzy refused to be intimidated: he had spent enough time on horseback to know how easily even a trained mount could be startled, and how simple a matter it would be, if he so chose, to spark the horse's hooves and set him to flight.

He would do no such thing, of course, but knowing that he could allowed him to stand in front of the heavyset beast and not flinch, or be intimidated.

"There is no need to be impolite, however," Jerzy said calmly. "I know why you are here."

"If you did not, you would be an idiot as well as a fool, and I had enough respect for your master that I assume you are neither of those things." Ranulf glared down at him, then, almost reluctantly, showed a brief, surprisingly open smile, even as he swung down off his horse, the leather creaking under his movements. Jerzy did not invite him into the House; and Ranulf did not react to the implied insult. House Malech and their local prince had always remained on amicable, if properly distant, terms, and while Master Malech had considered Ranulf a harmless pup, neither Jerzy nor Ranulf could afford to underestimate the other.

"I came of my own, rather than sending a messenger, or inviting you to my home. In these days . . . I was not certain you would feel comfortable leaving the safety of your yards. Indeed, you have not, since you returned home, not even to visit your own secondary yards. Most unusual."

He had been watching; had he bothered to note that Mahault had visited in Jerzy's place? Or did Ranulf believe that Jerzy had abandoned all but his primary vines? If so, then the prince was the fool.

"I am aware of everything that occurs in my soil," Jerzy said evenly. "And much that occurs outside it as well."

"Then we shall dispense with the verbal fencing, yes?" Ranulf stepped forward. Jerzy stood his ground. "You will have heard of the recent unpleasantness within The Berengia."

"Hunger and fear, and villagers near to rebellion against their lords. Yes. I have heard." Ranulf had not been listed among those refusing aid . . . but he had not been forthcoming with it, either.

"The world grows cold, Vineart, even as the season warms. Cold and menacing. The Washers are turning their hand to politics, and other lands look at us with hunger." He seemed uncomfortable making this speech, as though someone had prepared the words for him. "We owe it to our home to protect it—and I owe it to our people to protect you."

"You propose to protect me?" Jerzy let just a hint of skepticism show, tilting his head as though the thought had never occurred to him.

"I would offer the shelter of my name, the arms of my fighters, to defend your yards against any who would mean them harm."

"And in return? What would you have of me?"

"Nothing more than what your master and I had previously shared: The pooling of skills, to protect our people from harm. First offering of your wines . . . for a fair price, of course. Detta would not allow anything else."

"Of course." Jerzy moved the silver ring on his finger again, unable to stop himself. Ranulf's gaze followed the motion, and from the widening of his eyes, he recognized it.

"Your master had that commissioned from my silversmith, when he reached Mastery," he said, his voice brittle. "Do you claim it for yourself?"

Jerzy narrowed his eyes and studied Ranulf the way he might an unknown insect that settled on one of his vines. "It is none of your affair what I claim or do not claim, Lord Ranulf. The Commandments still hold, though others may seek to stretch them full out of shape."

The prince let out a huff of surprise, and Jerzy thought that he heard something else in there as well. Disdain, and perhaps a note of admiration. "You have no intention of allying yourself with anyone, do you, boy?"

"My master sought alliances. And he died for it."

Truth, in a way that Ranulf could understand, if not the entire truth. The prince's hard gaze rested on Jerzy, assessing him, then he gave another curt nod, and reached up to grasp his saddle, swinging up onto the horse's back without the aid of his stirrups. If he meant to show off in front of Jerzy, or impress him, it succeeded.

"The mountain passes and the ports are closed," he said. "None will enter The Berengia without our knowledge."

And none would leave, either. As warnings went, it had the distinct sound of a threat.

Jerzy smiled, a small, cold smile that refused to be threatened. "Sin Washer keep your road safe, Lord Ranulf."

He did not wait to see if the prince and his guards left, but turned and walked back up the path, his pace steady and firm, until he was safely within the open doors. Only then did Jerzy allow himself to exhale, his body shuddering like a winded horse.

"Detta," he called, raising his voice enough to be heard in the kitchen. "Have supper brought to my study, please."

"I don't understand. I mean, I understand why you didn't agree, because we've all seen how well that does not turn out, but why didn't you"—Mahault waved her fingers slightly—"use him, the way you used the Washers? I would think having the most powerful princeling in the area thinking he's deep in plot with you could be an excellent way to guard your flank."

They were gathered in Jerzy's study. A spellfire blazed in the hearth, giving off silent heat against the spring night's chill.

"It's not that I trust him any more or less than the Washers," Jerzy said, feeling the stress of the confrontation finally taking hold of his body and making him want to do nothing but lay down and sleep. He dared not, though: every time he dared sleep, he risked his control slipping, being drawn into the Root's embrace, and never escaping. "It's that I don't need him. Rather, I don't need to manipulate him. He spoke truth; he and my master worked together often as not, and I have some knowledge of how he thinks, and what he will do. More, he is not a bad man and has a care for his lands. He will be an effective barrier, should we need him, without my having to agree to anything."

"And then, if you do call on him for help, he will feel as though he's come out ahead, rather than suspecting he was played." Ao nodded and then tapped the pages of the dispatch that had arrived while Jerzy was dealing with their not-unexpected visitor. "That time may come sooner than not. There's more unrest in Iaja, and Corguruth." Ao's dark, sharp-cornered eyes, once filled with mischief, had shadows under them now, making his broad cheekbones even more prominent and narrowing his once-round face into something unfamiliar. Even his cheerful personality had sobered, the smile that used to snap with mischief now muted by worry and exhaustion.

Nobody noticed. Or, rather, they saw, but made no comment. There was no point telling someone they looked tired, or distressed. They all were tired and distressed, and increasingly dispirited.

"Serious?" Jerzy did not need to ask: he knew already, the same way he knew how many fingers were on his hand. As the days warmed and the blight did not ease, the reports had been coming steadily, a bird every third day or so carrying news of more illness or another outbreak of related violence. He could not heal everyone, nor could he let them come to him. Their own supplies were beginning to thin.

It was only a matter of time, now.

"Serious enough. The land-lord was set upon, and . . ." Ao let his words trail off, not wanting—or needing—to go into detail. They knew, too well now, what happened when the people turned on their lord.

"And there will be more, soon enough," Mahault said, her hands still in her lap, clasped so tightly that her knuckles had gone white. Two weeks before, a madman spewing fear and anger had riled the already-nervous populace of Aleppan to the point that they overran the palazzo, breaking down the Council chamber doors and destroying the furnishings within. Men had dragged her father the maiar to the gardens where Mahault, Ao, and Jerzy had once walked, and slaughtered him in the fountain until the waters ran red.

Mahault had not cried when the news came.

Jerzy's own eyes were dry as the winter soil. The cracks in the Lands Vin had been made clear; each of the eleven points were in a city already marked on the map that hung in front of them now. Each of the eleven cities had been targeted by Ximen's whisperers, their land-lord becoming erratic, or unpredictable, striking out until his own people turned on him. Eleven confirmed reports so far, of people driven to desperation and violence.

Ao's people had been invaluable in gathering the information; spreading their fingers across the trade routes, accessing the other trading clans, passing messages along with a speed that even messenger-birds could not match, finding their way in and out of lands where all traffic had halted.

"Eleven, in two months. It's as though the entire world has gone mad," Detta said from where she had been listening at the door. She carried a tray of tai in her hands and came into the study to set it on the desk, clearing a space for it among the maps and messages scattered there. The kitchen boy followed with a basket of meat-stuffed rolls, still warm from the fire.

"It has," Kaïnam said. His face, ever lean, had become even more drawn over the past month, his hand never far from where his sword would hang, even when he went unarmed within the House.

Jerzy stared at the map. Eleven riots since season-turn, eleven land-lords brought down by the people he was supposed to protect. In five of those, the Vineart who had allied with him had also been killed. There might have been other Vinearts killed, isolated within their yards; none of Jerzy's overtures had received responses. Whatever small willingness to share Malech had been able to tap had long run dry from fear.

A fear that had an all-too-real cause. This should be a season of birthings, not death.

"Where is it the worst?" Jerzy stared at the dragon, perched across the doorframe as though it were the only thing real in the world. There was a brush of something at the edges of his awareness, a rasping pass like the touch of leaves against skin, or soil underfoot, a lure like spice in the nose and summer's sunlight on his face, the quiver of magic in the air.

It was a now-familiar sensation even in Jerzy's waking moments, like the rustle of a rat in the granary that could not be evicted. The Root, the magic underlying the skin of the world: shattered, scattered, but still potent. All it took was the faintest hint of quiet-magic to escape, asleep or awake, and he was under siege. He was caught, unable to go forward, without being tangled in its grip.

There was a sense of puzzlement, and then the cool weight of the dragon slid against his skin, although the creature had not moved from its post above the doorsill. Jerzy took a few deep breaths, cautiously, and then relaxed: the barrier held. For now.

Jerzy did not want to think about what might happen if he let himself be caught. The very least would be that Ximen could use the connection to find him, strike at him from across the ocean. Worse . . .

"Worst?"

Jerzy started, hearing his own thoughts echoed out loud, then realized that Ao was responding to his earlier question. "Where are things the worst," he clarified, his voice tightened with frustration at having to explain what seemed obvious to him: What else would they be looking for? Did he have to do everything? He ran his fingers through his hair, resisting the urge to pull at the roots.

"We're not your slaves, Jer," Mahault said, her voice low but barely calm, even as the dragon cautioned, *Patience.*

Jerzy took a deep breath, forcing his fingers to unclench, letting his arms fall to his side. He was Vineart. They were not. But they were his allies. His friends. The word was still unfamiliar, but the comfort of it was not, any longer. Jerzy let his fingers gentle, his jaw loosen, and waited.

"Iaja," Ao said, answering his question without having to look down at the dispatches or back at the map. "The first alliance of maiars has shattered, and they hammer at each other as though they would erase any sign of them from the earth." He paused. "The Vinearts there . . . they're either under protection"—and Ao's tone made it clear he understood the word meant nothing more than servitude—"or they're . . . gone. Disappeared."

Iaja had once been the home of some of the most talented Master Vinearts in history, matching The Berengia in the strength of their vines. There would be time to mourn the loss later . . . or, Jerzy acknowledged, not at all.

"The islands along their coast have withdrawn into themselves, hoping to remain unnoticed," Kaïnam added, "while ships bearing the black banner sail unmolested, taking captives and loot, and disappearing back into the depths."

"Scavengers," Mahl said, disgust clear in how she spoke the word. "They're like wolves in midwinter; they feed on chaos. We can't worry about them; when order is restored, then the coastal lords will be able to hunt them down, as before."

"Assuming there are any lords left to hunt," Ao retorted. His people had been among the worst hit; he expected them to suspend most of their sea voyages soon, if they hadn't already.

Jerzy nodded, hearing Ao's words but already moving on past them. "Detta."

She stopped, waiting for his question.

"How much healwine do we have left?"

"Not enough," she said, knowing what he was going to ask, as a good House-keeper must. "If the violence comes here . . ."

"Refuse any new orders."

Detta's round face showed her unhappiness, but she bowed her head and left the room. It was contrary to everything Master Malech, and Master Josia before him, had decreed, but the reasoning was clear: they needed to keep enough for themselves.

"So far, Iaja seems to be taking the brunt of this Ximen's attacks, both physical and magical," Kaïnam said, "but his net is cast beyond that. It makes sense that either The Berengia or Altenne will be next. And since

Jerzy has taken up a stick and poked him with it . . . Jer, maybe you *should* have negotiated with Ranulf."

Jerzy schooled his face to look as though he was considering Kaï's comment and rubbed the back of his neck, aware of an ache that had not been there on waking. Rejected, Ranulf would do as the other princelings of The Berengia had already done and offer protection to one of the three other Vinearts who held lands within these borders. Soon, a rumor would float of the sole holdout within The Berengia, who considered himself above all alliances.

The sole holdout, from a House known for its bloodstaunch. From a House under suspicion of apostasy, and yet the Washers held back and did nothing, even as the House no longer shipped that bloodstaunch. . . .

Jerzy had no intention of relying on weapons or men-at-arms. This was a cold game he was playing; he was not sure the others, if they realized, would forgive him. But if Ximen could be suspected of whispering to the slaves, if the Root could find its way into the House, into his sleep, then not even his companions, not even Detta, could be trusted entirely.

"We still don't have the ability to hold off a real attack, much less launch anything," Mahault said. "The four of us . . . your slaves would be good only to slow troops down, not stop them, and the—"

"I am not worried about unrest from the locals," Jerzy said. "For Malech's sake, at least, we will have that much safety. And Ranulf will handle anything that attacks from outside the border." The lord was stubborn, willful, and like the rest of his kind, blinded by his own desires. But he would spend his last breath to protect The Berengia. Jerzy was counting on that.

"For now, there is peace, or at least the absence of unrest. But that will not last," Kaïnam said. "Even The Berengia will fall."

"It's a return to the old days, before Sin Washer." Ao wrapped his hands around his mug of tai, as though the warmth would take the chill out of his words.

"We have to stop it," Mahault said, fierce as a raptor, making the others respond even as they tried to remain calm.

Jerzy nodded slowly, twisting the ring on his finger. "We will." He sensed the anticipation the way he sensed the grapes, ripening on the vine. The fruit was ready for crushing. He turned in his chair to stare at the map, although his mind was elsewhere. "Ao, ready messages. Tell your people, and Kaï's, to stand ready for a command to strike, at targets of my choosing."

It was not the blow that landed that was dangerous, but the blow anticipated. Becoming a Master Vineart took skill, knowledge, and patience. If this worked, if he survived, he would have the right to wear Malech's ring.

If not, the ring would be the least of his concerns.

"We've put our parts of this in play," Ao said, leaning forward, his expression matched by the alert look in Mahault's eyes and the way Kaï stood suddenly straighter. "I think it's time that you tell us what you're planning."

Jerzy twisted the ring one final time and let out a long breath. He could not blame them—but he could not tell them.

"Not yet," he said. "I need you to trust me, a little while longer."

Chapter 14

*N*eth *had not* felt comfortable since returning to the Collegium. No, he amended that thought: he had not felt comfortable since he boarded that damned ship and chased after three children to the far beyond of the world. Since he had seen the living masthead on the *Vine's Heart*, that might either have been a spellcast mockery of Zatim Sin Washer's favor . . . or the true embodiment of it.

If one, it supported his orders, and his actions. If the other . . .

If the other, then his vows meant nothing, his life meant nothing, and he was as apostate as any, he and the others of the Collegium who had agreed to cast that name on another. For his own sanity, his ability to function, Neth had to assume that the figurehead had been an illusion, some aetherspell designed to put doubt and fear into their hearts.

When his party had ridden into The Berengia, they had been met by four other riders, including Brother Oren, who had reported that Vineart Jerzy had indeed returned to his master's House, and looked to be staying there, doing nothing out of the ordinary, nothing untoward. Further, Oren reported that he had spoken with the Vineart, and received a pledge that he would take no further action that would distress the Collegium.

Brion, at his left, had snorted at that. It was Brion's opinion that Jerzy could not help but distress anyone with common sense, and his companions even more so.

The desire to speak with Jerzy, to query him as to what had happened in Irfan, how he had set the fire that blazed so fiercely that it turned an entire sandy shoreline into an impassable glassy surface, to discover what drove him there, and then drove him back, warred with the orders, carried by Oren, to return to the Collegium.

Jerzy, it seemed, was no longer the Collegium's greatest concern.

And that, Neth admitted, striding down the corridor to the chamber where he had been summoned to gather, was perhaps the greatest cause of his discomfort. Something was wrong. Something he was not part of, was not included in. He could feel it in the very air of the Collegium.

"You doubt me?" A man's voice that caught at the edge of Neth's awareness, enough to make him turn his head to catch the response.

"He's a slippery one, even for a Vineart."

It was Oren's voice that caused Neth to check his pace, and slip against the wall, barely breathing. The voices had come from one of the rooms off the main way, a classroom, or office.

"He swore it on his master's ring." Brother Edmun, Neth identified the first voice. Mid-years, moderate of voice but fierce of temper. What business did he have with Oren?

"Brother Neth spoke truly, there is no malice in Vineart Jerzy's heart, only sorrow at his master's death. He has begun gathering allies, continuing the work his master started." Edmun paused. "I believe that he does in fact have knowledge of the source of our difficulties, and is planning a strike.

"And so, if we leave him be, he will do the difficult task of taking down the one who causes unrest."

"And if we leave him to it, and follow on his heels"—Oren's voice practically trembled in excitement, the anticipation of a student seeking to impress his teacher—"then we will be able to claim the glory of saving the Lands Vin for ourselves. Those within the Collegium who stand against us will have no choice but to silence their objections, and we will be able to guide the Collegium into its better destiny. And then we will deal with these Vinearts, who do not know their place within the greater balance."

Neth rested the back of his head against the tapestry and considered the pain that had started between his brows as dispassionately as possible, as befitted an Heir of Sin Washer. All the hesitations, the uncertainty, the arguments over apostasy and the direction the Collegium should or indeed might take . . .

Had he been so innocent, to not realize a schism had grown? That one of his own students was on the other side? Perhaps so.

He had hoped for better from Oren, had hoped he would be clear-eyed enough to see the long view. But then, he supposed the boy thought the same of him. And the idea that they should allow the Vineart to sully his hands, cross lines that they, Washers, were meant to maintain, and then come in after the fact and act as though they were somehow still clean-handed, despite having watched and done nothing to prevent it.

Worse, if Neth knew his brothers, and he did, it was unlikely that this was merely observed. The things he had seen, heard, for the past few years unfolded like a leaf in spring, and Neth was rocked by the understanding that so little had been left to chance.

No, his brothers had not caused this; they had not instigated the attacks, nor sent the serpents, not attacked the villages or vineyards. But they had taken full advantage of the confusion.

Jerzy had accused Brother Darian of complicity in the accusation of Vineart Giordan and himself of apostasy. Not directly, no; the boy had been too cautious, the way all slaves were, too careful, the way Vinearts became. No wonder it was so easy to suspect them, the way they protected themselves, protected their beloved yards . . . And was that not Sin Washer's Command? Were they not merely what they had been commanded to become? As soon to blame the bird for flying, or the fish for swimming. They were the balance, whatever others might claim. Vineart and Men of Power . . . Washers were merely the fulcrum, essential to the balance, but useless without the counterweights.

And he had been part of it, misdirected by forces within the Collegium. He had suspected they were there, the inevitable currents that moved any gathering of men, but had assumed he worked with the most powerful current. And now, it seemed, that he did not.

The other two continued their discussion, but Neth had heard enough, and moved on, forcing his body to move casually, normally, as he walked past the doorway and did not so much as glance sideways to indicate any interest at all in who else might be in that room.

A hundred thoughts worked their way through his brain, trying to see a way to stop or circumvent the plan he had heard unfolding, but without a better sense of who the players were, or how deep it went—Brother Ranklin? Was it possible? No, he would not, could not believe that—there was only so much Neth could do. He could not simply begin questioning every Brother in the Collegium halls, keeping a checklist of who said what. It would take too long, for one, and his brothers, clearly, were perfectly willing to lie.

There was only one thing he could do that would make any difference at all. The fact that it slid so neatly with his own thoughts might have been cause for concern—was he doing the right thing, or the comfortable thing—but in the end, it was the only option left. Reversing his steps with a casual turn, Neth headed not to his meeting, but the outer fields.

The Collegium was spread out over a flat valley, with cliffs at their back and a river alongside. The air was sweet-smelling, and the ground underfoot muddy, but Neth gave himself permission to enjoy the fresh spring air, putting aside his worries until he reached the end of the path, and the practice field. Brion was there as expected, working with a group of gangly boys who clearly did not know which end to fall on.

"Again," the Washer said, his thickly muscled arm pushing one of the boys forward. "And this time, try to remember to duck rather than standing there like a cow."

"Duck, cow, either way we're meat," one of the boys muttered, and Brion cuffed him hard against the back of the head. "You won't always have a solitaire for hire to protect you," he rumbled at them. "Nor will a brigand always recognize your robes in time to stop, or even care to. Even Sin Washer went down before knives, you young fool."

"A lost cause," Neth said, amused despite his worries. "As they all are . . . at first."

When he had taken Brion with him to confront Malech and young Jerzy, other Brothers had stepped up to teach the defense classes, but it was understood that Brion was the best. He had the stories to tell, the scars to show, to scare arrogant youths into cautious, prepared men. Neth had no right to take him away again, not so soon. Not when he would be needed.

But there was no one else he could trust. There was no *meme-courien* nearby to hire, it would take too long to summon one, and any bird enspelled to bring a message to House Malech could easily be intercepted in the same fashion. Only Brion, with his pragmatic view of the world, his ties to the outside world as strong, even now, as his oath to the Collegium, his knowledge of what was truly happening and not merely the stories carried back . . . only Brion could be trusted. More to the point, Brion had an excellent chance of actually making it there.

"I need you to take a message for me," he said when the class was dismissed, and Brion wandered over to see what the other man wanted. "To Vineart Jerzy."

Brion raised an eyebrow at that, but waited for details before asking questions.

"No one can know where you are going, or why."

It was a small thing, perhaps a useless thing, in this maddened world. But Neth was an honorable man, and Jerzy deserved to know.

*   *   *

ONCE, WHAT SEEMED like years ago, Kaïnam had spent the morning hours considering philosophical tracts or discussing the previous day's events with his sister, listening to her far-wiser evaluation.

He had never expected to be standing in an open field on a spring morning far from his island home, learning how to use magic to fight a war.

"To the skies, rise. To the winds, flow. Go."

Kaïnam swallowed the spellwine even as he uttered the final word, and lifted his hands palm up, as though releasing something.

Above him, two gray-feathered doves fluttered away, rising into the sky just as he had commanded them.

"And that's how you do it," Jerzy said, watching from his seat on the low stone wall. "No need to maintain a full coop for emergencies: any bird can be spelled to become a messenger if you have the correct decantation. Although I would not advise using a raptor, as they tend to become distracted by the sight of a rabbit."

"Useful to know," Kaïnam said dryly, still watching the birds flutter on their way back to the House, where Ao waited. They had gone to the far edges of Jerzy's yards, the stone buildings a distant blur on the horizon, across endless gnarled vines showing tiny leaflets against the pale-blue sky. In his home, even the winters were not this sere, the blues never so harsh.

Home. His father, dead. His brother, now Principal, taking the stone-carved seat and determining how Atakus might sail. He did not begrudge Nilëas the role. In truth, his second-eldest brother was an excellent choice, both experienced and energetic, and if not prone to deep thoughts, willing to surround himself with those who were.

Much like their father, in fact. A better Principal than he, Kaïnam, could ever have been. The thought stung, but that made it no less true. He still served Atakus. He still could protect it, in his own way.

"Can other creatures be used for messengers?" he asked, as much to distract himself as true curiosity. "A dog, perhaps? Or a horse?" Birds were too obvious, too easy for an archer or a hawker to take down from the sky. A dog could cover ground without notice, and who would think the horse, rather than the rider, would carry a message?

"Not a dog, no. Like a raptor, it's too likely to be distracted." Jerzy frowned, leaning back on the wall, comfortable as though he were lounging on a padded dais, and once again Kaïnam was struck by the thought that, were he to meet this man in another setting, he would still know him for a Vineart, even without the silver spoon that hung on his belt. The half-drowned boy he had pulled from the sea during a storm had died, as surely as the slave he had been before that was dead, and only the Vineart—cold, distant, removed from the world—remained.

That was a good thing, Kaï thought. What they were doing, the lures they were setting, it was no work for the innocent.

"A horse, though, that might work. It's something to think about." And Jerzy's mouth twisted a little, giving him a darker mien. "If we survive, that is."

Kaïnam had no response to that. He was getting ready to ride out to meet a messenger from the Scholars of Altenne, who had finally responded to Jerzy's request for a meeting. It was risky; their home marched alongside the Collegium, and it was not certain where their loyalties resided, which was why Kaïnam was going to meet them at a midpoint site rather than allowing them to come onto Jerzy's lands. But if the scholars were willing to add their knowledge, then the risk was worth it.

"I do not—" he started to say, when he was felled by a sudden, blinding headache.

Ships, crashing through a lightning storm where there was no rain. The sloping shoreline, so familiar it sent a pang through his breast, the tall white towers of the royal seat rising against the deep blue sky . . . men coming ashore, weapons drawn, met by Atakuan warriors, and the clash of steel, all seen from a distance, as though someone else watched, and did nothing. . . .

"We dare not interfere," a voice told him, a man's voice, echoing with the cawing of birds, their wings lifting the voice and carrying it to him. A sensation like spellwine, but harsher, smokier, filled his throat and nose,

gagging him. "*We cannot interfere. We have not the men, we are too far from home. We watch, we warn.*"

"Who are you?" he managed, even as the view swung around again, as though the watcher were on a boat that had hewed sharply starboard. Two ships, bearing banners Kaïnam did not recognize, a fluttering standard of black, red and gold.

The Exiles have returned the voice told him, fading out as though falling asleep, or moving away swiftly, then surged again. *This we tell you: the Exiles now hold Atakus.*

"Exiles?"

"It's a legend," Ao said, pouring a cup of *vin ordinaire* from the pitcher Detta had brought them along with a platter of dried meats and greens no one seemed interested in eating. "Just a legend."

"Tell me." Kaïnam, his head still aching, was in no mood for a drawn-out story. "Because that legend has just broken through Master Edon's greatest spell and overrun my home. They now hold access to one of the major ports, essential for all who travel that route, within striking range of the rest of the Vin Lands. If they belong to the enemy, if this is his first overt move, it was a masterful one, and we have no response to it."

"We have one response," Jerzy said quietly. He had recovered from the sudden intrusion into their heads faster, and his eyes had a peculiar shine to them that the others could not place. "The message was from Caul, the speaker one of those your contact has set to watch the seas."

Kaïnam nodded. "That accent, it makes sense. It would match their manners, too. But to send a message that way—Caul seems to have less resistance to using magic, at need, than they have always claimed."

"That was no magic of the Lands Vin," Jerzy said grimly. "I could recognize the source of the message, but not the means. Whatever legacy they use, it is not one I know."

Once he would have said that was impossible. Now, he wondered that he knew anything at all.

"Like the enemy?" Mahault said, her expression worried. They had not heard the shout, those in the House. Only Kaïnam, and Jerzy.

"No," Jerzy corrected her. "Different even beyond that. Whatever the Caulic king is up to, he has found a source of magic within his own lands that is not of Sin Washer's breaking. I dislike it, with all else, but it is a worry we have no time for, now." Caul, for now, was their ally—and one that had just proven both powerful and useful. Later, if there was a later, the source of their magic could be investigated.

"I must go to them." Kaïnam's worries coalesced into a sudden, solid determination. "I need to be there."

"How?" Ao was not unkind, but practical. "Even if you made it safely to the coast, you can't sail the *Heart* on your own, and by the time we rounded up a crew . . ." Unspoken but understood, that neither Ao nor Mahault could—would—go with him. Atakus was his concern, not theirs, except as part of the greater whole.

"Anyway, even if you were there, what would you do? Kaï, the Exiles . . . they are a legend, like I said. For them to come out of nowhere, like this, and attack Atakus . . . are we sure this unknown speaker, with unknown magic, can be trusted?"

"Tell me the legend," Jerzy said in a voice that brooked no denial or interruption.

Ao watched Kaïnam until the older man nodded his reluctant agreement, acknowledging the truth of the trader's words, then he shrugged, leaning back in his chair and stretching his legs out in front of him, the movement still stiffly awkward.

"Mayhaps two centuries ago, when Iaja was ruled by one lord, before the cities broke away, there were eleven families. Great Families, they were called. And they fought like prince-mages among each other, quarreling with politics and swords rather than magic, each trying to gain the advantage and put their own blood onto the throne.

"One family was smarter, or sneakier, than the others, though, and made an alliance with another family, planning a voyage of exploration that would win them lands that would set their families apart in fame and fortune and give them a clear, shared claim on the throne. A daughter from one and a son from the other would marry and bind the families together. One, they said, would be more powerful than two."

"If this had a happy ending, it would not be a legend," Mahault said.

"Truth. The ships of one family turned back halfway, returning to Iaja claiming a storm separated them from the others. True or not, no one could say. But the ships of that other family were never seen again, and their fortunes back home fell immediately, their eligible daughters married into other, lesser Houses, until even their name disappeared.

"But their banner remained, in the history books and the military rosters. Red, black, and gold."

Ao finished his story, and there was a pause.

"Ximen is an Iajan name," Jerzy said finally, thoughtful.

"Yes," Kaïnam said, his hand resting on his belt where his sword should hang. "Yes, it is."

Chapter 15

*J*erzy *did not* go to bed the night before, even after the others faded and went off, parsing the notes and books Malech and his master Josia had maintained, adding his own where it seemed useful or relevant. The discovery of Caulic magic, however used to their benefit, had unnerved him more than he had thought at first and driven home how fragile his own plans were. He needed to do more.

His skin was too pale and his eyes red-rimmed from exhaustion, his hand was sore and back muscles tight, and the study looked as though a storm had ripped through it, leaving wineskins and cups as debris, but when Mahault came to find him, midmorning, there was an air of satisfaction around him that she could not miss.

"Something's happened." Mahault took a chair, her eyes bright with anticipation.

"I know how to do it. I can find him." And not wait for him to find them.

"Him? Ximen?" Ao, who had followed Mahault into the study, went to stand next to Jerzy, looking down at the debris-covered worktable. His index finger poked at the debris, and Jerzy slapped the offending hand away sharply. "You tracked him using a feather?"

"A feather and a fang." Jerzy could hear the curl of pride in his voice, and then decided that he had earned it. "Although it's not a tracking-spell, truly." The addition of his own blood into the spellwine had been the connecting thread; a Vineart who did not know the weathervine trick of adding a drop would never have thought to do it. That final step had been easier than Jerzy had expected, the memory of Giordan leading the way, and after several failed experiments, he had finally felt the touch of what he looked for, a few hours after dawn.

He had been staring at his notes, trying to remember how to breathe, since then.

"Magic to magic, using his title and name, and the things that are tied to him, bone and blood, and the description of the flag . . ." Another Vineart, Jerzy could have explained what he did, or at least given them enough detail that they could find it themselves. Someone who had no touch of magic, not even the potential of slaves? It was like trying to describe the deepness of the sky to someone who was blind, or the pattering of rain on soil to a deaf man.

"It's tied to his name, and the sense of his magic, together," he said finally. "The way you react when someone calls you across a crowded room; I can make him turn around. Not physically. But the sense of him, marking him."

Even to Jerzy's ear it made no sense, but Ao, at least, didn't seem to mind not getting an explanation for once, focused more on the result. "So if you had enough information, you would be able to . . . find me anywhere?"

Jerzy stopped, his hands stilling as the idea struck him. "I . . . may be." It would be more difficult without the tang of magic to follow, but if he had something physical of the person, to stand in for the feather and fang, maybe. If he were able to . . .

"We could make a fortune, selling that spellwine. No, listen to me, Jer. Do you have any idea how much merchants would pay to be able to keep track of caravans with their goods in them? Knowing where they were when they arrived at market, or were loaded onto ships? And you can send this over the ocean . . . name the price, and it will be yours!"

"You are drooling," Mahault said, annoyed.

"Of course I am. Jer . . ."

Despite his exhaustion and near-quivering anticipation, Jerzy started to laugh. Nothing dampened Ao for long—not that the trader wasn't entirely serious about his proposal.

Some of the tension in Jerzy's body drained away, allowing him to speak more coherently.

"I don't know that I could actually incant it to a simple spellwine," he said. "But all right, if we survive this, I will consider it."

The likelihood of them actually surviving was small enough that it seemed a safe promise.

He had, as Kaï said earlier, poked their enemy with a stick. He could either wait . . . or he could poke harder.

Jerzy stared at the items on the table in front of him, and reached for the cup, taking a careful sip of its contents. The healwine burned in his throat, the bitterness too obvious; it had been sitting out too long and gone sour. But the magic was still strong, coursing through his body and banishing the exhaustion for a few hours longer. Long enough to do what needed to be done.

"Now if you must watch, be quiet."

They both shut their mouths with audible snaps, and settled against the far wall of the study. Jerzy had shoved the battered worktable against the wall under the maps. A series of bottles had been brought out of the cellar, and the surface was covered with tasting spoons and red-stained rags. He wanted nothing more than to throw a cover over the table, tuck himself into bed, and wake up to discover it had all been a horrid dream.

"Wind, first," he murmured to himself, putting all other thoughts out of mind. "Wind, to carry the spell. Fire, to fuel it. Earth, to ground it. Healspell, to bind flesh to flesh. Aether, to bring magic to magic."

And quiet-magic, to bind them all together within him.

The unblooded, feral grapes had given him that, he was starting to understand. Had changed him, opened something inside him, letting him sense the thing he had begun calling the Root, the living magic.

Magic makes the man. Gathering all the legacies together, stirred with the feral strength of the unblooded vines, the cold fierce magic that had been their birthright before Sin Washer made them . . . what? Jerzy did not know, and the not-knowing terrified him. But he thought of Ximen having access to all of that, not restricted to the legacies he could steal from his distant land . . . there would be no stopping the other man, then. That terrified Jerzy more.

He gathered the spellwines, lining them up each in a tasting spoon. The colors glinted at him, shading from the deep, heavy garnet of earth to the pale, almost translucent aether. A normal decantation would not have worked; even a Master Vineart would have difficulty collecting all five spellwines on his tongue, and still be able to control them.

Jerzy was no Master, but he knew these wines: three, he had worked the vines they came from, if not that particular harvest. The other two he had used before, that Vineart's work, the magic of those yards. The feel of the unblooded grapes in his mind, in his blood, told him that it could be done. That they were all legacies of the First Growth, all still connected by the Root. Not good, not bad, merely powerful. Dangerous, but needful. And that he, too, was part of the Root, connected by the magic within him.

That thought made him dizzy, so he pushed it away, concentrating on what was in front of him.

Taking a deep breath, he lifted his belt-blade, pressed it against the flesh of his wrist, where the slave-mark had once rested, piercing the skin. The tips of his fingers were too rough and hard, but the skin there gave way to vein, drawing forth a clear red drop of blood. He lifted his wrist to his mouth and licked at it, letting the blood touch his tongue, the taste salty-sweet.

Blood, to tie and bind the shattered pieces together.

Lifting the first spoon, he took only enough of the liquid to wet his tongue, letting it soak into the flesh. Earth, warm and spicy, welcoming and full. The scent of it rose into his nose, and he breathed it in deeply, trying to bring it into his entire body.

Then healing, cool and rounded, the taste of dark berries and fresh water, the nose of sunlight on dry stone. Fire, bright red and harsh on the tongue, with the nose of summer flowers in full bloom. Healing, tart and sharp, the greenest of the wines, the smell of rain and snow. And then aether. . . . He almost hesitated, his hand shaking as he lifted the spoon. The rasp of a cat's tongue, the sting of an insect's bite, the wet sweetness of overripe spring fruit, the dry scratch of riverstone, followed by a smell that seemed to belong only to aether, that he could not place or name, but knew for what it was, triggering an avalanche of memories in his brain.

Once he added his own blood to the mix, it acted as a paddle in the crush, his own body the vat, becoming something greater. The magic stretched and swelled within him, so ripe and potent he pitied those who needed a full mouthful to work it, who never felt the intensity, the depth of each wine, but only focused on the results. They used spellwines, but they never participated, were never caught up in how glorious every nuance, every layer of taste and smell, grew once it was released. . . .

The spellwines were all incanted, all designed for a specific use, but the freshly blooded magic within him slid underneath that, freed the essential magic from its shaping, and delivered it to him. Even other Vinearts, limited by their own walls, tied to the legacies the slavers delivered them into. Master Malech had never felt this, the sense of power thrumming within his veins, his skin the skin of the grape, swelling with every beat of his heart, the room itself seeming to sway around him.

Jerzy opened his mouth slightly and breathed in, letting the cool air slide over his tongue, opening the flavors even more, until the skin of his mouth tingled with it, and he could feel the magic surge in his blood, the quiet-magic answering the call. The room around him, the intent of the spell, it all faded under that, the dizzying feeling of spinning in place, driven by the magic until he could no longer feel his own body, but instead was part of something greater.

Not Master. Not Vineart. Something else. Something *more*. It was a step too far, he knew that, deep in his mind, but the understanding was so close, so tantalizing, he reached . . . and the Root beneath him stirred, and reached back, sliding its tendrils into his skin. . . .

"Jer?"

Jerzy grabbed at the noise, grabbed and held, building it into a solid floor under his feet, blocking the Root.

"Talk to me," he whispered, although he tried to shout it. "Say my name."

"Jer?"

"Jerzy." Another voice, lighter, like water flowing over rocks. "You are Jerzy. Jerzy of House Malech."

You are Vineart, a third noise added, and it was as though he had been flung hard up against a boulder, the spinning halted, his body still tingling from the effects.

You are a stupid Vineart, the noise added, and the rumble underneath was a familiar echo, the feel of a cuff against the back of his head, and Jerzy almost cried in gratitude.

"Jer?" Ao, worried. And Mahault, just behind him. Without opening his eyes, Jerzy identified them, even as he came back to his body, hands clenched hard against the wooden table, hard enough to dig splinters into his finger.

Vineart.

"I am . . . all right." He wasn't, not even close. "I let the magic . . . catch me up, a little."

No need to ever let them know how close he had come to being lost, how close he had come to falling into the Root, and . . . Jerzy cut that thought off. It did not happen; it was useless to linger. The spellwines waited. The Lands Vin needed him.

The last decantation he had used had only identified the feel of

Ximen. To find him, and hold him, he needed something specific, but inclusive, to tell the magic what he wanted of it, and give it shape . . .

Names. If magic made the man, names shaped them. "Ximen," he whispered. "Ximen, Praepositus. Vineart. Find, and bind. Go."

The magic swirled, and he almost lost his balance again, but steadied himself, this time intensely aware of the breathing of the two behind him, the weight of the Guardian in his chest, and the cool metal of his master's ring on his finger, binding him to this body.

A beat passed, then another, and Jerzy had a flash of doubts; had he misformed the decantation? Was the blend of spellwines too much? Had he used too little? Did he not—

Pain.

Jerzy staggered, his nails leaving marks in the table as he stumbled backward, his body arching forward as though taking a blow to the chest hard enough to fell a horse. Falling, endless falling into a void, the room no longer swaying but spinning around him, the rise of vomit in his throat, and the echo of sound around him, coming from all directions at once: present, possible, past . . .

The past, recent enough, the echoes still fresh in memory. The smell of warm dirt and horse sweat around him, the sound of metal clinking, the acrid taste of fear and anger, it surrounded Jerzy, swarming over him as the spell returned with what he had sent it to find, linking him to the one named Ximen.

And he felt that-which-was-Ximen die.

A sudden wash of relief—the enemy was dead—and shock—had he caused that? had he killed him?—ebbed with the realization that there was something else in that loop of magic, not held in the same manner but within it nonetheless. Something with the bloated stink of taint.

Something that yet lived.

Vineart. The awareness snarled the word at him, a streak of magic hurtling down the loop, blood-dark and rancid. Jerzy panicked, struggling to break the loop before that ill-intent found him, shedding the magic the way his master had once taught him, the second lesson ever, here in this very room.

If you can't control it, release it, he heard Malech say, his voice disgusted as he looked down at a younger, smaller Jerzy sprawled on the floor after a healspell made him throw up. *Never let it control you.*

have you now, you troublesome upstart.

The feel of the words was foul, the stench a physical thing, the hatred the other Vineart felt for Jerzy like a blow again to the chest, and Jerzy fell backward even as he felt hands catching him, supporting him, his eyes rolling back in his head, catching only a faint glimpse of the stone ceiling overhead.

"Guardian!" Not his voice—Mahault, calling, and the Guardian was there, wings stretched out, its long body forming a barrier, even as its long neck snaked forward and it spat fire along the loop, leaving it singed in its wake. Jerzy could just barely sense the flame reach its destination, singeing the other hard enough that he dropped away, howling in pain.

There was silence, save for the harsh sound of Jerzy's breathing, then Ao spoke.

"That didn't seem to work well."

There was another silence, and then Mahault let out a gasp that sounded suspiciously like laughter, and the two of them started to giggle helplessly, letting go of the stress now that they knew Jerzy was not dead.

The Vineart lay back on the floor, the Guardian having returned to its normal perch over the doorway, looking down at the three humans with a total lack of expression on its stone face, radiating a faint, almost imperceptible curiosity. It knew that the House had been threatened and that the threat had been sent away, but it lacked the details.

Jerzy closed his eyes against that curiosity, trying to sort the pieces himself. They had been misdirected, or their informant had: Ximen had been connected to the mage, but had not been the mage himself. Misdirected, to protect himself against discovery, should anyone question his tools, as Jerzy had. For some reason, the mage had killed this Ximen . . . but Jerzy had felt the magic that did it, felt the echo of the blow, the control that directed it, and he could use that again, name or no name.

The fact that the mage would now be able to find him as well . . . a grim smile moved Jerzy's lips. "Come and get me."

"Jer?"

"It's all right," he said, still not moving. He wondered what he would tell the others, still hovering impatiently, when there was the sound of someone outside the door and Kaïnam came in, a strange expression on his face.

Jerzy felt an odd sense of recognition flood him: the moment was just like the first day of Harvest, everything happening at once. And, like Harvest, you either acted, or failed.

You know the moment.

The Guardian sounded almost smug. Jerzy got to his feet quickly, ignoring the various aches and pulls of his body. "What?"

Kaïnam started to speak, then shook his head, discarding what he was going to say and starting again. "A *meme-courier* has arrived. From Caul."

"Vineart Jerzy."

Jerzy had never received a *courien* before; the one time a messenger had arrived for Master Malech, he had not been allowed to greet the *courien* or hear his message. Neither he, nor the others, had any idea how to address the other man, nor what level of courtesy should be extended. Unnerved from the encounter with not-Ximen, Jerzy decided to err on the side of being too arrogant rather than weak.

Therefore, he had Detta escort the messenger to his study, and waited below, letting his body recover from the encounter with not-Ximen before going up the stairs to greet his guest. The man stood in front of the great wooden desk, ignoring the chair that had been placed for him, his hands resting loosely at his sides, his simple uniform travel worn but otherwise clean and orderly.

Jerzy sat in his chair, leaned back, and looked up expectantly.

Meme-couriers were expensive to hire, but utterly trustworthy. They carried the same weight as if their client were actually speaking the words, and were, Master Malech had said, incapable of changing the wording they were tasked to deliver. It was not magic, but training, so deep they could not break it, not for love, money, or fear. For someone in Caul to have sent a message this way, rather than sending a messenger-bird or rider . . . it had to have been important.

"I bring to you greetings, Vineart Jerzy, from the Lord of Áth Cliath, the High King of Greater and Lesser Caul. These are the words the Lord of Áth Cliath would have you hear."

The High King—or his Spymaster, Mil'ar Atan? The High King could not be trusted. The Spymaster . . . could be trusted only slightly more. Jerzy did not show any reaction, merely tilted his head, indicating that the courier should continue.

"It has come to our attention, lord Vineart, that the island you indicated interest in has come under attack by forces which have neither of our better interests in their heart. In light of this, and with our own interests in mind regarding the reopening of those sea routes, we hereby offer the use of our own fleet to help retake the Principality in question, and to help defend it against further attacks, once it has been reclaimed.

"We are further aware that you guest within your House a member of the royal family of this Principality, and show him high regard. It would be our significant honor to allot him one of our ships, that he might take part in the liberation of his home, and ensure his people that we do, indeed, come with offers of aid, not interference."

Jerzy felt the urge to ask what the price for this gesture might be, but held his tongue. The courier could only repeat the words given him, not answer questions.

"In exchange for this, Lord Vineart . . ."

Jerzy allowed himself a raised eyebrow. There it was.

"We ask only that you allow us to call upon you in our occasional need, to discuss matters of mutual concern and commercial exchanges of shared benefit."

In other words, he could almost hear Detta mutter into his ear, *he wants first shot and best prices at our spellwines.*

Unlikely, considering Caul's historic stance on magic. And yet, clearly that time had also passed. If they would barter their magic for his . . . likely not. But the opportunity would be there, as Ao would say.

"The details of the offer are as follows. The warship *Fast Lance.* The warship . . ."

Jerzy listened to the man list the ships that would be part of this flotilla, and wondered what Kaïnam's reaction might be, if he were to agree . . . and what the prince might say if he refused.

HE FOUND THE prince in the courtyard, where Mahl had been sitting on the bench reading through dispatches, while Kaïnam, listening, dropped a handful of rounded stones, one by one, into the well. They plunked into the water deep below, the echo rising up the stone-built cistern. Jerzy listened to the echo, and judged the level of water to be within normal springtime range.

They stopped when Jerzy came out, letting him report on the *courien.*

Kaïnam heard him out, visibly tense. "He asked you to release me to his fleet?"

"In effect, yes."

"The arrogant . . ." Kaïnam fumed for a few moments, and then gave an elegant shrug that downplayed what they all knew, that he had been dying inside the past few days since that magic-borne message, needing to be on his way home. "He is arrogant, but correct. Without me onboard, or at the very least my seal of safe-passage, they would be treated as invaders by my folk, even once they cleared out the actual invaders."

And they offered him what he most desired: a way home.

"This offer comes suspiciously swift, days after they informed us of the Exiles' attack and return." Ao was polishing the side of his boot, worrying at a smear of mud that had dried on the leather, frowning at it as though it were the cause of all his concerns.

"If this is from the High King, we cannot refuse." Jerzy was not certain if the mage could have responded so quickly, setting such an invitation up to entrap them in turn. More, it did not have the feel of the thoughts he had encountered, the blind, relentless greed he had felt. This was more subtle, nuanced, the difference between a growvine and aether, earth, and air.

"The *courien* says he was hired by a man in plaincloth, bearing coin, not a letter of funds. That, to me, suggests our friend in Caul," Kaï said. "Either way, yes, I am not sure we have a choice."

"Can you trust them not to be invaders in truth," Mahault asked. "Once they've landed their fleet in your harbor?"

"Of course not," Kaïnam said, dropping the last of the stones in his hand. "It's just as likely I will become a royal hostage. But Caul is a pragmatic country, for all that they're madmen. If my brother tells them he would sooner see kin die than give up his diadem, they will understand he means it. And without me, they have little chance of succeeding to get to that point: Atakus did not survive unmolested all these centuries by being easy to enter. Even after these Exiles broke through the veil, there are safeguards that likely still stand." He paused, and looked at Jerzy. "Assuming that we do not believe that they, Caul, are in league with these Exiles?"

Jerzy shook his head, remembering again the feel of the mage's thoughts in his head, the anger in his veins. "He shares with no one."

Kaïnam dusted his hands, and leaned against the wall of the well, looking at Jerzy. His hair was tied back with a red kerchief, his clothing a plain shatnez weave that could have been worn by any farmer in The Berengia, and yet still he looked exotic, foreign. Jerzy blinked, as though expecting the sensation to pass, but it remained. Kaï's face had taken on a different cast, the proud nose and angular shape suddenly at odds with those around him.

Malech had carried such a nose, but it had looked hawkish, not regal. The vines had shaped him into belonging here, just as Jerzy, despite his distant origins, belonged here. Just as Mahault never would. In that instant, Jerzy knew that Ao would never return to his trader-people, whatever else happened. *Magic makes the man.*

"Then I see no other option."

"You'll leave us?" Mahl asked, her voice tight with anger. "Now, when we finally—when Jerzy finally has a real sense of our enemy, when we can finally go on the offensive?"

For the first time, Kaïnam looked discomfited. "Mahl . . . I must."

"Must what? Abandon us, walk away from our plans, our . . . we need you here!"

Jerzy felt the push of things unseen, growing below the surface. Mahault had walked away from her home city, her father and family, had seen the place where she was born fall to the mob, her father killed and her mother's fate uncertain. The price of survival, of doing what she thought was right.

Jerzy wondered if she was more upset at Kaïnam's having a home to return to than the fact that he was leaving.

"This is part of those plans, Mahl. You know that." The prince's voice was calm, too calm, and Mahault's hands gripped the papers in her lap so tightly they crumpled around her fingers. "Taking Atakus was only a first step: they will launch their ships, *Atakus's* ships, against us, next. Caul and Iaja have the only fleets able to compete, and Iaja has no interest in aligning with us. Caul does. They need me there to legitimatize their actions, and convince my brother to help protect the sea lanes from further attack."

Mahault set her chin and looked away.

"Mahl. This is what we've been waiting for. No successful offense has only one line of attack. The Exiles forced Atakus into isolation to make them vulnerable, give them a base to launch their own attack from, it has to be. My people can secure the sea for us and hold off that attack, but only if they are free to do so."

Jerzy watched, sensing that they were speaking a second language underneath that he could not understand, willing to let them work this out themselves.

The anger left Mahault's voice, but she was still unhappy. "I don't like it, you leaving us."

"Neither do I." The admission seemed to surprise Kaïnam, but he plowed forward. "I am a member of the royal family, Mahl. There are things I must do."

"I know." She didn't look at him, but the lines of her body softened slightly. "Jerzy, is there any way we can keep in contact, faster than pigeons? If the Cauls have managed it, perhaps a spellwine that could . . ."

"Master Malech enspelled his mirror to create a passage through which we could speak, but I do not know how." Again Jerzy felt the sting of an incomplete training, but it was a familiar pain, now, and overshadowed by the things he knew, wonderful, terrible things, that his master had not. "The Caulic messenger . . . I do not want to have to rely on them, or their magic, not knowing its source." There was already one mage out there, working horrors. There had been vines on Caul, once, but they died out long ago. The Root—did it stretch to Caul as well, even now? If not vines, what had it seeped into, that magic? It was a question for the scholars of Altenne; Jerzy needed to worry about more immediate concerns. But he would not put his trust in this new magic.

"I agree," Kaïnam said, responding only to what Jerzy had said out loud. "Allowing an ally to control correspondence is unwise. There is a windspell that carries messages," he added, "but it is . . . unreliable."

"Putting anything to the wind is risky," Jerzy replied with a shrug. "You can direct weatherspells but you cannot control them, not the way you do fire or earth." A drop of blood coaxed weathervines into obedience, gentled it for incanting. Blood-magic at the level the Exile Vineart used? Jerzy shuddered to think what he might accomplish, were he able to spread his malice on the winds via weathervines.

They would stop him. They had to stop him.

Mahault turned to Jerzy. "Your master reached you, before . . ."

"Used the Guardian as a conduit. Or the Guardian used him . . . I don't know how it works. It can find me, but I don't know if it could find *you*."

Jerzy paused a moment, and the other two waited, watching him, but there was only silence from the dragon.

"You're not part of the House," he said, finally. If Kaï took Ao with him, perhaps the Guardian would use the connection through Ao's grafted legs, but Jerzy couldn't bring himself to suggest it. They would be struggling enough without Kaïnam's steady sense and strong arm; he could not let Ao go as well. "I will try to enspell a mirror for you," he said finally, "and we will make it part of the Agreement with Caul, that they allow it, to keep us in touch."

"You trust them to hold to that?"

"As much as you trust them to allow you free run of their warship," Jerzy said.

And that simply, it was settled.

"The *meme-courier* is waiting for a response," Jerzy said. "Kaïnam, you will want to phrase it, on behalf of Atakus, and then I will give him my own response."

Mahault watched Kaïnam stride to the door Jerzy had emerged from, not hesitating a second further. "You think this is wise?"

Jerzy exhaled harshly, looking to the sky rather than meeting her worried gaze. "None of this is wise, Mahl. But it's what we have to do." He paused, and then gave her the only comfort he knew. "Seeds scatter. Roots remain." Longer than any of them had suspected.

She nodded. "And Kaïnam was right, rot him." She had started using Ao's favorite swear, although it made Jerzy flinch used this close to the yards. "We need more than one line of attack, ourselves. Jer, I have an idea. . . ."

THE COLLEGIUM WAS the size of a large town, or a small city, from the outer gate to the practice fields and the gardens that stretched down to the river, farmed by students as part of their meditation hours. Zatim's mother had been the god of the growing season, his father the lord of the Harvest, and spending time with their hands in the soil was as much a part of a Washer's training as learning Zatim's Commands and warnings. Hallways and classrooms, the Library and the training fields, the dormitories and the stables, all were open to any visitor who came seeking knowledge. Even the kitchens were open to any who might wish to walk through, although the cooks' tempers were often uncertain.

There was one place in the entire Collegium that was not open. One place that most residents knew existed, but had never seen.

The Cellar.

It ran underneath the Collegium itself, stone-walled tunnels and square-carved rooms like a maze, lined with wooden racks that were carefully labeled with a number that corresponded to a large leather-bound journal. The ink in that journal was browned with age in the earlier pages, a more vibrant black in the last, and noted almost five hundred years' worth of spellwines, bought, tested, annotated, and stored by the Spellkeeper of the day.

In a normal year, only a handful of Washers might access the wide, shallow steps into the antechamber. That afternoon, the sun casting long shadows behind them, four went down together. Brothers Ranklin, Omar, Isaac, and Neth.

There had been no meeting, no calling for opinions. Ranklin had appeared at his rooms, fixed him with that gaze that could still make Neth feel fourteen and uncertain again, and told him what would happen.

He had wanted to voice his dissent, to protest this madness, but it would have been pointless and kept him from being allowed to participate. So long as he was on the scene, Neth still held a faint hope that he might be able to control things, keep events from spiraling out of control.

Ranklin had taught most of the current brothers when they were gangly children, and was not fooled by Neth's acquiescence; yet he had included Neth in the group, anyway.

They were come to find a spellwine that would put an end to the chaos rising outside, bring the world back into order again.

The air was much cooler, below ground, away from the sun's reach, and the space echoed with deliberate silence, broken now by their presence.

"Brothers." The Spellkeeper was surprisingly young, lean and dark haired, rising from his desk with a grace that Neth was not sure he could have mirrored. His voice was rusty from disuse, but his pleasure on seeing them was real. "This is an unexpected but welcome pleasure. How may I assist you today?"

"We have need to look through your records," Ranklin said. "For a very specific spellwine."

"Of course. I will need the Vineart's name, and legacy."

"We do not know."

That stopped the Spellkeeper mid-movement, even as he was reaching to open the great volume on his desk.

"Ah. That . . . is considerably more difficult," he said regretfully, but with what Neth thought was a touch of anticipation in his voice. "What information do you have? Region? Legacy? Century?"

"It would be in the earlier archives," Omar offered. His ebony skin seemed a trifle ashen, although it could as easily have been the lighting as nerves.

The Spellkeeper had a definite gleam in his eye now, even in the dim spell-lights that illuminated the antechamber. "Indeed? An Ancient wine."

He had probably never done more than walk past those archives; there was no call for so-named Ancient wines, in this world.

"The Magewine," Isaac said. "The *ercenbalt* Magewine."

"Ah." The Spellkeeper let his hand rest on the tooled leather cover of the volume and breathed the still air in, out, and then in again. "Ah," he said again.

Not only ancient, but legendary. Vineart unknown. Legacy unknown. Only the name remained, less a proper name than a description, given by the scholars of Altenne long after the fact. Ercenbalt. Roughly translated, it meant "the courage of last hope." What it truly meant was "when all else fails."

THE CASK, WHEN located, was ancient as expected, but still solidly built, the wooden slats covered by layers of earthspells that protected against rot or decay. The sigil burned into the wood was one that Neth did not recognize, nor, according to the Spellkeeper, was it one listed in the journal of that century.

"We took in so many back then," he said almost wistfully. "Those were the grand times, full of excitement and magic."

Neth looked sideways at the Spellkeeper, as the others moved on ahead, the cask carefully loaded onto a wheeled cart. Clearly, he did not get aboveground much or listen to gossip at all. "Be careful what you desire," he said dryly. "Else you might be cast into the middle of it, and find it not so much to your liking."

"The decantation," Omar asked impatiently.

The Spellkeeper went to the wall of his alcove, drawing out another journal, this one far older, the leather heavier worn than the current edition. "The writing is faded, and the language slightly archaic."

"I thought that was part of your training," Isaac said. Unlike Omar and Neth himself, he seemed almost too eager to do this. His voice was thin from the stress, but to the Spellkeeper it must have sounded like disdain. His body curved in on itself, shoulders rounding, elbows turned in as though to cuddle the journal, or protect it.

Ranklin stepped in, his age and status stopping the argument cold. "Brother, your training is not in doubt, merely our own nerves. What is the decantation, please?"

"Root, bind. Leaf, curl. Magic, still. Go." He recited the words, and then shuddered. "It has the sound of an earthspell, but not the feel of it."

Spellkeepers were chosen not for their memory or their patience, but for their sensitivity to the power within the wines; without it, it would be impossible to find anyone willing to spend their days down here, but Neth had always suspected that it made them slightly odd.

"You need not worry," Ranklin said, his hand patting the younger man's shoulder gently, the paper-dry skin nearly translucent against the dark red of his robe, before turning to lead the way back up the stairs, having achieved what he came for.

"It has been over a century since that cask was last broached," the Spellkeeper said, frowning, still looking down at the journal page. "There is no guarantee that it will have remained intact. Be very careful with your testing."

"Of course." Neth was professionally reassuring, his entire demeanor tuned to giving solace, and the Spellkeeper, despite knowing all that, bought into it.

Men, even Washers, did not want to burden themselves with worries.

THEY RECEIVED THE occasional odd looks from students and teachers as they moved through the formal gardens, but no one was foolish or foolhardy enough to stop and ask questions. Neth could only imagine that his expression was at least as grim as that of his companions.

Ranklin's quarters had a door to the outside and a workroom that was their destination. His aide was there, looking anxious. Clearly he did not trust anyone other than himself with the old man. Neth had a moment's uncharitable, suspicious thought: was the younger, untried Brother a member of the schism? Was he worried not for the old man's well-being, but his own plots?

No. Ranklin was on the right side of things, for all that Neth disagreed with this decision. If his aide felt differently, he would have been wise to keep it to himself, and it was too late now.

"The Last Hope," Ranklin said. "Such a terrible name for such a terrible spellwine. Too much focus on how we are remembered, and not enough on what we are doing now."

"Are you saying we as a culture are pretentious, Brother?" Omar raised his nearly invisible eyebrows and waited for a response, clearly expecting a lecture such as they would have received as students.

"It would not be the worst thing I have said of our founders," he replied, but the laughter was faint, worried. It reassured Neth, that the mood was uneasy rather than jubilant. If they who were set on this thing were unsure . . .

"Place the cask there," Ranklin directed, taking a seat on the padded divan and resting his hands on his knees. He was old and fragile, but his eyes were still bright, and the mind was as sharp as it had ever been.

"Do you truly believe that this spellwine is . . . is the answer?"

Ranklin considered the question, as Neth had known he would, had expected no less of the old man, who had taught them all at one time or another. "The answer? No. But I do believe that it is *an* answer. Perhaps the only one we have."

"Harming the vines . . . it is counter to everything we have ever been. And the Vinearts are not the only thread in this knot."

"The men of power are as they have ever been, Neth. Suspicious, proud, cautious, and protective. Something has pulled them tight . . . that something is a Vineart. Whatever began this, began with magic. Only by bringing them all to heel can we return the balance to where it needs be.

"I do not choose this lightly. You, of all the others, you have seen firsthand the danger we face."

"Yes." Danger without, and within, although he did not say that. If Ranklin did not know of the schism, of his own Brothers, men he had taught now twisting that training for their own benefit, it might be possible for the old man to never have to find out. And if he did . . . then he had not spoken of it to Neth for a reason, and Neth would honor that.

Blind faith was not the way of the Brotherhood, but obedience honored Sin Washer's sacrifice.

They ranged themselves around the cask, sitting innocently on the low table, its aged wood a sharp contrast to the polished surface of the table. A tiny, pale gold spider crawled down one side, taking careful steps, no doubt shocked to find itself outside the cool, quiet environs of the Cellar.

"If this is to be done, it needs be done now." Omar turned to fetch a cup from the sideboard display, his hand reaching first for an ornate one made of glass, the colored bits sparkling like an artisan's toy, but then his hand moved to the left slightly and instead he picked up a simple hammered copper cup. When the others looked at him, he made a face, as though uncomfortable with his own actions. "This thing we do, it is not pretty. Pretty things should not be used for it."

Ranklin laughed, a soft exhalation of air that was not amused, but approving. "Even so, young Omar, even so. Come, let us do this."

"Let me," Neth said, stepping forward to take the cup.

"You did not agree with my decision," his old teacher said, surprised. "And now you volunteer to perform the decantation?"

"As Omar said, this is not pretty. Let it be done by one who knows firsthand the damage it will do." The other two had never visited a vintnery, had never spoken with Vinearts, conversed with them, or preached, or offered solace to their slaves. Neth knew what he was about to do and took the weight of that knowledge to heart.

If he was to be guilty, let his hands be bloody, as well.

The cup touched his hands, and his fingers curled around it, even as Isaac picked up the glass bulb that would draw the liquid from the bunghole at the top.

The stopper was newer than the cask, proof that it had been maintained over the years, and when removed the scent of the wine drifted into the room, musty and sharp, like the prick of thorns on the tongue. The bulb filled with liquid, a paler orange-red than he had expected, almost the color of rust on a hinge, or the faded cheeks of one of the portraits in the Main Hall.

Then it was being transferred to his glass, and Neth had to steady his hand or else let them see how it shook. With this decantation, he would bring a blight that would wither every grape on the vine, shake the confidence of every Vineart. . . .

"Ranklin! Stop this!"

The shout did make his hand shake, then, but thankfully Isaac had stopped pouring.

"You interrupt, in my private quarters?"

Three men stood in the doorway: Brother Weyland, a heavyset man from the lands north of Caul, and two others. Neth recognized them, although he did not know their names. They were looking at Ranklin, but their gazes flickered back and forth the way men do when they are expecting trouble—or out to cause some.

"This can wait."

"No, it cannot. I cannot agree with this."

That was surprising. If Weyland was a member of the schism, then he should—

"You think to act in half measures, as though that will solve this. The Vinearts must be brought to heel, not merely checked."

Ranklin remained seated, calmly observing the intruders. "Your wishes were too extreme. Our responsibility is to hold the Lands Vin together, not split them apart."

Something inside Neth hurt, hearing confirmation that his old teacher had indeed known of the schism and not stopped it.

The three men came into the room, their postures promising trouble, even as their words remained civilized. "This is our only chance to shatter the Second Growth, once and for all. To finish the job Sin Washer started."

"Apostasy," the aide whispered, astonished, horrified. "You blaspheme Zatim's Blood."

"I am *defending* it," Weyland roared, his long, white-blond mustache practically bristling with anger. "Vinearts were meant to be servants, not . . . not equals. The magic must be controlled. And not by lordlings or princes!" He stepped forward, clearly not thinking how his actions would be interpreted within the close confines of the chambers, with seven bodies already tensed.

Omar swung first, but Weyland blocked and countered, and then it became a melee, Ranklin falling backward, his voice, once so robust, barely able to make itself heard above the fight. Even as Neth watched, the old man stiffened, as though spasming, then fell limp.

Neth felt his breath catch, but he had no time to go to the old man's aid, even if there was anything he could have done. He sideswiped a wild swing and had barely enough time to note that none of his fellow combatants had taken lessons with Brion, when he found himself next to the cask.

The old, aged cask. Set high up on a table that was polished with care every morning. . . .

The oldest legends said that even after his death Zatim Sin Washer spoke with the first of the Washers, those whose hands had been washed in his actual blood. Neth had always thought that a fable, until the voice whispered inside his own ear. Harsh, almost foreign sounding, sharp like the crack of lightning, dense as the roll of thunder, and impossible to ignore or deny.

Stop it. End this. Protect my brothers, heir to my blood.

His hands lifted, touched, pushed, Neth watching them as though they belonged to someone else. The cask shifted, rolled, fell, shattered. The ancient slats of wood splintered, the noise enough to break through the violence and cause them all to turn, and stare. The floor, now coated with the brick-brown wine, slicked enough that those who tried to turn, to rescue even a drop of the precious liquid, slipped and fell, hitting the floor hard enough that they lay still; if still alive, unable to move.

Neth stood, and watched, and did not hear the voice again.

Chapter 16

*J*erzy *had not* slept at all in nearly three days, since the *meme-courier* had departed. Part of him knew that he could not continue that way, that sooner rather than later the healwine and the tai would force his body into collapse—or kill him—but even if he had been able to sleep without nightmares, there was no time for it.

"Master Malech gave me a mirror that would allow him to reach me, when I was in Aleppan. It was broken—when the serving boy tried to kill me, it was broken in the fight. I thought he had done it on purpose, to keep me from reaching my master . . . if he was in thrall to the mage, he might have been drawn by the scent of magic, not even knowing what it was."

He was talking too much, too fast. They already knew what they needed to know. Jerzy stopped, pushed his shoulders back, took a deep breath, not looking at the other three in the room.

"It doesn't matter. The important thing is that there is a spell that works through mirrors. This," and Jerzy indicated the mirror propped up against the wall, "has always been in Master Malech's study, propped up at an angle that reflected nothing. Not until the spell was decanted."

Mahault stepped forward, looking into the mirror. It was as wide across as Jerzy could reach, and almost as tall as he was—when he had first seen it, his entire length had fit easily within the silvered depths—framed by delicate gold and silver wires worked into lifelike vines. As Jerzy had said, nothing—not even her form, directly in front of it—reflected in the dull silvered surface.

"This . . . can be spoken through?"

"Yes." Jerzy hoped so, anyway. He had never used the small hand mirror Malech had given him, so he wasn't sure exactly how it worked. The boy he had been would not dared have asked Malech for specifics or details, but trusted that his master would tell him whatever he needed to know.

"And he would have . . . eventually," Jerzy said softly.

"What?"

"Nothing. I just . . . there is a notation in one of Master Malech's cellar books that I think is the right decantation." The problem was, the notation had not specified which legacy to use. It would not be a healing spell, Jerzy was quite certain of that, and Malech had not used weatherspells overmuch, so that was unlikely . . . that left fire, earth, and aether.

Earth seemed an odd choice, considering the mirror was not made of living things. He would put that aside for the moment. That left fire and aether.

"Aether is rare, and expensive. I would say that pointed to fire . . . except that Master Malech did not use this spell easily, so it would not have been of his making."

"So, aether," Ao said, confident as a master.

"That would be my thought."

"And you cast this decantation and it . . . does what?"

Jerzy ran a hand over his face, noting with surprise that his chin was scratchy. He did not have to shave more than a few times a week, but he must have forgotten. A quick look into a smaller mirror, faceup on the table in front of him, confirmed the suspicion. His chin was indeed covered with dark red stubble.

The mirror also revealed the fact that his eyes were blue-shadowed, and his cheeks hollow from stress and lack of sleep, and Jerzy thought that perhaps there was a reason that, for all its wealth, House Malech did not contain many mirrors.

"I'm not sure exactly what it does," Jerzy said slowly, reluctantly. "This mirror's old, older than Malech—he inherited it from his master, along with the yards. I think it . . . the decantation *should* form a connection between the large mirror and the ones I made for you." Mahault, Ao, and Kaïnam each stepped forward at that, and picked up one of the smaller mirrors: actually, three shards broken from a larger piece and the edges smoothed with a firespell so that they would not cut their owners.

"And then we speak into it, and you see us? Hear us?" Ao looked absolutely fascinated, while Kaïnam appeared slightly queasy.

"Yes."

"Amazing. If only they weren't so fragile—we would lose more on a caravan than we could recoup in sales, I suspect. Although . . ."

"Ao. This is not a tradesgood."

"Everything someone wants can be a tradesgood, Jer," Ao said in return, but his tone was light enough to be teasing. "All right, we can wait for another day to discuss it. Do whatever it is you're going to do."

"Bring me your mirror," Jerzy said, reaching for the aeatherwine flask. "Lean it against the wall, like that," and he indicated the wall opposite the mirror, so that the surfaces could reflect into each other.

Ao did so and then stepped back, while Jerzy poured the spellwine into his tasting spoon and lifted it to his tongue.

Aetherwine seemed to change its personality every time he tasted it. Here, it was smooth and sweet, almost overripe the way late summer fruit became when it hung too long on the tree. Jerzy let it soak into the surface of his tongue, breathing in the aroma until it filled his awareness and he could feel the odd tickling tingle of the spellwine beginning to rise.

Turning, he touched the larger mirror with his hand, letting the Guardian guide him as he imagined the mirror behind him, asking the larger mirror to recognize it, identify it, own it.

"Reflect and return," he told the larger mirror, waiting until the surface shimmered slightly in acknowledgment, and then turned to the smaller one. "Return and reflect." It took longer, the smaller sheet seeming to resist the order, until it, too, shimmered and fogged over. Jerzy felt a click inside him, as though the two surfaces had been pieced together, and swallowed the spellwine, his "go" barely audible even to himself.

"*Sometimes you command,*" he could hear Malech telling him, a long-ago lecture. "*And sometimes you coax. Knowing the difference can make all of the difference.*"

"Did it work?" Ao waited, staring at the smaller mirror with fascination.

"There's ever only one way to know," Jerzy said. He tried to hide his uncertainty, stepping back to allow Ao to reclaim the smaller mirror.

"So, what do I do?"

"Place your hand on the mirror, and repeat the decantation. Words, hear. Words return."

Ao repeated the spell, his voice steady, and the surface of his mirror cleared, reflecting first his own round face, scrunched up in concentration, and then fogged over again. When it recleared, it showed not Ao's face, but the lower half of Jerzy's body, where he stood in front of the larger mirror.

The larger mirror, on the other hand, now showed Ao's face.

"That . . . is the most incredible thing I have ever seen."

There was an odd lapse: Jerzy could hear Ao's voice behind him, while he watched the mirror-figure's mouth move, and then a second later, he heard the words again from the mirror's surface.

"Incredible," Ao said again, before Mahault stepped forward, her face bright with anticipation. "And now mine!"

Jerzy, still puzzling over the lapse between seeing and hearing, shook his head and turned around, directing her to put her shard where Ao's had been.

"I need you to stand between the two mirrors."

"What?" That made Mahault look slightly alarmed. "You didn't ask Ao to do that."

"Ao is already connected to the House." He didn't look at Ao's vine-grafted legs, but the implication was clear. "This . . . I need to . . . introduce you to the mirror."

This wasn't part of Master Malech's incantation: the understanding what needed to be done must come from the dragon: it knew more than even it was aware, absorbing it all those years of watching Malech work from its perch above the door. He would not trust the earlier *vina-*connection here. Not for this.

"All right." She stood in the middle, slightly closer to her own mirror, and waited, her hands at her hips and anticipation in every bone of her body.

This time, before Jerzy decanted the spell, he called up his own quiet-magic and, one hand pressed to the flat of the main mirror, extended the other toward Mahault. "Touch my hand. Palm to palm."

Her hand was cool and slightly sweaty, and when he invited the mirror to acknowledge her, something sparked between their palms, making her gasp, although she did not pull away.

"It's done?"

Jerzy nodded. "I think so." He dropped his hand and asked the mirror to find Mahault. The surface shimmered again, then showed Mahault . . . but from an odd angle, as though the mirror were placed by the doorway, not against the wall.

Mahault let out an exclamation of surprise and awe, as though she had never seen magic decanted before. "Ao's right. That spell is . . ."

"Is limited to those who are connected to the main mirror," Jerzy reminded her. "And it requires quiet-magic to operate."

"Oh."

"And, no," he said, before Ao could even open his mouth, "I hear what you're thinking and no, I don't know how to make the main mirror, and even if I did I would not try and change the spell so that anyone could decant it. There is a reason Vinearts are held to their vineyards, remember? And part of it is so that magic like this doesn't get into the larger world."

Ao started to protest, and Jerzy overrode him ruthlessly. "Don't you understand? *This is a prince-mage spell.* If anyone knew I had it, could use it, they would assume that *I* was the one behind the attacks!"

The truth of that silenced even Ao.

As he had a season before, Jerzy once again found himself standing at the edges of the House, watching his friends ride away. Kaïnam had departed that morning, to connect with the Caulic ships heading for Atakus. Now Mahault, too, was leaving, although merely heading northwest, following up on her plan to meet with the solitaires under Agreement with Lord Ranulf.

"You think that this will work?"

Mahault finished checking the saddle band, pressing her elbow into the horse's belly until it exhaled and allowed her to tighten the buckle, and turned to face the Vineart.

"I don't know. Keren said he would welcome another fighter, and not ask closely about my training. Once I'm there, I should be able to make some noise."

Jerzy had already set the cat among pigeons with the Washers; now it was Mahault's turn. Her plan had been simple: if Kaïnam was right, and their enemy was finally attacking by sea, then they needed to distract his attention, make him less able to protect the ships against Caul's attack.

A band of solitaires riding the Berengian coastline, calming fears and training villagers to properly defend their land, might attract more attention, and require the enemy to put more of his energy into that, allowing Jerzy more time to prepare.

"If Ranulf lets you redirect his hires . . ."

"If I choose my words properly," she said with a smile, "he won't have a choice. Keren and the others will present it to him as a finished Agreement."

"You've been spending too much time with Ao."

"Most likely," she agreed comfortably. "Jer . . ."

"It's all right." And it was. Unlike Mahault, Jerzy hadn't seen Kaïnam's leaving as any kind of betrayal, and he understood why she was riding off now. The fact that there was a hollow feeling in his chest had nothing at all to do with that, nor the fact that he had not been sleeping at all, recently. Every time he closed his eyes, the Root pushed at him, seeking entrance he dared not give. But the worry that chewed at him now was directed outward, not in. They would handle the physical world, the politics and power. Magic was his responsibility. His alone.

"Be careful," he told her.

"Survive to be paid, that's the solitaire way," she quipped, then pulled him into a rough hug.

And then she was gone, swinging into the saddle and riding down the road and out of sight.

The House was no quieter with her gone; the normal noises came from the kitchen, where Lil had everyone working on the day's meals. Jerzy looked to the right, toward his study, and then turned left instead.

The first time he had come into the House, the dirt of the yards still ground into his skin, his sweat smelling like the sleep house, the kitchen had been the single familiar thing he encountered. Shinier, cleaner, more controlled than the sleep house's kitchen, there was nonetheless a calming sameness to it.

Then, Lil had been one of the kitchen children, learning how to run a House from Detta. Now she was Cook, and the kitchen was her domain.

"And don't turn too quickly," she was instructing a small child sitting by the great fireplace. The towheaded youngster nodded, almost comically intent on his chore of turning the spit. Jerzy frowned; had

Detta mentioned taking on new servants? She must have, and he must have nodded, but he had no recollection of the event. Still. Detta was House-keeper precisely so that he need not. Just as he now left the physical details with Kaï and Mahault.

Lil saw him come into the kitchen and nodded, a tight gesture that didn't take her attention away from any of the other things occurring, turning to follow the action. "Roan, halve the dough, we'll need less bread this week. And get the meat from the icehouse before you begin the grinding. Will someone please stir that pot, before it overboils?"

Jerzy picked a meat roll off a platter as he sidled through, passing it from hand to hand so that it did not burn his skin.

"Vineart, there is break-fast already on the table," Lil said, knowing even with her back to him that he'd pilfered food. "Go eat."

Ao was at the table, a stack of papers at one elbow, a mug of ale at the other. He looked up when Jerzy entered the dining hall. "She off?"

"Yes. You didn't say good-bye?"

The trader looked down at the papers. "No. And I didn't say it to Kaïnam, either. You say good-bye, people think they've closed negotiations."

"She's annoyed with me."

"Of course she is."

Jerzy sat down, taking a bite out of the roll and wiping his now-greasy hands on his trou's leg. "Of course?"

"She wants you to do something already, make a move, finally launch your attack. Or at least tell her about what you're going to do, so she can see it laid out on a map and markers."

"I did tell her. I told all of you." The tai smelled good, a sure sign that he needed sleep, although he had managed to doze for a few hours the night before, once all their plans had been set in motion. He poured himself a mug and gulped it down.

Ao laughed, and looked up again from his notes. "Jer, the one thing I've learned is that you Vinearts look open and guileless, but you're as deep as your damn roots, and twice as tangled. And you don't even realize it. You think you are being obvious, but all you've done is talk around them and assume we'd pick up on it. And Mahl? Mahl's not really a subtle creature."

Jerzy frowned, feeling as though either he or Mahault, or both, had just been insulted, but not sure how.

"But you understand?"

Ao was not subtle by nature, but he understood an indirect question the way only a trader could. "Yes. They think you're planning on distracting our esteemed enemy with side feints and potential attacks, weakening his tools, and then bringing it all down with your magic. But you're not."

"I'm not."

"No." Ao poured himself more ale from the other pitcher, and took a long sip. "You're going to let him attack you, trap him on your own soil. Everything else, everything we're doing with ships and soldiers, it's illusion, a diversion to cover what is truly happening. The only thing that matters is you, and him. The only thing I haven't figured out is how you can be sure that he will come here and not destroy you first."

It did not surprise Jerzy that Ao understood. Or that the trader would not ask directly for answers, although he had to be aching with curiosity.

"I have something he wants," was all the Vineart said.

He sounded confident, but inside Jerzy could feel his nerves stretching thin. Once he had become aware of the Root, had felt its pull, he had to be on guard against it constantly. If Jerzy let it touch him again . . . he did not know what would happen. To him, to the Guardian—to all their plans.

There was, as Kaïnam had said of the Caulic offer, no real choice.

Jerzy pushed his hands against the table, feeling the muscles in his back creak and stretch.

Blood had broken the First Vine, once, but now the Exiled mage used it to make his magic stronger. The Root responded—to that, to the strange new magic of the Cauls, to something entirely different . . .

possibly even to Jerzy himself, Apostate, the multiple legacies he should not have, seeping into him, changing him.

Perhaps the Root had always been there, waiting only to be noticed.

"All things follow," he said. "Seed to stem, stem to vine, vine to fruit, fruit to wine. Logic and pattern."

Ao started to say something, then lifted his tai to his mouth and sipped, instead, merely watching.

Blood made magic stronger. The blood of man. Man makes the magic. Magic makes the man.

Jerzy's head ached, but he kept hold of the thought, trying to learn its scent and shape. Sin Washer's blood had been what broke the Vine, soaking into the soil and shattering the magic at its Root. Sin Washer had broken the First Growth, had created the smaller, less powerful legacies and Commanded Vinearts to stay within their own yards . . . to prevent this. To prevent what he, Jerzy was . . . or was becoming. Blood magic. *Prince-mage.*

In order to do what needed to be done, blood would be the least of it. If he gathered the legacies further into his quiet-magic, if he let the Root twine around him, shatter and change him, how much worse could it become? How much worse would *he* become?

Trust yourself.

The Guardian, who had been quiet since before he enspelled the mirrors, sounded firmly in his head. Aware of Ao sitting across from him, gaze bright and curious, Jerzy declined to respond verbally, but did send back a strong sense of utter unhelpfulness. How could he trust himself, stretched this far to breaking?

What would he be, when it was all done?

Chapter 17

THE ATAKUAN SEA

There were seven ships in the Caulic fleet assigned to Atakus, all sleek monsters with a full complement of crew and captains who seemed to have both the fear and respect of their men. Kaïnam, even after a ten-day to familiarize himself, was both impressed and envious: his people were, by their very nature, a seafaring folk, but they specialized in sleek little racing ships and fishing fleets, not warships.

Perhaps, if they had . . . No. It would have made no difference. Their enemy came not with cannon and sails, but whispers and a dagger.

"Prince Kaïnam. The Captain requests that you attend him."

After so long on the mainland, it was almost odd to hear the more formal cadences of his native tongue, although the sailor who stood in front of him had an atrocious accent.

"I shall be along soon," he responded, not lifting his attention from the papers in front of him. The sailor nodded, gave an odd half salute, and left the cabin.

The Captain would not tell him anything that he did not already know: they had reached Atakus. Kaïnam could read sea maps and star charts; more, he *knew* in his bones, as they reached his homeland. The sense of tension within him grew, the closer they sailed.

Kaïnam was glad that his brother had been elected to be Heir, he admitted to himself now. Traveling with Jerzy, working with Ao and Mahault, he had discovered that his training, his abilities, were best used in conjunction with others, not as sole leader.

Had it always been that way, the natural inclination of his talents? Or was it merely the situation, the unforeseen, impossible association with Vineart Jerzy, pushing him into previously unmapped routes?

Kaïnam did not know, and the not-knowing bothered him. He knew that there were things Jerzy omitted, details of his plan left out, and while he knew the Vineart had valid reasons . . . it left him feeling exposed. He, Kaï, was a plan-maker, methodical, precise, and not easy with the improvised leaps or turns his life seemed determined to make.

Aware that others were waiting on him, Kaïnam gathered the maps together and placed a sail weight on top to keep them from sliding off the desk, then stood. A glint caught his eye from across the room, and he paused. The mirror, still wrapped in the cloth he had packed it in. A corner had come unbound, and the silvered surface caught the sunlight that filtered through the single, tiny window of his cabin.

Should he report in? Other than the occasional roaming sea serpent, they had encountered little of interest in their journey so far, and while Jerzy had asked him to note any details of this magic Caul seemed to be using, he could tell the Vineart only that none of the sailors seemed to know anything of it, and the Captain merely shook his head and changed the subject whenever Kaï mentioned magic—perfectly normal behavior for a Caulian.

No, he had nothing to tell Jerzy, and while he hungered to know how things progressed in The Berengia, if anything had happened, Jerzy would have activated the mirror on his side. Kaïnam checked each morning when he arose, using the mirror to shave with, to avoid suspicion, if anyone were watching, but the telltale shimmer had not appeared.

Reaching for his surcoat—embroidered with his family's sigil of tree and vine that he had taken to wearing while onboard the *Moon of Chance* to remind the sailors of his status and position—Kaïnam laced it up quickly, made sure that his hair was neatly pulled back in its queue, and went to see what the Captain wanted.

"So glad of you to join us, Highness."

Captain Padrig looked like a smooth courtier, his clothing immaculate and his face as smooth-shaved as Kaïnam's own, but the moment he opened his mouth, salt fell out. Bitter, witty, and foul-mouthed, with no respect for any title save his own, he nonetheless had a keen mind, and the two of them had fallen into a wary but amicable respect.

"It seemed the least I could do, your Captainship. I do hope that you have something of interest, to drag me from my slumber?"

Snide courtesies observed, the Captain merely pointed to the portside, where a heavy layer of clouds lay on the horizon. "I believe that is our destination."

The other six ships had ranged up behind them, allowing the *Moon*, with the flag of Atakus flying just below that of Caul on its mast, to take the lead. Anyone who might be observing through the veil of magic would see, and know who came to visit.

"How do we play this?" the Captain asked now. "Do we run up the red flag, or no?"

The red flag was for fair-sailing and negotiation. A ship approaching the harbor—any harbor—that did not run either the red-banded flag of Negotiations, or the white banner that indicated assistance needed, might be an enemy intent on battle. Padrig was asking him if they were assuming the Exiles still held Atakus, or not.

The spell-veil still held, although it was clearly weakened by the fact that they could see the mists around Atakus, if not the island herself.

Was that because the Exiles did not know how to maintain it? Or was the fact that it was back up at all proof that Master Vineart Edon was alive, and working still to protect Atakus?

There was no way to know.

Kaïnam took a deep breath, and watched the low clouds gather and roll. If you knew what you were looking at, it was obvious that this was no natural cloud formation: it moved differently, felt differently. Weatherspells, wrapped around the island . . . a Master Vineart's work.

Jerzy believed that the enemy mage came from the Exiles, that this assault on Atakus was merely another prong in their attack. But Jerzy also said the Vineart had no weathervines.

Was Jerzy wrong? Had Master Edon reclaimed control of his spell, thinking to protect Atakus from further invaders? Who would they face, when they sailed into Atakus's harbor: the Exiles, or Edon, unaware it was rescue reaching for him? Or some yet-unknown Vineart who had taken advantage of the unrest?

The latter seemed unlikely, from what little Kaïnam knew of spellwines. Could Jerzy have created such a thing? Logic said no: no matter the quiet-magic he still did not quite understand, Jerzy was too young, untrained. But Kaïnam remembered the way he had incanted the spell-mirrors, the way he had saved Ao's life when he would otherwise have bled out from his wounds, and thought perhaps Jerzy could.

No matter who or what waited, when it came to magic, the Cauls had it right: it was best to be wary. The Caulic spy had not reported the Exiles' ships leaving Atakus's harbor.

"Strike all the flags," he said. "Until we know otherwise, assume Atakus remains in enemy hands."

Padrig nodded to the cabin boy who had been waiting quietly, and the lad jumped up and dashed to the foredeck to let the signalman know what orders to give the other ships.

"We'll need your knowledge now," Padrig said. "To get past that barrier, s'not enough to know it's there; we need to calculate every handspan of the bay, ensure nobody wracks up on th' barriers."

Kaïnam had no need to check maps: the main bay, although large enough for the entire seven ships, was ringed by a natural formation of stone, ensuring that the ships would have to enter the bay one at a time.

"I've been working on that," he said now. "Or did you think I spent the days we've been at sea filing my nails and braiding my hair?"

"D'ye really want me to answer that?" The Captain had terrible teeth, his gums raw and his breath worse than a month-dead fish, but his smile had surprisingly gentle humor in it.

"You'll want to stay a few degrees to the left, for now," Kaïnam told him. "And then—"

There was a shock, as though the ship had—impossible—struck something in the deep water.

"Deep Proeden," Padrig swore, even as they grabbed at the rail to steady themselves. "What was that?"

Kaïnam knew, even as the shout came up.

"Serpent!"

Unlike the beast that had come up underneath his *Green Lady* when he originally fled Atakus, this beast was a true monster. Its neck rose from the water, bearing a head the size of a longboat, and by the time its sloped shoulders came into view, the great milky-white eyes were even with the crow's nest, the view from the deck of a half-open maw lined with black and filled with teeth that, Kaïnam knew, could snap a man's legs off.

"Aim and fire!" Padrig shouted. Kaïnam had seen the crew drill during the voyage but was still impressed by the way sailors turned into archers at literally the drop of a rope—and even more impressed by how others stepped forward to fill the essential roles so that the ship was at no time unmanned. Iaja might be known as the land of sea travelers, but Caul earned their reputation as sea fighters.

Kaïnam thought, briefly, of returning to his cabin for the spellwines he had stored there: more than the cask of heal-all, there was also a flask of firewine that would put a burn to the serpent's hide, if he set it to a bowsman's arrow. No. The archers had their tools, and there might be a need for it, later. There was another way to fight off the beast, if he could only convince these stubborn Cauls. . . .

Padrig strode from the small shelter to where the steersman was manning the wheel, barking orders that were relayed to the men hauling canvas overhead, and Kaïnam followed, hot on his heels. He had fended off a smaller cousin of this beast—or perhaps even this very beast if they grew that fast—with only a fishing spear. It would take considerably more than that to drive off this serpent.

Even as he thought that, the great head darted close, under the riggings of the ship next to them, and snatched a hapless sailor off the deck of that ship.

The crunch could be heard, even over the shouting and the creak of the ships as they turned about.

"Warn the other ships to watch for more." Jerzy had seen two off the coastline of The Berengia, and there had been several during their voyage on the *Vine's Heart*. They had no way of knowing how many had been created, or if they could breed.

Kaïnam tried to imagine a sea where serpents this size roamed and bred freely, and felt ill.

"Magic will drive them off," he said. Jerzy had kept them clear while sailing to Irfan and back. If he could just get the Captain to crack and admit he had access. . . .

"We have no magic," Padrig said, but it was such a quick response, Kaïnam suspected it was more reflex than truth.

"I know you have magic," he said, softly in case any of the other sailors were listening, in case it truly were such a secret, hoping if so that the captains were in on it. "Your High King used it to reach us, to invite me here. I will not believe he sent you out without the same."

High King. Spymaster. In Caul, Kaïnam suspected, they had become the same thing, when it came to orders such as these.

Padrig swallowed, his throat working nervously, even as he kept all of his attention on the archers and their prey. The beast had been pricked a dozen times already, and had learned to be wary of the ships, but it still swam too close, darting its head down now and again, trying to snatch another sailor from the deck.

"It's not for the likes of us," Padrig said. "Not for this. It's aether-magic. Spirits fired with salt and soil, an' carries messages, clears the vision, finds your way. But only them as are trained can use it, not like spellwines. 'Tis not for the common man."

Jerzy would doubtless be fascinated. Kaïnam had more immediate concerns. "But someone on this ship can use it?"

Padrig did not hesitate. "On the *Rose of Kilaarn*. The witches sail there."

"Silent gods bless you, Captain," Kaïnam said, and left the man there, looking for one of the ship's scramblers, the small boys who ran messages up and down the rigging, and occasionally from ship to ship. They were mostly pressed into service in the battle, fetching arrows and refilling bolts, but Kaïnam grabbed the arm of one, a wiry-muscled child who couldn't have been more than eight, and pulled him gently aside.

"I have a task for you, boy. You need to get a message to the *Rose*. Can you do that for me?"

In normal times they would have used flags to signal back and forth, or sent one of the pigeons that roosted below the mast, but nobody would be looking, even if they could spare a sailor to handle the flags, and a bird would be snapped out of the air by the serpent before it cleared the bowsprit. A scrambler, though, could move fast and low enough to not be seen. Hopefully.

"Aye mil'ar," the boy said. He was a dark-skinned creature, with hair the color of the sun at summer's set, and for a moment Kaïnam wondered if the boy shared any family lines with Jerzy, the only other person he had ever seen with hair that shade.

"Good lad. Get this message to the *Rose*, then. 'The beast is magic. Magic sends it back.' Can you remember that?"

The boy looked at him as though he had lost his mind, and Kaïnam laughed despite himself. "Go then," he said. "Be quick."

He was not, in fact, particularly worried about the beast, even as it bumped up against the hull again, sending men staggering. One serpent, no matter how large and fierce, against seven ships? But the beast was tenacious, and while the fleet would win its way through eventually, there would be damage taken in the process; damage they could not afford. The Caulic magic could possibly ease their way. Could. Not assured. But they had to try.

With a magic that the Exiles could not predict, that even Jerzy could not identify . . . Caul's magic could be a double-edged blade. He would need to be careful how it pointed.

Allies for this fight only a voice whispered in his ear, feminine and faintly familiar, and Kaïnam sighed, acknowledging the truth of it. Tomorrow that blade might be pointed at him. Still. For this fight, it would be useful. He went forward to stand with the Captain.

"We need to lure it closer," Padrig said, when he saw who it was next to him. "We're shooting every blasted bolt we have, and losing half of them into the sea. If this keeps up, even if we kill the beast, we'll be ill-equipped to make a forced landfall—men onshore would slaughter us before we were close enough to draw swords.

"Do you think they control this beast, or is it sheer bad luck it comes at us now?"

"I don't know," Kaïnam said. "We suspect they have the same master, the beasts and these Exiles, but how much control he holds . . . that we don't know."

WAKE!

The last time a summons like that had woken Jerzy from sleep, he had been a new-chosen student, and the yards had been infested with glow-root. This time, even asleep Jerzy knew it was the Guardian calling him; he was aware of the nature of the attack before his eyes were open, calling out orders even as he swung out of bed. It was martial, not magical, an expected development, but he would not underestimate the threat for all that.

Ranulf had let these men slip through. They were a threat only to

Jerzy, not The Berengia at large. That told him how to handle this.

"Gather everyone into the courtyard." The center of the House was open to the sky, but any bolts or arrows that were sent over the rooftops, he could handle. Trou, shirt, belt looped twice, boots jammed onto his feet, and Jerzy was moving, not toward the courtyard but the front hall.

They are coming up the road.

"I know." This was his land, he could feel them, once their hooves and boots hit his soul. He did not know who they were, but he knew what they wanted.

An image came to him, a dragon-shaped fireball, followed by a wind driven by great wings.

"No." He rejected both suggestions. "If I meet their force with magic, they will consider themselves justified. If I meet them, man to man . . ." What he, whose only physical skill was with a cudgel, could do to impress armed soldiers, Jerzy did not know, but instinct—and Kaïnam's teaching—told him that it was the right move.

"Make sure Ao has his bow," he added. "And then join me outside." A stone dragon would be enough magic to remind these intruders who they dealt with, but the Guardian's size, that of a large dog, would keep it from being overt.

Tactician. The word came with a hint of surprised approval, and Jerzy grinned tightly, echoing Ao's words of not so long ago. "I learn slow, but I do learn."

He exited the House, slowing his body so that by the time he passed under the ever-green arch of leaves that marked the House proper, he looked as though he were merely out for his usual pre-dawn stroll.

Thirty. All mounted. Armed. The Guardian swooped overhead, so Jerzy assumed that the others had been hauled out of bed and sent to the courtyard, and promptly put them all out of his thoughts.

And one ahead, on foot. The dragon's mental voice was surprised, but not alarmed.

"Vineart Jerzy."

The man who stepped out of the shadows was tall, broad-shouldered, dressed in brown riding leathers over a dark red tunic, and was not a stranger.

"Washer Brion." Jerzy stopped, looking up at the other man, who was easily an armspan taller, if not so overwhelmingly muscular as Jerzy remembered. He did not think the other man had somehow shrunk, so he must have grown again. "Are the Washers part of this?"

"No." He shook his head, and Jerzy saw that his face was stubbled and blue-shadowed, as though he had not seen a bed or washbasin in some time. "I was sent with a message, and a warning. I seem to have arrived in time to give the former, but not the latter."

"You knew about this?" Jerzy raised a hand to indicate the horsemen coming toward them at a slow, inexorable walk.

"Not them, precisely. But that there would be trouble. You have made a number of people both within and outside the Collegium uneasy, it would appear." He glanced backward, gauging them with the eye of a fighter, not a Washer. "You could quell them with a single spell."

"Two spells, perhaps. I am hoping that will not be necessary. Spellwines are not meant to be used as weapons." Telling a Washer that seemed suitably ironic.

"Aye, and men of power are not supposed to covet the vineyards or the magic they contain," Brion said grimly, turning so that he fell into position at Jerzy's left shoulder. "Nobody listens to us anymore."

Jerzy laughed, suddenly feeling oddly light-headed. Maybe it was the lack of sleep, or the insanity of facing down a troop of solders unarmed, or maybe it was the relief, unexpected, unanticipated, of having that spot at his shoulder not be empty . . .

He had not realized, until then, how much he missed Kaï and Mahault, not merely as companions, but sparring partners, informing his plans merely by being there.

The feel of air moving over them made Brion look up into the sky, just in time to see the Guardian descend. A creature of magic, it did not need its wings to actually fly; the arm's-length span on either side of its body were stretched out for maximum visual impact rather than flight, its neck stretched out, and its body elongated as stone talons wrapped themselves around Jerzy's right shoulder.

Friend?

"You will stand with me?" Jerzy asked Brion, not sure how to answer the dragon's query.

"I dislike ambushes, and overwhelming odds," the other man said calmly, still watching the approaching troops, assessing their armament and appearance.

"A Vineart's life is risk," Jerzy said. "Every year, we watch and wait, never knowing what the Harvest will bring."

"And was this your moment of choice?" They might have been having a conversation about a horse, for all the emotion in Brion's voice.

"Slaves do not have the luxury of choice," Jerzy said, matching his tone to the Washer's. "The Harvest comes when it comes, and we must be ready." He lifted his head and singled out the lead rider with his gaze.

"Welcome to House Malech," he said, projecting his voice over the distance without raising it to a shout. "You are far from home, and dressed for battle. Might I enquire why?"

That, he noted, seemed to surprise then. They had not expected to be met head-on, and certainly not with civility.

"You have ceased to supply my lord with bloodstaunch." The leader was an older man who, with his helmet off, revealed grizzled hair, close-cropped like a professional soldier and a face seamed with wear.

"I have." Detta had not informed him of any complaints, but she might have decided there was no point to it, in the face of all else.

"We need it." The soldier's voice was heavy, accenting words differently than Jerzy was used to. Not Berengian, not Aleppan, but similar . . . Iajan?

"There is none for offer."

A few of the horses shifted with a jangle of harness and gear, indicating that their riders had tensed up.

"You refuse us?" The speaker's accent grew thicker. Iajan, definitely.

The hardest hit of the Lands Vin. The Exiles' target. Did his master suspect it?

Jerzy forced his body to relax, the pressure of the Guardian's talons on his shoulder as comforting as the soil beneath his soles. Underneath him, the Root stirred, searching for him, the magic within him. If Jerzy called on it, he would be able to drive these men from his land . . . but he would never escape, himself. "This is my land. These are my decisions. Do you claim the right to make those decisions for me? Here, in front of a Washer?"

Brion was not wearing his robes, but the color of his undertunic and the belt around his waist, with the single wooden cup, should have warned them.

From the way their leader glanced down, and then pulled his head back slightly in surprise, it had not. They had been so focused on Jerzy. . . .

The Guardian shared with him an image of Kaïnam—the prince's long black hair was no match for Brion's grizzled warrior's crop, but he was a swordsman, tall and broad-shouldered, enough that, if they had been warned Kaïnam was here, they would have expected to see him at Jerzy's side, not this stranger-Washer. Their error, and now they would be off balance.

"We need bloodstaunch."

Had the man's voice been an entreaty, a request, Jerzy would have backed down. He had never meant to withhold from those in need, merely protect his own people, and draw the enemy's attention to him. But the Iajan *demanded*, arrogant as a lord up on his horse.

"There are many things in life that we need," Brion said, and his tone had slipped from his normal rough growl to a smooth, polished tone so much like Washer Neth's that Jerzy suspected it was taught them in their Collegium. "We are not always granted those things."

"I am not looking for Solace," the Iajan said. "Merely what is due us."

"Due?" Jerzy's plan to remain calm and use words, rather than magic, sparked and died at that. "You claim a thing due you?"

On his shoulder, the Guardian lifted its wings higher and stretched its long neck skyward, opening its muzzle so that the riders could see the row of serrated stone teeth.

There was the metal-on-metal snick of a sword being pulled from its sheath—not Brion's, as the Washer remained still beside him, waiting.

"Be very careful what you do, here," Jerzy warned, his voice quiet, but again pitched to carry. "You are not in your lord's House, but mine." A Vineart was master nowhere save his yards, but there he was absolute.

All three sides of the balance, Washer, lord, and Vineart, were locked for a moment, waiting.

"Your kind have caused this," the Iajan said with bitterness, practically cutting the words off with his teeth. "You brought this sickness to the lands, magicking up monsters and illness, tearing my home apart, causing brothers to come to blows, and then withholding healspells desperately needed . . . and you, Washer. What have you done to help any of us?"

It was the same question Master Malech had asked, and Jerzy, again, had put to Neth. What had the Washers done?

In response, Brion reached over his shoulder and drew his sword partially from its sheath, enough so that the riders could see the hilt clearly, and no mistake. "This Washer will send you crying for home, boy," Brion rumbled, and then added something in a language that Jerzy did not recognize; Iajan, from the way the riders reacted.

"So be it," the Iajan said, and spurred his horse forward without warning, not even bothering to draw his own sword, clearly meaning to trample Jerzy before he could get out of the way.

Even as Brion stepped forward on a slant, coming between Jerzy and the horse, his sword flashing free of the scabbard and swinging forward, the Guardian took to the air, wings stroking enough wind to set Jerzy's hair fluttering in the backwash.

Now.

"Not yet," Jerzy said under his breath, even as the horse swung away from Brion's sword and the other riders armed themselves and came forward. "Not yet . . ."

Mil'ar Cai's lessons came back to him, and the sword-blows that came his way drew forward a matching movement, sending him forward and back, always a hair's breadth from the edge. Not to attack, but to use the attack as a defense. Occasionally a blow landed or a horse knocked into him, but he kept on his feet, always moving, ducking into the blow rather than away, confounding the soldiers who were used to meeting other men with swords and horses, not a single, slender figure who moved like a ghost. Swearing cut through the whistling, clanging sound of blades, Brion yelling at the top of his considerable lungs.

"And your sisters swill with pigs," he informed them, adding something else in Iajan that made at least one rider spur his horse directly for the Washer, and never mind the others in his way.

Ao is on his way.

"Rot," Jerzy swore. What part of "stay put" did he not understand?

All of it, likely. Jerzy should be thankful that Lil hadn't insisted . . .

There was a sense of regret, and faint amusement coming from the dragon, and Jerzy swore harder. "Of course."

Ducking underneath a horse's head, he reached up and grabbed the mane, his fingers tangling in the course, short-cut hairs. He ran a little, to keep up, then used the momentum and pulled himself up behind the rider, grabbing the knife at his belt and holding it to the other man's throat.

"Hold!"

His voice carried, startling them. The fighting—really more of a shoving match at this point, as none of the riders seemed inclined to kill Brion, even as he laid them out with the flat of his blade—ground to a halt. The Guardian took its position on Jerzy's shoulder again, settling slightly, putting more of its weight on the bone, but not enough to damage him. Jerzy managed not to wince.

A noise drew his attention, and he saw Ao, still wobbly on his grafted legs, coming down the road, Lil a few steps behind him. They both carried naked blades, although Lil clearly had no idea how to use it, holding it the way she would a kitchen knife. He shook his head slightly, and hoped they understood. *Stay there. Don't interfere.*

"Who sent you?"

The soldiers muttered and glared at him, but nobody spoke. Jerzy lifted the blade slightly, feeling the skin's resistance under the blade, and asked again, "What lord sent you."

The man under his blade, their leader, answered. "Diogo de Reza."

Jerzy, trained to recall ten hundred incantations and as many decantations, only took a moment to recall the name from the dispatches. Iajan had formed an alliance with a local Vineart, who had not been seen since, then taken on another who had likewise disappeared. More, it was rumored that Diogo had been part of the consortium that had put a price on Master Malech, payable after his death.

They had not been responsible for Malech's murder: that would be laid at the feet of their enemy. Jerzy told himself that, even as he reached up with his free hand to stroke the Guardian's rough stone skin the way a hunter might his hound.

"Go back to your master. Tell him that in The Berengia, Sin Washer's Commands are still in force. I hold my yards from no man, I take orders from no man, and I do not take well to being threatened."

The man flinched, and Jerzy knew, through no magic save observation, that there was something wrong in Diogo's House, something centered in the lord himself.

"I cannot return . . . you are withholding—"

The Guardian hissed, a low, hot sound, and the man's jaw snapped shut as though it had been knocked by a solid blow. Jerzy had never heard the dragon make a sound before, but it seemed the least of surprises today.

"I would advise that you go," Brion said, his sword arm relaxed, but ready, the blade tinted red where he had scored an opponent. Unlike Ao and Lil, he knew how to use his weapon. "It would not be well for Iaja to fall under the Brotherhood's displeasure, in these difficult times."

Their leader scowled but barked a command in his native tongue, and the others put up their weapons, nudging their horses into a more orderly position. "Sahr Vineart. Sahr Washer. My temper, my concern for . . . the intensity of my lord's orders . . . overwhelmed me. This unfortunate incident . . . is entirely my fault."

Jerzy doubted that. Whatever illness had befallen Diogo, his orders had been specific. They had come, armed and in force, and been too ready with violence. Working the vineyard, a slave learned that if there was an infestation or weakness in one portion of the yard, it was likely repeated elsewhere. So, too, with men: if Iaja were reaching into The Berengia for what it could not find at home, then other land-lords would escalate as well.

Just as the people turned on their lords, in fear, the lords would turn on Vinearts. The Washers were turning on themselves. And the Vinearts? Who had the enemy Vineart planned for them to turn on?

A Vineart cannot turn.

Jerzy ignored the Guardian for a moment, staring at the Iajans, then looked up, to where Lil and Ao still waited.

And then he understood. In making them, Sin Washer had doomed them. His kind would turn inward, self-destruct, unable by their very nature to strike out, unable to even look beyond the boundaries of their walls. There would be no Vinearts when their enemy was done; none save himself, untethered by the Commands. A return to the days of the prince-mages—with none to check his desires.

None save Jerzy.

"Lil." Jerzy did not raise his voice, but it carried well enough for her to hear, and she stepped forward, cautiously.

"Have Detta select a half cask of bloodstaunch for our visitors. As a gesture of friendship."

Lil looked stormy, but nodded, turning and walking back up the path.

"Thank you, sahr." His erstwhile hostage's words were grudging, but the look in his eyes was guardedly grateful.

A half cask would not do much, but it could, at least, ease suffering. A quiet voice like Kaïnam's told him that this was not a wise move, long term: the soldiers would remember only that the Vineart had given them what they came for and not the fact that they had not been able to take it by force.

Long term was not his concern, today. Jerzy could not bring himself to turn them away entirely, no matter the cost to his plan.

"You will camp on the road outside my lands," he said. "And when the half cask is brought out to you, you will leave. If you remain, if even one of you remains . . ." He reached for a memory of Master Malech, cool and stern, and then he smiled.

The Iajans did not wait to be told a second time to leave.

THE VINE-MAGE HAD not meant to kill the Praepositus so soon. Still, the second wave of ships had sailed, his poppet onboard, and it would suffice. The slave he used had been too short, the skin not quite the same color, anyone who knew him well would know it was not Ximen. But those closest had stayed behind—save two of his spawn—and the blood and scrapings he had taken from the corpse were enough to cover a multitude of flaws. All else could be blamed on stress, or sea air—and any who questioned could so easily, shipboard, fall over the side.

The vine-mage took a sip of the spellwine, the deep rich fruit salted with the blood added during the incantation, Ximen's own blood, to tie the magic more firmly to the flesh. "My breath, his flesh. My thoughts, his voice. Go."

Shipboard, he felt the poppet stir, pausing mid-conversation. The sound of the water below creaking hulls, the stink of saltwater and unwashed flesh, struck the vine-mage as strongly as if he were there himself.

"What reading?" The poppet's voice was not quite right, and the vine-mage frowned. Never mind that none had the wit to question it, the failure irked him.

"Steady as she sails, my lord. The vine-mage's protections hold."

The vine-mage severed the connection, feeling the sense of the ship fade. That was all he needed to know. When they connected with the first fleet, the poppet knew to contact him.

It had taken the vine-mage years of trial and error to discover what parts of the body were needful to create a true poppet, rather than merely binding an existing body to his command, but it worked. For a while, anyway. A poppet capable of movement and reaction would only stay animate for a few weeks, at most, and then fall apart, but a few weeks would be enough. They would be well at sea when someone discovered the body, decaying from some unknown illness.

And when word was finally sent back to the Grounding, after the ceremonial grieving, the vine-mage would have a hand in choosing the next Praepositus, one who would be a biddable assistant in what was to come.

Yes. The death might have come too early, but it would all be well, in the end. The only irritant remained that unknown Vineart.

It had challenged him, taken his pieces off the board, against that fool Esoba. It smelled of power, of the spellwines he himself did not possess, that he needed to reach his goal. And yet it had eluded him, using the sea to hide itself. It had escaped him, sliding into his awareness and then out again, while he was occupied with Ximen. It knew too much, had touched too deeply, and escaped unscathed, with the vine-mage not knowing how much he had learned.

That was not acceptable. There could be no one to challenge him, when he finally stepped onto the old world's soil. Ximen had worried too much about prestige and politics, the military might of small men, but the vine-mage knew all that mattered was control of the magic. Once he could dig his own hands into the vineyards of the old, could feel the magic that filled that land, so far from this shattered fragment, nothing would be beyond his capabilities. He had made the vines here powerful through the sacrifices, but they were still too hard to work, too stubborn. The old world vines, trained for centuries, would yield power to him as he had only imagined. . . .

Nothing could stand in his way. Nothing could be allowed to stand in his way.

Turning away from the poppet, he walked over to the worktable, and picked up a flask of spellwine, pouring a small dose of the dark red liquid into the shallow, flat-bottomed cup next to it. Earthwine, the only legacy that had grafted properly in this land, taking to the wild vines like a babe to a foster teat. Strong and rich, smelling of dirt and spice, the scent of the hot summer winds, nourished and tamed by blood, it reached for its native lands, binding the old and new together.

On the shelf above the table, there were four small domes of glass, each one protecting a bit of hair, or flesh, or peeling of nail. The one to the far left had scrapings of skin, taken from under the fingernails of the Irfan merchant. He had not been a total disappointment, after all.

"One bird down, two birds down, and the hunter shall have a feast," he said, almost singing it, as his narrow fingers scooped up the dried bits of flesh and placed them in another dish. Hand that had touched hand, skin that had brushed skin, and the feel of the bright-burning Vineart in his mind. "Little magic bird, soon you will be in my net, I will pluck your feathers and crunch your flesh."

All he had to do was wait, and be ready. When the Vineart fluttered its wings again . . . he would have it.

Chapter 18

They're doing what?"

Brion leaned back in his chair, looking far more like the soldier he had once been than a Washer. "You disturb them" he said to Jerzy, ignoring Ao's indignation for the moment. "You disturb anyone with common sense," he added, sipping at his *vina*, causing the other two people in the room to laugh, quietly.

"This break within the Collegium is none of my doing."

"No, of course not. Men are men, no matter they wear robes or trou. There are days I think we should hand it all over to the women; solitaires are wondrously practical creatures, and House-keepers such as your Detta would no doubt run the world far better than we."

Detta, seated in one of the chairs, let out an amused snort and looked pleased.

"But that is neither here nor there," Brion went on. "Brother Neth felt that you should be warned that the Collegium plans to use you thus. But I think that you had already anticipated that?"

Jerzy had chosen not to sit behind the desk in his study for this meeting; Brion had met Master Malech, and Jerzy did not think that he would impress the Washer, trying to mimic that pose. Instead, he had Roan arrange chairs so that all four of them—Brion, Jerzy, Ao, and Detta—were able to see each other equally.

Detta had been surprised when Jerzy asked her to remain, after she reported the delivery of the half cask, but had taken her chair and listened intently as the others, while Brion reported on why he had been sent.

"I had not planned that far," Jerzy admitted, looking down into the depths of his own *vina*. He had been focused on the moment, on building everything to the point where the other Vineart would have no other options, making Jerzy the clear and obvious point to strike. After that . . . With luck, Ao and Kaïnam's people, and the solitaires, would be able to hold the peace while the Lands Vin recovered.

"It works, though. It all works," he said, thinking out loud, trying to see events the way Kaïnam would. "If he does in fact have whisperers among the Washers, he will know that they are in disarray. Iaja tears itself apart, The Berengia begins to crumble. His ships, his men hold Atakus. And he knows I am watching, now. Closing in."

Brion started to ask a question, but Ao shook his head sharply, and the Washer subsided.

"He has set himself in motion," Jerzy went on. "Magic has a weight to it: once a spell is decanted, it cannot be stopped, just as wine spilt cannot go back into the flask. He must follow through, or risk losing control."

"And then you will destroy him?"

"No," Jerzy said, finally speaking out loud the plan he had carried for weeks. "Then I invite him to destroy me."

"You're mad." Brion had his back against the wall, his shoulders firm, one hand resting on his belt, and he looked more like a fighter, like a solitaire or a soldier, than any Washer. "You—we—have an enemy who can reach across oceans, who can manipulate men and beasts, send magic that you cannot trace . . . and you would invite him into your own home?"

Brion did not understand. He could not. Jerzy looked to Detta, who had remained silent while the Washer ranted. Her round face was closed and still, her usual vigor dimmed by shock and dismay.

"You would bring this . . . taint, here? Into the vineyard?" She shook her head, her short, graying curls swinging with the movement. "Oh, Jerzy . . ." She would not say no, she knew it was not her place to say what would or could be done here; Jerzy was Vineart. But she clearly was not comfortable with his decision. "Master Malech—"

"Master Malech is dead."

Malech could not have understood Jerzy's actions, either. He had been a Master Vineart, but master of only two legacies; he had never touched an unblooded vine, had never felt the great Root stretching underneath his feet. He would not understand the temptation, the desire, that drove their enemy.

"Master Malech is dead and there is no one else. The mage saw to that." Baiting traps, setting lures, pruning the strongest branches rather than the weakest so that the vine itself was weakened.

Jerzy ignored the shimmer of the Root deep below, carefully calling on the quiet-magic within him, tasting the dark fruit and cool stone on his tongue and in his throat, sour and deep like no legacy he could name, a forbidden blend of wines.

Apostate, he was. Firevine, and Healing, the legacy of flesh, the vines he had been called to. Weathervines, given to him freely by Vineart Giordan. Three of the five, and the unblooded grapes of Irfan filling in the spaces, the reassuring presence of the Guardian somehow touching him with the spells used in its creation: Growvines, the legacy of earth, and Aether, the rarest of them all.

Sin Washer had broken the Vine to keep any one man from such power. But power would find its own way; quiet-magic gathered the legacies, binding them within the Vineart . . . five legacies and quiet-magic, once called blood-magic, bound together under one will. . . .

Jerzy had shied away from what that meant, even as he crept into the thick of it, used it, built his plan around it.

Apostate.

Forbidden.

Mage.

"Ao."

The trader had been waiting patiently—patiently as he could, anyway—waiting for Jerzy to give him something to do, and looked up expectantly when Jerzy spoke his name.

"I need you to round up the slaves, all the workers, and take them north, to the firevine yard." Any attacks would be brought against the House itself, not the smaller yards; the Guardian's protections would extend and hold there.

Ao was already shaking his head. "No. Sending them away, fine. Smart. But I'm not leaving. Not while you're staying here."

"I need you to do this."

"Rot you do." Ao scowled at him, clearly angry. "Let Detta take them. I'm staying."

Jerzy didn't want him here. He wanted them all gone, away. Safe, like Mahl and Kaïnam; tucked away where they could do good, after.

"We stay," Brion said flatly. "Whatever you plan to do . . . there are those who wish you ill, beyond your—our enemy. You will need someone to guard your back. Vineart for magic, soldiers for war. That is how it has always been."

Jerzy rubbed at his forehead, where he could feel the pain beginning to build again, a dry, throbbing ache that not even a healspell could ease.

No one could be protected.

"I don't want you here," he said, as though they cared at all what he wanted.

"Maybe not," Brion said. "But you need us. And if I know one thing about you, Vineart, it is that you will do what is needed."

Yes. He would. Jerzy twisted the silver ring on his finger, then nodded. "Detta. Take the wagons, load them with whatever you will need." He saw no need to instruct her further; she knew better than any what supplies she would require. "Any who can ride, take horse. The rest can walk. Leave now."

He looked up to see her gaze on him, a steady, assessing look so very similar to the one she had given him that first morning when Malech had brought him into the House.

A year past. Barely more than a year, a Harvest gone.

Much changes in a season.

The dragon had a point. Everything changes, in a season. But the cycle remained the same. Jerzy clung to that, the hope that this too would turn and return, and not shatter.

Ignoring the other four, who had begun discussing the practical matters of such an exodus, Jerzy got up and walked over to the mirror leaning against the far wall. The silvered surface was tarnished, the reflection wavy and uncertain, but he could sense the magic within it, close but unlike the magic that moved within the Guardian. The Guardian was a magic beyond him, but he had created smaller versions of this mirror, had extrapolated from the original spell, without previous knowledge. If he stretched, if he reached . . . could he create another Guardian?

And once he knew how to create . . . could he destroy, as well?

The quiet-magic shifted within him, and he felt dizzy, overly potent. This was forbidden, against Commands, for a reason. Too much hold ready, ripe with power. If he decanted this, unleashed it, could he then bring it back under control?

He placed his hand flat on the surface and let the quiet-magic gather on his tongue, murmuring the decantation that would bring Kaïnam to him.

The surface darkened, then swirled, silvery strands like water in a storm, until the entire mirror was the color of an overcast day.

"Kaï?"

The princeling appeared in the mirror, his face turned as though responding to someone else, then whipping back to Jerzy.

"What's wrong?" Kaï's skin was flushed, his long dark hair tied back, and a streak of something that might have been blood crusted across his jawline, but he appeared unharmed otherwise, more distracted than dismayed by Jerzy's summons.

"It's time." He had not detailed his plan to Kaï—had not had the details to give him then—but the other man did not need to know what he was about to do, only what was required of him. "I need you to hold their attention there, as best you can."

Kaïnam showed his teeth in something almost a grin. "Hold their attention? I think that we can arrange that, O Vineart."

As before, the sound of Kaï's voice came after his mouth moved; Jerzy wondered what he had missed in the spell to cause the delay and then dismissed the worry. It worked; that was all that mattered.

There was a shout, muffled, and Kaïnam turned his head to the left again and the grin became even more bloodthirsty. "Speaking of which, I'm needed. Fair winds, Vineart."

"Good Harvest," Jerzy replied, but the connection had already been broken.

"They've encountered the enemy," Brion said, and Jerzy almost jumped, not having realized that the Washer had come up beside him. "Who does he ride with, and where?"

"Atakus." Jerzy saw no reason to hide the facts from the other man; Kaïnam was of a family of princes, and as such it was his right to enter into direct battle. "Sailing with a Caulic fleet."

Brion's eyebrows went up at that news, but he merely nodded. "A logical alliance. These Exiles were the ones responsible for the destruction of their ships?"

"We believe so."

"And what you believe, the Caulic king is certain of. You realize that once they have a foothold on Atakus, they will not relinquish it easily."

"Kaïnam is aware of that." Jerzy's tone was dry, disinterested; if the Washer was looking for some sign that Jerzy was taking a further interest in the matters of men of power, he would be sore disappointed.

Jerzy placed his hand back on the mirror, this time invoking Mahault's mirror.

But the silvery swirl remained in motion, never clearing to display the solitaire. Jerzy pressed his palm more firmly against the surface, as though he could somehow force the connection, letting the quiet-magic fill his mouth and slide down his throat, to no avail.

For whatever reason, the spell-connection could not form.

"Jer?"

If Mahault had been too busy to respond, the mirror still should show where she was, or more particularly where the mirror was. It was possible that the spell was too weak to work, or that the mirror itself had been damaged, as Jerzy's had back in Aleppan; they were delicate things, and Mahault had been riding hard.

Or they might be blocked. Had the mage sensed his connection to Kaï, and followed the spell?

"Detta, go now. Everyone needs to be out of here by sundown."

"Jerzy, that's . . ." She stopped, and did not argue further. "It will be done." For a large woman, Detta could move swiftly when she wished, and by the time Jerzy turned to Brion, she was already gone.

"If you insist on staying, be useful," he said to the Washer, who took no visible offense. "I need your eyes on the vintnery, with the slaves gone."

"What am I looking for?"

"Anything. Riders, birds, a wind that feels wrong. Anything that changes, anything that feels wrong. Ao, do the same for the House."

"And if we do see or feel something?" Ao asked.

Jerzy smiled, but unlike Kaïnam's grin there was no humor in it at all. "Run."

THE SUMMONS FROM Jerzy had come at a good time; they had just slipped past the spell-barriers and into the harbor, but engagement had not yet begun. There were enemy ships anchored there, their lines generations old even though the construction was new. They were voyagers, not skirmishers; any battle to come would be on land rather than sea, and so Kaïnam had returned to his tiny cabin to change from shipboard wear to leathers and boots more suited to swordplay and fending off arrows. He did not know what weapons the Exiles might choose, but he would be as prepared as possible.

When the bellow came for landing parties, Kaïnam removed his hand from the mirror's frame, and dropped it carelessly onto the cot, a shiver of anticipation running through him. It was not how he had thought to come home, but it was time.

Whatever Jerzy was doing, back in The Berengia, he would give a fair distraction, here, oh, yes. No more magic. No more caution.

His sword belt in hand, Kaïnam went to join the Caulic fighters.

"THAT WAS TOO easy."

"Easy?" One of the sailors, his blade held at an awkward angle, as though to keep the blood crusting on its edge as far away from him as possible without dropping it, echoed Kaïnam's words with disbelief. "We had to slaughter them."

"Exactly." Kaï's hair had come loose at some point during the battle on the sands, and he walked with a slight limp where one of the Exiles had gotten a blow behind his left knee before dying. "They were strong fighters, lean and well-trained, and yet they met us on the beach, where there was no advantage to them. And then, when things went badly, they did not retreat to the walls, where they could have held us off. Why?"

The four men with him had no answer, but he had not expected any. A logic problem of the sort his sister used to set before him: X ships in the harbor meant there had probably been Y men, total. His people were sailors and fisherfolk, mainly, not warriors, but Kaï could not see Y men being enough to subdue the entire island, if it roused itself against the intruders.

Why had it not? His father dead, his brother new to ruling . . . had he been ousted by the intruders? Had they used such violence, that none dared resist? A hundred and ten possibilities flickered through Kaïnam's mind as they moved cautiously up the white marble steps, so familiar, become so strange. Beyond the gate, his family's residence lay. The rooms where his father held council, where his sister had taught him patience and observation, where his brothers and he had play-fought in the long hallways, guided and humored by the guards . . .

Where he had last walked, sneaking out of his own home, against his father's command, against all honor, to seek the truth of their enemies.

Kaïnam could feel his heart beating too strongly, his skin tight with anticipation. Would his brother meet him beyond those doors? Armed Exiles, springing a trap? He wished for more sailors at his back, but they were needed to secure the rest of the city and the ships in the harbor, that none could escape.

The great carved doors were open, as though Atakus were still an island at peace. Kaïnam stepped into the Great Hall, his sword in hand and five fighters at his back.

"Welcome home, Prince Kaïnam."

Whatever he had expected, it had not been that.

"Master Edon."

The Vineart stood, not in the center of the hall, but off to the side. It was not modesty that set him there, Kaïnam knew instinctively; the light coming in through the door angled in such a way to set him in a warm glow, the wall behind him shadowed, as though he were emerging from the darkness, bringing the light with him. It was a masterful trick, but Kaïnam was his father's son, and he had been taught to observe by his sister, who had been called the Wise Lady. He knew stagecraft when he saw it.

Suddenly too much became clear.

"You betrayed us. You sold Atakus to the Exiles." Bile seared his heart, made his throat clench against the words, but he remained alert, his body primed to react given the cue.

Edon knew him well and made no move that might invite attack. "I betrayed no one, Prince Kaïnam. Your father and I acted as one, as we always had."

"No. My father would never countenance this."

"Lord Ximen is a most persuasive man," Edon said, now stepping forward from his pool of light. The cane he always carried with him was held, not as a walking stick, but as a younger man might hold a fight-staff. Kaïnam noted it, but did not react.

"His plan for a new world, to wipe away the weakness of the old, would have brought Atakus into its full power, given us the standing we have always been denied, treated merely as a waystop for greater lands. Your father welcomed that chance. Had he not died." Edon looked sorrowful for a moment. "He was my friend, Kaïnam. I mourn his loss."

Kaïnam believed him. That belief changed nothing.

"He would not have countenanced my sister's murder."

"That was none of our doing," Edon said sharply. "None of Ximen's doing. He did not approach us until that day. We have enemies, even then, even now, who would see us fall. They struck against your sister, seeking to reach your father. Ximen promised your father revenge against them, if he would open our ports to their ships, and only their ships, giving them safe harbor."

Kaïnam swallowed, his throat sore and his voice hoarse with agony. "And you, Edon? What were you asked to pay, and what have you received in return?"

"Freedom." The old man hit the stone floor with his cane, as though to emphasize his words. "Ximen's new world will wash away the restrictions of Command, allow magic and power to re-form as once it was. Not for me, my boy—I am too old, too set. But those to come? The Vinearts who will inherit my vines? They will become as they should be, as they were meant to be."

"Sin Washer forbade it." Kaïnam wondered, suddenly, what had become of the Washer who had been trapped on Atakus when the barriers were cast. Had he known what insanity Edon bore within him? Had he survived, hiding, or had he spoken out and been killed?

"Sin Washer was a god, and the gods are silent. They have removed themselves from our daily concerns, and so we no longer concern ourselves with them. Or would you prefer they return, moving us to suit their whims?"

"No." Kaïnam did not. If this had in truth been his father's desire . . . if he had stayed, if he had listened to the old man, and not declared his acts mad, would he have been taken into their confidence? Would he now, in his father's stead, rule Atakus, as was his right as Named-Heir?

"Where is my brother, Edon?"

"Waiting to see you, my prince. But first, you must decide. Where do you stand?"

"Ximen is dead," Kaïnam said instead. "Ximen was a tool of the mage you feared, as you were tools, manipulated and destroyed in the use. That mage ordered my sister killed, Edon. He drove you into his trap, and has no intention of giving you anything in return."

"You know nothing of this," Edon said, but his aged, once-familiar face showed a moment's hesitation.

"I have traveled far, Vineart. I have seen magic greater than yours. I have been tangled in this mage's web myself, and won free. I know what the Exile's mage wants, and that he has no intention of sharing it with any other."

Kaïnam knew no such thing; he spoke the words a voice whispered in his ear, soft and feminine, with the tang of sea air and saltwater. But the voice was not calm, was not measured but enraged, and it filled him with such a deep sense of betrayal, of burning hatred, that it was almost as though the hatred alone lifted his arm and drove the blade up, deep into the Vineart's chest.

The old man looked at him, unsurprised, unworried, his hands reaching up to grasp at the blade, not as though trying to push it away or block the already delivered blow, but letting his gnarled, age-wrinkled fingers rest on the metal. As Kaïnam stared, blood flowed from the wound, dripping along the burnished metal and staining the tips of the old man's fingers. One hand lifted from the blade and reached out, searching for skin to paint on, in some obscene replication of Sin Washer's gift of Solace. A gift, or one last spell, a dead man's curse?

It was too far, the distance of the blade separating them. A heavy exhale, a gust of hot wind, and the old man's body slumped and slid backward, taking the sword with it, out of Kaïnam's shock-slacked fingers.

Kaïnam stepped back, letting go of the hilt, the body falling back onto the floor, out of its pool of light and back into the shadows, a crumpled swirl of robes, the blade still jutting from the flesh.

Done, a voice whispered in his ear, the touch hot and cool at once, stinging and soothing against skin coated with cold sweat. It was his sister's voice, the remnant, the last fading trace that had pushed and prodded him since her murder, but he did not recognize it, no longer wrapped in the gauze of humanity. Too long gone, too far removed from the wisdom of her living compassion, in death her soul turned hard and unforgiving.

He had been manipulated, on all sides.

Stomach roiling, head dizzy, training taking over when his mind could not function, he bent forward, curling his own fingers around the hilt and pulling the metal from flesh, ignoring the sound it made coming free, ignoring the fact that he had just killed a man he had known his entire life, had trusted, as much as he had trusted anyone outside his family. A man who had betrayed everything Kaï had been raised to defend.

"Lord Kaïnam?"

One of the sailors behind him, his voice uncertain. Kaï had forgotten they were there.

"Secure this place. And find my brother." If he yet lived. If Edon had not murdered him as well, in the name of freedom. If the enemy, too, had not used him.

Kaï looked down at the sword in his hands, gleaming with death, and wondered how much it hurt, if that pain would blot out the one already resting in his chest.

Chapter 19

Solitaire."

"I am not . . ." Mahl sighed, and gave up. She rode with the solitaires, and she was female. They would not understand the difference. "Yes?"

"Lord Ranulf's orders, and you are to secure the Valle of Bedurn."

"Of course." The order was not unexpected. Bedurn had not risen against Ranulf—yet. But they had a mill, and cattle yet left. Soon enough the mill would run out of grain and the cattle would be eaten, and they, too, would feel the jab of hunger turn to anger, and anger to violence.

"That it's come to this . . ." She turned to Keren, who had walked up even as the rider trotted away. "I meant to strike against our enemy, when I came to you, to roust the people against the danger, not . . . not this."

"Lords command. Solitaires . . ."

"Follow?"

"Carry through." Keren looked out over the road, the rooftops of Bedurn visible in the distance, the red tile and gray stone peaceful in the morning air, faint wisps of smoke rising from the ovens and forge.

"This is what we have come to," Keren agreed. "Better us than his troops, who would take as their due whatever fell into their hands."

That was why Ranulf had them at this duty: a solitaire would enforce, and subdue, but she did not abuse. Jerzy had been right; Ranulf was a good prince. It was merely that the situation was . . .

Bad. Very bad. Mahault felt the tug of worry low in her gut, that she was doing the wrong thing, in the wrong place. The confidence that had driven her here was long gone, and every morning she woke wondering how the battle fared back home.

"I was wrong," Keren said, still watching the distant rooftops.

"What?"

"I was wrong, and I will not say that often. You should have been a solitaire . . . but this is not the world that happened in."

"Keren, I—" Mahl tried to find the words to defend herself, to explain, but the older woman shook her head. "There is no shame, Daughter of the Road. We must do what we are called to. Go. Fight where you are needed."

"HERE. EAT, BEFORE you fall over."

Jerzy looked up at the wooden platter being held out to him, and then lifted his gaze further to Lil's face.

"Why are you still here?"

Lil met his glare evenly, unfussed, as though she had been taking lessons from Detta. "You really thought I'd run away?"

"It's not running . . ." He shut his mouth with a snap, feeling teeth click against each other in frustration. No. If he had thought about it at all he would have known that Lil would not leave. That Detta left only because he gave her a direct order; more, that she knew he was counting on her to do as he asked. Lil . . .

A Vineart stood alone. A Vineart showed no weakness. A Vineart made no attachments beyond his yard.

Tradition. Command. He had broken so much else, what were these but more things to fall aside?

"Eat," Lil said again, pushing the tray at him. "Or I'll worry."

"You'll worry anyway," he said, but allowed her to place the tray down on the desk, reaching for a slice of bread and dipping it into the shallow bowl of honey. The thick sweetness was the perfect antidote to the heavy weight of spellwines on his tongue, and woke his appetite. Suddenly ravenous, he reached for the pile of sliced cold meats, and Lil stood and watched with satisfaction as the platter was picked clean.

"All right, then," she said, picking up the debris. "Better." She hesitated, platter in her hands, and then took two strides to where Jerzy sat and bent forward, placing the faintest of kisses on the top of his head. "You can do it," she said, her voice softer than he could ever remember hearing it. "You can."

Jerzy closed his eyes against a prickle of heat, and when he opened them again, she was gone.

A Vineart stood alone. His the duty. His the burden. No one else should bear it.

With a sigh, he leaned back in his chair, focused his gaze on the Guardian, resting patiently over the doorway in its usual niche, and felt his heart, beating too quickly, his skin, too slick with sweat. The food helped, and a series of deep breaths, as Malech had taught him, brought his body and mind alike to a calm stillness.

Within that stillness, Jerzy reached for the quiet-magic again, swirling it the way he would newly crushed mustus, drawing the magic up and then punching it back down again, letting the sense of himself float down into the earth, sliding just above the root he could feel spanning the Lands Vin; not enough to rouse it, not enough to risk himself, but leaving a trail that, should anyone be looking, could be followed back to him.

The world was askew, but within himself, the balance rested: power and control.

He was done waiting.

Five tasting spoons were lined up in front of him on the desk, the remaining clutter of papers, tasting spoons, and pens pushed to the side, out of reach or risk of spill. Each contained a single legacy: earth, weather, fire, flesh, and aether. He had not tasted them, merely pouring a measure into each and letting the sense of them rise into the air.

Sin Washer had forbidden this, had restricted them to a lifetime of learning one or two legacies, put the combined strength of unincanted *vina*, the overpowering magic of the First Vine, out of their reach. And yet . . . Jerzy recognized each legacy as he touched it, and it in turn knew him.

What had happened, between the Breaking of the Vine and the rise of Vinearts? Not only the loss of the First Growth; there had to be more, that subverted the will of Zatim Sin Washer and made this possible.

Jerzy thought he knew. Quiet-magic. The thing that moved slave to Vineart. The thing that had appeared, according to Master Malech, only after the shattering of the vines, the transfer of power from prince to slave. A Vine might be shattered, but roots, denied access one way, grows another.

The quiet-magic would bring all five legacies together within him, mimicking the strength of the First Growth, matching the blood-soaked strength of the Exile. His, to use.

He had woken that morning, knowing it was time. The Exile was over. The mage was looking for him.

Vineart.

The whispered word was both reminder and instruction. He did not taste any of the spellwines; there was no need. A Vineart knew the vines, and the vines knew him. Allowing his body to relax back into the straight-backed chair, he rested his right hand over his left, the silver ring heavy on his finger, a reminder that, while he did this on his own, he was not alone: Malech, and Josia, and Filion, the Vineart who had trained Josia, all the way back to the first of that line, the unknown slave, the Vineart-to-become who, in the aftermath of the Breaking, had discovered that a vine whispered to him and made his blood shimmer with magic.

His, the direct legacy, the birthright denied. What he was about to do was forbidden by the Washers, by two thousand years of tradition.

Jerzy took a deep breath, and rejected tradition.

Spice. Warm spice, the flavors of all Iaja and Aleppan, the islands of the Southern Sea. Dry stone, and warm earth. The cooler herbs of The Berengia and Altenne, fruits both sharp and smooth, mingling in his Sense, filling his nose and mouth with an awareness of their power.

Jerzy felt an instant of panic: it was too much, it would overwhelm him, it would destroy him. He almost broke away, denying the legacies, when the Guardian's whisper slid into his ears and lay itself across his chest.

Vineart.

Yes. His own voice, as soft a stone-whisper as the dragon's, responding and acknowledging the searching tendril of the mage, still distant, still searching, and then going beyond, taunting the other, leaving a trail behind. He let the mingled magics envelop him, allowing his own awareness to become secondary, just as he had the morning when Master Malech plunged him into the vat of mustus to see if it would claim him.

The slave-mark on his hand had turned to a Vineart's mark, that day. What sort of mark would he wear, when this was done?

Then that question, too, fell away, as any sense of Jerzy fell away, the magic sliding into him, flooding him, filling his skin with magic like the flesh of the grape primed for Harvest.

As he drifted, it was as though part of him spread throughout the entire vineyard, carried by root and stone, soil and stream. He was the solidity of the House, the dry flavor of the earth, the solemn strength of the vines, inhuman and yet not cold, not uncaring . . .

Careless magic. Power. Strength. The core of magic, curled deep within the world, reaching up through endless, countless roots, shattered and broken, but never gone. Waiting for someone, some slave, to look up and see beyond his walls. . . .

Yes. This was the lure no blood-mage would be able to resist. Everything that lived within him. Everything that breathed with his breath. He was House Malech, and House Malech was him.

And House Malech had become a prize the Exile could not resist.

THE HOUSE WAS uncannily silent. Ao had not realized, as he moved through the house, how accustomed he had become to the natural noises of the Household, from the steady hum of the kitchen to the distant shouts and sounds of the slaves working outside, the wagons that occasionally rolled up and down the cobblestone road, and the sound of voices that rose and fell throughout the day, Mahault's clear tones, Kaïnam's more formal accent, Detta's clipped, exasperated voice, and Jerzy, slower than the others to speak but his voice, deeper now than when they had first met, carrying over all others. Odd, that it was only when they were gone that he could identify them.

Like his legs, he had never appreciated them until they were gone.

He rubbed at one leg, almost expecting it to feel like flesh through the cloth of his trou. The wood underneath was smooth-hewn and polished, carved to mimic the exact lines of a natural leg, and it flowed with enough vigor that he could move it, simply by desiring to walk, or bend, or rise . . . but it was not flesh. It was not real.

His flesh had been washed down the gullet of a sea serpent, half again the size of the *Vine's Heart* and three times as toothy. When he slept, he could still hear the splash it made as it rose up out of the water, echoing through his dreams, turning even the most pleasant fantasy into a shadowed horror.

He had made his choices, struck his Agreements, and he would not go back on them. But, even more, he would not allow a man who would loose such creatures on the world to gain even one more handspan of power. He would die, first.

"Jer, I hope you know what you're doing."

He had no desire, at all, to die.

*   *   *

"WHAT ARE WE looking for?"

Brion looked at the young girl who had appeared, walking alongside him. She was slender, with her hair tied back into a neat braid, the red kerchief that was so common in this land tied around her neck in a simple knot, her clothing worn but clean, her hands likewise. A servant, but one who held herself like a House-keeper, her eyes clear and her voice steady. Lil, the others called her.

"I have no idea," he admitted, even as they matched steps along the road that bisected the vintnery, separating yard from House, from the stables and paddocks at the crest of the hill, down to the end where it joined the main road. The sky, a clouded blue that afternoon, now filled with purple shadows as the sun dipped below the treeline, and the air filled with the sound of birds making their evening calls.

"Shouldn't we watch the vineyards?"

Brion hesitated, and then shrugged. "I had thought to do so, but . . . something warned me off." He waited for her to scoff, but the girl nodded.

"With all that's happened . . . I imagine the yard would welcome no strangers, now. We built Master Malech's pyre there; he will protect it."

"You believe that?"

"Detta says she can still sometimes feel old Master Josia around the House. Vinearts don't leave, she says. They sink into the roots, and grow into the wines."

"I'm not sure I find that comforting in general, but today? I hope that you are right."

Lil shivered despite the thick jacket she had thrown over her shoulders. "Whatever happens, it's coming. Soon. I can feel it. I can . . ." She let out a snort that might have been amusement. "I can feel it. Like a storm coming over the ridge, the way the animals get upset. A prickling in my skin."

"The Vineart said, if we saw or sensed anything, we should tell him, and then leave."

"We can't help him," she said. "Not really. The strongest spellwine, the best decantation, and we'd still be useless. Master Malech was warned, and it still came in and struck him dead inside his own House. Jerzy . . . whatever he's doing, we can't help him, or protect him, or . . ."

"So why are you here?"

"I am House Malech," she said, simply. "I was born here; my father was an overseer for one of the southern yards. I will not abandon my Vineart."

"Hm."

"Why are you here, Washer? You came to deliver a warning; that warning was given. You could leave with a clear mind, return to your own people. And yet you stand with us, even though your sword and your prayers are useless. Why?"

Brion stopped, staring up at the House, the pale stone a ghost in the dusk, the windows of the upper level dark and abandoned.

"We are commanded to different roles," he said, still looking at the House. "Generations trained to obedience, told that obedience is all that keeps the world from returning to disaster. But still we find ourselves here, hounded from without and torn apart within, by hiding, narrowing our focus until all we could see were our own fears. I cannot think that was what Zatim wished."

"What if it was?"

Brion looked away, finally, his gaze sliding over the vineyards, the distant shapes of the sleep house and storage sheds, and then back to his companion. His skin prickled, the same unease she had mentioned overtaking him as well. "Then he was wrong."

THE VOICES, THE faint worries and fears of the others carried through the still air where Jerzy lingered, neither swimming nor floating but merely existing in a pose of nonanticipation, letting each minute flow of magic swirl and settle into him. Far below, the Root stretched, reaching, looking for power to match its own, to feed and be fed from. The world Root, the source Root. The remnants of the shattered Vine, the First Vine, seeking to grow whole once again.

His enemy had found that Root, fed it with blood, coaxed it into cooperation. But he needed more. His goal was not power, but sole power. Total control.

The shimmer of Jerzy's magic along that Root would bring his enemy to him . . . but he could not let himself become entangled in it. Balance. Control. A Vineart stands alone. Now, here, Jerzy finally understood. It was not a command to be separate, to be lonely, or isolated, but to be complete.

That the Root was far more powerful than he was did not matter, only that Jerzy held control. Only that he remained master of himself.

The sense of exultation, of restless, relentless energy, surged through him, all five legacies coming to the fore, pushing for space, the similarities overlapping where their differences chafed, leaving behind rough patches that felt like bruises to Jerzy's Sense. He let the sensations wash through him, until his skin became liquid, his bones pure magic. Was this how a prince-mage felt, the power of the First Growth to command with a thought and a word?

Even as he held control, a shiver grew in his wine-saturated bones, deep in his groin, radiating outward until his spine arched and his fingertips ached with the sensation, his breath coming faster and harder until the Guardian slammed into his awareness with a warning.

Storm.

The sense Jerzy got was not of weather but rather a disturbance, an unsettling. He turned, swirling within himself, to follow the Guardian, deep in his sense of the quiet-magic, awash in his own blood, and felt it as well, shivering through the ground. It was not entirely unfamiliar: the Exile had scented him, had snatched at the lure.

You.

Jerzy's eyes opened, contained again within his flesh, aware of where he sat within his own study even as he retained a sense of the depths of magic swirling around and within him, the connectedness of it all. His breathing was still too quick, his heart racing and his limbs shaking. There was a dizziness in his head, and he could not quite focus.

"Guardian."

A request, and the smooth, cool strength of the stone slid into him, steadying him, keeping him within the stillness. The quiet-magic flowed over that calm, coating it, pushing it gently into his own bones. The awareness he'd had of the entire vintnery, the feel of the others outside, faded; still part of him, but not a distraction, and he was able to find the mage-storm, racing along the roots of the world, toward him.

It differed from his, this storm. He could taste the lack of weather-vines, the way Lil could tell when a spice was missing. But the hole was filled with the dark tang of stolen blood, surging like a heartbeat, steady and slow. The fear he had not felt before surged at that sound; it was too steady, too calm.

Had the Exile even noticed that its tendrils within the Lands were being counterattacked? Was the loss of Atakus barely a distraction, the rebuffs of his attacks here, driven off by the solitaires, a counter-ruse of his own?

It no longer mattered. Harvest came when it was ready; the Vineart could only act, or lose.

This deep within the magic there was no taint, no wrongness within the storm, merely power. Pruned of human concerns, it merely existed, waiting to be used.

Jerzy closed his fist around the sense of it, felt it coat his tongue and fill his nose. Power.

Here I am, he thought, the stone weight of the Guardian taking his challenge like a spear, direct into the enemy's awareness.

The reaction was immediate.

Before, when he had encountered the Exile's work, it had carried the taint of rot and decay, of oversweet fruit gone bad, the coppery tang of blood overpowering any freshness or delicacy. Here, there was none of that, merely a wave of power, deep and rich, thick and heavy, as unstoppable as a storm at sea, wind and spume combining to toss any ship foolish enough to challenge it into splinters. For an instant, Jerzy was back on the doomed ship in just such a storm, only the vessel being threatened was himself, and there was no one left to rescue him, as Kaïnam had lifted them from the sea.

In that instant, Jerzy knew that he had been wrong.

He was not strong enough. Even with his access to the five legacies, the power Vinearts had grown out of the splintered bits of the First Growth . . . it was not enough. Whatever legacies this mage had access to, they had been twisted in a way that Jerzy's quiet-magic could not match.

Not alone.

Not alone.

The realization hit at the same time he felt cold claws grip him, pulling him back and up, giving him space to breathe, and think.

Take.

He had already taken of the Guardian, to the point where he could feel the stone of its body underneath his own flesh, the cool, calculating tick of its thoughts a counterpoint to his own. And he knew, in that same way, what the dragon was saying.

Take what was needed. Take what would bring him to match with the Exile.

Blood.

The thought was enough to find them; the slaves, halfway to safety, some riding, some walking, all tired but trusting in Detta, trusting that the Vineart had sent them to another vineyard, that all was well, all would be well.

They belonged to the vines. They belonged to him. Jerzy could reach out the way he had touched the two slaves earlier, dry them of what he needed and leave husks behind, and no one would point a finger or whisper, even if they knew. Even if they knew, no one would gainsay his right, or his need.

Sin Washer had broken the First Vine with his blood.

A drop of a Vineart's blood, mixed with a cask of weatherwine, tamed their stubborn nature and brought them into the Vineart's control.

The Exile mage had taken the blood of others, had mixed it with his vines, somehow . . . reversed what Sin Washer had done, to bind rather than shatter. Jerzy could not follow it, the Guardian had no sense of how it was done. But he could sense the strength within the slaves, now that he looked for it. Blood-magic. Malech had told him they had called quiet-magic that, once. In the blood. In the blood of the grapes, in the blood of the Vineart . . . in the blood of slaves who might someday become Vinearts.

Stolen.

Not the magic itself, but the potential. The strength to use and control the vine-blood. Jerzy's anger felt like cold rain, pelting against his skin, even as another, deeper part of him saw how it could be done.

Take.

The swirl of magic intensified, an almost painful pressure within him, reminding him that while he paused, the Exile drew closer, emboldened.

Take, and survive.

The Guardian was basic. Survive. Protect. Jerzy thought of the force he had touched, so much stronger than his own, and imagined it spread out not only over the vintnery but all of The Berengia. Smothering the hills of Aleppan, the sun-washed cliffs of Atakus, so clear from Ao's description, the distant plains where Ao's family built their caravans, and the wild, untamed interiors of Irfan . . .

Despairing, Jerzy reached out, and took what was needed.

Chapter 20

The storm hit just as Mahault turned off the main road and headed up the cobblestone drive into the vintnery. She barely had time to slide off her horse and coax it to the ground before the winds would have knocked them both sideways.

The weather had been fair all the way back, her pace driven by a worry she could not name. Once Keren had released her, she had known only the need to be here, her feet set in the soil of the vintnery. It made no sense: she had no ties to the Vinearts save friendship with Jerzy, and yet she returned, with as little hesitation as she had shown the afternoon she helped a scared youth escape her father's hall, and turned her back on all that had been, and whatever might have become.

Three times now, she had turned away from the future she dreamed of, chosen another road. And all those roads came to the same place: House Malech.

Scrabbling at her pack, she slipped it loose, taking her blade from its tie-down, and left the horse to its own devices. Staying low, she was able to move with the wind, the gusts practically pushing her toward the stone structure of the House. The thought that she was being herded came and went: this storm had no interest in her. It was magic, and magic meant Jerzy.

"Aipe!" she yelped, as her arm was caught up, and she had almost drawn the blade in reaction when another hand came down and held her steady. "At ease, woman." The voice was not familiar, but it had an air of command she responded to, letting her muscles slacken and the sword remain undrawn.

"You're the maiar's girl."

"I am Mahault." The stranger had a soldier's haircut and a face that looked like it had seen the hard end of something a few times too many. What was a fighter doing here?

"My name is Brion," he said, as though sensing her suspicion. "Washer Brion." Before she could react to that, he dragged her farther, into the alcove of two trees, where they were slightly protected from the storm. "I stand with Vineart Jerzy," he said. "In this moment, at least. What news from beyond?"

"Riots," she said, reporting as she would have to Keren, without hesitation. "Uprisings in towns across the Lands, as though the people have lost their minds. There is no need for monsters any longer; the people see them behind every door, under every wave, and strike without thought. And the lords' men strike in return, seeing only the threat of rebellion, securing even peaceful towns against the fear of later upheaval.

"It has to end."

That was why she had come back: nothing she did made a difference, out there. If she stood with the solitaires and the prince's men, it would merely be to cut down frightened men who had no business holding anything more martial than a plow.

"I think it will," the Washer said. "Jerzy sent them all away, intending to lure this mage to him." They both looked back, careful to remain out of the direct wind. "I believe he has succeeded."

Mahault chewed at a fingernail, worrying the tip as she glanced from the House to her companion. "What can we do?"

Brion shook his head and sank down to his haunches, resting his back against the tree. "Wait."

The sense of distance was staggering. Jerzy stood at one end of an empty plain, the ground hard under his bare feet, turning and then turning again, trying to comprehend. The air was dry and cool, nothing breaking the emptiness out to an impossibly distant horizon, in all directions. Isolated, impossibly barren, Jerzy had never seen anything like it, not even the furthest ocean stretch had been so empty and depressing. This land would eat sounds, not echo them.

Somewhere, elsewhere, bodies fell, blood dripping into the soil, each drop sliding through stone the same dry white as the Guardian's form to reach roots hungry for the magic within. And Jerzy, in turn, pressed down on his soles and felt the roots surge up into him.

These were his lands. His slaves. He commanded, and obeyed.

In this place, Jerzy was dressed in worn trou, the material stained with dirt, the lace worn and frayed, his sleeveless tunic a hand-down, washed so many times its original color had faded to a yellowish white. A slave's outfit, more comfortable and familiar than any fine cloth he had worn since. A red kerchief was tied around his neck, sweat-stained despite the cool air around him.

Jerzy looked up into the sky. Thick gray clouds filled the overhead space, matching the featureless brown plain. If there was sunlight hidden behind the clouds, it could not be seen, making the shadowless light all the more strange, the landscape that much more barren.

"Guardian?"

His voice sounded flat, his mouth awkward, and, he realized, the awareness coming as though he had always known it, that he was not real. This was not his body, this was not a plain, those were not clouds overhead.

Even as he became aware of that, the ground rumbled and split, the brown soil shaking aside as thick, gnarled roots shoved their way up from the surface. Jerzy took a quick step back, but the roots appeared there as well, trying to curl around his bare ankles, the rough surface burning his skin where it touched him.

"Guardian?" he asked again, but there was no answer, not even the cool weight that usually accompanied the dragon's awareness.

"You are alone."

The voice was soft, coming from somewhere to Jerzy's left, and he turned around quickly, caught off guard and unprepared.

"Quite alone." The speaker was tall, cloaked in a hooded robe that fell past his knees. His feet, Jerzy noticed, looking down, were also bare, the skin wrinkled and twisted as the roots around them.

Even as he watched, those toes lengthened, digging themselves into the soil, burrowing like grubs. Jerzy jerked back, nauseated.

"All alone," the voice repeated, and the softness became mockery. "Strong, yes. Stronger than any other. But I am stronger yet, stronger than you can ever know."

"Show yourself," Jerzy said. "If you are so strong, stop hiding."

A sudden gust of wind rose and pushed the hood away.

Jerzy had not been sure what to expect. The calm, weathered face looking back at him was not it. An angular chin and cheekbones, deep-set dark eyes, and hair fading from a high forehead, rumpled and graying: he could have been anyone, any stranger on the road, any farmer or trader in his unadorned clothing. No belt wrapped around his waist, no tasting spoon or flask rested at his hip. Daring greatly, Jerzy reached out and caught the man's hand, turning it to look for the Vinemark.

The entire back of the man's hand was covered in a wine-colored splotch, darker and pushed in at the middle, jagged around the edges. It looked unhealthy, and Jerzy recoiled, dropping the hand as though it was covered in plague-spot.

"You called me," the mage said, lifting his hands palm upward, mocking the act of surrender. "And so here I am. I give you the opportunity of facing me, of offering up your skills against mine. Are you not honored?"

He knew. Cold sweat flooded Jerzy, making his stomach churn and his gorge rise. He knew that Jerzy, no matter what he had done, what offering he had taken, the slaves dropping without a sound as he pulled their strength from them, could not stand against his long-soaked strength. He was taunting the Vineart, the way a cat might play with a bird before dispatching it.

"Shall we begin?"

That was the only warning Jerzy had, before the battle was joined. A curve of the mage's hand, a muttered phrase, and magic slammed from the ether, the giant cat's-paw that had attacked him once before, only here the claws no phantom but real, bone-white and sharp, and swiftly coated in red from the cuts it left across Jerzy's face. He staggered back, stumbling over the roots that had stilled for now, poised as though somehow listening to the sounds of mage-war around them.

Jerzy retaliated instinctively even as his body moved back, slapping the cat's-paw with a wave of quiet-magic, but he did not have a spell ready, could not control the quiet-magic here, in this unfamiliar place, distracted by the strangeness, the unechoing silence, and the paw returned for another blow, the air moving with a hint of the taint in its wake.

The Exile stood still, his face showing only a derisive pity.

"You should have kept running," he said. "If you had run, you would not have seen me coming, and I might have been merciful." He shook his head, making a tsking noise. "I cannot allow challenges, Vineart."

The cat's-paw shimmered, becoming more solid, and swooped down again. Jerzy fell and rolled on the dry soil, his hand catching onto one of the roots in his way. It burned him, an impossible heat that somehow did not hurt but dug into him, touching the legacies gathered within.

Unblooded. Like the vines of Irfan. Not the First Growth, not quite, not after so many centuries shattered, but untamed, yet untouched by Sin Washer's curse.

The Exile laughed, reaching down to grab hold of one of the roots, pulling it until the brown length reached hip high. "Decades I have worked to tame this, to bring it to my service, not serve it. You, wrapped in must-nots and restricted by your own foolishness, you are too weak to manage it, too soft to do what had to be done."

All for nothing. He had invited the blow, and been unable to counter it. His plan shattered, and despair filled him instead.

"Give me what I want, and the end will be gentle," the mage said. "I can, too, be kind."

The word was like the prick of his blade against his skin, and memories flooded Jerzy: the feel of the Overseer's lash against his neck, readying the killing blow, the touch of magic in his skin as he ended a dying slave's life for mercy, the taste of the feral vines in his mouth as they crept up around the prisoner's neck, wringing the life from him as Jerzy's hatred and fear overflowed his control, the feel of a weapon in his hand and the surge of anger as he protected what was his own. The smell of the taint rising up from his own skin, the stink of his sweat, and the blood of others, leeching into his flesh.

"No . . ."

The mage, over him, laughed, misunderstanding the horror in his voice.

A Vineart stands alone. A Vineart must be rested, yet stressed. Harsh conditions make a more powerful crush. His master's voice, then others, whispering through the dry air. *Control.*

A slave did not know kindness. A Vineart was not gentle.

Vineart.

Apostate.

Jerzy.

Brother.

He stood alone, but he was not alone.

"Give way, and you will feel no more pain."

"No," Jerzy said, his spoken voice a dry growl, the quiet-magic he had summoned earlier coalescing into the stone-shaped spear, this time wreathed in sharp, serrated thorns. Earthspell and growspell, bound together. They were not his legacies, but they responded to his need, and Jerzy knew that, taint or no, the Guardian had not abandoned him.

The Guardian, here, in this place, was not without, but within.

Jerzy rose to his feet, smooth and easy, stone in his feet anchoring him to the ground, the bits of vine still caught in his hand warming him.

The Exile mage took blood, took life, and forced his vines to obey, to grow to his training. His magic was obedient to his will, powerful in its arrogance.

Jerzy did not command; he served. Like the vine itself, he survived.

He could not force the moment of Harvest, only wait for it. He would not force his vines to obey, only ask.

Help me.

He had not consciously spoken, summoning strength, had not even known what he was asking, but the words flowed from him, through the Guardian, into every alert creature of House Malech.

And they gave, not blood, but solace. The other side of Sin Washer's sacrifice. The surviving slaves' surrender, their instant obedience to his quiet-magic. Detta's rough affection, as sure and steady as the turn of seasons. Ao's outrageous confidence. Mahault's calm reflection. Lil's unwavering belief, cut with a gentle mockery like clear-running water. Even Brion's devout belief, tempered by worldly knowledge. All his, in that instant.

It was not enough. It did not change his magic, did not empower him.

But it reminded him why he was here.

The clothing of a slave. The isolated, sere plains . . . He had come here, and brought the Exile with him, lured the other to this place. His own choosing, even if he had not recognized it, at first.

Here was where it would all end.

Jerzy stepped toward the Exile, his body falling into a graceful glide that would have done his weapons master proud. Not to take the blow, but to slip under it. Not to strike the target, but bypass it, force it to turn and follow, until it could not strike at him but for harming itself.

Those earliest lessons from Mil'ar Cai, the warcraft from Kaïnam, the tradecraft from Ao, the sword lessons from Mahault. The scattered legacies of a shattered vine.

The shattered magic that had formed him.

Jerzy called the quiet-magic now, his mouth flooding with moisture so suddenly he almost gagged on it, the sour-sharp taste too intense to be mastered. Magic made the man.

In that instant the cat's-paw slammed down and Jerzy stepped again into the Exile's space, forcing him to divert the blow or take a share of it himself, but before he could react Jerzy was stepping back again, delicate as a cat, his tongue laden with the magic he needed.

Man made the magic.

There was no decantation for what he needed, no spellwine ever incanted to do what must be done. Tradition said it could not be done. Every handspan of his being said it *should* not be done.

None of this was evil. The unblooded vines, the root itself, the sense of all five legacies swirling within him, their power separate, but working in concert the way he had been told they could not, should not . . . None of it was wrong. Only forbidden.

Against Sin Washer's Command.

Sin Washer, who had broken the prince-mages, destroyed their power, reduced magic to a thing to be bought and sold, used by any who had the coin, controlled and restrained.

But magic would not be denied expression. Quiet-magic, blood-magic, was proof of that. The magic wanted to be whole; the legacies let him use them, but they used him as well.

Jerzy's head ached; there was no time to think, no chance to sit back and contemplate, even as the magic rose within his mouth, he was casting it out against—not the cat's-paw, but the source of it, his blow the heavy hooves of a draft horse, rearing back and coming down, the thundering noise of bone and flesh, even as the cat's-paw's claws caught him across the ribs and sent him sprawling facedown into the dirt.

What they were doing . . . magic. Not spellwines, not decantations, but pure magic, subject only to his command.

This. This fullness, this stillness, this exhilaration, was what it had meant to be a prince-mage.

"You feel it. You know." The Exile should have been crushed under the blows, but he came back, his shattered face folding and unfolding like leaves, the bones re-forming.

None of this was real. Everything was real.

Jerzy got to his feet, reaching this time for fire, binding the smoky warmth into a cage, then filling it with the crisp, hard taste of weather-legacy and letting it leak slightly, just enough . . .

The way the Exile turned, almost scenting the air, let Jerzy know that the final lure had been taken. Time to Harvest what had been sown.

"You know what we have been forbidden, all this time. Why? So that fools born to particular Houses should determine our fates and our worth? That a godling, out of anger, should say what we may or may not do?" The mage spat blood onto the dry ground, thick and black. "Sin Washer did not care for us, Vineart. Sin Washer *feared* us."

"You say 'us,'" Jerzy said, panting heavily from the effort of holding the magic contained, pausing, not using it despite the weight of it within him. "You mean . . . 'you.'"

"Why, yes." The Exile sounded almost surprised, a mockery of true emotion. He wiped his mouth with the back of his hand, leaving a smear of black blood across his chin. "Why, yes, I do."

His bloody hand raised, and Jerzy could sense the taint building now, the swirl of thick sludge that had been sliding throughout the Lands Vin focused inside that upraised hand.

The roots rising through the ground sang in the wind, blood calling to blood, sacrifice to sacrifice. Brutal, and powerful. None could stand before it, all must give way, or be destroyed.

Jerzy reached within himself again and touched the memory of the unblooded vines. No less brutal, more so because they did not care, they did not bow to the Vineart's desire but had to be fought, tamed. Sin Washer had shattered the First Growth, but he had also made it easier to mold, to control. Why?

Magic makes the man. The man makes the magic. Sin Washer had known all this. Jerzy touched the Root, looking not for power but fullness, and he understood. Magic of the earth, and blood of man. If the balance between the two shifted, if one became too great . . .

Zatim had seen the danger. He had not been a god, but a mortal. A prince-mage, great with power, so great that the magic had become him.

But unlike the vine-mage, he had seen the horror of what he had done.

The First Growth had been shattered, the Root reduced, constrained by Zatim's blood. But he had not been able to destroy it utterly, not without destroying the magic itself and forever undoing the balance. So it lay hidden in their blood, the quiet-magic . . . until someone looked up and out beyond the walls and saw what could be had for the taking. . . .

The unblooded vines had been only a hint of what they had lost. Jerzy almost lost his focus at the thought, but the Exile shifted and drew his attention again.

Balance, not control.

"I have what you want," Jerzy said, the growl now barely a whisper, opening the cage of fire a little more. "Are you strong enough to take it?"

As the Exile's magic roared into him, Jerzy did not resist, but rather gave way.

"Come on!"

The Washer grabbed Mahault by the shoulder and hauled her forward, the two of them running in the sudden break of the wind, aiming themselves for the great doors of the House. Only one was ajar, the other closed tight for the first time that Mahault could remember, but they managed to make it through and into the relative safety of the entry hall before collapsing on the floor.

Behind them, someone slammed the remaining door shut, even as the wind picked up again, the noise like a scream, wrapping around the house and battering at its walls.

"What's going on?" Ao, his wide eyes showing too much white around the edges, his hand gripping a wooden staff as though he were ready to take on an army of invaders, waiting only for something to actually appear.

Lil had been the one to shut the door, although there was no way to actually bar it: a Vineart did not worry about such things when constructing his house; there were no bolts or bars to be seen.

The light through the narrow, colored glass windows changed and moved, as though something were moving outside the House. For all they knew, for all they could tell, something was.

"Put that thing down," Brion said to Ao wearily. "You're more likely to hit one of us than anything useful."

Ao glared but lowered the staff until it rested on the ground, using it to support his weight. "What's going on?" he repeated. His voice shook a little, but none of them could claim better. "I thought Jerzy was going to lure the other mage here?"

"He did."

"But . . ." Ao glanced at the windows. "That?"

"You've not much traffic with magic, have you?"

"My people . . ." Ao started to say, then shook his head. "Only what I've seen Jerzy do. This . . ."

"We should find him," Lil said. "If he needs our help again . . ."

None of them spoke, feeling helpless. They were here because they could not bear to leave, but there was nothing they could do.

"If he needs us," Mahault said, "he will find us." She rested her back against a tapestry-covered wall, welcoming the cold, hard surface as an antidote to what was going on outside. "I hope Kaï's all right." They had no way of knowing, not until a message came.

Chapter 21

*J*erzy stood in the featureless plain. The clouds were low overhead, the soil at his feet bare and brown. The roots were gone, returning into the deep stone where they had lain for two thousand years.

He could feel them, still.

He could not feel the Exile.

It had happened so swiftly, exactly the way Mil'ar Cai had taught him, allowing his enemy into his own space in order to bring him down. But he had done nothing, had not struck, had not raised magic against magic.

Jerzy had let the mage inside, had opened himself and given way. Like his first test with the mustus, when it had judged the slave and claimed him, he did not fight, did not resist, but gave way, let it sink into every space within him, remake him . . . and in the remaking, take on what was Jerzy, too.

The mage had tried to take Jerzy, had followed him down to the tangled roots of the world.

No man could destroy the Root. Not even Zatim.

The Root had taken its own.

Jerzy closed his eyes against the unreal scene, trying not to remember.

Still, the taste lingered, layering on his tongue and coating his throat, reminding him of the draught he had swallowed. A Vineart did not hold power, but the power held within him.

It could have been him. It still could be him.

Jerzy had not expected to survive. Now, the magic pressed from within his veins, demanding to be used. Jerzy gasped for breath, and felt something sharp under his ribs. He had broken something, somehow, in that last attack.

He raised a hand, pressing his palm down against the sharpness, and imagined it healed, the pain gone.

And it was, as simply as that.

Sin Washer had been no god, but he had not been a man, either. He had been a prince-mage, the greatest of his time, and he had seen what magic and men, unchecked, would become.

He had shattered the Vine to protect humanity from itself. From *himself.*

The Root, awoken, had been the blight Jerzy felt in the land, drawing from all other crops, all living things. The devastation the legends spoke of, the dying, and rebellion. . . .

And now the Root had come to the surface, had been fed, had been allowed to re-form. In him.

The thought made the world spin, and his stomach threaten to rebel.

Vinearts were commanded to abjure power, to restrain themselves within the limits they were given. But now the taste of that power lingered in his mouth. Sin Washer had not intended Vinearts to have the quiet-magic, but the magic had kept its hold on them, through blood and bone, the shattered fragments still part of them. If Jerzy wished, he could call it, could do as the Exile had done, and bind it to him.

The Command to respect limits, not to interfere with things beyond his lands . . . It did not matter that Jerzy had not meant to bring the legacies together. It did not matter than he had done so only to protect the Lands Vin. How long would he hold to that, if he could reach across oceans and influence men within the safety of their own walls?

Magic makes the man. Once learned, it could not be unlearned. He would carry this with him, forever.

Jerzy sighed, allowing his hand to fall back onto the ground, opening his eyes to the pale sky overhead. In this sere land, the magic existed, and did not exist. He could remain here, keep the knowledge to himself, let it die with him, and not risk returning the world to the days of prince-mages again.

Vineart.

The Guardian's voice, soft as clay. He could ignore it, push it into the soil, re-form it to his desire. He could . . .

Vineart.

Then, again: *Jerzy. Jer.*

Ao. Mahault. Lil. Their voices, distant but insistent. Calling through the bonds of heart and vine. Their hands on him, his actual flesh, somewhere Else.

Vineart. Not the Guardian, that time, but Kaïnam, his voice cool and distant, demanding an answer. The lord of his own land, once again, reaching through the mirror, bloodied but whole.

They were not clay, not stone, but flesh, aching and sore. He owed them so much; he owed them everything.

Safer to stay here, reject their voices. Safer to protect them from himself.

A Vineart stood alone. A prince-mage cared nothing for others, cultivated only his power.

You are Vineart, a voice said to him, the soft whisper of leaves and the burst of fruit, the tang of blood and tears and the quick flare of pride. *And now you must be more.*

"Sin Washer?"

Who could say a man who had become a god could not speak past his death. But there was only silence in response, and Jerzy half-convinced himself he had imagined it, all of this a delusion, a phantasm of magic and exhaustion.

Jer.

Ao's voice.

Jer, come on.

The feel of hands on his other-body, urgent and gentle. The sound of a muffled sob, and a harsh curse, then the taste of healwine splashing into his other-mouth.

It would be safer to stay. Easier to stay.

His friend called to him again, willed him to return. They had sacrificed so much. . . .

He did not want to be a god. He did not want to be a sacrifice.

A slave survived.

Jerzy stared at the sky, tasted the rich magic against his tongue, and sighed, letting himself sink down into the soil, until the Root bound him up, and took him away.

He came to in his bed, the coverlet heavy against his bare skin. His lungs felt inflamed, his eyes swollen, and his thoughts sharp and painful as glass shards.

You live.

"What do I do now?" he asked the Guardian, his mouth barely moving around the words.

You live.

"But I . . ."

Only you know.

The weight of it was already within him, the truth bitter as spoiled mustus and even as the door cracked open and he heard the sound of Detta's steps and felt her hand cool on his forehead, he knew.

A Vineart stood alone. Even with friends, companions: the burden was his. Would always be his.

"Welcome home, Vineart," his House-keeper said, and he opened his eyes, and tried to smile.